TERROR ON AN ENGLISH ROAD

A truck came roaring along the narrow road in front, and as Harry watched it slithered violently to a halt and a Negro leapt out of the passenger seat, trotting swiftly toward his car. To Harry's astonishment, the man was carrying an ugly-looking handgun, complete with a metal silencer.

"Open the door," the man snapped sharply.

Swallowing hard, Harry flicked up the door lock and the Negro slid into the passenger seat, holding the gun menacingly at Harry's head. There was a gleam in the man's eyes as bleak as death itself. "Start up the engine," he ordered. "Follow that truck."

Harry watched the lorry reverse recklessly into a nearby field, and set off at high speed along the narrow road ahead. The simplicity of the operation was breathtaking. If the people who had seized him were the same group which had kidnapped his son—then one thing was searingly clear.

They were professionals to their fingertips.

BLOOD RIVER

Bob Langley

BANTAM BOOKS

NEW YORK • TORONTO • LONDON • SYDNEY • AUCKLAND

BLOOD RIVER

A Bantam Book / December 1990

ISBN 0-553-28781-8

Published simultaneously in the United States and Canada

Bantam Books are published by Bantam Books, a division of
Bantam Doubleday Dell Publishing Group, Inc. Its trademark,
consisting of the words "Bantam Books" and the portrayal of a
rooster, is Registered in U.S. Patent and Trademark Office and
in other countries. Marca Registrada. Bantam Books, 666 Fifth
Avenue, New York, New York 10103.

BLOOD RIVER

One

The patrol made its grisly discovery on the morning of March fourteenth, fifty yards south of the Angolan/Namibian border. It was a routine patrol made up of men from C-for-Charlie Company of the South African Defense Force commanded by Sergeant Cohen du Preez, and for several days they had been scouring the scrub-covered Namibian frontierlands, watching for nationalist guerrillas drifting in from the north; now, with dawn breaking, the men were anxious to get back to camp and snatch a few hours' rest before stand-to at dusk that evening.

In a dried-up riverbed choked with boulders and clumps of thorny scrub, Private Behrens, twenty-two years old, spotted a series of animal scratchings on the crumbling topsoil. Protruding from the surface, almost indistinguishable from the sandy shale background, rose a rusty rotor head and a pair of splintered helicopter blades. The blades were attached to a metal coupling, and from the alignment of the bearing assembly and the unmistakable bulging of the defile floor, it was clear the main body of the aircraft lay buried just beneath the ground.

As Sergeant du Preez studied the evidence of his patrol's discovery, he guessed at once what had happened. The aircraft, out of control, had hit the bluffs with the river in full flood, and the surface mud had hardened into a thick crust, providing a highly effective camouflage.

Sergeant du Preez ordered his patrol to unclip their digging tools and for more than two hours they labored in the blistering sunlight, scraping away the earth until they had uncovered the machine's outer fuselage. It was an American-built Sikorsky, capable of carrying thirty-six fully armed troops or eleven thousand pounds worth of equipment. Tilted slightly on one side, its nose cone shattered into a gaping hole, it still maintained a strange aura of life, as if in some indeterminate way the days of interment had encapsulated the sights, sounds, and smells of its final moment.

As Sergeant du Preez eased cautiously through the gap in the aircraft's nose cone, the stench of putrefaction almost made him retch. It was totally pervading, a foul, inescapable odor. Sergeant du Preez knew the smell well. He had encountered it many times during his boyhood, hunting with his father on their ranch in Natal. It was the smell of death, of rancid decay.

Surprisingly, most of the main cabin had remained intact, and from his position in the flight cabin Sergeant du Preez could see the entire interior unobstructed. The Sikorsky had not been built for comfort, and the metal bulkhead and drive shaft carried an air of functional austerity. The passengers were still strapped into their bucket seats, their bodies in various stages of decomposure. Their partially disintegrating faces looked grostesque, too unrecognizable to be termed human, and du Preez steeled himself as he studied the macabre array of grinning skulls, rotting cheeks, and loose, molding hair. He counted six corpses in all, including the pilot. Some were lying against the bulkhead. Two wore uniforms bearing the insignia of colonels in the U.S. Army. Du Preez could see their wristwatches and medallions gleaming in the sunlight drifting through the cabin windows.

He was about to withdraw when he spotted a dusty briefcase lying on the deck. Frowning, Sergeant du Preez picked it up and, holding the lid shut with his free hand, backed thankfully into the fresh morning air.

The smell of death still lingered in his nostrils as he fastened the briefcase flap and tossed it to one of the troopers watching from the rim above. Two hours later, he radioed the news of their discovery to his army base at Ruacaná. At three P.M. the briefcase was picked up by light aircraft and transported south over the Orange River. At four o'clock in the afternoon, under the category F.21, the highest security code in the military manual, it was delivered to the eighteenth floor of the Metlife Building on Roeland Street in Cape Town, headquarters of the South African secret police.

Robben Island is South Africa's Alcatraz. Originally a leper colony, it was converted in 1962 into a maximum security jail where important political prisoners could be sealed off from the outside world. Surrounded by treacherous South Atlantic currents, the island's inmates can see the awesome spectacle of Table Mountain rearing above the sprawl of Cape Town barely six miles away, but it is the proud boast of the Robben Island authorities that throughout its entire existence no prisoner has ever managed to escape.

The ordinary convicts are accommodated in

large communal barrack huts, but the more "dangerous" political detainees are confined in a special sealed-off top-security wing overlooking the lime quarries. That March, a frail, aging black man occupied a private hut in the area known as Section A. The hut was guarded constantly day and night, and no one, not even top-ranking prison officers, was allowed to enter without authority at the highest level.

Joshua Matshoba was arguably South Africa's most celebrated prisoner since Nelson Mandela. Like Mandela, he had been educated at the University College of Fort Hare, and had joined the African National Congress Youth League while studying geology in Johannesburg. In 1960, after the official banning of the ANC, Joshua Matshoba had organized a series of protests and strike meetings which, for eight breathtaking days, had brought the country virtually to its knees. Placed on the government's "most wanted" subversive list, he had run rings around the police for almost eighteen months, surviving a series of remarkable adventures which had captured the public's imagination and turned him into a living symbol of rebellion and dissent. Arrested during a police raid on an isolated farmhouse, he had now served more than twenty-five years in South African prison cells. Slight in stature, with implacable dark eyes and bushy gray hair, he looked at first glance like a harmless and disarmingly ordinary old man, but the South African authorities were under no illusion about Joshua Matshoba's charismatic influence and kept him in strict solitary confinement.

On the morning of March fourteenth, barely four hours after Sergeant du Preez's discovery on the Namibian border, Joshua Matshoba was escorted to the prison yard for his daily exercise period. It was part of Robben Island procedure that Matshoba exercised alone, and always under the watchful eye of a strong security accompaniment. The day was cool, tempered by a fresh breeze from the open sea. Fleecy clouds danced unhurriedly eastward, and sunlight gleamed on the distant rooftops of Milnerton and Bloubergstrand. As Matshoba stepped into the compound, filling his lungs with air, he glimpsed the glass-domed machine gun turret where uniformed sentries studied him blandly over the deadly gray barrels of their Swedish M-45s. He paused, frowning, as an aircraft began weaving its way unsteadily toward the high-wire perimeter fence across the narrow strip of wind-tossed ocean. It was a Vosper D-Hawk with a white fuselage and large red crosses painted on its wingspan. Matshoba realized at once the pilot was in serious trouble. A column of swirling black smoke trailed from the aircraft's tail and the stricken machine looked like a wounded bird as it lunged and dipped toward the prison yard in a series of rapidly descending arcs. A shout rang out as one of the guards spotted the approaching biplane, and within a minute every head in the enclosure was craned breathlessly upward, transfixed by the life-and-death drama taking place in the air above. The plane looked so helpless, so chillingly alone, that despite the misery of his personal condition, Joshua Matshoba felt a wave of compassion for the unknown pilot battling desperately for survival. There seemed no way on earth he could keep his aircraft aloft as, stuttering and hiccupping, he came limping toward them, losing altitude with each passing second. Over the foreshore he tottered, straddling the lime quarries and the high rocky cliffs, and then, as the spectators below watched dry-mouthed, the blazing aircraft suddenly plunged in a full-power dive toward the dome of the machine gun turret. For a moment, Joshua Matshoba stood mesmerized; then, sensing the inevitability of impact, he flung himself to the ground, burying his face against the hard pitted earth. The plane hit the turret head-on, a ball of flame erupting outward along its fuel tank, filling the yard with the stench of blazing gasoline. The roar of the explosion seemed to lift the top off Matshoba's skull, and he felt the ground shuddering beneath his cheek as fragments of splintered fuselage showered the compound in a deadly tattoo. Lifting his head cautiously, he saw the entire machine gun turret had disappeared. In its place, the charred and twisted wreckage of the blazing aircraft protruded from a nest of smoke-blackened timber. Acrid fumes belched from the caldron's interior, drifting like fog across the open yard. Above the crackling of the flames, Matshoba detected a strange high-throated roar which baffled him for a moment; then, through the churning smoke columns, he glimpsed something grotesque drifting above the high-wire perimeter fence. As he watched dumbfounded, a helicopter emerged, hovered momentarily, and began its difficult descent. Around him, the prison guards shouted in alarm. As the helicopter settled in the middle of the compound, two metallic objects dropped from its hatch and rolled across the ground.

"Grenades," somebody bellowed in a voice half crazed with panic.

The guards dived for cover, the grenades exploding in flashes of blinding phosphorescent light, filling the yard with a heavy white gas. Moisture sprang to Matshoba's eyes and he felt his nostrils prickling as he began coughing and retching compulsively. Through the gloom, he glimpsed figures spilling out of the helicopter hatch, their faces shrouded in bulky gas masks which imbued them with an eerie, almost elephantine appearance. A wave of hope swept through Matshoba's wiry body as they came running toward him, spreading out in a ragged uncoordinated line. Still coughing, he struggled to his feet and staggered frenziedly forward to meet them.

The rattle of incoming machine gun fire, when it came, was like the death knell of a dear and valued friend. Matshoba saw dust spurting from the earth as the bullets traced a frenzied pattern across the open exercise yard, and the nearest figure spun dizzily, his arms flailing at the air in a frantic gesture of protest and pain. Matshoba saw the man catapult over, thudding into the earth in a thick cloud of dust.

Rat-tat-tat-tat-tat-tat. The coughing stutter was almost continuous now, flat and toneless on the sun-drenched air. Through the swirling smoke patterns, gas-masked figures danced and twitched macabrely, decimated by the blistering hailstorm of machine gun fire.

Realizing his danger, the helicopter pilot made a desperate attempt to lift his machine into the air. He managed a rise of barely fifteen feet before the awesome fuselade shattered his pitch control rod, and Matshoba watched dry-mouthed as the bulbous machine reared backward, somersaulting over. It hit the ground with a stomach-shuddering impact, and the metal hull ballooned outward in a blinding spasm of crimson flame.

Gasping for air, a guard seized Matshoba by the scruff of his neck, thrusting his pistol under the hapless man's chin. Matshoba caught the rank odor of the man's gamy breath. "When will your friends ever learn?" the guard hissed, panting hoarsely.

"Nobody gets off Robben Island—not unless they're carried out."

Matshoba stared dumbly at the twisted wreckage of the blazing fuselage. Then, with an air of resignation and defeat, he bowed his head and allowed himself to be escorted meekly back to his prison hut.

On the evening of March fourteenth, nine hours after the discovery of the helicopter wreck on the Namibian border and five hours after the abortive attempt to break Joshua Matshoba out of Robben Island prison, Karel Van Brero, head of BOSS, the Bureau of State Security, South Africa's notorious secret police force, sat in the cabinet room in Cape Town and watched silently as the president sifted through the papers recovered from the disinterred briefcase. Though the president's features remained impassive, Van Brero's years of experience as an investigator and interrogation officer told him his worst fears had been justified. The papers now being scrutinized by the head of the South African state were not forgeries, as Van Brero had first suspected, but genuine top-secret documents whose existence was known only at the highest government level.

Van Brero was a hard-line right-winger, policeman by profession, racist by inclination. Though he had been a key figure in bringing the president to power, regarding him as a creature much the same as himself, solidly committed to keeping the country's balance of power in the hands of its 4.9 million white minority, Van Brero had begun to regret his influential support. The events of the past few months appeared to have changed the president's attitude in small and subtle ways. While the president remained outwardly as staunch as ever, Van Brero had detected what he considered to be conciliatory phrases creeping into the president's speeches. The escalating wave of violence and, most important of all, the condemnation of the rest of the world, had clearly had a sobering effect on the head of state's thinking. Van Brero knew there were circles in the government—powerful, influential circles—which wanted the dismantling of the entire apartheid system, and in Van Brero's mind such a move would be tantamount to treason. He was an unimaginative man, narrow-minded and insular. His only concern was a burning determination to maintain the concept of white superiority.

"It is true, *menheer?*" he asked in a quiet voice.

The president looked at him, squinting slightly in the desk lamp's glow. His face was full, his features prominent. "You do realize, Karel, that this is a matter of the greatest delicacy?"

"But is it true?"

The president sighed. "Don't sound so accusing, Karel. We are on the threshold of revolution. Unless we contain it now, we stand to lose everything."

"With appeasement?" Van Brero declared derisively.

"Not appeasement. Compromise. We have to face the unpalatable truth that the old ways are already over. We must cut our losses before it becomes too late."

"In my experience, nothing in the world was ever achieved by weakness."

The president gave him a sour look. "You'll never understand," he said, "that there's a marked difference between weakness and diplomacy. Mediation is what politics is all about."

"This kind of mediation will destroy our country forever."

"Are you really so blind, Karel, you can't appreciate that this is our only hope? It offers us an insurance, a guarantee for the future."

Van Brero looked scornful. "With Option 24? The daydream of a lunatic."

"It's ambitious, I'll grant you that."

"*Preposterous* is a better word. In a more stable atmosphere, you'd have laughed it out of existence. It will never work, *menheer*."

The minister sighed. He liked Van Brero, but the police chief lived in a closed and blinkered world, intolerant of change, immune to outside influences. It made him a difficult man to deal with.

"We're stuck in a blind alley," the president said patiently. "Option 24 offers dignity instead of defeat, a chance to safeguard South Africa's future in the face of a hostile world."

Van Brero's voice sounded soft, quivering with emotion. It was clear he was holding on to his temper with an effort. "*Menheer*, let me tell you something. My great-grandfather fought the British at Ladysmith and Spion Kop. He poured his blood into this land, and he expected us to preserve it, to retain the Afrikaaner consciousness. What you're doing is a betrayal of everything he lived and died for."

The president rubbed his eyes wearily with his fingertips. "No one in this country cares more about the Afrikaaner consciousness than I do, Karel, but there's a rabble out there trying to tear our society to shreds. We might hold them back for a year, ten years, twenty, but sooner or later, South Africa will go the same way as Kenya, Rhodesia, and the Belgian Congo. Unpalatable though it may seem, we have to extend the olive branch while we are still in a position of strength."

Van Brero snorted. "You think these people give a damn about your olive branch? It's power they want, total and absolute."

"Karel," the president said patiently, "you heard about the Robben Island raid this morning? The terrorists used an aircraft to crash-bomb the machine gun turret in an attempt to break out Joshua Matshoba. It's no longer a raggle-taggle scarecrow army we are facing. They have sophisticated weapons, and they're learning to use them more effectively with every day that passes. That's why we have to press ahead with the PAC talks. And that's why we have to pin our hopes on Option 24. The men in the helicopter wreck were members of a special task force returning to Zimbabwe, three Americans, two British. They'd been carrying out exploratory discussions with representatives of my personal staff in Pretoria. Now, we are in a position to commence phase two, a direct meeting between senior negotiators in a neutral country. If their dealings prove successful, it could pave the way for a major summit conference in the spring of next year."

"You call that diplomacy, *menheer*? Negotiating with a gun at your head?"

"Karel, we are living in a hostile world. If we intend to protect the things which are sacred to us, we must learn to compromise."

Karel Van Brero sat back in his chair, conscious of a deep and bitter sense of betrayal. The chilling fabric of the president's philosophy filled him with panic and dismay. He was silent for a moment as he studied the head of state thoughtfully. Then he said, "You do realize, *menheer*, that the helicopter crash was no accident?"

The president frowned and shifted uneasily on his seat. Leaning forward against the desk, he locked his fingers together, a sure sign he was becoming nervous. "I thought you said the fuel tank exploded."

"That was our initial impression. The forensic people suggested it could have been a leakage or"— Van Brero's eyes glittered—"some kind of missile."

"The ANC?"

"Who else? We checked the briefcase documents for fingerprints and ran the results through our computer."

"And?"

"Most proved negative, as you'd expect."

"Most?"

Van Brero's face looked bland. "One set checked out. The prints belonged to a man named Elliot Chamille, a notorious terrorist. We have a complete dossier on Chamille's activities at our Roeland Street headquarters."

The president moistened his lips with his tongue. His cheeks had suddenly gone several shades paler. "Karel, if this is some kind of elaborate scaremongering designed to sabotage the PAC talks, I warn you it's extremely ill-advised."

Van Brero looked unabashed. "*Menheer*, we believe the briefcase documents may have been read, or even copied, by members of the terrorist forces, and placed back deliberately in position."

"That would be . . . most compromising," the president admitted.

"The ANC will never stand by and let you negotiate, *menheer*. They'll use this knowledge for their own political ends. You'll give them a coup that will resound around the world."

The president sat back in his chair. He was enough of a politician to realize there was a chilling truth in what Van Brero said. He toyed with the papers in front of him with his finger as he came to an unwilling decision.

"I'm going to beat them at their own game," he whispered, "I'm going to move quickly, before they have a chance to interfere."

Van Brero looked exasperated. "Call it off," he urged. "At least postpone it to a safer date."

"I'll not jeopardize our country's future by abandoning everything we've worked for," the president declared stubbornly.

He reached for the telephone and punched out a number. "I'm putting the operation into motion tonight."

In the early hours of March fifteenth, a convoy of transport trucks left Krugersdorp outside Johannesburg and, flanked by heavily armed troop vehicles, headed south toward Cape Province. The convoy was unusual for two reasons. The first was the size and strength of its military escort, and the second was that no one, not even the convoy commanders themselves, had the faintest idea what the cargo contained. Preparations for its transfer had gone on for months in advance, carried out by high-ranking government officials, all of whom were trusted members of the South African *Broederbond*. Forms and documents had been signed and countersigned, signatures of people who no longer existed passing unnoticed through the tortuous administrative labyrinths. So complex had been the mass of confusing material, so intricate the authorization transactions, so bewildering the departmental clearances, that their origins proved virtually untraceable.

At half past two on the morning of the fifteenth,

the convoy set out along the N1 motorway and arrived at Cape Town's Duncan Dock early the following day. Here, the cargo of wooden crates— stamped FARMING MACHINERY—was loaded into the hold of a waiting merchant vessel, the bulk carrier SS *Arcadia*, and precisely at noon, the *Arcadia* set sail for the open sea accompanied by six battle cruisers and two squadrons of British-built "Sea King" helicopters. Twelve miles from shore, the escort commanders received orders to return to base and, puzzled by the pointlessness of the exercise, withdrew obediently, leaving the SS *Arcadia* to continue her mysterious voyage north alone.

A cold wind blew through London. It lifted the canopies of the shop fronts and scattered spray from the fountains on Trafalgar Square. Outside the South African embassy, a small group of demonstrators, miserable and bedraggled, huddled together for warmth as they solicited signatures from passersby for anti-apartheid petitions. Two raincoated policemen watched them in silence, reflecting wryly on the trials and discomforts of their chosen profession. The demonstrators, drawn from an assortment of anti-apartheid groups, had sworn to maintain a twenty-four-hour vigil until democracy was at last established in the Republic of South Africa.

Ezekiel Dhlomo, a young black student from Luanda in Angola, stood with the others, stamping his feet in an attempt to keep his circulation going. Though he had lived in England for almost three years now, he had never come to terms with the soul-chilling cold of a British spring. Cold he had experienced many times before in Africa, but something about the British weather seeped into a man's vitals, numbing his bones and blood. He was contemplating the misery of his position when he spotted a cavalcade of limousines swinging around the central reservation on Trafalgar Square. He counted three vehicles in all, black and featureless, their windows shaded to keep out the sun. They moved in convoy, ignoring the frenetic urgency of the midday traffic, their pennants fluttering as they drew to a halt at the embassy's side entrance in nearby Duncannon Street. The motorcade's arrival aroused Dhlomo's curiosity. The men who spilled from its doors carried, he realized, the unmistakable hallmark of BOSS undercover agents. He saw a thickset figure clambering out of the center vehicle, and an exclamation of surprise burst from his lips. Turning to his companion, he snapped, "Give me the camera, Toby, quick."

Dhlomo darted into the narrow side street and, slithering to a halt, raised the camera to his left eye, swiftly clicking the shutter.

"*Magtig*," one of the security guards swore. "Grab that bastard quickly. *Dié pikswart een.*"

Dhlomo saw the security guards moving swiftly toward him and, spinning on his heel, sprinted diagonally toward the opposite side of the street. Dodging to the left, he scrambled up a narrow cutting which he knew led eventually into St. Martin's Lane. An alley opened on his right and he darted into it, cartwheeling over a cluster of dustbins directly blocking his path. Garbage spewed across the alley floor, and as Dhlomo struggled to his knees a boot thudded with an almost stupefying force into the side of his narrow rib cage. Eyes bulging, he rolled over, hugging his chest and gasping for air. Figures clustered around him, kicking the garbage peremptorily aside. "Bloody Kaffir," a voice grunted with a heavy South African accent.

Dhlomo saw a man stoop down and pick up his camera from the ground. With a curt, almost dismissive gesture, the man tore the film from the metal spool, tucked it into his pocket, and hurled the camera against the wall. He looked down at Dhlomo with an expression of undisguised contempt. Dhlomo had never seen such hatred, such pure indivisible malice, in the eyes of a human being before.

"*Bobbejaan*," the man breathed.

And moving swiftly, yet with a meticulously timed precision, he kicked Dhlomo twice in the face. Dhlomo's world seemed to lose definition, blurring into a filmy haze with neither density nor perspective. He groaned softly under his breath as the South African security men strode brusquely out of the alley.

The British headquarters of the ANC, South Africa's resistance movement, stands in the borough of Islington, directly facing the metropolitan police station. At first glance, there is little to distinguish it from the row of grocery stores, launderettes and tumbledown restaurants which flank the property on either side, and a casual passerby might be forgiven for imagining the premises to be unoccupied, for the windows are kept meticulously boarded and no number or inscription appears on the outside door. On the morning of March eighteenth, in an upstairs room overlooking a narrow backyard, a small group of people sat watching silently as Dhlomo's swollen features were tended by an African nurse. With the exception of two young white women, the observers were universally black, and their eyes looked strangely flat and emotionless as they listened to the droning of traffic in the street outside. Their leader, a small, middle-aged African named Archibald Themba, studied Dhlomo intently as the nurse applied a dressing to his ravaged cheek.

"You are quite certain about this?" he hissed.

Dhlomo nodded, exasperated. He still felt dizzy from the impact of the security agent's boot, but mingled with his light-headedness was a sense of indignation at his associates' expressions of disbelief. Only Themba, solid, phlegmatic, pensive, had refrained from challenging his story, and it was Themba questioning him now, his small eyes sharp and inquisitive.

"It was him," Dhlomo breathed. "McAuley, I'd recognize him anywhere."

"You saw him close?"

"Six feet, maybe less."

"It could have been someone who looked like McAuley. How can you be so sure when all you got was a glimpse?"

"He was surrounded by security men," Dhlomo exclaimed. "You think they'd go to all that trouble for a look-alike?"

Themba took a deep breath and, rising to his feet, ran his fingers through his crinkly black hair. "So it's true. McAuley's here in England."

"That's impossible," a woman stated. "The British would never let him in."

"He's got British approval. American too."

"I don't believe it."

"We have the evidence," Themba said. "We didn't believe it at first. We thought it must be some kind of trick. We looked for proof, confirmation. Now, it looks as if we've found it."

His eyes glittered with suppressed excitement. "Call Sipho and tell him to get over here. We must get a message through to Africa at once."

Two

The sound of voices woke Kate abruptly. Shrill and excited, they echoed in the hot African air. At first she almost ignored them, for such disturbances had become commonplace during her four-month stay in the Mozambique guerrilla camp, but something in the voices' timbre alerted Kate's senses, and she rose to her feet, ducking her head beneath the low-thatched roof beams.

She was a tall woman, slim and supple— "gawky," the schoolteachers had called her during her early years of adolescence. But those days had passed; with the attainment of womanhood, her body had filled and rounded in all the right places, and now, clad in shirt and slacks of simple bush khaki, she carried an air of inescapable allure. Her cheekbones were high, her features delicately sculpted, and in the pale glow of the hurricane lamp, her long hair, coiled into a single braid, looked blue-black and shiny.

Kate Whitmore was a British nurse. For four months she had braved the flies and heat of Mozambique, where African Nationalist guerrillas were waging a savage war against the forces of apartheid, using her knowledge and expertise to repair the ruined bodies which filtered back daily across the South African border.

Now, as she peered into the African night, she felt her pulse quickening as she glimpsed people running frenziedly across the village compound. Robed women stood among the primitive straw huts, yodeling shrilly as they watched a ragged band of bloodstained men hobbling out of the surrounding trees. Something in the newcomers' gait, a hint of urgency, of desperation, set Kate's senses tingling. They carried the air of men on the run, fugitives, escapees. Prey. Though the guerrilla camp was fifteen miles inside the Mozambique border, Kate knew only too well the South African Defense Force would ignore international protocol if they were hard on the trail of retreating resistance fighters.

She had little time to consider this point, however, for dimly through the darkness she spotted Dr. Rasgeldi sprinting toward the medical hut, his baggy corduroy trousers flapping inelegantly around his bony legs. Discerning Kate in the hut doorway, Rasgeldi called across the deafening melee. "Hurry, Miss Whitmore, they are bringing in casualties."

Kate needed no second bidding. Emergencies brought out her resolution and strength. The soldiers were laying the first of their wounded comrades on the operating bench as she burst through the medical hut door. The man had been shot in the throat and was clearly unconscious. He lay with his head thrown back, his eyes closed, his chest rising and falling rapidly. As his lungs battled frenziedly for air, a terrible gurgling sound emerged from his half-open mouth. Dr. Rasgeldi examined the injuries earnestly, his slim Asian face filled with fervor and concern. He swabbed at the blood pumping rhythmically down the front of the man's sodden combat shirt. "The bullet's clipped his windpipe," he declared in an urgent voice. "He's drowning in his own blood."

Kate watched as skillfully Dr. Rasgeldi sliced into the wounded man's throat, opening up the wound to permit a freer intake of oxygen. The man's chest steadied as air at last began to permeate his tortured lungs.

"I need Sodium Pentothal," Dr. Rasgeldi announced.

"We only have one ampule left."

"What happened to the reserves?"

"They're finished. We're still waiting for replacements from Beira."

Dr. Rasgeldi sighed. "Bring it quickly, then. And God help the men who follow."

Her brain reeling, Kate pressed gently on the syringe plunger, watching the wounded man relax as the Sodium Pentothal flooded his bloodstream. How easy it was for these people to die, she thought wryly. They faced extinction with a stoicism she found difficult to comprehend, let alone emulate. It had seemed such a noble idea in the beginning, her private war against apartheid. She'd had something to offer, something real and tangible, her experience as a British nurse. "But you are not one of us," the ANC representative had told her frankly when she'd volunteered her services at ANC headquarters in London. "Why should you risk your life, your liberty, for a people who are not your own?"

"The fight against oppression is universal," she had answered proudly.

And she had meant it, every word. But four months of entombment in the squalid little guerrilla camp had had a profound effect on Kate's psyche, and she had come to realize that the process of freedom was neither simple, straightforward, nor, in terms of human suffering, even necessarily desirable.

In the pale sheen of the hurricane lamp, she watched Dr. Rasgeldi's fingers working dexterously. He was a brilliant man, his training honed by months of frontline surgery. How many doctors could claim such experience? she reflected. How many had undergone such a testing and purifying baptism of fire?

She helped him fix the dressing in place and signaled to the soldiers to carry the unconscious man into the shelter of an adjacent hut. She barely had time to swab down the operating bench before a second casualty was placed in position, and with a familiarity which only years of experience could generate, she went through the harrowing routine, sponging incisions with sterile towels, staunching hemorrhages with a gleaming hemostat. An hour passed. Two. Kate worked feverishly, moving from casualty to casualty with an air of almost stupefied absorption. Another young man was placed on the operating table, and she felt her spirits blanch as she gazed down at his horrific injuries. His left leg had been almost completely shattered below the knee-bone, and strings of shredded flesh danced macabrely around the splintered bone flakes. Rasgeldi's assessment was obvious and immediate.

"We'll have to amputate."

Kate hesitated. "Without anesthetic?"

"The limb is riddled with shrapnel. Unless we take it off, he will almost certainly die of blood poisoning."

Dismayed, Kate stared down at the young man's face. He was scarcely more than a boy, and his blue-black cheeks were beaded with sweat and dotted with ancient tribal marks. His body shivered in the first convulsions of traumatic shock, and his eyes, yellow and feverish, focused on Dr. Rasgeldi's face with an entreaty that made Kate's senses melt.

"Stand at my side," Dr. Rasgeldi commanded. "I'll need you to clamp the bleeders."

Swallowing, Kate took up position by the young man's leg. She hated this, she thought, the maiming and mutilation, the true cost of the Peoples' War.

Dr. Rasgeldi nodded to the soldiers surrounding him. "Hold him down," he ordered.

Leaning forward in the flickering lampglow, he made his initial incision, slicing through the layers of outer tissue. The young man screamed, his voice rising in a shrill, steadily escalating scale, and a foul odor prevaded the air as his sphincter muscle gave way.

Suddenly Kate felt the earth shudder. It was a strange sensation, like the effects of an earthquake very far away. The hurricane lamp danced on its roof nail and smoke fumes drifted through the open doorway. Almost simultaneously, the hut vibrated under a stomach-churning explosion, and Kate glanced at Dr. Rasgeldi, her muscles tightening in alarm. "The South Africans," she breathed.

Dr. Rasgeldi gave no answer. Cheeks glistening, he was hunched over the wriggling boy, his slim hands dark and bloody as he sliced at flesh and muscle tissue imperviously.

Boom-boom—boom-boom. Kate heard the deep sonorous roar of heavy artillery, the deafening explosions of shells landing in the tiny encampment, the shrieks of terror and alarm as the villagers stampeded in panic.

She shut her mind to the pandemonium outside and leaned forward to sponge the incision clean, clamping the bleeding vessels and fastening them off with catgut. Dr. Rasgeldi used a second scalpel to slice through the red fibers punctuating the muscle barrier, and Kate followed his movements, swabbing, clamping, tying off, working deeper and deeper into the rapidly widening wound.

She heard the rhythmic stutter of machine guns echoing above the barrage's din like the buzzing of angry insects, and her fingers trembled as she inserted another clamp. She could see fear and consternation on the faces of the guerrillas who were holding their squirming companion in position. They wanted to run, that was horrifyingly apparent, and Kate didn't blame them—she was desperate to flee herself. Her insides trembled at each fresh shuddering explosion, but somehow the absorption of the task at hand held her stubbornly in place.

Rasgeldi was working like a man in a fever, throwing delicacy to the winds, paring flesh around the central nerve column as Kate probed for constantly pumping arteries.

Wheeeoooowww. The whistle was shrill, high-pitched, unmistakable. Inside the hut, the guerrillas froze into a silent tableau, waiting, counting, praying. For a fraction of a second, the whistling seemed to stop, and Kate, holding her breath, imagined the shell had somehow passed them by. Then, strangely and unaccountably, she saw the contents of the hut whirling around her head as if struck by some strange and demonical whirlwind, and for no reason she could clearly explain, she was lying on her back on the hard earthen floor while pieces of human flesh mingled with chunks of ruptured roof thatch spun around her dizzily. A wave of white-hot air swept her body and her ears rang as a deafening explosion split the night. The din seemed to go on and on, like a record player on which the needle had stuck. I'm dying, she thought, and in some strange and indefinable way, she felt her body and mind separate. Someone was calling her name: "Kate, Kate . . ." and, blinking sharply, she saw it was her mother. Then the voice grew deeper, took on an urgent, more masculine timbre, and peering upward through the charred rubble, Kate spotted a black soldier crouching above her in the spiraling smoke fumes.

"You okay, missy?" he demanded hoarsely.

She propped herself up on her elbows, glancing around the decimated medical hut. Across the compound, she could see blinding flashes as the incoming shells kicked up great mushrooms of earth and debris. A tree leapt into the air like a piece of splintered matchwood.

"Dr. Rasgeldi?" she croaked hoarsely.

"Dead," the man told her in a flat voice. "They all dead. The patient too."

Kate glanced down at her body, covered with dirt and rubble. Blood stained the front of her khaki bush shirt, but a quick exploratory examination revealed the blood was not her own. Her skin was bruised and scorched but otherwise intact, thank God. Everything in its rightful place.

The black man seized her under the armpit. "We got to hurry, missy. Soldiers coming fast."

Kate staggered to her feet, feeling her senses lurch as she glimpsed armored troop carriers lumbering through the churning smoke columns. The South African Defense Force.

Machine gun fire scythed across the open compound, and a man, running, seemed to falter in full stride, somersaulting forward, his body ripped almost completely in two. The thatched huts blazed furiously like a series of macabre beacons.

Leaning heavily on the guerrilla's arm, Kate

began to hobble through the maelstrom of devastation, a wave of lethargy sweeping her limbs. She
gritted her teeth, willing the feeling to pass. I am not
a maiden aunt, nor a lily-livered weakling, she
thought. I am alive by some astonishing and unbe-
lievable miracle, and I intend to go on staying alive,
shock or no shock.

She thought of Dr. Rasgeldi. He'd been so kind,
so compassionate, so caring. Now he was gone,
snuffed out like a candle flame, his gentle eyes
locked forever in the blue-marbled insentience of
death.

A shot kicked up the earth at her feet, and she
glanced fearfully around. Soldiers were flitting like
specters between the armored personnel carriers,
their uniforms flickering in the glow of the dancing
flames.

"They've spotted us," she exclaimed, struggling
to hobble faster.

Her companion dislodged himself from her
grasp and, turning, crouched expertly on one knee,
bringing his rifle into alignment. It was an ancient
battle-scarred Enfield, and Kate watched in wonder
as the guerrilla worked the bolt, ejecting a used
round and chambering a new one with fluid dexterity. Cer-*aaack*—gently he squeezed the trigger, and
through the swirling smoke columns in front, she
saw a soldier crash headlong into a tree, his skull
erupting into a bloody halo.

"Come," the black man snapped, steering her
furiously toward the river.

Kate saw the clay bank looming up and slithered
down it, too crazed with terror to worry where she
was placing her feet. She reached the shore and
tottered into the shallows, wincing as the cool water
sloshed against her fevered ankles.

"Head for the scrub," the black man ordered, panting sharply in the warm night air.

"What about you?"

"I will hold them on the bluff while you get under cover."

"No," she hissed angrily. "I'll not leave you here alone."

"Move, woman, you think I want to die for nothing?"

She hesitated, blinking as the sweat streamed remorselessly into her eyes.

"Go," he shouted, his voice almost at fever pitch. "I will follow as soon as you reach the opposite bank."

Gasping, Kate turned and began to splash through the slow-moving current. At its deepest point, the water scarcely reached her knees. She could see the scrublands ahead, and the prickly thorn bushes where the crazed tribespeople had faded into the sanctuary of the African night.

The rattle of a machine gun made her skin twitch. She saw spurts of water leaping into the air as bullets scythed through the frothy waves ahead. Then—*crack crack*—she recognized the heavier, throatier roar of her protector's Enfield firing back, keeping the first sporadic wave of South African troops pinned down on the steep clay bluffs above.

Kate saw rocks looming out of the riverbed and danced over them, scrambling up the grassy embankment. The scrub gathered around her, gray and comforting. She paused behind a thorn bush and, turning, cupped her hands to her mouth. "I'm under cover," she yelled as loudly as she could.

The black man rose and pounded furiously for the river. He ran disjointedly, balancing the rifle across his chest. He looked like an athlete, lean and

trim, despite the frenzied urgency of his movements.
She watched as he reached the water's edge and
sprinted through the shallows, his legs kicking up
great fountains of feathery spray. She could see his
face clearly, the features lit by the flickering hut fires
above, his mouth open, sucking at the air, his eyes,
yellow and intent, fixed on the scrub ahead. He
reached the central current, his pace slowing as the
deeper water washed at his calves and ankles.

Kate saw figures rising on the bank above. Her
stomach knotted and a wave of sickness spread
through her lower body. "Nooooo," she bellowed.
But it was a pointless exercise, an empty indictment
hurled against the wind. The shot, when it came,
seemed almost anticlimactic. A marksman had lined
up the fugitive comfortably in his sights, relishing
the moment, enjoying the feeling of power a simple
squeeze of his finger gave him.

Crack.

Like a ballet dancer executing some intricate
and meticulously practiced pirouette, the black man
whirled, his spine arching in a graceful, delicate
curve before crashing forward into the current and
floating motionless facedown, blood eddying from
his combat jacket in a series of macabre ripples.

Tears stained Kate's smoke-grimed cheeks. She
wanted to scream out loud at the futility and injustice of the moment. The man hadn't deserved to
die—wouldn't have, if he'd run like the others.
Staying behind, he had helped her escape, but that
solitary act of deliverance had cost him his life.
Crouched in the darkness, her body shuddering
under the dry racking sobs, Kate stared at the figures
framed along the riverbank and her lips parted in a
silent snarl as she felt a new emotion replacing the

terror threatening to engulf her. Cleansing and purifying, she recognized it for what it was.

Hate.

Through the long hours of darkness, the land
repeated itself endlessly. Stumbling along in a
dreamy haze, Kate scarcely knew where she was
going anymore. Her body ached in every limb, and
her legs had lost all semblance of natural sensation.
She ignored the monotonous sprawl of stunted scrub
and impoverished syringa trees, concentrating on
the simple overriding task of placing one foot me-
thodically in front of the other. At some point during
the night she caught up with the straggling remnants
of the fleeing tribespeople, but though they nodded
at her in welcome, no conversation passed their lips.
Morning brought her out of her reverie. She was a
strong woman, always had been, not just in the
physical sense, but mentally too. She'd gone her own
way, made her own decisions, knew how to handle
herself, how to deal with the world and the crises it
presented. But last night had been the first time in
her life she had experienced the reality of being
under fire. Before, she had only seen war second-
hand—the mangled bodies paraded daily for her care
and attention. Now, the horrors of the fight glowed
luminously in her memory. She was no coward, God
knew, and no shrinking violet either, but she
wouldn't be human if she didn't feel in the dim
recesses of her mind some vague tremor of apprehension and disgust.

The brightness of the day brought fresh warmth
to the ragged band of fugitives, and Kate, struggling
along with the rest, heard a welcoming shout in the
trees ahead and the unmistakable yodeling of tribal

women. The scrub fell back and she glimpsed a clutter of tin-roofed huts arranged in a starburst around a central compound. One sported the inscription, written in English, OJUBYU FIRST CLASS CAFÉ AND RESTAURANT BAR. Kate recognized the place in an instant. It was Plaatje, a refugee settlement some twenty-four miles inside the Mozambique frontier. A wave of relief flooded her exhausted body as she stumbled into the central compound. A young boy on a motorcycle sat watching the approaching fugitives through narrowed eyes. He was slim-cheeked and bony-shouldered, his slender body clad in a ragged bush shirt and a pair of faded, heavily patched jeans. "Please," he said in heavily accented English, "is there a Miss Whitmore here?"

Kate frowned, pausing in her stride. "I am Miss Whitmore."

The boy stamped on the starter pedal, revving his engine into life.

"You must come with me at once, please."

"On whose authority?"

"Bishop Sepamla's," the boy said.

Kate had heard of Bishop Sepamla, a distinguished African religious leader, an outspoken critic of apartheid, and, if the rumors were to be believed, a high-ranking member of the ANC ruling council.

"Please," the boy repeated urgently, "my instructions are to bring you as quickly as possible."

Kate longed to rest and bathe, but without a word she hooked one leg over the motorcycle's pillion saddle and slid her arms around the young boy's waist. Opening the throttle, he drove out of the compound, and Kate felt the slipstream bathing her cheeks and throat, molding the bush shirt against the contours of her fevered body. There was something strangely cleansing about the wind, she thought, as if it could blow her mind clear, scatter forever the tortured images which still clung in her stupefied brain. Though the sun's heat steadily intensified, she felt little discomfort, for the vehicle's movement cooled her body and limbs. For more than an hour they followed a network of gravel roads, and just before noon she glimpsed a township looming up, the buildings ramshackle and delapidated, their walls bolstered with Coca-Cola signboards and corrugated metal sheets. Men sat in the shade, drinking beer out of dusty bottles, their eyes following implacably as the motorcycle roared along the sprawl of narrow back streets.

Kate spotted a whitewashed church standing alone in an isolated meadow. It looked strangely incongruous, its tall spire contrasting sharply with the tumbledown squalor of the houses surrounding it. Her driver drew to a halt at the building's entrance and, without turning his head, motioned her brusquely inside.

She clambered from the pillion saddle and walked up the narrow steps, pausing on the veranda to tap lightly on the door.

"Please come in," a voice said warmly.

Puzzled, she stepped across the threshold, narrowing her eyes at the sudden transition from daylight to semidarkness. A man stood in the tiny vestry, small, dapper, spectacled, his black face framed by the filtered light from the stained-glass window. "Miss Whitmore?"

"I'm Kate Whitmore."

"Welcome to Nunkwa. We were afraid you might have been killed."

"I almost was," Kate answered dryly.

The man sighed in commiseration. "We heard the news of last night's raid. I understand they

scored a direct hit on the medical hut. Poor Dr.
Rasgeldi. He dreamed always of liberation for our
people."

"Are you Bishop Sepamla?"

The stranger nodded, indicating an open door,
and Kate followed him into the tiny office. It was
stark and businesslike, as if its occupant disliked
ostentation in any form. There were no paintings, no
ornaments, not even, she noted with surprise, religious icons or crucifixes. It was as if the room had
been scoured deliberately bare.

At a stove in the office corner stood a Negro in
an immaculate gray suit. Kate stared at him, fascinated. He was the most handsome black man she had
ever seen. Tall, lean, devastatingly attractive, he
exuded an air of assurance which made him appear
oddly aristocratic.

"Permit me to introduce Elliot Chamille, one of
our most gifted young officers," the bishop said.

The handsome black man smiled winningly.
Somehow, everything he did carried a kind of inherent gracefulness, as if his movements and manner-
isms, even the tilt of his chin and the angle of his
eyes, belonged to some superior species. "Would you
care for some coffee?" the black man inquired.

Kate nodded, and taking a pot from the stove, he
filled a metal mug and pushed it into her hand. She
sipped gratefully, feeling a flush of warmth spreading through her lower stomach.

"Please be seated, Miss Whitmore," Bishop
Sepamla said. "I gather you've had a rigorous jour-
ney. The experiences of last night . . ." He paused.
"Who can tell the trauma such incidents generate? It
is enough to say that we understand and sympathize.
Unfortunately, though we would like to give you

time to recuperate, we need your help and we need it quickly."

Kate frowned in puzzlement as she slumped into the nearest chair. "Are you sure you've got the right lady?"

"I believe so."

The bishop perched himself against the edge of the desk, gazing down at her. He did everything, she noticed, in an overly precise way, but unlike the handsome young black man whose gracefulness was instinctive, the bishop's seemed strangely contrived.

"I am going to ask a great favor of you," the bishop said gently. "You have been a considerable help to us already. Without your support, it is unlikely Dr. Rasgeldi would have been able to continue his work among our people in the front line. However, I now need you to take a more direct involvement, to become not merely a purveyor of mercy, but in effect a combatant."

Kate frowned, cradling the coffee mug in her palms. "You're asking me to fight?"

"In an oblique sense. You will not be called upon to kill anyone, if that's what's worrying you, but your life—and I must make this point piercingly clear—will be placed in extreme danger. Please understand, I would not make this request if it were not a matter of the most supreme importance."

"I'm a nurse, not a soldier," Kate exclaimed helplessly. "I've never in my life even handled a gun, let alone fired one."

The bishop rose from the desk, pressing his fingertips lightly on its top. Like everything else he did, the gesture seemed strangely measured, as if he carried an inborn appreciation of the moment. "You know a man," he said, "called Harold Fuller?"

Kate heard her own intake of breath. For a

moment she couldn't be sure she had heard correctly. "Harry?" she echoed.

The bishop nodded, his eyes sharp and discerning. Kate shook her head in a helpless gesture. "I don't understand. What in God's name can Harry have to do with the struggle in South Africa?"

"You do know him, Miss Whitmore?" The bishop's voice was gentle but insistent.

Kate nodded, sighing.

How long had it been? she wondered. Two years? Three? A lifetime. And yet, inexplicably and perversely, the simple mention of Harry's name sent her pulse pounding, her senses racing. She thought she'd gotten over that, regrets, disillusion, the things which went with a love affair gone sour. But you didn't get over Harry. He was too real, too tangible, too—she searched for the word—too bloody infuriating. She'd loved him, passionately, profoundly, unarguably, but they just hadn't been suited. Different temperaments, different personalities. It had hurt her deeply when the relationship had broken up.

"This man—" Bishop Sepamla said diplomatically, "you were once very close, that is true?"

"I loved him," she answered simply.

The bishop inclined his head. "Did he, as far as you are aware, feel as strongly about you?"

"I believe he did. We were too different, that's all. They say opposites attract. Well, that might be true in the beginning, but when it comes to living together, you need some kind of contact, some kind of neutral ground. Everybody does."

"How would you describe Harold Fuller's character?"

She hesitated. "Difficult. He's prickly and short-tempered. He's also kind, generous, and loyal. Politics don't interest him a jot. He lives his life on his own terms, works hard, drinks a bit too heavily, keeps himself extremely fit. For relaxation, he plays the cello, not too badly either. His specialty is improvising on fugues by Bach. In some ways, he's the most complete man I've ever met. In others . . ." She shrugged. "He's existing in a vacuum. He doesn't give a damn what the rest of the world is doing."

Summing people up wasn't easy, she reflected; a few terse sentences scarcely conveyed the complex attitudes and thought processes which made up a human being. Yet in Harry's case, she had thought about him so often, analyzed him so much, the process seemed simple and straightforward.

"He's not, then, the kind of man you would describe as motivated?"

Kate laughed dryly. "In the things which matter—matter to Harry, that is—he can be as motivated as the next man, but most of the time he regards the world and everything in it as one long interminable game."

"He's unlikely, then, to be sympathetic to our cause?"

"He doesn't even think about your cause. In Harry's world, South Africa doesn't even exist. That's what broke us up, in the end. He just couldn't understand how I could get so involved. I couldn't accept how he could remain so detached."

The bishop took a deep breath. Somewhere outside, a woman was singing. It was an African hunting song, and her voice sounded cracked and discordant in the hot morning air.

"Mr. Fuller has a young son, I believe," the bishop said softly.

"Tim? Tim will be . . ." Kate calculated quickly, "almost ten this summer. He lives with his aunt in Coventry and travels up to join Harry for weekends and holidays."

Bishop Sepamla strolled across the floor, bowing his head in silent study. He paused for a moment as the stained-glass window cast dappled patterns of orange and green across his crisp white shirt. "We are about to launch an important operation," he said in a gentle voice. "It is both delicate and dangerous, and poses a serious threat, not only to the lives and well-being of the people who will undertake it, but also to the future of our armed struggle. If we succeed, however, we will achieve something we've been struggling toward for over twenty-five years: the release of Joshua Matshoba. Miss Whitmore, I want you to be part of that operation."

Kate swallowed hard. Elliot Chamille, the good-looking young black man, stood watching her closely. Well, she thought, it's what you wanted, isn't it? To become involved. To do your bit. For the cause. For the people.

"I'd like to help," she whispered, "in any way I can."

The bishop turned. In the light from the window, he was smiling warmly.

"Good," he said, "I hoped you would see it our way."

Moving to the cooking stove, he picked up the coffeepot and filled another spare mug. Her answer seemed to have released some tension within him. His movements had lost their measured air; they looked natural and spontaneous. He spoke without looking back at her.

"We're sending you to England," he said.

Three

The airport official was a fussy little man who looked as though he carried the troubles of the world on his shoulders. He came through the door of the VIP passenger lounge as Waldo Friedman was finishing his third martini. Leaning over Waldo, he molded his customarily pained expression into a look of passable agreeableness and said, "Your plane is ready to leave now, Mr. Friedman."

Waldo nodded, draining his glass. He did not usually drink so heavily so early in the evening, but he hated flying at the best of times, always had. It was an experience he had never grown used to, and for a man in Waldo's position—political analysis specialist, Section 10, Control Group Foreign Affairs, U.S. State Department—fear of flying was an embarrassing liability.

He rose to his feet and picked up his briefcase. He was a small man, thickset and solidly built with hair balding markedly above the temples. His expression was grave, but it was a simulated gravity, for Waldo was not by nature an unhumorous man; experience had taught him, however, that for individuals like himself, who lacked the benefits of natural dignity and poise, a serious countenance was the best alternative.

He followed the airport official out to the concourse, accompanied by a small entourage of plainclothed security men. The jet stood waiting at the side of the runway, its pale wings catching refracted slivers of light from the setting sun. It was a private flight authorized by the Secretary of State himself, which indicated, Waldo felt, the seriousness with which Washington regarded the affair.

Beyond the aircraft, he could see the lights of the city reflected in the dour March sky. Waldo had almost reached the boarding steps when a commotion from the airport entrance caught his attention. Frowning, he paused and glanced across the runway. A cavalcade of limousines came streaming across the tarmac toward him, flanked on both sides by motorcycle patrolmen. The wail of a police siren split the air, and Waldo saw lights flashing on the roof of the leading vehicle. Puzzled, he watched as the motorcade drew to a halt, and a tall, distinguished-looking man with sandy crewcut hair clambered out of the middle car. "Mr. Friedman?" he inquired in a polite voice.

Waldo nodded.

"If you could spare a moment, sir, the president would like a word with you."

Waldo sucked in his breath. For a moment he couldn't be sure he had heard the man correctly. He had met the president only once, and that had been at a crowded political rally in a perfunctory exchange which had lasted, Waldo estimated, approximately eight and a half seconds.

His pulse quickened as he stepped toward the center limousine. Taking off his hat, he leaned down to peer through the open door. The president smiled affably back at him, his features creased and familiar. "Hello Waldo," he said in a friendly voice. "Sorry to butt in on you unannounced, but my security advisers hate it when I set up too many prearranged appointments."

Waldo felt curiously tongue-tied as the president patted the seat beside him. "Get in, Waldo," he ordered pleasantly.

Settling himself against the leather seat cushions, Waldo slammed the door. He seemed mesmerized by the president's presence, and stared dumbly at the warm eyes and affable grin which, through press and television appearances, had become as familiar as Waldo's own. The president beamed at him with the air of a benign uncle. "Excited, Waldo?" he asked.

Waldo shifted uncomfortably in his seat. "Apprehensive, sir. It's quite a challenge."

"And a responsibility. Don't ever forget that. What happens in London is important to the entire world."

"Well, these are little more than exploratory talks," Waldo began.

The president silenced him with a lift of his hand. "The seed is small, but with luck, the tree will grow strong. Exploratory or not, it'll be up to you to find some point of contact, some common ground. It's the first time we've managed to get the South Africans to the negotiating table."

"McAuley has a reputation for being a difficult man," Waldo remarked cautiously.

"At least he's a moderate, a non-Afrikaaner. Most important of all, a non-*Broederbond* member. He's our only hope, Waldo. Don't alienate the man. He alone can persuade the South Africans where their future lies."

"I do appreciate the trust you've placed in me, sir."

The president grinned amiably. "Trust, Waldo? Not simply trust. Hope. The hope of mankind. The hope of the entire free world." He sighed, leaning back in his chair. "If we can get the South Africans to agree, at least in principle, to the dismantling of apartheid, it will be the pinnacle of my career. I'll go down in history, Waldo."

Waldo blinked. He'd imagined the president to be above such tawdry considerations at personal ambition. "Let's not get too optimistic, sir. We've a long way to go before we can say there are tangible grounds for progress."

The president's greatest asset was his natural grace and charm, and he used it to full effect now, smiling a boyish smile which lit up his entire face. The years melted away, and suddenly he looked young again, the creased skin scarcely noticeable against the flashing teeth and sparkling eyes.

"I know what you're thinking, Waldo. Is it the talks I care about, or what they'll do for my reputation and career? Well, presidents are human like everyone else. You can't bestow immortality on a man just because you elect him to the White House. I admit I have a personal stake in this. But that doesn't alter the fact that the future of millions of people rests upon your skill and diplomatic integrity. That's why I'm counting on you, Waldo, and that's why I considered it important to come here tonight and wish you luck."

Waldo heard the screech of an incoming jet. The wind picked up, blowing a few drops of rain against the limousine windshield.

"I want you to feel free to call me direct at the White House if you run into problems. Just give your name and you'll be linked through to either my

private suite or the Oval Office, wherever I happen to
be."

The president's eyes focused on Waldo's face
with a disturbing intensity. It was like the culminat-
ing point of an actor's carefully measured perfor-
mance, expertly timed, meticulously executed. "You
are on the brink of changing the world, Waldo. I wish
you God speed and bon voyage."

Smiling, the president held out his hand, and
with an air of confusion Waldo realized he was being
dismissed. He swallowed hard, grasped the prof-
fered palm in his own, and muttered, almost inau-
dibly, "I'll do my best, Mr. President. You can count
on that."

Still blinking, he clambered into the chill
evening air and watched the motorcade cruise
slowly back across the tarmac, the sirens of its escort
echoing over the distant wail of departing jets.

"British Airways announces the arrival of its
ten-forty flight from Lusaka. Will all passengers
please pass through the immigration hall and make
their way to the baggage reclaim department on the
lower floor?"

Despite the warmth of the airport terminal, Kate
shivered involuntarily as she glanced through the
windows at the swirling sky outside. It seemed
strange to be back in England again. She had
dreamed of it often during her long months in the
guerrilla camp, reflecting nostalgically on the familiar things which had once been part of her daily life:
the roar of traffic, the odor of diesel fumes, the sight
of store windows glistening in the frosty air. But now
the frenetic atmosphere of the airport building frightened her. She'd forgotten what it was like to be

surrounded by so many people. Had she made a terrible mistake? It had been a spur-of-the-moment thing, ill-conceived, badly thought out. She was a nurse, a minister of mercy. She eased pain, imparted solace. She had no right to indulge in reckless adventures which stood little chance of fulfillment and which, in any event, represented a flagrant violation of the laws of her native land.

She went through the Customs hall in a daze, pushing the baggage trolley containing the two suitcases of clothing she had purchased in Lusaka. They were a strange crew, and no mistake: two young Africans, Timol and Malheiro, who spoke in a language Kate barely understood and who seemed unable to take seriously, even for a moment, the hazardous undertaking on which they had embarked; an English mercenary, Robet De Brere, tall, bony, cynically sardonic; Elliot Chamille, their leader, charming and sophisticated—and herself, she thought, she mustn't forget herself. She was the strangest element of all, the one person here with nothing tangible to gain. De Brere was risking his neck for the money, the Africans were doing it for the cause. But God knew, it wasn't her cause, not when you came right down to it. She hated apartheid and everything it stood for, but she was a foreigner, an outsider, an Englishwoman with a world of her own.

As they came through the Customs gate, a heavyset black lady in a bright floral dress stood waiting for them in the arrival hall. She smiled as Elliot walked toward her and gently kissed her hand. He did it with a natural inherent gracefulness, raising her wrist to his lips without bending his head.

"Hello, brother," she said in a throaty voice. "You still look as gorgeous as ever."

"Melody, you get younger every year."

The woman laughed delightedly. "I get fatter by the minute. It's a bad place to live, London. Too many temptations." She slapped her belly with one pudgy palm. "Viktor calls me his African bulldozer."

"What you need is a few weeks on old-fashioned mealy-meal."

"If I tried that, Viktor would throw me out on my ear. He likes something he can hold on to in bed."

Chuckling, Elliot introduced his four companions. The woman's expression sobered as she greeted them formerly, one by one. "We have a place for you to spend the night," she said. "Sorry about the dramatics, but it's wise to be cautious. London is swarming with BOSS agents."

She led them to a battered old car in the parking lot outside. "Toss your gear in the trunk," she told them cheerfully. "And don't be put off by the body-work's appearance. It runs better than it looks. Viktor uses it to transport pigeons up and down the M.1."

Squeezed between Malheiro and Timol in the rear, Kate gazed wonderingly through the window as they chugged among the early evening traffic. The streets looked strange after the sparse emptiness of the Mozambique bush. They swung left off Penton-ville Road and the buildings grew seedier as they picked their way through a labyrinth of squalid little terraced houses. Children, predominantly black, played around the streetlamps, their breath steaming in the chill spring air. The woman drew to a halt in front of a ramshackle apartment block which looked, at first glance, as if it was falling to bits. "It's not exactly the Ritz," she said apologetically, "but you'll be safe here, and after all, it's only for one night. The basement flat belongs to Kamil. He's in prison at the moment, so he lets us use it whenever we need to. You'll find food in the refrigerator and money in the gas meter. Help yourselves to what you need. There are four bedrooms, which means two of the men will have to double up. Don't answer the telephone unless the caller rings three times, and dials again. Is that understood?"

They nodded silently, and opening the car door, the woman led them across the pavement and down the narrow flight of steps. The apartment was dusty and filled with stale air. "Been left too long." The woman opened the windows. "Viktor's supposed to clean the place regularly, but I have a feeling he spends most of his time at the betting shop. Anyhow, if there's anything you need, just give me a call. The number's on the telephone pad."

They thanked her, and Kate chose the smallest bedroom, dropping her suitcases on the narrow bunk. She felt tired, she realized, too tired even to eat. The long flight from Lusaka had worn her out. A small washbasin stood against the bedroom wall, and gratefully Kate stripped off her dress, draping it across the narrow bed. She eyed herself in the wall mirror, running her fingers through her long black hair. She didn't look like a dangerous revolutionary, she thought. She didn't look like anything at all, except perhaps—and God knew, she wasn't too coy to admit it—an alluring young woman. At least, men seemed to consider her so. She'd never had trouble with men before. They'd flocked around her like flies during her student days. She'd enjoyed their cajolements, their flattery, she'd be a fool to deny it, but all she'd ever cared about had been Harry Fuller. Testy, irascible, lovable Harry. He went at life like a battering ram, happy to accept the world as it was, exploiting its vagaries instead of trying to alter them. He'd been exasperated by her sense of obligation, and she in turn had been disillusioned by his lack of commitment. Yet, despite everything, she'd admired his great raw appetite for living. And she'd loved him dearly. Loved him still, if the truth were known. You didn't live with a person for three years of your life, then blot him out as if he had never existed. She felt sorry for Harry, sorry for what she was doing to him now.

Kate glanced up as the door clicked softly open. Leering at her crookedly was the British mercenary, Robert De Brere. She'd had little contact with De Brere since their departure from Lusaka, but several times she'd caught him watching her from the corner of his eye. Now, glimpsing the expression on his face, she felt a sudden tightening in her stomach.

"What do you want?" she asked in a cold voice.

"Just making sure you're nicely tucked in."

"Get out," she ordered. "This room is mine."

Chuckling softly and stepping in, he glanced over his shoulder and closed the door behind him. Despite the evening coolness, his skin looked shiny with sweat. "You're not being very friendly."

"I'm tired, I'm irritable, and I want to rest. Is that too much to ask?"

"I just thought we might have a little talk."

"Can't it wait until tomorrow?"

"Dodgy. Once the action starts, we might not get another chance."

"Please go, Mr. De Brere," Kate said with a sigh.

"Mister?" he echoed. "Very formal, aren't we?"

"We have enough on our hands as it is without setting up added complications."

"Well, that's just it." He grinned as he moved toward her. "Seeing as how we're the only white people on this team, I thought it might be a good idea if the two of us stuck together, gave each other moral support, so to speak. You know what these Kaffirs are? They get very excited when the pressure starts. Things go wrong, we may have to depend on each other, you and me."

"I'm surprised you fight for them if that's how you feel."

"I'm a businessman, like everyone else. I take what I'm worth on the open market."

"And don't give a damn what you're doing here."

He laughed dryly. "I offer good value for the money. As long as they're footing the bill, they know they can depend on me. I'm an extremely dependable fellow."

Reaching out, he ran one finger down Kate's cheek, bringing it to a halt just beneath the rim of her jawline. "Extremely dependable," he echoed.

She stared at him coldly, her eyes dark and hostile.

"Did anyone ever tell you you're a very beautiful woman?"

"Is that your idea of originality?"

"You know, you'll find me likable, if you'll only give me a chance."

"I doubt that."

He chuckled. "I have a feeling that despite that ladylike exterior, you're just praying some man will come along and tear you down off your pedestal."

Calmly and insinuatingly, his hand slid down the slope of her shoulder, probing beneath the lacy rim of her slip. She felt his palm crushing the soft flesh of her breast, and a surge of anger coursed through her.

"Get out of here," she ordered softly.

De Brere grinned. "It's going to be a long and dangerous trip. We might as well make the most of it."

"Get out of here this instant," she repeated in a warning voice.

He laughed, a strange flush entering his cheeks. With no trace of haste, Kate raised her right hand and thrust her thumb into the sternal notch directly beneath De Brere's thorax. She pushed steadily, increasing the pressure with her wrist, and De Brere, eyes bulging, gave a helpless choking sound as he reared backward. Without hesitating, Kate moved forward and in a neat, infinitely precise motion, kneed him skillfully in the crotch.

De Brere's body crumpled in front of her. He sucked in his breath, mewling deep in his throat, and his shoulders stooped like a question mark as he stumbled against the bedroom wall.

The door swung suddenly open and Kate saw Elliot Chamille standing on the threshold, jacket off, sleeves rolled up. He glanced at Kate and then at De Brere. "What's going on here?"

"Mr. De Brere's just had an unpleasant turn," Kate told him primly.

Elliot's eyes narrowed, noting the anguish in the Englishman's eyes.

"Has he been bothering you?"

"Not really. Mr. De Brere is a romantic at heart, and like most romantics, he sometimes finds the intrusion of reality a little hard to bear."

"Get out," Elliot ordered De Brere in a quiet voice.

The Englishman grinned painfully, struggling to recompose himself.

"Watch her, soldier, she's a terror. My voice'll probably be three octaves higher in the morning."

"Out," Elliot repeated, and clutching himself, De Brere shuffled chuckling through the door.

Kate walked to the bed, tugged her house-robe

from the open suitcase, and pulled it on. Elliot watched her, his face cool and composed. "He's a dangerous man; you shouldn't encourage him."

"I didn't encourage him," she snapped angrily. "I've hardly even spoken to the idiot."

"How on earth did you manage to subdue him so easily?"

She shrugged. "I used to work in the emergency ward of a big city hospital. We got the lot, drunks, addicts, weirdos. Learning to defend ourselves was a matter of course."

"You're quite a lady," Elliot said. "Maybe he'll think twice before he tries it again."

"What's he doing here anyhow? How can you trust a man like that, a mercenary, selling his services to the highest bidder?"

Elliott's eyes crinkled with amusement. "Oh, De Brere's a roughneck all right, but he has a simple code he always adheres to. He remains loyal to the person who's paying him, and he's very good at his job. He knows the business inside out. He's the kind of patriot you can always rely on, providing the money's good."

"He's not even African, for God's sake."

"Correct, but then, neither are you."

She stared at him coolly. "I'd have thought there's little question of where my loyalties lie."

"You're right. I'm just pointing out the parallel, that's all. If it makes you feel any better, I'm not African either. I'm an American."

She blinked. "American?"

"Sure. Detroit, Michigan."

"But I thought—"

He laughed gently. "That I came from the Homelands? Well, I do. Like Kipling's ladies, all blacks are kinsmen under the skin."

"You don't even talk like an American, for God's sake."

"A simple precaution. In my profession, it's often a good idea to disguise your origins."

He was a strange man, Kate reflected, examining him curiously. His face was sensitive and aesthetic, but there was a gleam in his eyes which suggested some primitive, primeval force. Though they'd spent several days working together in Mozambique, their relationship had been strictly a professional one. She'd found him easy to get along with, gentle and humorous, yet oddly distant in personal terms.

"Do you realize I know practically nothing at all about you?" she said.

"The less we know about each other, the safer for everybody."

"But you know about me. You'll have read my file. Don't tell me the ANC doesn't keep book on all its people."

His lips twitched. "Sure, I've read it. But it doesn't tell me much. You can't learn the truth about a human being from a few clipped phrases on a briefing sheet."

When he smiled, it was difficult not to respond. She could sense the strength in him, a dark pulsing power which seemed to generate through his long, athletic body. Curiosity filled her. Something about Elliot Chamille seemed oddly out of place.

"Why did they choose you for this job?" she asked.

He shrugged, his eyes still twinkling. "They must have figured I'm the best, I guess."

"In my opinion, you don't even belong here."

"No?"

"I mean, you don't belong in Africa, you don't belong with the movement."

"How's that?"

Kate considered for a moment. It wasn't easy to put her finger on, but she knew she was right. "Let me put it this way. Me, I specialize in lost causes. Anything—famines in Ethiopia, earthquake victims in China. It's a kind of disease, I have to get involved. My father spent his entire life fighting for the underdog. I suppose he started me on the path of rebellion, and I just never grew out of it. But you—you're too cultured, too refined. The deprivations of the Third World belong to a different universe."

"Despite what you think of me," he said softly, "they are still my people."

"Is it really so strong, that sense of kinship?"

"I wouldn't be here if it wasn't."

The humor was back again, but mingled with it was a kind of elusive sadness. "It's impossible for a white woman to appreciate the black experience," he told her. "But one thing at least we can relate to. The apartheid system diminishes us all."

"Aren't you worried? If this thing comes off, you'll be on the front page of every newspaper in the world. If it doesn't you'll be dead."

He chuckled. "I never think about consequences. Bad for the digestion."

"You're a cool one all right."

Her eyes narrowed as she spotted a vivid strawberry mark on his forearm.

"You've hurt yourself."

To her surprise, he quickly tugged down his shirtsleeve, fastening the cuff.

"What is it, a scar?"

For the first time since they'd met, he looked faintly uneasy. "It's nothing. A birthmark, that's all."

A flush of embarrassment spread across his cheekbones, and he ran his fingers through his crisp black hair. "Look, I'm sorry about De Brere. I'll see he doesn't bother you again."

"Don't worry, I can take care of myself."

"I realize that. But it's been a long flight, and we've got a heavy day in front of us tomorrow, so why don't you get some rest and we'll talk again in the morning?"

She frowned as he stepped outside, closing the door behind him. Long after she had gone to bed, Kate lay awake thinking. She hadn't been mistaken. The mark on Elliot's arm had been a scar, and the look on his face had been fear. She had to confess Elliot Chamille was not only an attractive man. He was also an enigma.

Inside his room, Elliot stared moodily at the ceiling, rubbing his forearm with his fingers. He'd thought it over, that part of his life, thought he had reached a point where time had salved the anguishes of the past, but nothing had faded. It was his private hell, his secret malaise, and Kate Whitmore had brought it back with devastating force.

Fool that he was, he'd let the woman get to him. She'd looked so tantalizing standing there, her hair tangled, her body clad in a filmy silk slip. There was something fascinating about her self-assurance, about the way she'd handled De Brere. Elliot admired self-assurance. He had worked so hard to attain it, he seldom failed to appreciate it in others, especially women. Especially women like Kate Whitmore, he thought. Funny, he'd never noticed her beauty before. That first moment he'd seen her, stepping through the door of the tiny church, she'd looked like something the cat had dragged in. Now, her closeness disturbed him deeply. There were different sensations in making love to a white woman, he reflected, different textures, different body scents. Kate Whitmore had—he hesitated to use the word, but he could think of no other way to describe it—class.

Something else she had too. Humanity. Commitment. She believed in the cause. She didn't know—couldn't—that Elliot's feelings of philanthropy had undergone a traumatic transformation. No more innocence for him, he thought. They'd destroyed innocence, as they'd destroyed everything else. Now he was doing it for the same reason as De Brere, for money, materialism, financial gain. He rubbed his forearm moodily. How would Kate Whitmore feel if she knew the simple truth? he wondered. Would she understand and commiserate. Would she soothe his fevered brow? He shook himself dourly. What are you rambling about? You came here to fight a war. You haven't time for trivial diversions.

But the idea was intriguing, whichever way he looked at it, and he lay for a long time thinking deeply before he finally dropped off to sleep.

Four

Harry hung back, hunching his shoulders as he watched Jackson stalking him like a panther. Dimly, his mind registered the ropes at his rear, the blunt outline of Acuum, the coach, watching owlishly from the ringside, the odor of disinfectant from the bucket on the floor below, but his eyes, sharp and penetrating, focused on Jackson inching in for the kill. Jackson threw a left which Harry blocked easily, but feinting to his left, the stocky Liverpudian caught Harry with a vicious jab to the stomach. Harry heard a roaring sound in his ears, and a wave of sickness spread through his lower body. He pulled in his guard, retreating desperately toward his corner while Jackson followed, swinging his fists in a series of wild uncoordinated punches. Harry dodged and parried as best he could. Then, with an incredible streak of luck, he caught Jackson with a glancing blow on the side of the jaw. Jackson danced back, shaken, and Harry lunged in to the attack, driving his opponent backward by the sheer savagery of his onslaught. He could hear Jackson panting as Harry pounded his body and skull unmercifully. Reaching the ropes, Jackson tried to fall into a clinch, but Harry, avoiding his grasp, caught him with a vicious uppercut that snapped back Jackson's head and dropped him smartly to his knees.

The coach's whistle blew, and Harry let himself relax, filling his lungs with air. He tugged the leather headguard from his skull and leaned forward to help Jackson to his feet. "You okay?"

Jackson nodded. He looked disgruntled, as if Harry had insulted him in some strange and indeterminate way. Because Jackson was ten years Harry's junior and at least fifteen pounds heavier, Harry knew he felt humiliated at being forced to the canvas by a man he regarded as physically inferior.

Harry rubbed his stomach as he clambered through the ropes. He was a tall man, heavy-shouldered, with a thatch of unruly dark hair. Tugging on his robe, he shuffled toward the gymnasium door where Bill Mackey stood waiting, his squash racket tucked under one tracksuited arm. Bill was Harry's closest friend. They played tennis together, fished together, roamed the Cumbrian hillslopes together, and sometimes, when Harry's moods grew too somber to control, drank themselves into a stupor together. Bill's bald head gleamed faintly under the fluorescent lights and he grinned as he glimpsed the expression on Harry's face.

"I'm getting too bloody old for this game," Harry complained, massaging his stomach tenderly.

"You were too bloody old years ago, only nobody dared tell you," Bill said with a chuckle, following Harry into the shower room. "Why don't you take up a gentler hobby, like stamp collecting or butterfly hunting?"

"Boxing's good for the soul. It works out the aggression."

Bill switched on the shower, peeling off his sweat-sodden tracksuit.

"That's the trouble with you, Harry. You think you're Peter bloody Pan."

Harry sluiced himself down and dried his body with a vigorous towel rub. By the time he'd dressed, the ache in his stomach had eased off considerably, and he followed Bill into the chill March night, his feet crunching on the cindered parking lot. They could see the hump of Carlisle Castle framed against the mottled night sky. Mist hung between the street-lamps, and drunken singing echoed among the department stores.

"Fancy a beer before you go home?" Harry asked.

"Can't. Susan's got guests in tonight. Some of her colleagues from the office."

He glanced at Harry sideways. "Why don't you come along? Spot of company won't do you any harm. Better than going back to that big house alone."

Harry grinned. "Still trying to match me up, Bill? Who've you got waiting this time? Some spinster from the local flower club? Susan's idea, I'll bet."

Bill shrugged in embarrassment. "She did mention something about a very nice girl just dying to meet you."

"Why don't you tell your wife I'm happy the way I am? You know the old saying: Once bitten, twice shy."

Bill was silent for a moment, staring thoughtfully at the windblown, rain-spattered sky. Across the street, the rows of rain-soaked houses seemed to huddle together for comfort and warmth.

"Still thinking about Kate, Harry?"

"Kate? Haven't thought about her in months."

"Pull the other one, sunshine."

Harry glanced at Bill sharply as he reached his car. Fumbling in his pocket, he leaned forward to open the door. "Bill, what happened between Kate and me was a mutual decision. We split up, we didn't desert each other. It's no tragedy. I've got my work, I've got my music. I'm happy."

Bill paused, stubbing at the ground with his toe. "You can't blame Susan for getting concerned. You're just not the bachelor type, Harry."

"I'm the same man I always have been. If I'm not complaining, why should anyone else?"

"Okay, forget I ever mentioned it. See you tomorrow night, squash club, seven o'clock."

"Marquess of Queensbury rules. Loser buys first pint."

"As always. Drive safely, Harry."

Bill waved as he strolled toward his car.

But driving out of town, Harry felt the depression building up inside him. Damn Bill, he was too bloody intuitive for his own good. Was his loneliness really so apparent? Friends, they only tried to help, but there wasn't anything Bill could do. Or anyone else, for that matter. The emptiness inside him was like an emasculating force. Three years it had been, longer, and still the hurt remained. Was it possible, he wondered, to love one woman to such an extent that without her the whole of life became some kind of brittle farce? People said time healed everything, but time hadn't eased his pain or satisfied his loss. He was like a zombie, not even a human being anymore, just an empty spiritless shell, scoured of emotion. He'd loved her too much, that was the truth of it, and love at such an intensity was too searing to be contained. They'd quarreled almost from the start, pointless, meaningless battles which had left them mentally bruised, emotionally scarred. But perhaps, in some strange and indefinable way, it had been their very polarity which had drawn them together, their sexual antagonism which had molded and cemented their relationship. After all, he'd never been much in the mating stakes. No charm, no eloquence. No ambition either, not in the customary sense. He hadn't done badly—area manager for British Rail—not a job to be sniffed at. Plenty of men who'd give their eyeteeth for a job like that, but the truth remained—and he might as well admit it—most people would find his career choice baffling. There'd been a time—nearly eight years ago—when his brother Richard had suggested a partnership in his building business, and Harry had turned him down. Richard simply hadn't understood, and Harry couldn't blame him for that. You had to see the railroad the way Harry saw it. In his youth, it had seemed so vigorous, so alive, so romantic. He could still recall with a biting nostalgia the steam locomotives butting their way up the 1 in 80 from Kendal to Oxenholme, and the classic Claughtons dragging their twelve-wheeler L&NWR carriages, all over the daunting hump of Shap summit. It had seemed the only future he'd ever wanted. But would a woman regard it so, especially a woman like Kate Whitmore? Nothing romantic about the railways today. Electrified lines, functional diesels. The trains just didn't breathe life anymore. A woman might be ashamed of that, ashamed of a man who would pin his existence to something so ordinary and mundane. She was a fighter, Kate, no question on that score. He'd admired her spirit always. No weakening. No compromise. Had her principles and stuck to them resolutely. A woman in a million. But principles didn't make an easy companion, and his own bloody temper had done the rest.

If he could turn back the clock, would things be any different? He doubted it, but he'd give his mind and soul for a chance to try. Kate, he thought, watching the headlamps pick out the hedgerows at the side of the road, if I could win you back, where in God's name would I find you now?

Kate sat in the battered old car and watched the traffic building up around her. People scurried along the pavement, hurrying home from work. There was an air of bustle and purpose which seemed strangely reassuring. A sense of deep foreboding had settled on Kate since early morning, refusing to be dislodged. She felt guilty for what she was doing to Harry, guilty for what she was doing to Tim. Tim was Harry's son, a bright boy with quick, intelligent eyes and a fertile, imaginative brain. She hadn't seen him for more than three years and her pulses quickened at the thought of their reunion. She liked Tim, found him something of a kindred soul, sympathetic and receptive. Unlike Harry, who always scoffed at her commitment to impossible causes, Tim was gentle, sensitive, kind.

Her breath quickened in her throat as she spotted a solitary figure in a dark blazer and gray flannel slacks drifting through the school gate on the opposite side of the road. She could scarcely believe how tall he'd grown. He's almost a man, she thought, feeling tears springing into her eyes.

"That's him," she said softly.

Sitting behind the driving wheel, Elliot examined the boy gravely.

"You're sure?"

"Of course I'm sure."

"He's older now. He'll have changed."

"It's him, I tell you."

Something in her voice made Elliot glance at

her, his dark eyes shrewd and perceptive. For a
moment he studied her in silence, then his features
softened. "Don't feel guilty. The boy won't be hurt.
I've given you my word. And it's a small price to pay
for an old man's freedom."

He smiled encouragingly. "Hurry now. You
don't want to lose him in the crowd."

Kate clambered out of the car and crossed the
busy side street, dodging among the traffic. Pausing
at the curbside, she watched as Tim strolled casually
toward her. Suddenly he stopped, his eyes widening
in astonishment. She tried to smile, but her lips
seemed frozen into a nerveless fudge.

"Kate?" he whispered, his voice barely discernible above the shouting of approaching schoolchil-
dren.

"Hello, Tim."

He ran toward her, and suddenly she was hugging him hard against her chest, laughing and crying
by turns. "I almost didn't recognize you," she
choked. "You've grown so big."

"I thought you were in Africa."

"I've just got back."

His face looked flushed and earnest. "Have you
called Dad?"

"Not yet. I . . ." She hesitated. "I wanted it to be
a surprise."

She ran her fingers through his tousled hair.
"Don't you ever use a brush or comb? You're just like
your father. A pair of scarecrows together."

His face looked flushed and earnest. "You *are*
coming home, Kate? You *are* back to stay?

She smiled, fighting back the tears. "We'll see,"
she said.

"It'll be just like the old days, the three of us

together. Dad only keeps me here because he thinks
I need looking after."

"Tim," Kate said, "I have some friends I'd like
you to meet."

"Friends, Kate?"

"They're nice people. You'll like them."

His eyes flashed with excitement. "From Africa?"

Kate nodded.

"That's great. I've never met anyone from Africa
before."

It was the moment she dreaded, the first tenta-
tive act of betrayal. Once taken, she knew there
could be no turning back. Tim reached up, slipping
his hand into her own, and she felt the tears streaming down her cheeks as, filled with confidence and
trust, he accompanied her across the narrow roadway.

"I've been trying to reach you all morning,"
Harry's secretary said as he stepped through the
office doorway. "Simon said you'd gone up to Lock-
erbie."

"That's right. We had a baggage car derailment
blocking the Glasgow Central express. Afterward, I
had to dash down to Penrith on a hot axle job. What's
up?"

"Your sister Mildred called. She says it's urgent.
Something to do with Tim."

"Okay, I'll give her a buzz. In the meantime,
Vera, get on to Blagdon and see if that cargo can be
switched to another unit, will you?"

Harry felt uneasy as he picked up the receiver
and dialed his sister's number in Coventry. He hoped
Tim hadn't been getting into trouble again. He was a

sensitive boy on the surface, but he didn't take too
kindly to school discipline. Harry knew he was the
despair of the teachers, but he hoped—fingers
crossed—it was nothing more than a phase, a stormy
interlude through which the boy would eventually
pass. When Mildred's voice came on the line, Harry
immediately sensed the tension in her.

"Harry? I've been trying to reach you for hours."

"I've been out. What's happened?"

"It's Tim," Mildred said. "He's disappeared."

"Disappeared?"

"He didn't come home from school last night.
I've been worried sick."

"Why didn't you call me right away?"

"I didn't want to worry you, Harry. It's not the
first time he hasn't turned up for supper. Sometimes
he goes fishing with the other boys. But when it got
to midnight and he still hadn't arrived, I knew
something was wrong."

"Did you call the police?"

"I had to. He's never stayed out so late before.
Harry, I know this sounds ridiculous, but the police
believe Tim has been kidnapped."

Harry heard the rattle of Vera's typewriter in the
office next door.

"Kidnapped?" he echoed.

"Some of the children saw him getting into a car
with a strange lady after school last night. The car
was driven by a black man. They noticed it particularly because of its delapidated condition."

"But why would anyone want to kidnap Tim?"

"Money, Harry?"

"That's crazy. If it's ransom they're after, they'll
get pretty lean pickings from me."

Something rattled in the station yard outside,
and glancing through the window, Harry saw a

patrol car draw to a halt on the cindered parking lot.

"Looks like the police are here."

"Try not to worry, Harry. It could be perfectly innocent."

"You don't really believe that, Mildred."

"I feel so awful, as if I've let you down in some unthinkable way."

"Don't. We can't wrap Tim in cotton wool."

"He'll be all right, Harry. I know he will."

"Stop worrying, Mildred," Harry said reassuringly. "I'll call you back as soon as I find out what's going on."

His hand was trembling as he put down the receiver. It was like some kind of bad dream from which he would soon awaken. Millionaires had their sons kidnapped, not area managers of British Rail.

Harry met the policemen at the top of the stairs. There were two constables and a plainclothed detective. They were all young, the detective particularly; he was fresh-faced and red-haired with a smattering of freckles across his sunbaked cheeks. "Mr. Fuller?"

Harry nodded.

"I'm Detective Sergeant Fisher. May I introduce Constables Hendricks and Wright?"

"You've come about my son."

"You've heard the news, then?"

"Just that he's disappeared."

"Mr. Fuller, we believe there's a strong possibility your boy might have been kidnapped. He was observed last night getting into a car with a lady and a Negro."

"I know. My sister called."

"Any idea who those people might be, sir?"

"None whatsoever."

The detective pushed his hands into his overcoat pockets. His face looked bland, the features planed into simple uncompromising lines. "I'd like to extend our sympathy, Mr. Fuller, and offer our assurance that we'll do our damnedest to get your son back safely."

"Thank you, Sergeant. I appreciate that."

"In the meantime, I must ask for your cooperation."

"Of course. Anything you want."

"First and foremost, have you any idea who could possibly benefit from kidnapping your boy?"

"Not a clue," Harry admitted.

"No particular enemies, no one who might have a grudge against you, that sort of thing?"

Harry shook his head. "You don't suppose it's sexual?"

"Unlikely," the detective said. "Not with a lady in tow. What about the boy's mother? Might she be the type to attempt an escapade like this?"

"Tim's mother died at his birth," Harry said bluntly.

"I'm sorry, Mr. Fuller, I thought you were divorced. Forgive me for asking this, but what about your financial state?"

"Area managers of British Rail aren't exactly Greek shipping magnates. Forget about the money angle, officer. If that's what they're after, they've kidnapped the wrong boy. I'm comfortable all right, but not enough to make it worthwhile risking a jail sentence."

"In that case, we'll need a detailed description of your son's personality, character, habits, a list of his friends and associates, and any information you can give us, Mr. Fuller—letters, diaries, that sort of thing. Perhaps you'll accompany us to your home."

Harry frowned. "My home?"

"Our strongest hope is that the kidnappers will try to establish some kind of contact, and if they do, that's where they'll call you. Too many people at the office to interfere. We'd like you to sit by the telephone while we sift out the relevant details."

"Right," Harry said. "I'll get my coat."

His mind was racing as he followed the policemen into the parking lot outside. There was a feeling of unreality about the affair, as if it was something he had read in a newspaper somewhere, absorbing, arresting, but in no way pertinent to himself. And mingled with the unreality, there was something else Harry recognized. Guilt. His sister's telephone call had been an indictment of sorts, for he'd had no right, however logically he'd reasoned it out, to parcel Tim off to some nameless and idiotic school in far-off Coventry. A boy needed his father, that was an inescapable fact. He'd considered himself too busy, too bloody engrossed in his work to bring Tim up in a decent and proper manner, but he'd been wrong, tragically and inexcusably wrong. If anything happened to Tim, Harry knew he would never forgive himself.

"You lead the way, Mr. Fuller," the detective called in the station yard. "We'll follow in the patrol car."

Harry drove in a daze through the Carlisle suburbs and along the network of country roads which led to the little village of Wetheral. It was a beautiful day, cold but sunny, the air tempered with the first delicious hint of spring, but Harry scarcely noticed the broad fields or the purple hummocks of the distant mountains. He felt sick to his stomach, and his hands, gripping the steering wheel, trembled relentlessly. Tim, he thought. God Almighty, if anyone hurt his boy, he would tear their throats out, law or no law. You loved a son in a way you could never love any woman, he told himself morosely, not more deeply maybe, but differently; he was part of yourself, part of your own flesh and blood, a living entity in his own right yet with some intrinsic quality with which you identified and understood. Before Kate, Tim had been Harry's sole reason for living. With Kate gone, he was all Harry had left in the world.

In the rearview mirror, he could see the police car trailing doggedly in his wake, the faces of its occupants strangely inscrutable as if they had composed their expressions to match the gravity of the case. The road bobbed and dipped, winding its way along a riverbank, and as Harry topped a small humpbacked bridge, a tractor clattered out of a nearby field and stalled abruptly behind him, blocking the police car's route. Harry sighed, pulling his vehicle onto the grassy verge. He could see the tractor driver fumbling desperately at his controls.

A truck came roaring along the narrow road in front, and as Harry watched, it slithered violently to a halt and a Negro leapt out of the passenger seat, trotting swiftly toward his car. To Harry's astonishment, the man was carrying an ugly-looking handgun, complete with a metal silencer.

"Open the door," the man snapped sharply.

Blinking in disbelief, Harry shot a quick glance in the rearview mirror. Behind him, the tractor driver was still struggling to get his engine going, his bulky vehicle blocking the patrol car completely from view. Swallowing hard, Harry flicked up the door lock and the Negro slid into the passenger seat, holding the gun menacingly at Harry's head. There was a gleam in the man's eyes as bleak as death itself. "Start up the engine," he ordered. "Follow that truck."

Harry watched the truck reverse recklessly into a nearby field, and set off at high speed along the narrow road ahead. Switching on the ignition, he trundled off in its wake, his fingers sweaty on the steering wheel. This can't be happening, his brain screamed. The incongruity of the situation seemed almost comical, as if he'd become the victim of some highly dubious practical joke. A quick glance in the rearview mirror showed the police car still in position, patiently waiting for the tractor driver to move away. The simplicity of the operation was breathtaking. If the people who had seized him were the same group which had kidnapped his son—and Harry could think of no other logical explanation—then one thing was searingly clear. They were professionals to their fingertips.

Farmhouses lay tucked among the pasture folds, their whitewashed walls picturesque and appealing in the bright March morning. The vehicle in front kept up a steady pace, swinging into the dips and curves with an ease and familiarity which suggested to Harry the driver had scoured the route meticulously beforehand. "Where are we going?" he asked in a quiet voice.

No answer. The Negro never seemed to blink, that was the unnerving thing. Except for the shuddering of the car, he might have been carved out of stone.

Harry shot him a quick sideways glance. "Is my boy all right?"

Silence.

Harry felt a stir of anger. "If anything's happened to Tim, you bastard, I'll ram that pistol down your gullet, silencer and all."

There was no change in the black man's expression. He looked strangely detached, as if Harry as a human being didn't exist at all. In a curious way, the man's very lack of emotion seemed terrifying. He would squeeze the trigger, Harry felt sure, at the drop of a hat.

Ahead, the road bobbed sharply over a narrow bridge, and Harry saw the truck pull onto a gravel track winding tortuously through a patch of woodland. He took the turning without a word, dropping his speed as his vehicle bucked and lurched over the rough uneven surface. The trees closed in, shutting off the river and the road behind. Ahead, the track came to a halt in a broad loading bay used during logging operations. The truck stood parked to one side, facing back the way it had come.

"Pull up here," the Negro commanded coolly, and without a word, Harry swung the car to a halt, backing alongside the other vehicle. He switched off the engine and looked at his captor expectantly, trying hard to keep his features unafraid.

"Get out."

Dappled sunlight filtered through the tree branches as Harry clambered into the morning coolness. The air smelled clean, and his nostrils caught the odor of rising pine sap. Straightening into the sunlight, the Negro leaned across the car roof and jerked his head to the left. Harry squinted through the trees. He could see the river curving toward the adjacent pasturelands. A figure stood on the grassy bluffs, waiting patiently, and without a word Harry began to stroll toward it, picking his way along a narrow track winding through the clinging underbrush. There was was something strangely familiar about the thick hair and supple body, and a faint breathlessness gathered in Harry's diaphragm. As he approached, the figure turned, head at an angle, cheeks slightly slanted, and Harry felt his senses lurch. A strand of hair, tossed by the breeze, fluttered across the sunbrowned face, and with a neat, almost unconscious gesture, Kate flicked it back, studying him intently. "Hello, Harry," she said.

A series of shudders ran through his astonished frame, and he felt his vision wavering like the first warning symptom of a massive migraine attack. Kate, he thought. His eyes scarcely registered her beauty. He'd visualized it so often in anguished postmortems into the errors of the past that he took it now for granted, noting instead the changes in her— hair longer, skin more deeply tanned, noting too the hint of strength in her soft gray eyes, the willful determination confronting him challengingly. She'd always been strong, he knew. Not a lady to mess with. He'd liked that in the beginning, but afterward it had exasperated him, for there was no give in Kate, no chink of weakness to breach the formidable barrier of her convictions.

"Kate?" he whispered in a choking voice. "What in God's name are you doing here?"

Her smile still lingered, its humor sad—directed not so much at him as at the curious circumstances in which she found herself. Her eyes were gentle and familiar, yet filled with that unstoppable force which had caused him so much bafflement in the past.

"What's going on?" he demanded. "Why was I brought here at gunpoint?"

"We had no choice, Harry. The police had you under observation."

"Where's Tim?"

"Safe."

"Safe where?"

"Don't worry, he's being well looked after."

She tilted her head. "You might at least look pleased to see me."

"Pleased? For God's sake, I want my boy."

"Your boy is fine. I'll explain everything in just a moment, but first I want to look at you."

She moved toward him, scrutinizing his face. "You've filled out a bit, Harry. It suits you."

"You haven't changed at all," he said. "Still the same old Kate."

"Is that a note of complaint or approval?"

He sighed. "I want to know why you've put me through this ridiculous charade," he insisted.

"It was necessary. You'll understand why in a second or two. You know I'd never hurt you, Harry, not intentionally anyway."

"Why not? You hurt me often enough in the past."

"You think it was all one-sided? You think you have a monopoly on pain?"

"At least I loved you," he growled.

She cocked one eyebrow mockingly. "Love, Harry? You wouldn't recognize love if you saw it walking down the street. You live in a world of your own making. Anything outside that, you dismiss contemptuously. You never tried to understand that I was different. You never compromised, never reached out."

He snorted. "You expected me to welcome that bunch of do-gooders you called friends?"

"You might at least have been civilized about it. They were human beings, real people, Harry. Committed. They cared."

"Phonies to a man," Harry snapped.

Kate's eyes flashed with anger. "At least they didn't live their lives in blinkers. They didn't accept the world as some kind of immutable force. They tried to change it, fight injustice, fight oppression. They weren't like you, big and macho and self-sufficient. You never gave a damn about anything, Harry, except enjoying the individual moment."

"I cared about you," he said softly.

She sighed, some of the fury draining from her eyes. "I'm sorry I couldn't be the helpless little woman for you, Harry. That's what you needed. Someone traditional who'd iron your shirts and mend your pants. I didn't belong in your world any more than you belonged in mine."

Harry hesitated. A couple never truly loses that strange and elusive intimacy, he thought. Living together becomes a culture in itself, with its own subtleties of expression, of communication.

"Three years we haven't seen each other," he said, "and here we are, quarreling already."

She smiled. "I've missed you, Harry. I've missed you terribly."

"You're the one who walked out, remember."

"There was no other way. We were killing each other, slowly and surely. It was like living with a time bomb, couldn't you see that?"

"We could have talked it out first."

"Talk?" She gestured helplessly. "We could have talked until the cows came home, it wouldn't have changed a damned thing. You can't help being you, Harry, and I can't help being me."

Harry ran his fingers through his unruly hair. Now that the shock of confrontation had passed, his nerves were beginning to steady a little. He glanced back through the trees. He could see the Negro watching them closely over the car roof. Two other men had joined him, both black, Harry noticed.

"Who are your friends?"

"Colleagues."

"With guns?"

"They're soldiers. Freedom fighters."

"Terrorists, you mean."

She glared at him hotly. "Everything I say, you pigeonhole into some contemptuous category of your own choosing. Those men are members of the South African resistance movement. They're fighting for the future of their country, so don't sneer at them, damn you. I can't stand your macho bloody Cumbrian superiority."

Harry's face hardened. "Are they the bastards who kidnapped my son?"

Silence.

"Are they?" Harry repeated in a cold voice.

She nodded.

"Then I don't give a damn what they're fighting for. I'm against them, tooth and nail."

"Listen to me, Harry," she pleaded softly. "Before you close your mind completely, at least listen to what I have to say."

"Go ahead," Harry told her. "But by Christ, it better be good."

She folded her arms across her breasts as if the chill March wind had sliced insidiously through her padded parka. The sunlight cast shadows across her nose and cheekbones. It picked up the glossy sleekness of her hair, illuminating it in gentle nuances of refracted light. Her voice, almost indiscernible, seemed to tremble slightly as she began to speak. "It's true they kidnapped Timmy. It's true too that I helped them."

She raised one hand as she heard his intake of breath. "Please," she whispered. "Let me finish. I give you my word your son will not be harmed. You know perfectly well that whatever else I might be capable of, I would never, in a million years, hurt Tim."

"Not you maybe, but what about those lunatics over there? They're fanatics. Capable of anything."

She stared at him calmly. "You've got to trust me, Harry. Tim will be released untouched. You have my sacred word on that. They gave me a personal undertaking before I agreed to cooperate."

"Undertaking?" Harry snorted. "What the hell is an undertaking to men like that? They'll lie to you or anyone else if they think it'll help their tinpot cause. Their ethics are as malleable as the circumstances demand."

"What do you know about ethics?" she exclaimed. "You never had a noble thought in your entire life. You live for yourself, Harry, for your own personal gratification. Do it if you want to, but don't sneer at men who are prepared to die for their ideals."

Harry hissed in annoyance. There was something indefatigable about Kate. He knew from bitter experience that when her mind was set, she was unshakable as a rock.

"You were talking about Tim."

She hesitated, sighing. "We need your help, Harry. We need it badly. We're on the threshold of what could be a major victory."

"And this in some way involves my son?"

"Not in a direct sense," she admitted. "It's you we want. Your knowledge, your expertise. Howard McAuley, the South African foreign minister, is paying a secret visit to London. He's come to take part in exploratory talks with British and American diplomats. Their aim is to bring about the dismantling of apartheid."

Harry listened expressionlessly. His eyes offered no indication of what he was thinking.

"McAuley's a moderate," Kate continued. "It

was McAuley who sold the idea, at least in principle, to the South African prime minister. We have in our possession photostated documents which set out all the details. It's a sellout, Harry. Oh, it'll bring an end to apartheid, true enough, but not in any immediate sense. The system is to be phased out gradually over a period of twenty years. Blacks are to be admitted into the administration on condition that they can compete on a white man's level. The principle of one-man-one-vote will only be adhered to when everything else has been accomplished to the satisfaction of the South African ruling classes. That could take thirty or forty years, Harry. The British and Americans are jubilant. They think getting the South Africans to the negotiating table is a major step forward, but they're wrong. The people won't wait. They want their freedom and they want it now, by force, if necessary."

"You've come to assassinate McAuley?" Harry whispered.

"Assassinate?" Kate blinked. "What d'you take me for, a murderer? No, we've come to kidnap McAuley. We're going to trade his life for the release of Joshua Matshoba."

Harry took a deep breath. Across the river he could see a farmer plowing in a distant field; seagulls followed his tractor blades, trailing through the air like a billowing white cloud. "Where do I come into this?"

"According to our information, McAuley intends traveling to Scotland before the talks begin. He's making what I suppose you'd call a sentimental journey. His great-grandfather came from a tiny village in Ayrshire. McAuley's a difficult traveler. He gets sick at the drop of a hat. He dislikes flying and he dislikes driving. The plane trip from South Africa

was an unpleasant necessity, but following a request
by the security forces, British Rail has agreed to lay
on a special train to carry him from Euston to
Glasgow. We know the journey is imminent—in fact,
we're expecting it within the next few hours. What
we don't know is what time it's scheduled to leave
and arrive."

Harry nodded grimly. "I see."

"You're the Carlisle area manager. They
wouldn't dispatch a special train through your section without informing you personally."

"That's true."

"We need the details, Harry. We must have the
exact time the train will pass through Carlisle."

"Then what?"

Kate's eyes saddened. "I'm sorry," she said gently. "There's something else we must ask of you. Just
south of Carlisle, there's an old branch line running
through the hills to Broadstruthers in the Scottish
border country. We want you to arrange for the
minister's train to be diverted along it."

"Impossible. The Glasgow main line is electrified. You can't divert a train without a diesel unit
standing by to take over."

"The minister's train won't be electrified. They're
afraid an unexpected power cut might leave it stranded.
They've laid on a Class 47."

"But the Broadstruthers branch line hasn't been
used in years. It's probably too delapidated to take
the weight of a modern locomotive."

"It won't be for long," Kate said. "A few miles
north of the turnoff is a spot called Simonbridge
Junction, where the old Kielder line used to run. The
track's been torn up now, but the junction's still
intact. We'll stop the train on the viaduct."

"In the middle of nowhere? There's only one

road up there, you idiot. They'll run you to earth before you've gone five miles."

"We won't be using the road," she told him calmly. "At Simonbridge Junction, we'll be within striking distance of the Border Forest. Four hundred square miles of Norwegian spruce, Harry, spreading across the hills and fells of north Northumbria. An army could lose itself up there for months. They'll never find us, never."

Harry whistled softly under his breath. "You've thought it all out."

She nodded. "It'll work, Harry. It's got to. There's too much to win, too much to lose. All we need is your cooperation."

"And if I refuse, you kill Tim, is that it?"

"For God's sake, Harry, why do you never listen to a single thing I say? I'm asking this as a personal favor. If you still feel any affection for me at all, then I beg you, on my knees, Harry, to help us stop a terrible act of injustice. Joshua Matshoba is innocent. All he ever did was demand dignity for his people. On that alone, they've held him in prison for over twenty-five years."

"If it's my noble nature you're appealing to, why in God's name did you snatch Tim?"

"Can't you see?" she exclaimed. "We did it for you, Harry. We did it to protect your name. When this is over, they'll realize we had to have inside help. It's your cover, Harry. No one will condemn a man who's forced to cooperate against his will."

Harry stared at her icily. "You little fool," he breathed. "You naive, trusting, ignorant little fool. You think I live in a blinkered world, a world of my own making, but my God, nobody could be so blind, so completely and unutterably lacking in awareness. They're using you exactly as they intend using me.

They'll give you their word, they'll give you anything you ask for, anything that gets the job done. But refuse to cooperate, and they'll snuff Tim out as unthinkingly as they'd swat a fly."

The wind caught his hair, fluttering it across his forehead. She could see the muscles tightening beneath his jawline. "All right," he breathed. "You've given me no choice. I'll not risk my boy's life for the sake of some faceless South African politician. I'll help because I have to. But I'll tell you this. You've made a mockery of everything we ever had together, everything I believed in. Whatever happens, whether we secure Joshua Matshoba's release or not, I'm going to see you suffer for what you've done to my son."

There was no mistaking the hatred in Harry's features. Kate stared down at the river so he wouldn't discern her dismay.

Five

Waldo Friedman stepped from the shower and reached for his robe, grimacing slightly as he caught a glimpse of his reflection in the bathroom mirror. He was not, by any stretch of the imagination, an imposing man, he thought; his nose was too long, his ears too big, and he'd begun to develop an unsightly bulge around his middle. But then, he had to admit ordinariness had always been one of his strongest assets. A man too positive, too physically commanding, stood little chance in the field of diplomacy. People—especially politicians—resented dealing with advisers who came across as smartasses, and if Waldo had any commendable quality at all, it was his ability to appear agreeable, unimposing, and compromising. Throughout his early career, he had remained studiously in the background, serving at embassies in Stockholm, Warsaw, Santiago, and Rome, making friends, courting premiers, but impressing no one in particular. At the State Department in Washington, where he worked, he was regarded as a shrewd, incisive professional, a man who understood his country's problems and took great care to see they were never exacerbated. But in dealing with people, Waldo was unfailingly friendly and courteous, a manner he had developed to a meticulous art. It had paid off too, all things considered—political analysis specialist, Foreign Affairs, was not a post to be ashamed of, even if his earlier ambitions had followed a more extravagant course. And if the PAC talks came off, if he succeeded in bringing some semblance of order and sanity to the turmoil in South Africa, he knew it could prove the crowning point of his career.

He frowned as, stepping into the sitting room, he heard someone tapping on the hotel suite door. He had dismissed his security men earlier in the evening, considering their presence unnecessary since London was one of the few cities in the world in which he felt relaxed and at home. Nevertheless, his mission was extremely delicate, and he was cautious as he padded across the room.

"Who is it?" he demanded in a loud voice.

"Mr. Friedman?"

"This is Friedman. What do you want?"

"I thought I'd introduce myself. Charles Palmer, head of Section 4."

Waldo hesitated. He had heard of Palmer, who was something of a legend in the British security service. In 1972, he had taken over from Sir Martin Salisbury after testifying to the Franks Committee investigating leaks of classified material under the Official Secrets Act. Since then, he had honed his department into a finely tuned machine, revitalizing the entire British intelligence network. A bachelor and a misogynist, Palmer was known to be a career man, dedicated to his work and protective of his anonymity.

As Waldo fumbled with the lock and eased open the door, a hand appeared in the aperture, clutching a plastic ID card. Waldo studied it for a moment, then stepped back, waving his visitor across the threshold.

At first glance, Charles Palmer reminded Waldo of the late Ronald Colman. He was small, gray-haired, and inherently graceful. His features were sharp, his skin pale, and he was dressed in an immaculately cut pinstripe suit which could only have been tailored on London's Saville Row. Palmer exuded an air of well-bred civility which suggested the archetypal English gentlemen, but something in his eyes made Waldo hesitate; it was nothing he could put a name to, but Palmer's gaze carried a directness which convinced Waldo his guest would be a bad man to cross.

"I'm Friedman," Waldo said, holding out his hand, wincing impulsively as he felt the wiry strength in the slender artistic fingers.

Palmer glanced around the room in surprise. "You're alone, Mr. Friedman?"

"I dismissed the Secret Service men. I feel such a fool when they're hanging around. I'm an administrator, not a politician. Too much attention makes me nervous."

"Just the same, aren't you being a trifle reckless?"

"Nobody's likely to blow my brains out, if that's what you mean. In State Department terms, I'm what you call a "dancer." I dance to the music, whichever way it's played. That makes me a very minor official indeed."

"It's not often I meet an American so uncharacteristically modest."

Waldo smiled. "You shouldn't categorize us, Mr. Palmer."

"Nevertheless, my department has a WP.14 on you. That's a very high-security classification indeed. Somebody at the top clearly wants you protected."

"Well, a great deal depends upon these talks. If they break down, there'll be some red faces in Washington and Whitehall."

Waldo opened the cocktail cabinet. "Can I offer you a drink?"

"I'll have a whiskey, if one's going."

"Scotch or rye?"

"Malt, please. No ice."

Waldo was silent as he filled the glasses. He knew Palmer was studying him closely. Despite his sophisticated appearance, the Englishman's eyes seemed to miss little, and Waldo was willing to bet Palmer had made a lightning assessment of his character which was probably as near the knuckle as it was possible to get.

"What brings you here?" Waldo asked, handing Palmer the whiskey.

"Just a social call. I thought I ought to, in the interests of international cooperation."

"You caught me just in time. As a matter of fact, I was planning a little visit of my own."

"Indeed?"

"Thought I might drop in on McAuley. Sort of break the ice before we get down to business."

"Is that what you call 'dancing'?"

"It's what I call diplomacy." Waldo smiled. "I find it works wonders at the negotiating table if you've met your opposite number beforehand."

"Well," Palmer drawled, "in this particular instance, you've drawn a blank, I'm afraid. Mr. McAuley is leaving London tonight."

Waldo blinked at him. "Leaving?"

"He's traveling to Scotland. British Rail have laid on a special sleeper."

"Why, for God's sake?"

"Sentimental reasons. His great-grandfather was born up there, I understand."

"I see," Waldo murmured, disappointed. He had been counting on operating in his usual manner, making contact, setting up relationships, establishing points of agreement before the hard bargaining got under way.

"To be honest," Palmer admitted, "it's not purely a nostalgic visit. The Scottish journey was prepared by our diplomatic people as a simple precautionary measure. If these talks extend beyond the end of the week, it's just possible someone will recognize McAuley—a reporter, a photographer— and wonder what he's doing here."

Waldo nodded, understanding. "You'd find that a little embarrassing."

"*Difficult*'s an apter word. There'd be some rather tricky explaining to do. However, no one's likely to question the motives of a man retracing his roots. The British are an incurably romantic race."

Waldo glanced down at his drink, swirling the liquid lazily in the glass. "Well, it looks as if I'm a bit premature. I guess I'll have to sit on my thumbs for a while."

Palmer looked sympathetic.

"If you can stand the company of a doddering old man, my club in Knightsbridge offers some of the finest fare in England, and I'd be delighted to have you as my guest."

Waldo stared at him in surprise. Palmer's face suggested arrogance and disdain, yet Waldo had a feeling he was not at all the way he seemed. Suddenly, Waldo liked him. He grinned as he tossed back his drink. "Sounds terrific," he said. "Give me a minute to put on my things."

*   *   *

Harry drove in a daze through the network of country roads, his brain in a turmoil. His meeting with Kate had destabilized him completely; the suddenness of her reappearance, the preposterous undertaking on which she had embarked, had created a vacuum in his mind, smothering thought processes and response patterns alike.

Harry Fuller was a simple man. His attitudes toward people were surprisingly uncomplicated. He valued loyalty above all things. Harry's allegiance to his friends was constant and unshakable, and nothing in the world appalled him as much as an act of deceit, a breach of faith, a treacherous deed. Yesterday, he'd believed that without Kate, some essential part of himself had been summarily amputated, leaving him not wholly alive anymore. Today, he hated her with a searing passion. Love and hate were interchangeable, he reflected. You seldom hated any enemy as much as the friend who betrayed you, and Kate had committed the unpardonable sin. She had put his boy in jeopardy. For that, he wanted revenge. It was a smoldering truth, hard, immutable, impossible to escape. Once this was over, once Tim was safe, once he was clear of the squalid little mess, he would make Kate weep for what she'd done to his son.

He saw the house emerging in its little patch of woodland, a fine Georgian-built residence of Cumbrian sandstone which he'd bought for a song seven years' earlier, and which—in the beginning at least—he had renovated and refurbished proudly. But some of the life had gone from the place after Kate had left. He'd lost interest, that was the top and bottom of it. Now the house looked run-down and neglected.

Harry could see the police car waiting as he pulled into the front drive. He switched off the engine, and Detective Sergeant Fisher came strolling toward him, looking puzzled. "We wondered where you'd got to."

"I was lost in the clouds," Harry admitted. "When I glanced in the rearview mirror, you'd vanished."

"Damn tractor held us up for nearly ten minutes."

"I'm sorry, I shouldn't have scuttled ahead like that."

Fisher pursed his lips. "You must've taken an unusually roundabout route. We've been waiting here for ages."

"Well," Harry said, "I went back looking for you. Thought I'd better. Visitors find the signposts around here hellishly complicated."

"I see. In that case, shall we go inside, Mr. Fuller? If the phone rings, you ought to be on hand to pick up the receiver."

Harry hesitated. "Look," he said reasonably, "suppose I give you the door key and let you wait for the kidnappers to call?"

Fisher frowned. "I don't quite follow."

"I have to get back to the station. We've got a special train coming through from Euston. Top security."

"Funny you didn't mention that before."

"It must have slipped my mind in the turmoil of Tim's disappearance."

"Surely, under the circumstances, somebody else could handle things?"

"You don't understand. The line must be kept totally clear. They need my personal authorization."

Fisher examined Harry impassively, watching

with a policeman's shrewdness for small imperceptible signs of anxiety or distress. Harry met his gaze,
struggling to quell the tension in his stomach. Detective Sergeant Fisher was nobody's fool, Harry knew.
"Very well," Fisher said at last. "Give us the key and
I'll call you at the office if anything happens."

"I do appreciate your support," Harry told him.

Fisher stood watching as Harry started up the
engine and drove back the way he had come. There
was no expression on the detective's face, but his
eyes looked deep and thoughtful. He whistled
soundlessly in the cool morning air, then he muttered, "Something's wrong."

Constable Hendricks glanced at him with surprise. "Fuller?"

"He's defensive and he's frightened. Somehow
or other, he's been got at."

Hendricks frowned, eyeing Harry's departure.
He was a slow-witted man who survived by following the instincts of his superiors. "What should we
do, d'you think?"

Detective Sergeant Fisher came to a quick decision. "Send Tony into the house. Tell him to sit by
the telephone and monitor all incoming calls. We're
heading back to Carlisle. Whatever happens, we're
not letting Fuller out of our sight."

In the hour before midnight, Euston Station
looked deserted. A few derelicts sat dozing about the
wooden benches, but the concourse was unusually
empty of passengers. Commander Dameron of Scotland Yard's Special Branch, tall, muscular, balding,
watched with approval as his men checked the
entrance route to Platform 14 and signaled their
colleagues to proceed with the boarding.

"This way, Minister," Dameron said politely, taking McAuley's arm.

McAuley was a small man, but he moved with a deceptive grace which suggested to Dameron he kept himself scrupulously fit. He was, Dameron had discovered with surprise, both affable and engaging, accepting the commander's security precautions with a patient, if somewhat wry resignation. Commander Dameron felt less benevolent toward the small group of South African secret servicemen, five in all, agents of BOSS, the notorious undercover police force whom the South African authorities had insisted accompany the minister's entourage. They were led by a detective named Tazelaar, a thickset man in his early forties, whom Dameron had disliked on sight. He'd heard ugly stories of the way BOSS agents carried out their work—stories of whippings, beatings, and even, in some cases, cold-blooded murder. But it was more than gossip which fashioned Dameron's attitude. Something about Tazelaar made him feel uneasy. The man seemed strangely unhealthy. His languid eyes carried an absence of emotion, as if his body functioned with the unfeeling consistency of a well-oiled machine. If anything existed inside the blunt dome of his skull, Dameron had seen little evidence to suggest it. Nevertheless, he had to admit the scale of the enterprise was impressive. Five BOSS undercover agents, seven Special Branch detectives—twelve armed bodyguards to safeguard the welfare of one man. Howard McAuley should be the safest politician in England, thought Dameron, though he reflected that he would have felt a good deal happier if he'd been allowed to keep the affair exclusively British.

McAuley paused as they passed a group of

workmen stacking newspapers on a wooden trolley. "Are they the morning editions?" he asked.

"I believe they are, sir," Dameron answered politely.

"Can I get you something, *menheer*?" Tazelaar inquired.

Dameron stared at him sourly. Despite the brutishness of the man's appearance, Tazelaar was the most insufferable crawler the detective had ever encountered.

"See if they have a *Financial Times*, will you?" McAuley asked, fumbling in his pocket for a coin.

Tazelaar stopped him with a lift of his hand. "That will not be necessary, *menheer*."

Tazelaar spoke briefly to the little group of workmen and, dropping a fifty-pence piece on the trolley top, presented a newspaper to McAuley with an extravagant flourish. Dameron glowered at him as they continued their progress through the ticket gate and down the ramp to the empty platform. Bulky and expressionless, Tazelaar eyed the Englishman shrewdly from behind. He sensed the man's resentment, recognized it, understood. All his life he had aroused feelings of distaste, revulsion—even fear—in other people, but on a job like this, he couldn't afford such friction. Everyone had to work together, that was the only sensible way. He felt gratified at his own refusal to respond. It was, he considered, a victory of sorts. He had no intention of fueling the commander's flame.

Jan Tazelaar had learned to sublimate hostility in the same way he had learned to sublimate sex, seeing in one the road to divine punishment, and in the other a staircase to an incalculable hell. This concept had been planted in Tazelaar's mind by his father, a devout, fiery bear of a man who had run his family like the scourge of God. The Tazelaar farm in the Orange Free State was the only home young Tazelaar had ever known until, at the age of fifteen, his youthful body bruised and battered from his father's attempts to thrash the devil out of his soul, he had been dispatched to his grandmother's home in Doornfontein, a suburb of Johannesburg overlooking Joubert Park. Tazelaar had regarded his change of environment as a sign of blessed deliverance and would have been happy, he felt sure, if it hadn't been for the stubborn conviction, printed indelibly deep within his psyche, that he was in some strange way irreversibly depraved. The dark rages which smoldered inside him filled him with a kind of supernatural dread, and he regarded his fury as a weakness of sorts, a complex anomaly which made him feel like an outcast from the whole human race.

In the English school in Newtown, the pupils had ridiculed his harsh Boer accent, and on three separate occasions, as punishment for speaking in the Afrikaaner tongue, he had been made to stand at the front of the class with a pair of woolly donkey ears dangling from his skull. During his formative years, he had developed an inherent hatred for everything British, but the admonishings of his father, coupled with the biting sting of his father's *jambok*, had convinced him such aggressive emotions were deeply and profoundly sinful, and he had concentrated on promoting an attitude of benevolence and goodwill.

He had joined the police force, not out of any deep-rooted conviction, but because it had seemed the thing to do at the time. Finding the proximity of his grandmother too constricting, he had moved to Cape Town, coming forty-second out of two thousand applicants taking the Police Academy exami-

nation in 1962. A laconic man with a detective's eye
for detail, he had risen swiftly through the ranks,
transferring to BOSS at the instigation of the *Broederbond*, the secret society which dominated every
level of South African administrative life.

Tazelaar took to his duties with the impassioned
fervor of a committed evangelist, finding in the
protection of the South African state a perfect outlet
for the fiery rages which had ravaged his earlier life.
Having obliterated from his mind all traces of overt
aggression, he viewed the interrogation of black
detainees as an affectionate act, designed not merely
to break the prisoner's spirit, but to "settle his mind"
in much the same way as an indulgent father might
discipline a wayward child. Priding himself on this
tolerant attitude, he beat their skulls with knuckle-
dusters, pounded their flesh with truncheons, applied electrodes to their mouths and genitals—doing
it always, he assured himself, with a true and genuine love in his heart, a lasting compassion for human
frailty.

It seems incredible to credit the fact that Jan
Tazelaar, psychotic and obsessive, could have risen
to such a dizzy and responsible rank in any security
service in the world, but Tazelaar's ability to control
his emotions made him a difficult man to define.
Withdrawn, introspective, unfailingly remote, he
had a reputation—one he was secretly proud of—for
never losing his temper in public, and he was
determined not to ruin that now as he followed
Commander Dameron down the ramp to the railway
platform where their train stood humming softly,
preparing for departure. Tazelaar counted four carriages in all, and frowned.

"What's this?" Commander Dameron said to the
British Rail official.

"The front coach belongs to the minister," the official explained. "The others are mail vans bound for Glasgow. It's an expensive business, running unscheduled trains. We have to economize as much as we can."

"Anyone accompanying the mail?" Dameron demanded.

"Only the guard. He's already been cleared by your security people."

Dameron nodded, satisfied, and stepped back to let McAuley aboard. Tazelaar followed, his eyes sweeping the platform in one last precautionary gesture, and fifteen minutes later, with its precious passenger safely esconced, the train pulled out of Euston Station and started its long fateful journey north.

Sitting at his desk, Harry felt weariness threatening to engulf him and leaned forward, rubbing his eyes with his fingertips. Ten hours he'd been waiting here, and still no news of the minister's train. He was beginning to wonder if Kate had gotten her facts wrong. It wouldn't be the first time, he reflected wryly.

He peered at Vera, his secretary, sitting at her electric typewriter. The morning's derailment had created a mountain of paperwork, providing Harry with a welcome excuse for remaining in the office, but he could see Vera was becoming desperately tired. "Seen the time?" he said gently.

She nodded. "Almost midnight."

"Shouldn't you be getting home?"

"Work's got to be done, Mr. Fuller," she told him gamely.

"You've worked quite enough for one day. I'll tidy up any loose ends."

Vera hesitated. "I don't like leaving you here alone."

"It's what I get paid for."

She shook her head. "You're too conscientious, Mr. Fuller. It'll be the death of you yet."

She ran her fingers over the typewriter keys, then reached for the dustcover and tugged it on. She looked relieved as she rose to her feet.

"I'll see you in the morning, then."

"Not too early, Vera. Take a few hours off."

"Lunchtime all right?"

"That's fine."

"Just leave any typing in the in-tray."

Gathering up her things, she walked into the outer office and Harry felt glad when she'd gone. It made things easier somehow, being here alone. He could concentrate on his hatred, fuel it, nurture it, soothe himself with thoughts of what he would do to Kate after the emergency was over. But Vera returned a moment later, clutching a sheet of paper, and something in her face sent Harry's senses racing.

"This'll make your day," she said sympathetically, handing him the telex message. "A Class 47 Down Special. I hope you weren't planning a night on the tiles."

Harry took the sheet from her hand, scanning the details quickly. Folding the telex, he pushed it into his pocket and rose to his feet, seizing his raincoat from the office wall peg.

Vera looked at him with surprise. "Where are you going?"

"I have to make a phone call."

"Why don't you do it from here?"

He winked. "This is private. I don't want anyone listening on the party line."

She chuckled. "So you *were* planning a night on the tiles, after all."

"That's the trouble with you, Vera. You see through me like a crystal ball."

The yard was deserted as he scuttled down the metal staircase. He made his way to the nearest telephone booth and, slipping a coin into the slot, punched out the number Kate had given him. There was a click on the line and a masculine voice said, "Hartley and District Express Packaging Company."

Harry took a deep breath. "It's on its way. Estimated time of arrival, 0355 hours."

Putting down the receiver, he stood looking at it for a moment. There could be no turning back now, he thought.

His hands were trembling as he left the phone booth and strode back into the station yard.

Sitting in the patrol car, Detective Sergeant Fisher watched Harry vanish into the darkness and stubbed out his cigarette in the dashboard ashtray. "Now there's a curious thing," he remarked to Constable Hendricks. "Why would a man with an office full of telephones go to the trouble of dialing from an outside booth?"

Hendricks grunted without answering as Fisher spotted a second figure emerging out of the gloom, trim, high-heeled, raincoated. He recognized Harry's secretary, Vera.

"Miss Walton," he called, sliding down the window. "Detective Sergeant Fisher here. I wonder if I might have a word with you?"

The woman paused in her stride, staring at the

patrol car uncertainly, and Fisher opened the door, clambering into the lamplight. "It's important, Miss Walton. Truly."

Sighing, she strolled toward him and he waved her inside. "The air's terribly damp tonight. We don't want you catching a chill."

Vera was silent as she settled herself against the seat cushion. Fisher offered her a cigarette, but she shook her head. He studied her thoughtfully, letting his instincts do the work.

"Working late, Miss Walton?"

"Emergency. We had a derailment this morning. We've been trying to catch up."

"That shows commendable zeal."

"I don't mind overtime. I get paid for it. And besides, it goes with the job."

"Mr. Fuller's job too?"

"Of course."

"I see his office light is still burning. It does seem an awful lot of trouble for one little derailment."

"Oh, that isn't the derailment. Mr. Fuller has to stay behind because we have a Special coming through."

"Ah yes, of course. The one from Euston."

She looked puzzled. "You know about that?"

"Mr. Fuller told us earlier. As a matter of fact, it's the reason he hurried back to the office in the first place."

Vera's mouth opened and shut uncertainly. "That's impossible," she whispered. "The telex only just arrived."

Fisher frowned, glancing at Constable Hendricks. "Let me get this straight. Are you saying Mr. Fuller has just learned about that train?"

"Literally this minute."

"But surely, as area manager, he'd be in a position to know if anything unusual was happening on his section of the line."

"He can't have known about this one. The decision has only just been made. I read the telex myself."

Detective Sergeant Fisher took a deep breath and sat back in his seat, staring at the car ceiling. His eyes looked feverish in the glow from the streetlamps.

"Miss Walton, I'm going to ask a very great favor. Are you expected anywhere?"

"Expected?"

"I meant is anyone waiting for you at home—a companion, a mother, someone who might be distressed if you fail to arrive on time?"

"I'm . . . I'm single," she said. "I live alone."

"Good. I realize you've had a long and tiring day, but I want you to return to the downstairs office and, without Mr. Fuller's knowledge, elicit some important information for me."

Vera looked startled. "I can't do that."

"Why not?"

"It would be . . . disloyal."

"Hardly disloyal, Miss Walton. You'd be helping police inquiries, doing your duty as a responsible citizen. I need to know who authorized that train, and what, precisely, it is carrying."

She looked doubtful. "At this time of night, London will be virtually unmanned. It could take hours to get an answer."

Fisher's face looked bland. In the darkness, his eyes fastened on hers with an almost mesmeric intensity. "That's all right, Miss Walton, we have all the time in the world."

* * *

The cottage stood in a remote mountain valley, flanked on one side by tawny hills and on the other by open farmland. It had been, Elliot deduced, the home of some shepherd or forgotten gamekeeper, but in recent years the building had been modernized and turned into a holiday retreat for wealthy families from the cities of Newcastle or Carlisle. The emptiness of its surroundings had made it a perfect operations base for Elliot and his companions, and they had broken in the evening before, making themselves comfortable for the long hours of waiting ahead.

Elliot stood at the window, staring gloomily into the darkness. There'd been no word from Harry Fuller, and he was beginning to wonder if they had made a ghastly mistake. Fuller was worried about his boy, deeply worried, but he was also tough and indefatigable, a fighter—Elliot had recognized the signs. Who knew what a man like Fuller might be capable of?

Elliot shook himself, glancing at the others dozing on the chairs and sofas behind him. Kate was sleeping peacefully, wrapped in a blanket, her black hair ruffled untidily across her face. She looked beautiful in repose, he thought, and smiled wryly to himself. Biology again. Why was he so attracted to the woman? He hardly knew her, when you came right down to it. A few days' training in Mozambique, a brief stay in London's West End—hardly the perfect basis for a significant relationship. And yet, in some strange elusive way, he felt as if he'd known her all his life. She carried that air about her. Indomitability. It was all there in those classic cheekbones, that delicate nose and slender neck. Her strength. Her commitment. Her utter refusal to compromise. He admired that.

You always admired the things you couldn't have, he reflected, seeing in them the fulfillment of a need that existed more in imagination than cold hard fact. And yet, imagination often transcended fact. It was purer, nobler, even to some degree more satisfying. It had been the story of his life, he thought ruefully.

Elliot's childhood had not been a happy one, though to outside observers, his background of wealth and privilege must have seemed a blessed and unparagoned state. His father, a wealthy industrialist who had made his name initially in the property business and later as the head of a thriving automobile conglomerate, had brought up his family with a sanguine belief in the superiority of their lineage, and among the Detroit Negro community they had been known as the Kennedys of Michigan. Elliot had four brothers and two sisters, all of whom were older than he by a margin of at least eight years. Being the youngest member of such a distinguished household did not, to Elliot's mind, produce any tangible advantages, for almost from the moment he was old enough to appreciate such things, he had been both awed and intimidated by the radiance of his brothers' intellect, by the splendor of their material success, and most of all by the staggering and unquenchable arrogance emanating from their pores.

His father had made a point of turning each mealtime into an intellectual debate, introducing a topic of some current interest and obliging his sons to discuss it in the belief that such exercises sharpened their minds and galvanized their senses. Woe betide any offspring who expressed ignorance of the subject at hand, or who failed to dissect it with what their father considered suitable astuteness and originality. Elliot had hated such gatherings, for the loquacity of his brothers had made him feel both dim-witted and inadequate.

At the age of eighteen, Elliot had been sent by his father to complete his education in Paris. Elliot had loved Paris. From his first moment of arrival, the elegant boulevards, the graceful symmetry of the buildings, the air of bustle and purpose which flooded the French capital seemed to electrify his senses, and freed from the constrictions of his family, he threw himself into Parisian life with a heady abandonment. He was determined to hone his personality into one which would enable him to compete, in both an aesthetic and material sense, with his four celebrated brothers, and cultivating the company of top designers, he discovered subtly the correct way to dress, buying his suits from the most distinguished tailors and making, in the process, a reputation as an elegant and sophisticated young man about town. He studied French wines, sampling the finest vintages and learning to recognize the good from the indifferent. He attended lectures on art, music, philosophy, and science, applying his mind with such dedication that within two years he could talk knowledgeably and articulately about almost any subject under the sun. Most of all, he employed his stunning good looks and considerable charm in the pursuit of the feminine sex. Where girls were concerned, Elliot had no hang-ups whatsoever, physical, racial, religious, or puritanical. He liked them all, small girls, tall girls, rich girls, poor girls, white girls, brown girls, plump girls, skinny girls, pursuing the mysteries of the flesh with a commitment matched only by his thirst for enlightenment. From morning till night, his apartment was strewn with a constant litter of discarded brassieres, lacy slips, and filmy transparent panties.

These diversions, however, did not interfere with the more serious business of living, and he proved himself an exemplary student, reinforcing his tutors' faith by publishing, in one year, a definitive work on Michigan's animal and plant life and another on the architecture of the New England colonial period. A natural athlete, he represented the Sorbonne at the Fontainebleau Games, and later competed with distinction in Avignon and Marseilles, winning the coveted Zabala Trophy at Montbard Stadium. As the years rolled by, he learned the subtleties and intricacies of a world he had scarcely known existed, becoming elegant, cultured, and articulate.

Throughout this idyllic period in his life, Elliot had little contact with the hordes of ragged black people who flocked the city streets, struggling to eke out a living by selling trinkets and curios to the tourists. Elliot was as removed from the poorer sections of his race as a medieval lord might have been from his starving and scavenging subjects. He did not consider the problems of racial prejudice or his people's fight for equality, until two things happened which had a dramatic effect on his outlook and well-being. The first was a chance meeting on a Parisian boulevard with a cadaverous-looking black man who was stopping passersby with a series of plaintive entreaties. Glimpsing Elliot approaching, the man stepped forward, rubbing his stomach. "Please," he hissed, "I have not eaten for nearly three days. I am so hungry."

Elliot was startled, not so much by the words themselves as by the obvious integrity of the man uttering them—he clearly *was* starving and, being black and probably an illegal alien into the bargain, was being *allowed* to starve by the great mass of passersby. The man's need touched Elliot, and fumbling in his pocket, he pushed all the money in his possession into the Negro's disbelieving hands. But this act of charity did not lighten Elliot's mind, and for days afterward he pondered on the beggar's haunted and ravaged features. It seemed incredible to Elliot that in a civilized twentieth-century society a man could be permitted to starve simply because his fellow inhabitants considered him some kind of inferior being. There were, he realized, people of his own race, his own color, who were suffering deeply for no other reason than the immutable nature of their genes.

The second incident occurred several months later, and proved the catalyst which changed Elliot's life. In a gaming house on the Rue Dargin, he defeated at cards a rich young man from Versailles whom Elliot knew vaguely as Marcel Le Gras. Rueful, but philosophical at his loss, the Frenchman courteously invited Elliot to join him in a glass of champagne.

"You're quite a card player," Le Gras said pleasantly. "A born winner, if I may make the observation."

Elliot inclined his head, acknowledging the compliment.

"In fact, you seem to be a winner at everything you do."

"Luck," Elliot suggested modestly.

"I wish I could cultivate such luck. The ladies find you irresistible."

"Ah, that is my devastating élan."

The Frenchman chuckled warmly. "You're an

extraordinary fellow, M'sieur Chamille, there's little doubt of that. It's such a pity you're a nigger."

It was the first time in Elliot's life he had ever been confronted by the fact that there were people in the world who did not see him as an individual, but as a representative of a species which belonged, by the simple consequence of its color, to the lower levels of existence. He had grown to manhood in the sincere and unshakable belief that he was somehow a cut above the ordinary man, a superior creature whose inherent nobility was right and proper in the natural scheme of things. The insanity of the insult, the mindless asinine folly, outraged his senses and steeled his resolve. Now he realized where his true vocation lay and, from that moment on, pledged himself to the deliverance of his people, wherever they happened to be.

Traveling to Africa, he had joined the movement, embracing it with a passion it was difficult to define. In the early days, his absorption had been total. He had pamphleteered, organized strikes in the mining areas of Germiston and Kempton Park, fashioned bombs for the heartland of the Western Cape, and trained resistance fighters in the guerrilla camps of Angola and Botswana, learning to survive in a violent and often unprincipled world. He had severed his last links with affluence and devoted himself to the path of glorious insurrection. But men changed, he reflected mournfully, and he too had changed. Reality had set in. Disillusionment. The fragmented nature of the black cause, the deadly rivalries within the groups themselves, the struggle for power left no easy answer, no right-vs.-wrong solution.

In the streets of Soweto one October evening, this conviction had confronted him in an experience he was never to forget, one which would have a profound and debilitating effect on his later life. Elliot and an ANC colleague, Alan Modipane, had been confronted by a group of scarecrow figures carrying rifles and Swedish Carl Gustav submachine guns. The intruders were members of AZAPO, the Azanian People's Organization, a resistance group engaged in a bloody feud with the outlawed ANC. Dusk was gathering as the ragged insurgents fanned out to block their captives' retreat from the rear. Children, heads plastered with henna, gathered at the fringe of the tight little throng, their eyes wide with fascination and wonder. Drawn by the scent of drama, the Soweto residents collected around them in a ragged group.

The AZAPO fighters were led by a wiry little man with a fanatical glare. "What are you doing here?" he demanded.

"Walking," Elliot answered simply.

"You are not welcome in Soweto. You are enemies of the people, counterrevolutionaries, part of the oppressive colonial oligarchy."

Elliot was not unduly alarmed. He harbored an innate confidence in his ability to talk himself out of tricky situations, but the wiry little fanatic was both malevolent and adamant. "We must put these traitors on trial," he declared to the gathering at large.

The "trial" took place in the open area in front of the local hospital. Their accuser delivered a flow of impassioned invective designed to inflame the spectators' senses while Elliot listened in silence, his mind deep in thought. When the man had finished, Elliot rose to his feet and, clearing his throat, proceeded to decimate his prosecutor's arguments with consummate skill. He used the same revolutionary rhetoric, the same slogans, but with a new and devastating force. "Is this what we've come to, squabbling among ourselves? Our struggle is not directed at each other, but against those who seek to dominate us, the corrupt, murderous, oppressive politicians. We are a liberation movement, not a bunch of adventurers or terrorists. We must work as allies against the common enemy. Everyone, men and women of all ideologies, should present a united front in order to create the power factor which will free our people."

Elliot's persuasive style had the desired effect. Impressed by his words, the listeners declared him innocent, but when it came to Modipane's turn, their attitude hardened considerably. With mind-shaking stubbornness, Modipane remained recalcitrant and defiant. Standing in the circle center, he faced his accusers in dignified silence while the tiny fanatic ranted and raved, whipping the observers into a kind of hysteria. Modipane's refusal to acknowledge the authority of the court aroused the Africans' fury, and when the moment came to declare their verdict, the decision was unanimous.

"Execute him," they howled.

Elliot leapt to his feet. "This has gone far enough. How can we hope to overthrow the despots if we murder our own people?"

"It is not an act of murder, but of retribution," the little fanatic maintained coldly. "The man is a traitor to the movement."

"You're crazy. He believes in the same things we do, he fights for the same cause."

"Execute him," the fanatic howled.

Powerful hands gripped Elliot's arms and shoulders, hauling him back, and he watched stricken as Modipane was bound from head to foot. Rubber tires filled with gasoline were pushed over the helpless man's shoulders and set summarily alight while

Elliot, crazed with horror, saw the flames spiraling around his friend's motionless body.

"Let me go," Elliot screamed.

Twisting and struggling, he tore loose from his captors and beat at the fire with his bare hands. Modipane barely responded, that was the terrible thing, and as Elliot pummeled the twisting spirals of flame, the melting rubber clung to his arms, leaving a scar that would never fade. Then hard hands seized him again, holding him down in the dust, and sobbing impotently, he lay watching as Modipane squirmed out his life in a maelstrom of pain.

Elliot could never forget the anguish of that moment. He had merely to close his eyes to see it again, Modipane blazing like a roman candle, the AZAPO leader leaping and dancing around the circle of fire, and the people—his own people, the very ones he had come to liberate—laughing and applauding like spectators at some grotesque burlesque show.

Something happened to Elliot after that. His attitude changed. His convictions. It was like a loss of innocence. Though he continued to fight for the cause, his motives took on a more personal note. He became cynical. Materialistic.

He was filled too with an inner conflict which could never be resolved, for his helplessness seemed to diminish him in some way as a human being. He developed a mindless, almost pathological fear of fire. Whenever he saw fire, he went into a cold sweat, he just couldn't help it. Its very presence seemed an abomination, the antithesis of life itself. He knew he could no more expunge his guilt than he could go back now, prodigal-like, to the comfortable affluent life he had left behind in Detroit, for having witnessed fire's torment, he feared it as a sane man might fear the prospect of hell.

The sound of the telephone brought Elliot out of his reverie. He turned, blinking, and began to move to the outside passageway, but De Brere beat him to it, rising from his chair and flinging open the door. Elliot heard the click of the receiver being lifted.

Elliot waited, the breath catching suddenly in his throat. His mind was sharp and alert, his memories of the past forgotten. He had no time for reminiscing, he thought. He had the future to think about.

When De Brere returned, his eyes were flashing, his cheeks flushed with excitement. Elliot looked at him expectantly.

"We're in business," De Brere said with a crooked grin.

At the station switchboard, Vera Walton plucked the headset from her ears and sat back in her chair, frowning frustratedly. "It's no use," she declared. "Nobody's answering."

Detective Fisher looked undismayed. "There must be someone about, Miss Walton. Euston Station doesn't shut down completely. There'll be baggage handlers, platform staff."

She sighed in irritation. There was no doubting the policeman's authority, but he had no right to encourage her to betray her trust. It seemed dishonest somehow, hiding her activities from Mr. Fuller. "You're asking for specialized information, and that means management level at least."

"Try every number you've got. If we can just make contact, perhaps someone down there will be able to put us in touch with a figure of authority."

"Sergeant Fisher, that could take all night. Can't you simply contact your people in London and tell them to approach the station direct? It would save a great deal of effort."

"I'd do that like a shot, Miss Walton, if I had anything tangible to go on. To tell the truth, I'm not at all sure what it is I'm looking for. I've got a feeling at the back of my nostrils that something is wrong, and that feeling's never let me down yet, but if I involve the Met boys at this stage, then end up with nothing to show for it, the guv'nor will have my guts for garters."

He patted her wrist encouragingly. "Bring Miss Walton a cup of black coffee from the automat machine," he said to Constable Hendricks. "And use the rear staircase. I don't want Fuller realizing we're inside the building."

The officer nodded and scurried off, clattering along the narrow passage. Fisher turned back to Vera, his eyes strangely bereft of emotion.

"Now, Miss Walton," he said in a gentle voice, "shall we try again?"

Through the long hours of darkness, the train sped remorselessly northward, negotiating upgrades, tunnels, and bridges alike, clattering gamely into the chill March night. Inside the minister's carriage, Commander Dameron listened to the rhythmic clicking of the wheels and reflected that never in his life had he encountered a coach as luxurious as the one in which they were riding. Someone said it had been designed for members of the Royal Family, and Dameron could easily believe it. Its walls were exquisitely padded with rich velvet upholstery, there was a private bar, liberally stocked, a separate bedroom complete with shower, and a sumptuous four-poster which Dameron would never have believed if he hadn't witnessed it with his own eyes.

He sat in a brocaded armchair, his legs stretched comfortably in front of him, a glass of brandy cupped pleasantly in one palm, ruminating on the endless pleasures the rich and powerful accepted as a matter of course. How the other half lived, he thought. There were moments, even in the life of a simple policeman, when he was allowed to glimpse, however fleetingly, a world he could scarcely begin to imagine, let alone aspire to.

"You look a little pensive, commander," McAuley, the South African minister, said.

Dameron shifted in his chair, faintly embarrassed. He liked McAuley, had been agreeably surprised by the man's casual and friendly manner, but conscious of his position, he was careful not to appear too familiar. "I was just thinking," he confessed sheepishly, "how easily I could get used to all this."

The minister chuckled. "Luxury's illusory, Commander. It soon loses its appeal when you're surrounded by it all the time."

"That's easy to say, sir, when you've got it."

"You surely don't imagine I live like this at home?"

"I thought all South Africans—white South Africans, that is—were mini-capitalists."

"You've been reading too many press reports. Don't you appreciate how they distort things?"

"I've had a few dealings with the press," Dameron admitted.

"It's the media who are to blame for what's happening in South Africa today."

"You really believe that?"

"Of course. Left to our own resources, we would have sorted out our problems years ago."

Dameron looked at him dryly, swirling the brandy around his glass. The minister's face was square and fleshy, his nose hooked, his mouth bloodless. His eyes were uncomfortably sharp, as if he had a facility, despite his charm, for observing, discerning, dissecting. "You do not believe me, Commander?"

"With respect, sir, I don't think any privileged class in history ever rescinded its power willingly."

"You're a cynic, Commander. Learning from the past is the most admirable quality of the human race. How do you think our civilizations survive? I'm unfailingly optimistic about the inherent goodness of mankind."

"It's easy to see you haven't led a policeman's life, sir."

"You disagree?"

"How would you explain the excesses of Hitler, Genghis Khan?"

"Aberrations. We are not immune to fanatics, Commander, but our basic goodness brings us through."

McAuley paused as a scuffle behind him caught his attention. A wasp, trapped inside the carriage, was buzzing furiously among the drapes and padded upholstery. It executed an intricate aerial ballet, wheeling and dipping above the detective's heads, its droning mingling with the rhythmic clacking of the wheels. One of the detectives swatted it with his arm.

"What's the bloody thing doing here at this time of year? It's not even April, for God's sake."

Conscious of being under attack, the wasp began careering backward and forward in a frenzied effort to escape. The detective rose to his feet, rolling up a sheet of newspaper. To the amusement of his companions, he began pursuing their unwelcome guest around the clattering railroad carriage, swiping at it furiously. He was a big man with a prominent beer-drinker's paunch, and Dameron chuckled at the absurd spectacle of his shivering belly as he wheeled and lunged at the elusive little intruder.

"Go on, Arch," one of the man's colleagues yelled, welcoming the diversion.

Red-faced and sweating, the detective pursued his prey laboriously, swinging his paper in a series of wild uncoordinated sweeps, but the wasp darted always just beyond his reach.

"Leave the insect alone."

The command was like the hammer of God, and Dameron jumped impulsively in his chair. At the far end of the car, Tazelaar, the South African, had risen to his feet and was glaring at the shirtsleeved detective with a fury which brought the man to an abrupt halt.

"It is one of God's creatures," Tazelaar said in his thick South African accent, "frightened and bewildered. It means you no harm."

His powerful body quivering with rage, Tazelaar looked dangerously out of control, and the detective swallowed, glancing uncertainly at his companions. For a moment, the only sound in the crowded carriage was the wasp's buzzing as it scoured the walls for a means of escape. It settled on the window frame, and as Dameron watched, Tazelaar inched forward and gently, tenderly cupped his hands around its tiny perch. "Come, my little beauty," he crooned. "No one will harm you."

Picking the insect up, he opened the window and released it into the buffeting slipstream.

McAuley smiled at Dameron in triumph. "You see, Commander? Major Tazelaar is a policeman too. He has seen the seamy side of life, perhaps even more graphically than you, but he has never lost his basic human goodness."

Dameron didn't answer. There was something in Tazelaar's manner he found disturbing, a hint of madness, of psychotic obsession.

McAuley finished his drink and rose to his feet. "Well, gentlemen, I think I shall retire. I have a hard day in front of me in the morning, and I regret to say I'm still suffering a little from jet lag. Please make use of the cocktail cabinet. There's no sense in losing your rest and feeling miserable into the bargain. If you need anything, just tell my valet. He's been instructed to ensure you are well looked after."

They rose to their feet as McAuley made his way to the tiny bedroom, echoing "Good night, sir" in a respectful chorus.

Moving to the bar, Dameron poured himself another brandy. "In the interests of international cooperation," he said with a grin, "I think we should all take Mr. McAuley's advice."

Kate pushed her shoulder against the horse's rear, forcing it unwillingly up the last few feet of narrow ramp and into the cramped conveyor box. Clearly unhappy at being confined, it nickered in protest as she flung up the tailgate, fastening it into position. Kate could hear the others cursing as they struggled to load the protesting animals. Horses could be the most difficult creatures on God's earth, she thought, stubborn and recalcitrant—rebellious too, when they had a mind to be. They had bought them, together with the truck and conveyor-trailer, from a group of Irish gypsies south of Rugby, and she had an unhappy feeling the horses would prove the most difficult part of their entire operation.

De Brere grinned at her in the darkness, his wild face curiously disheveled. She'd scarcely spoken to De Brere since he'd made his ill-fated advances in London, but her coolness had done little to temper his enthusiasm. He seemed to bear her no ill will, that was the surprising thing. If anything, his manner was even friendlier than before. "Nasty creatures, aren't they?" He grunted. "Never could stand them myself. How anyone can love horses baffles me."

"We need them, De Brere," Kate answered coolly, displaying more conviction than she felt.

"Think so? If you want my opinion, they'll give us nothing but stick."

"It's wild country up there. We must have some kind of transport to get ourselves around."

"Sooner rely on my two feet."

He moved around the conveyor box, fixing the couplings in place, and Kate ran her fingers through her long tangled hair. She still felt sick after her confrontation with Harry on the bluffs near the river. It had been an unpleasant and unsettling experience. Seeing him again had taken her breath away, as she'd known it would. He'd always had that capacity, even in their bitterest quarrels. And now he hated her, that was blatantly apparent. She'd had no right to involve Tim, no right at all. Causes were one thing, but people counted too, particularly people you cared about. Like Tim and Harry. Aggravating, infuriating, irresistible Harry. He'd changed a lot, she reflected. Not so much on the outside, not so she'd actually have noticed if they hadn't gotten into a free-for-all. His hair was graying a bit, but that was only to be expected, and in any event, it made him seem more attractive in a funny sort of way. Not that Harry had ever been a pretty man. Rugged, maybe. Interesting. But his features were too chiseled, too Mount Rushmore–like to ever be construed as classically good-looking. He wasn't a bit like Elliot Chamille.

She heard a clanking sound as Elliot attached the horse trailer to the rear of the battered truck. She could see his breath as he panted in the chill night air. His handsome face was obscured by shadow. He was a strange one, Elliot, and no mistake. Difficult to analyze. Unlike the Americans she'd met in London and Africa. Didn't even talk like them, that was the puzzling thing. International, was Elliot Chamille, a complex mixture of different cultures, different societies. Where Harry was explosive, Elliot was controlled. Where Harry was earthy, Elliot was refined. And yet, there *was* a kind of earthiness in Elliot Chamille. It was something you couldn't miss, that hint of animalism in his makeup. All he had to do was move into her presence and her knees felt wobbly, her stomach weak. Even his voice had the capacity to make her thrill; it was deep, vibrant, strangely disturbing in the way some particular piece of music might be disturbing, galvanizing the senses, inciting the emotions.

Harry too was physical, but where Harry's persona was like a kind of shambling irascible bear, Elliot was a panther, sleek, sure, irresistible.

The irony was not lost on her as she stood panting in the darkness, a woman who had returned to find not merely the expected upheaval of an old love resurrected, but the bewildering havoc of new feelings, new sensations—sensations she could scarcely begin to understand, much less attempt to control.

She heard a muffled thumping noise as one of

the horses began to kick at the vehicle rear, and De Brere swore volubly.

Elliot grinned at her, his teeth gleaming through the darkness.

"Don't just stand there, give him a hand, you idiot."

Forgetting her confusion and the ordeal ahead, she hurried urgently forward to help.

Charles Palmer's club was muggy and cheerful, a pleasant sanctuary from the chill spring night. Waldo found himself relaxing as he studied the dapper British security chief curiously. Palmer was wading his way through a plate of fresh asparagus, dipping the tips in melted butter and slicing off the ends with an air of delicate fastidiousness. Palmer was an enigma, Waldo decided, elegant—almost foppish—on the outside, but cold hard steel beneath. He had, however, an engaging manner, and Waldo felt secretly pleased McAuley's journey to Scotland had placed him so unexpectedly in the company of this fascinating little intelligence man. "I dine here several nights a week," Palmer confessed. "It's one of the few pleasures I have in life. I like the noise, the company. It stops me feeling lonely."

"I wouldn't have thought you the lonely type." Waldo smiled. "You're too convivial."

"Do you really think so? I'd never have described myself as outgoing. Please don't get me wrong—I like people as much as the next man, but I do have a tendency to withdraw into my shell."

He patted his lips with a napkin. "I never married, you know. It was a big mistake. There were ladies who were . . . very nice to me, but I lived for my work. It was all I ever cared about. Now . . ." He shrugged ruefully. "In a few years' time, I'll reach retirement. I haven't the faintest idea what I'll do. I have no interests outside the security service. Once, years ago, I was fond of veteran cars. I had a six-cylinder Hispano Suiza, but it got smashed up on a visit to the Lake District, and I haven't had another since."

"Ever sat on an aircraft and tried to guess what the other passengers do for a living?" Waldo asked.

"Occasionally."

"Well, if I'd seen you in different circumstances, I'd have put you down as some kind of academic. A college professor, a mathematician. Maybe even a Shakespearean actor."

Palmer smiled thinly. "In my profession, part of the secret is looking ordinary. It's a skill you acquire for survival's sake. Besides, you're not exactly typical yourself. I'd never label you a professional mediator."

Waldo chuckled. "There aren't too many of us around. Not at government level anyhow."

"Must be a difficult job," Palmer commented, watching him with that faintly disinterested gleam Waldo had already recognized was a sign Palmer was fishing for information. He too, in his own mild way, had learned to spot the small, indiscernible signs which betrayed a man's true motives and intentions.

He speared a slice of venison with his fork and popped it into his mouth. "Mr. Palmer, I've spent my entire life deciphering people's expressions. It gets to be second nature after a while. You're curious, I can tell. If you've got something on your mind, why don't you go ahead and ask? You might be surprised at the result."

Palmer smiled wryly. Picking up the wine bottle, he carefully refilled Waldo's glass. "I should have had more sense than to cross swords with a professional. You're quite right. I *was* on the point of probing you."

"You're puzzled about my visit here."

"Something like that. You and McAuley—an interesting combination. If you want the truth, as an intelligence man, my role is to look, listen, and say nothing, but I'm a human being too, Mr. Friedman, and I can't help being curious. I like to know what's going on."

"I can't jeopardize these talks by discussing their nature beforehand, you must realize that."

"I quite understand."

"However"—Waldo smiled disarmingly—"I can tell you this. If we reach an agreement, it'll be the first step in a historic decision."

"The dismantling of apartheid?"

Waldo's voice assumed an injured tone. "You knew all along."

"A simple process of deduction, that's all. I can think of nothing less which would induce the governments of Britain and the United States to invite the South African foreign minister to secret talks in London. The thing which puzzles me is the security level. McAuley's being guarded like a member of the Royal Family. From whom, for God's sake? Hardly the ANC. Surely they'll welcome the talks as a step in the right direction."

Waldo's face looked grave as he toyed with his wineglass. "You're wrong," he said. "If the ANC knew what we were up to, the chances are they'd be deeply unhappy. The secret of mediation is compromise, leaving a man room to maneuver, and the South Africans know that. That's why they're coming to the negotiating table. They see the future fraught with disaster, and they're determined to bargain now, while they're still powerful enough to stipulate the rules. It's a shrewd and clever move, when you come right down to it. They'll concede in principle the necessity for bringing an end to apartheid, but make damned sure they safeguard their interests every step of the way. They're demanding from us the lifting of certain trade restrictions, and also our influence in placating the ANC, but at this delicate stage, where we're simply, in effect, exploring the possibility—the likelihood—of reaching an agreement, we're keeping the conference firmly under wraps. If the ANC discover what we're up to, they could well try and abort the entire thing."

"I see."

Palmer's face was thoughtful as he reached for his wineglass. "We'll have to make sure that doesn't happen, then, won't we?" he said with a secret smile.

Commander Dameron heard the radio humming softly and, opening his eyes, sat blinking in the plushly upholstered armchair. A sour acidic sensation lay heavily in his belly—brandy, he remembered, from the hospitality cabinet in the carriage bar.

The clicking of the wheels brought him back to consciousness, and his head throbbed as he glanced around the railroad coach. His fellow detectives had arranged themselves about the cluttered interior and were now sleeping peacefully, their bodies relaxed, their features composed. There was no sound except the uneven droning of a solitary snorer and the radio's persistent hum.

Dameron groaned as he eased himself out of the chair and stumbled toward the mahogany table. He felt hollowed out inside like a man in the throes of

postcoronary trauma. Unforgivable it had been,
drinking like that, especially on duty, but train
journeys bored him, always had.

He flicked the radio switch with his thumb,
grimacing at the bitter taste of bile in his mouth. He
should have had more sense, a man with his experience. Have to watch it in the future. No more
brandy. Sleep it off, with luck, before the train
reached Glasgow station. He didn't want the minister
thinking he was under the weather.

"Dameron here," he said, speaking into the radio
microphone.

There was a faint crackling on the receiver set,
then a voice broke through, shrill and distorted.
Dameron recognized the tones of Commander Wirth,
his associate officer in Scotland Yard, London.

"Where have you been, for Christ's sake?" Wirth
demanded. "I've been trying to get you for the past
hour."

"What's wrong?" Dameron inquired innocently,
rubbing his left temple with his fingertip.

"Nothing's wrong. But you had me worried,
Jack, when I couldn't get any response. Why didn't
you answer?"

"I was busy," Dameron lied blithely.

"Damn fool. I might have issued a full alert."

"Doug," Dameron said calmly, "what is the
purpose of this call? Are you checking up on me for
some reason?"

"Just maintaining contact, Jack. Regulations."

Typical of Wirth, Dameron thought. Fussy and
meticulous, he followed his instructions to the letter.

"What do you expect to happen on a moving
train, for Christ's sake?"

Wirth's tone softened, taking on a conciliatory

note. "Easy, Jack, just doing my job. Where are you, anyhow?"

"Somewhere north of Warrington, I imagine. Who cares? I'll call you the minute we arrive in Glasgow."

"Don't get mad, Jack. I have to write something in the situation report, otherwise, Granahan'll skin my hide."

"To hell with Granahan," Dameron growled. "Don't use this radio again, unless you've got a definite reason. That's an order."

Scowling, he flicked the transmitter switch and turned unsteadily toward his armchair. As he did so, he stumbled, almost dragging the radio from its perch. Muttering under his breath, he straightened it with studious care. Then, sighing, he flopped back into his seat.

He didn't notice, as he settled down to sleep, that in his clumsiness he had tugged loose one of the radio's vital leads.

Harry sat in his office, staring numbly at the opposite wall. He was filled with a sense of profound foreboding, a feeling which, having started, doggedly refused to let him go. Like Faust, he had sold his soul to the devil. The worry of Tim, the shock of confronting Kate again, the unexpected emergence of his past had disorientated his senses. Kate had given her word the boy would not be harmed, but Kate, despite her strength, despite her experience and commitment, was an innocent in such matters, and Harry knew better. He had seen the implacable gleam in the eyes of the Negro. Killing would mean nothing to such a man. The black was a fanatic, and like all fanatics, would go to any lengths, including the murder of an innocent young boy, if he thought the act would assist his cause.

But it was more than the Negro which worried Harry. He felt guilty, that was the size of it, guilty because he was culpable. In Harry's experience, these things didn't happen in real life. But what was real life, when you came right down to it? Everyone's was different, and if there was any similarity at all, it lay in its capacity to unseat, to confound. Take Kate, for example. She's gone the entire route in her day—anti everything—nuclear power, Irish partition, the Vietnam War. Causes were fuel to Kate's flame. She really cared, that was the crazy thing. But now her extremism had jeopardized his boy, and that made Kate his enemy. He could feel his hatred like a palpable force. It rose inside him when he visualized her. That body which had, in the past, given him such pleasure and fulfillment, now aroused revulsion and fury. He recalled past snubs, forgotten resentments, plucked them out of the air. You couldn't explain a thing like that, the way love could turn to hate in the twinkling of an eye, the way you could care about a person more than anything else in the world, and then, suddenly and inexplicably, you wanted to hurt that person so badly your skin started to crawl at the mere thought of it. Whatever happened, whether they grabbed McAuley or not, he asked only one last thing of life.

A chance to get his own back.

Sitting in a bar at Palmer's club, Waldo saw the waiter approaching with a telephone on an extended lead. "Mr. Palmer," the waiter said. "Call for you, sir."

Palmer smiled at Waldo apologetically as the

waiter plugged the wire into its socket on the adjacent wall. "Sorry about this. I rarely get a chance to digest my meals in comfort. One of the burdens of the job, I'm afraid."

He picked up the receiver, and Waldo heard a voice at the end of the line.

"Mr. Palmer?"

"This is Palmer. To whom am I speaking?"

"Commander Wirth, Special Branch, sir."

"Yes, Commander, what can I do for you?"

"It may be nothing, sir, but we've had a phone call from a Detective Sergeant Fisher of Carlisle police. He's investigating the kidnapping of a young boy, the son of a British Rail official. The man is the area manager for the Carlisle region, which, as you know, encompasses the main Euston-to-Glasgow line."

Waldo felt a tremor of uneasiness pass through his stomach as the commander outlined the events of the afternoon. He described Harry's disappearance, his strange behavior regarding the minister's train, and his mysterious call from the public telephone booth.

"I don't know if any of it's significant, sir," the commander concluded, "but the thing that's worrying me is, I can't seem to reach our people protecting Mr. McAuley. Someone appears to have switched off the radio's power."

When Palmer spoke, his voice sounded unnaturally hoarse. "Listen to me, Commander. There may be a perfectly rational explanation for these events, but under the circumstances, I think it unwise not to take precautions. How far has the train now progressed?"

"Well, judging by the time, it should be approaching Preston."

"I want you to get on to the station authorities and have it stopped at once. Tell them to use their transport police, and place the carriage under heavy guard until we can get a relief squad into the area."

"Very well, sir," the commander answered crisply. "I'll see to it right away."

Palmer put down the receiver and shrugged at Waldo, smiling reassuringly. "One of the things I've learned in this business is never leave anything to chance."

"You think it's coincidence?"

"Of course it's coincidence. I'd stake my pension on it."

But Waldo noticed Palmer's hand was trembling as he reached for his brandy glass.

Six

Sitting at his desk, Harry heard the telex machine clattering in the outer office and, scrambling through, tore off the paper sheet, carrying it to the light. His muscles tensed as he scanned the lines of print. They were stopping the train at Preston Station. Jesus, he thought.

His first reaction was one of hope. If the train didn't come, the kidnap couldn't go ahead, and if the kidnap didn't go ahead . . . But Harry felt sweat beading his skin as he stared into the station yard outside. Terrorists weren't reasonable men, he reflected. Ruthless and fanatical, they killed with mindless indiscretion. Who knew how they might respond? They could murder Tim in a fit of pique, of frustration and rage.

Harry came to an unwilling decision. Walking back to his own office, he picked up the telephone and punched out a number. The line crackled, and a voice came on at the other end: "Preston Station."

"Give me Bender," Harry said.

"I'm sorry. Mr. Bender isn't here at the moment."

"This is Harry Fuller at Carlisle."

The voice lost its formal tone. "Harry, how are you? It's Frank Pridemore, the station manager. Mr. Bender had to go home. His wife's not well."

"Listen, Frank, the London police have been

trying to get you on the telephone. There's something wrong with the Preston cable."

Pridemore's voice sounded surprised. "That's odd. They called me barely ten minutes ago."

"This is an emergency," Harry said. "You've got a Class 47 Special approaching on the Down line."

"That's right. It's nearing the station now. We're planning to hold it on Platform 3."

"Don't," Harry told him urgently. "The train musn't be allowed to stop."

Pridemore's voice sounded puzzled. "I don't understand. I've had direct orders to keep it under heavy guard. We've a squadron of transport police standing by."

"The situation's changed. The train musn't be impeded in any way."

"I don't know, Harry. The commander who phoned me was quite emphatic."

"Frank, this is extremely important. That train is carrying a distinguished foreign diplomat. Special Branch detectives have reason to believe an attempt will be made to kidnap him somewhere near Preston."

"Jesus Christ."

"Listen to me, now. Under no circumstances must the train be halted."

"But this is contrary to everything I've been told."

Harry cursed under his breath. "Frank, tell me something, do you recognize my voice?"

"What's that?"

"Do you recognize my voice, for Christ's sake?"

"Yes, Harry, of course I recognize your voice."

"The commander who called you from London, did you recognize *his* voice?"

"How could I? I'd never spoken to the man in my life before."

"So who are you going to obey?"

There was a long pause at the end of the line while Harry stood fuming with impatience. Somewhere outside, he heard the rattle of boxcars as a goods train clattered through. Pridemore sighed as he came to a decision.

"You, Harry," he said compliantly.

Harry felt relief flood through him. "Then get on with it, for God's sake. That train must be crawling up your backside by now. Switch those signals. You're wasting precious time."

Pridemore stood on the platform and watched the smoky outline of the approaching diesel. He had just made it, he reflected, panting. Another minute and his call to the signalman would have been too late. The urgency of the situation baffled him completely. His life as a station manager was, as a rule, a perfectly ordered affair, revolving around the simple everyday problems which running a railroad engendered. The secrecy surrounding this solitary express had aroused his curiosity. He wasn't being nosy, he told himself, he just wanted to see what the fuss was about.

The train slowed, the driver cutting his speed as he thundered through the empty station. Glimpsing Pridemore huddled near the platform edge, the driver sounded his whistle in a shrill discordant salute.

Pridemore watched the train rattle past, its carriages vibrating as they clattered over the connecting points. Only the leading coach showed any signs of life. Pridemore could see slivers of light peeking through the drawn blinds from the scrupulously concealed interior.

As the train cleared the station platform, the driver opened up his throttle, gradually picking up speed, and Pridemore stared after it in puzzlement, watching it vanishing steadily into the night. Shivering a little in the chill, he thrust his hands in his overcoat pockets and crossed the platform toward his brightly lit office. It was, after all, he thought, a perfectly ordinary train. He could see no imaginable reason for making such a fuss.

Kate blinked as Elliot stopped the car and switched off the engine. She peered about her uncertainly. Beyond the glow of the headlights, the land lay cloaked in total darkness. She could see the grassy verge at the side of the road, a wire fence, a line of telegraph cables. Nothing else. In the silence, the world seemed curiously unreal.

"Are you sure this is the place?" De Brere asked from the rear, his face obscured by shadow.

Elliot nodded.

"The junction's about three hundred yards to our left. There's a viaduct there. It'll give us a bearing."

"What happens if the train doesn't stop?" Kate whispered.

"We'll make it stop. We'll light a fire on the line."

Kate shivered. There was something so certain, so determined in Elliot's manner, she had the weirdest feeling he hadn't once paused to consider the consequences. Elliot's eyes softened, glimpsing her uncertainty. He smiled in the darkness, and she felt her senses melt. He could turn on the charm in an instant, she thought, he really was the most extraordinary man.

"I know you're scared. We all are," he whispered.

"Not you," she said, her breath steaming on the chill night air. "I can't imagine you ever feeling scared."

"You're wrong. I've learned to hide it better, that's all."

He reached over and squeezed her hand. "Trust me."

She nodded, and he glanced into the rear where the others sat watching him owlishly. "Okay, everybody out. Get the horses unloaded and saddled up. Judging by the schedule, the train should be here inside an hour. We don't want to be caught with our pants down if the driver turns up early."

Kate's legs were trembling as she stumbled into the darkness.

Waldo felt his stomach tense when he saw the waiter approaching with the telephone for the second time. Putting down his coffee cup, Palmer picked up the receiver, nestling it against his chin. "Palmer here."

Waldo heard the voice at the end of the line. "Mr. Palmer, Commander Wirth again. I'm sorry to disturb you, sir, but there's been a new development."

"What's happened, Commander?"

"The train, sir. It didn't stop at Preston."

Palmer frowned, and Waldo felt a tremor of uneasiness.

"The station manager claims he received instructions from Harry Fuller in Carlisle to keep the line open," Commander Wirth said.

Watching Palmer closely, Waldo saw a tiny pulse begin to throb beneath the Englishman's left eye. "Does Preston come under Fuller's jurisdiction?" Palmer said.

"No, sir. But the Preston area manager had left the station premises, and Fuller managed to convince his assistant there was some kind of fault on the telephone cable. He thought he was following our orders."

"Any joy on the radio transmission?"

"Not yet. They seem to have switched off the power."

"Dammit, Wirth, what do your people think they're playing at?"

It was the first time Waldo had seen Palmer display actual emotion, and a small knot of worry gathered in his chest. Something was happening, something he scarcely dared contemplate.

Palmer reached up and began to rub his temple with his fingertip. His eyes were closed and he was breathing hard, filling his lungs with air.

"Commander," he said in a voice Waldo noticed was at least two octaves higher than its normal level, "listen to me carefully. I want you to contact the Carlisle police and tell them to arrest Harry Fuller at once. Tell them to occupy the signal box and place the train in strictest quarantine, is that clear?"

"Yes, sir."

"After you've done that, I want you to call the authorities at Heathrow Airport and arrange for a special plane to fly me to Carlisle."

"I'll do what I can, sir," Waldo heard the commander promise.

Palmer looked at Waldo apologetically as he

replaced the receiver. He was trying to appear calm, but Waldo knew his brain was racing. "I'll have to leave you, I'm afraid. Things seem to be getting out of hand. The waiter will call a taxi to take you back to your hotel."

"Forget the taxi," Waldo muttered, pushing back his chair. "We'll fly to Carlisle together, Mr. Palmer. I have a stake in this too, remember, and I wouldn't miss it for the world."

The sound of police sirens made Harry jump. I'm getting windy, he thought. A bundle of nerves, I'm turning into here.

He tried to relax, listening placidly to the distant screeching, waiting for it to fade into the night. But the sirens didn't fade. They grew louder, more insistent, and with a flush of alarm Harry rose to his feet. They were coming for him, he realized, knowing it as surely as he'd ever known anything in his life. Striding to the door, he glanced into the passageway outside. Two men were scuttling up the staircase toward him. Harry recognized Detective Sergeant Fisher and the uniformed constable, and something in their faces told him he hadn't been mistaken. Slamming the door, he turned the key and stood for a moment gazing wildly at the wall. Grabbing his parka, he darted to the rear exit and clambered onto the fire escape outside. There was no question of throwing himself at the mercy of the authorities, of pouring out everything he'd done and knew. He was an integral part of the terrorist plot. It wasn't merely Tim's well-being in jeopardy now. He had his own skin to think about.

He rattled down the metal staircase as the roar of police sirens grew deafening. A convoy of patrol cars burst through the narrow entrance gate, their head-lights flooding the station yard with light.

Harry ran toward the perimeter wall, moving by instinct almost, feeling his limbs operate with an air of curious detachment as he took the wall at a gallop and dropped deftly to the other side. He was in a narrow alley, flanked by metal dustbins.

Gasping for breath, he sprinted toward the distant opening, the lamps blinding him as he burst into the brightly lit street. Too much glare, he thought impulsively, and, scuttling across the road, ducked into a nearby lane. He felt safer in the darkness and, pausing, leaned against the lane wall, holding on to his side. What a mess, he thought darkly. The whole damned thing was falling to bits around his ears. He was a criminal now, a fugitive from the law.

And what about Tim? Without his father's complicity, Tim wouldn't stand a chance. He had to think. Work things out. Concentrate. They'd stop the train, that much was certain. They were probably, at this very moment, ordering the signalman to switch the lights to red. He had to circumvent that somehow. It was the only chance Tim had.

Harry saw a car parked in the shadows ahead and staggering toward it, he wrapped a handkerchief around his fist and quickly smashed the window. Opening the door, he expertly joined the connecting leads behind the ignition switch. The engine roared into life.

Harry's body was shaking as he slithered behind the steering wheel. He had one last chance, he thought. A million-to-one shot. A miracle, if he pulled it off, but he had to give it a try. Tim's life depended on it.

He slipped off the hand brake, engaged the gear,

and, with his heart thumping wildly, thundered off into the night.

Commander Dameron felt someone shaking his shoulder and grunted, opening his eyes. It was Rogers, his assistant, clutching a mug of coffee.

"Shame to wake you," Rogers said with a grin. "You were snoring like a trooper."

Dameron shook himself as he straightened in the chair. He took the coffee mug, cradling it gratefully between his frozen palms. "Christ, it's cold," he muttered, shivering.

"Bloody South Africans turned off the heating."

"What for?"

"Too stuffy, they claim."

"How's the time going?"

"Nearly four. We'll be approaching Carlisle shortly."

"Anything happening?"

Rogers shook his head. "Quiet as the grave."

Dameron felt the coffee spreading a flush of warmth through his empty stomach. Better, he thought. The effects of the brandy were at last beginning to disperse. His head still throbbed a bit, but the sickly feeling had gone. Served him right, anyhow. He deserved his backside kicked for drinking on duty. "How's McAuley?" he asked.

"Sleeping like a baby."

Dameron grunted as he sipped at the coffee mug. "Then all's right with the world," he muttered.

Harry stopped the car and sat in the darkness, breathing hard. There was nothing to see beyond the range of his headlights. The road, flanked on either

side by open fields, looked completely deserted. He
closed his eyes and opened them again, his cheeks
flushed, his pulse unsteady. A close-run thing, he
thought. They'd almost nabbed him back there—
would have, if he hadn't been so sprightly. He'd shot
through the streets like a man demented. No patrol
cars, thank God. The entire police force appeared to
have centered on the station yard. Now he had to
work quickly if the situation was to be salvaged.

He opened the door and clambered into the
night. The engine was still running, making an
irritating clatter on the predawn air. Harry opened
the hood, tugging the connecting leads apart, and as
the car spluttered and died, the headlights flickered
out, enveloping him in darkness.

Wiping his lips with the back of one hand, Harry
squinted into the gloom, discerning dimly the outline of a wire fence. He groped his way toward it and,
with some difficulty in the filtered starlight, clambered over to the other side. He could see the
railroad tracks gleaming above the embankment. He
felt his way along the grassy verge, pausing as he
glimpsed, directly in front, a strange shape material-
izing out of the gloom. His heart hammered wildly as
he recognized the outline of the tiny railroad shed.
Bang on target. It had been pure guesswork, choosing
his spot on the road back there. A miracle, locating
the hut without a flashlight. Maybe his luck wasn't
played out, after all.

The shack was locked, but the door jimmied
easily, and Harry switched on the electric light,
blinking as the sudden glare dazzled his eyes. The
shed was filled with tools used by the track mainte-
nance gangs. Harry rummaged about until he found
what he needed: a screwdriver, a large wrench, a
metal cutter, and a heavy iron crowbar. A flashlight

stood on the wooden tea cupboard and, switching it on, Harry hurried back into the night, picking his way along the metal track, stepping expertly from sleeper to sleeper.

He saw the points ahead and, placing the flashlight carefully on the ground, knelt down and examined the junction carefully. The track had been "clipped and scotched" to secure the points out of use. In accordance with railway regulations, the movable blades had been bolted to the main line, and metal "fishplates" riven to the rail ends. A wooden wedge had been driven firmly into the joints.

Harry went to work with his saw, slicing through the heavy padlocks. It took him almost an hour to cut the padlocks loose, knock out the wedge with his crowbar, and remove the rail bolts with his giant wrench. He was sweating heavily by the time he'd finished.

Rising to his feet, he jammed the crowbar between the blades and threw his weight against its metal shaft. Pushing, heaving, gritting his teeth, he felt the points beginning to slide and concentrated the bulk of his strength in his arms and shoulders, willing the blades to move. There was a faint creaking sound, then, with a gentle click, he felt the rails switch alignment and slip securely into position. Gasping, he stood staring down at his handiwork. First hurdle surmounted, he thought grimly.

He left the crowbar where it was and, picking up the flashlight, shuffled down the track until he discerned the signal tower framed against the sky. The switching of the points had caused the lights to switch to red, but there was still a telephone connecting the tower with the signalman at Carlisle station. Harry had to put it out of action. Clutching

the screwdriver between his teeth, he clambered up
the metal ladder and prized open the control box
door. His breath steamed on the freezing air as he
studied the complex array of wires under the flashlight beam and, working swiftly, toyed at the leads
with his screwdriver.

In the distance, he heard the first faint drone of
the approaching train and his stomach twitched as
he slammed the control box door. Just in time, he
thought thankfully. Another minute, and they'd have
passed me by completely.

His senses tingling, he slithered back down the
metal rungs.

Commander Dameron frowned as he felt the
train beginning to slow. No doubt about it, they were
drawing to a halt, the rhythmic clatter of the carriage
wheels muffled by the harsh screech of the locomotive brakes. Behind him, the South African, Tazelaar,
rose to his feet and fumbled in his holster for his
pistol. Dameron glared at him. It had been a sore
point, and one he knew his superiors had conceded
unwillingly, allowing the South Africans to retain
their handguns. If the bloody fool was going to
brandish his revolver at every opportunity, there'd
be hell to pay when the news got back to London.

"Put that away," he snapped in an angry voice.
"Where the hell do you think you are, back on the
old Transvaal?"

Tazelaar ignored him, his languid eyes dark and
wary. He stood bracing himself against the moving
carriage, the pistol barrel pointing toward the floor.

"What is going on?" he demanded in his thick
South African accent. "You said there'd be no stopping until we got to Glasgow."

"That's right, but we can't avoid the unexpected, you idiot. It could be anything—an obstruction, a faulty signal lamp, a goods train blocking the line. Waving a shooter around won't do a damned bit of good. Now put it away before you blow somebody's toes off."

He glanced at his followers as the train shuddered to a halt. "Wake McAuley," he ordered. "Tell him to get dressed."

He pulled back the blinds and squinted into the night. They had halted in the middle of nowhere, that was his immediate reaction. He could see flat fields reaching away in the eerie starlight. The driver had clambered down from the locomotive cabin and was standing at the side of the rails, chatting to a tall, heavy-shouldered man clutching a flashlight in his fist.

Dameron opened the carriage door and leapt deftly into the darkness. He walked toward the driver, his senses tense and alert. "What's happening?"

The driver, a small man with lifeless receding hair, indicated the figure standing in front of him. "This is Mr. Fuller, sir, the Carlisle area manager. He says we're being diverted."

Commander Dameron glanced suspiciously at the newcomer, his gaze registering a muscular face and dark intelligent eyes.

"Diverted where?" he demanded. "We've had no warning of any diversion."

"The order's just come through," Harry said. "There's some kind of flap on with the Carlisle police. They think there may be an attempt to spring your diplomat off the train. I'm rerouting you to the east, around the city outskirts. You'll rejoin the line a little farther on."

Dameron frowned. "Do you always divert your trains in such a dramatic manner?"

"Hardly. But then, our trains don't always carry such unorthodox passengers."

Dameron looked at the engine driver. "Shouldn't you have some kind of link with the signalman?"

"Only the lights," the driver explained. "When the red light's flashing, my locomotive brakes come on automatically."

"Then what?"

"Usually, I climb out of the cab and talk to the powerbox via the phone on the signal tower."

"Why don't you do that now?"

"Can't. Telephone's out of action. I tried."

Dameron felt a stab of uneasiness. He didn't believe in coincidence. Eighteen years as a policeman had taught him that circumstances which interweaved were rarely accidental.

"You came here alone?"

"I thought it best," Harry said. "We've been told the train has top-security clearance."

"Do you recognize this man personally?" Dameron asked the engine driver.

"Mr. Fuller, sir? Of course. I've worked under him for years."

"Any ID?"

Fumbling in his pocket, Harry produced his B.R. identity card. Dameron studied it in the flashlight beam, then nodded, satisfied.

"Okay, let's get things moving. It's making me nervous, standing here."

He watched Harry follow the engineer into the driving cab, then reached up, dragging himself back into the leading carriage. He could see the others watching expectantly as he slammed the door and pulled down the blind. "Diversion," he explained. "There's some kind of scare on."

"Scare?" Rogers echoed.

"They think there may be an attempt to hit the train."

"Jesus."

"They're rerouting us around the city boundaries."

Tazelaar glanced at his South African companions. "Why didn't they warn us by radio?"

Dameron grunted. He was wondering the same thing himself. Shouldering the South African aside, he examined the radio set carefully. His fingers located the loosened lead. "Christ," he muttered, "no wonder."

Slotting the lead into position, he flicked the transmitter switch and spoke into the microphone. They heard a crackling sound on the receiver, then Commander Wirth's voice broke through loud and clear. "Where the hell have you been, you bloody fool? I've been trying to contact you for nearly an hour."

"Radio's been buggered," Dameron said. "I'll explain later. Tell me about the diversion."

"What diversion? What the hell are you talking about?"

Dameron hesitated, and a feeling of uneasiness started in his stomach.

"We've just been stopped by the Carlisle area manager, a man named Fuller. He's taking us on an alternative route around the city. A precautionary measure, he says. Something to do with an attempt to halt the train."

"Jesus Christ," Wirth breathed, his voice riven with hysteria.

Dameron's cheeks blanched as he stood, legs

braced against the shuddering deck, and listened in
dismayed disbelief while Wirth outlined the events
of the past few hours.

Inside the powerbox, the atmosphere was tense.
Twenty-two police officers stood behind the signalman, watching the display panel on the opposite
wall. The panel showed in vivid detail the network
of railroad tracks lacing the surrounding area. Col-
ored lights indicated the location of approaching
trains. It was four-thirty in the morning, and only
one unit was actually moving; the "train describer,"
a tiny aperture at the panel's rim, displayed the
unit's reporting number as 1Z82, the Class 47 Special
carrying Howard McAuley from Euston to Glasgow.
To everyone's consternation, the lights had suddenly
and unaccountably switched from orange to red.

"I don't understand it," the signalman confessed, "Red indicates the track circuit's occupied,
but there's nothing else on the line for miles."

The police superintendent, a thickset man with
thinning gray hair, muttered under his breath. It
wasn't often he got orders direct from Special
Branch, and he didn't want a screw-up, not with
London involved.

"Could there be some kind of blockage, d'you
think?"

"Unlikely. Not unless it's deliberate. Of
course . . ." The signalman looked doubtful.
"That's Armathwaite Junction where the old loop
line around the city starts. We used it as a detour in
the old days, if we were carrying out engineering
operations inside the station precincts. It links up
with the disused track to Broadstruthers in the
Scottish border country."

"Are you saying the train might have been diverted?"

"It's possible. Mind you, somebody would've had to tamper with the points."

"Can that be done?"

"Difficult. But if they knew the layout . . ." The signalman shrugged.

"Terrorists would know. They'd make it their business to know."

"Then that's the only explanation."

The superintendent swore. "How can we stop this bloody train?"

"You can't. It'll be halfway around the city by now."

"There must be an intercepting road somewhere."

"Well, the line hasn't been used for years, so the driver will have to take things slowly. The Birkethead bypass runs parallel with the track at Simonbridge Junction. You've a good chance of cutting him off there, if you hurry."

The superintendent didn't answer. Boots clattering, he was already leading the stampede down the staircase outside.

Dameron stared at the door connecting the forward carriage with the locomotive rear. They'd tried in vain to smash its lock, but the heavy sealing bars remained stubbornly in place. They had hammered loudly on the wall panel with the metal fire extinguisher, but there'd been no response from the control cabin on the other side. They had pulled the communication cord, but evidently Fuller had managed to disconnect it. To all extents and purposes, they were, Dameron realized with frustration, effectively isolated from the unsuspecting engine driver.

Tazelaar's face was sullen. "We are prisoners on this carriage?"

"That's about the size of it," Dameron admitted frankly. "Fuller must have helpers ahead. We've got to stop the train before we reach his rendezvous point."

"How?"

Moving to the window, Dameron slid it open and leaned outside. He could see the locomotive directly in front, its flanks caked with grime and feathery scorch marks. Lights gleamed inside the cabin windows, but there was no way of attracting the driver's attention, and no percentage in it even if he could. Fuller was a muscular man. If it came to the push, he could overpower the engineer and take over the controls himself. As area manager, he probably knew how to operate a locomotive.

Dameron came to a desperate decision. "Someone will have to go over the roof."

The detectives looked at him uncertainly, and Dameron felt his facial muscles slacken. "Let me rephrase that," he corrected. "*I'll* have to go over the roof."

"Don't be a fool, Jack," Rogers said. "You'll break your bloody neck out there."

Dameron spat into the night and, taking out his pistol, checked it grimly. "I'm no hero," he admitted. "If you've got a better idea, I'll be happy to hear it."

Rogers faded into silence and Dameron nodded, sighing. "That's what I thought."

He turned to the window, wincing as the chill air battered his fevered cheeks. He must be crazy to even think of this, he told himself. But it was down or out, win or lose. Without McAuley, his career was finished.

He leaned out, filling his lungs with air, and, reaching up, grunted softly as his fingers located a narrow drainage channel tracing the rim of the sloping roof. Easing his body through the open window, he gritted his teeth as the icy wind bit through his flimsy sports jacket. It took his breath away, stunned his senses, made his eyes swim and his ears echo with its bellowing clamor. He held on grimly, propping his toes against the window ledge, hauling himself desperately upward. The ·wind seemed to be everywhere, heaving and straining like a living force bent on his destruction. He was too old for this, he reasoned. Forty-two last birthday. He'd been crazy to think he could do the Errol Flynn bit.

He felt a flurry of raindrops driving against his face and, shaking, reached up, seizing the protruding curve of a ventilator on the side of the carriage arch. The wind caught his jacket, whipping it right and left. Transferring his weight, he wriggled and slithered, working himself bit by bit across the apex of the shuddering roof. He was shivering all over as he lifted himself cautiously to his knees. His flimsy platform seemed to dance alarmingly beneath him. Something loomed in the darkness ahead, and his stomach cringed as he recognized a bridge. Hurling himself flat, he felt its stone arch brushing his shoulders and spine, and gulped, tensing his limbs, expecting at any moment to be swept away by the buffeting slipstream. Then the train was past the bridge. Move, he told himself angrily. You can't stay here. Your fingers will freeze.

Choking desperately, he pushed himself to his feet and spread his legs, struggling for balance on the shuddering rooftop. This was the bit he dreaded, the jump for the locomotive's rear. Braced against the wind, the carriage surface slippery and treacherous beneath his feet, the narrow opening looked like an awesome chasm. Backward and forward he tilted, the wind blasting his body as he poised himself for the moment of takeoff, then sucking in his breath, he jumped forward as hard as he could. He caught a momentary glimpse of the rails flitting by below before his heels touched the locomotive rear and he struggled desperately for balance. Unlike the passenger coach, the engine's roof arched steeply, and its surface felt like glass. It took every ounce of Dameron's concentration to keep himself from toppling over as he inched gingerly toward the vehicle's nose. Something loomed in the night ahead, and with a chill of horror he recognized the framework of another bridge. Desperately he tried to duck, his heels slithering on the shiny rooftop. I'm falling, he thought.

He hit the engine roof, digging his fingers against the metal casing. Skin ripped from his ravaged hands as he slid helplessly over the side. A narrow pipe ran vertically down the engine's flank and Dameron grabbed it, his body swinging wildly over the flashing embankment, directly level with the driving cab window. He could see the engineer sitting at the controls, and Fuller, the manager, directly behind him, peering through the windshield ahead. Swallowing hard, Dameron fumbled for his pistol and hammered its butt against the reinforced panel. Nothing happened. He hammered again, and this time the pane shattered, showering the cabin with splintered glass. Harry and the driver looked up, startled. "Stop," Dameron screamed in a strangled voice, thrusting his pistol through the jagged shards. "Stop, you bastard, or I'll spread your brains across the bloody windshield."

Riven with the astonishment, the driver needed

no second telling. Muttering under his breath, he reached forward and quickly applied the brakes.

Elliot shivered as he picked up another log and tossed it into the fire. Twisting and crackling, the flames spiraled upward, hurling sparks into the crisp March air. Elliot's body seemed filled with a strange sense of dread. It was nothing he could put a name to, nothing tangible or real, but the fire produced within him a kind of vacuum in which thought and illusion intertwined. In his mind he saw the dusty streets of Soweto with evening falling, a ring of black faces jeering in the sunset, Modipane's features blistering and charring, and the horror of the moment seemed to dissemble Elliot's senses. He glimpsed his friend's eyes, the sealed lips, the horrible disfiguring as the fire leapt higher, licking its way up the helpless body, and suddenly the past seemed more real, more lucid than the present. Sweat sprang to his cheeks, glistening through the smoke, and De Brere looked at him worriedly. "You okay, soldier?"

Elliot nodded, swallowing hard.

"You look bloody awful."

Steeling himself, Elliot picked up another log and thrust it into position. He couldn't make sense of it, a fire this size—nothing really, just a few wood knots tossed together to get up a blaze. But it didn't matter. In Elliot's mind, fire—any fire—was something he couldn't abide. And there was no point fooling himself he was getting over it either, forcing the qualmies back where they belonged. He'd never get over it, never. Just as he'd never get rid of the scar. Well, he hadn't time for this. He had to pull himself together. This was now, this was real, and he had a job to do.

Thirty feet away, standing with the horses, Kate heard the train like a distant echo. Carried by the wind, its clatter bore a strange eeriness, like a macabre lament from centuries past, plaintive and forgotten.

"It's coming," she called softly.

She glanced back at the track where the flames were dancing higher. It looked impressive enough, the fire, but would it be enough to hold the train? The driver would be wary, cautious, conscious of his special cargo. How could they be sure he wouldn't simply blast his way through?

A tremor of alarm rippled through her as the roar of the train faded to a murmur. Something had gone wrong. She peered at Elliot, who was squinting into the darkness, his head cocked, listening intently.

"It's stopped," she breathed.

Elliot nodded, running his fingers through his crinkly black hair. She understood his dilemma. If they moved off to investigate, the train could easily pick up speed and their moment would be lost. If, on the other hand, they remained where they were, the driver, for whatever reason, might decide to reverse.

Elliot came to an unwilling decision. "Get mounted," he snapped curtly.

Kate's stomach quivered as she seized the bridle and clambered weakly into the saddle, glad now of the endless hours of cantering and galloping she'd indulged in during the long years of her Cumbrian youth.

Elliot led the way as they loped through the gate of the adjacent field, and leaning back in the saddle, Kate flexed her knees, struggling fiercely to hold her mount in line.

* * *

Dameron shepherded Harry and the driver through the door of the minister's coach, following swiftly, thankful for the strong arms which reached down to assist him. His body felt numb, but he took care to keep his features studiously composed. He'd be damned if he'd let that bastard Tazelaar see how scared he'd been.

McAuley was studying the prisoners with an air of casual curiosity. He seemed unabashed by the events of the past few minutes. If anything, Dameron thought, his eyes looked livelier than ever, as if the prospect of danger infused him with some strange sense of exhilaration.

"What on earth is going on here, Commander?" McAuley asked.

"I don't know yet," Dameron admitted softly, "but I intend to find out."

"These gentlemen look respectable enough."

Dameron had to admit the minister was right. The area manager particularly appeared remarkably calm and resigned, though the engine driver was shaking a little. The driver's voice rose shrilly as anger dried the mucous on his vocal membranes. "Bloody fool," he snapped. "It's a wonder you didn't cause an accident, smashing the window like that. It'll have to be paid for. That's British Rail property."

"Shut up," Dameron ordered.

The man glanced at Harry uncertainly as if seeking some kind of moral support, but Harry's face remained impassive. He was studying Dameron through flat expressionless eyes.

Dameron thrust his pistol into its leather holster and picked up the radio receiver. Wirth's voice broke through the crackling static. "Jack?"

"We've stopped the train," Dameron said.

"Anybody hurt?"

"Negative."

"Fuller?"

"Under arrest."

"Good work, Jack. And the minister?"

"McAuley's fine."

"Where are you now?"

"Just north of Carlisle, on the old Broadstruthers branch line."

"Excellent. There's a police convoy on its way from Carlisle to meet you. Look through the window on the right. Can you see a road?"

Dameron tugged back the blind. "There's one hugging the railroad track," he declared.

"Great. When the police arrive, transfer McAuley to a patrol car. He's to be taken to Carlisle station and held there until Charles Palmer turns up, understand?"

"What about Fuller?"

There was a pause on the transmitter and they heard Wirth muttering under his breath. "Stick him in one of the cells," he said at last. "We'll let the security boys figure out the charge. That's what they get paid for."

Trotting through the darkness, their horses' hooves muffled on the soft crumbling earth, Kate and her companions glimpsed the outline of the train ahead. The great diesel stood humming softly, steam from its valves spiraling into the crisp night air. There was no sign of the engineer. Motionless, the locomotive looked emasculated somehow, as if the sudden impromptu halt had robbed it of dignity.

Elliot coasted the rim of a dried-stone wall, his

lithe body supremely graceful as he guided his horse with subtle movements of his thighs. A natural horseman, Kate thought. A natural everything, Elliot Chamille. Rarely had she encountered a man so completely at home in any surroundings.

She saw Elliot jerk his mount abruptly to a halt, and almost ran into the back of his mare as she hauled hard on the reins, reaching down to pat her horse's neck reassuringly. She glimpsed lights flashing on the road ahead and, to her dismay and disbelief, heard police sirens splitting the night in an eerie clamor.

They sat holding their horses fiercely in check, watching a stream of patrol cars screech to a halt alongside the motionless locomotive. Dark figures spilled into the gloom, clambering over the wire perimeter fence.

Kate felt a wave of defeat sweep through her body. "We're too late. Something's gone wrong."

Elliot's eyes glittered. She could feel his anger matching her own.

"Fuller, it's got to be."

"Harry wouldn't. I'd trust him with my life."

"Who else knew, for God's sake? It had to be Fuller."

"No," she cried, "I'll swear it wasn't Harry."

Elliot cursed as he battled to keep his mount under control. His rage and frustration seemed almost more than he could bear. He'd worked so hard to get things going, planned, plotted, improvised. He glanced around the darkened field. Cattle lay sleeping all around them, and Elliot frowned as a startling thought occurred to him. It's crazy, he thought. But his senses were racing, his body tingling.

"Spread out," he hissed. "Get those cows on the move."

Kate frowned in puzzlement. "What good will that do?"

"The police can't turn their cars on the road. They'll have to back into the field here."

"So what?"

"So when they do, we'll treat them to a good old-fashioned North American rodeo," he said with a grin.

Harry stood silently in the railroad coach and watched the little group of policemen approaching the open door. They looked resolute and business-like, their faces molded into the no-nonsense expressions of men who disliked having their routine disrupted and were determined to see that somebody suffered for it. Leading the entourage was a thickset man in superintendent's uniform, his cheeks baked red by the sun and wind.

Harry sighed gently. Circumstances couldn't be worse, he reflected. Lunatic, it had been, trying to do things single-handed. Put Tim's life at risk. He should have ducked out when the first of their crazily laid plans started going awry. Absolved himself. Cut and run. But he hadn't. For whatever reason, he had pressed on stubbornly and was now in deep and serious trouble. Damn fool that he was, he'd risked everything—his career, his freedom, his entire future—on a preposterous gamble only an idiot would have taken. How would they view it in the courts? Would they regard Tim's kidnapping as extenuating circumstances? He hoped so. He had damn little else to fall back on.

The superintendent drew to a halt at the carriage step. Standing on the ground, his chin just level with the carpeted deck, he peered up, shading his eyes against the lamplight. "Commander Dameron?"

"I'm Dameron," said the tall balding man who had clambered over the locomotive roof to arrest Harry and the engineer. Harry eyed him with an air of grudging respect. There was no disputing the commander's guts. There was no disputing his temper either, Harry reflected, glimpsing the look in the detective's eyes.

"Superintendent Messner," the policeman said. "We have orders to take your passenger into protective custody."

"How many cars have you got out there?" Dameron demanded.

"Seven."

"Can you double up your men and leave one of the vehicles empty?"

The superintendent looked puzzled. "Why?"

"Taking care of the passenger is our job, superintendent. I'd like my own team to accompany Mr. McAuley to police headquarters."

The superintendent considered for a moment and Harry could tell he was weighing the wisdom of refusal against the indignity of losing face. In the end, he decided to comply.

"Take the second vehicle," he offered. "I'll squeeze my men into the other cars."

"What about us?" asked Tazelaar, the South African.

Commander Dameron grinned at him. "Sorry, chum, there's just no room. Looks as if you'll have to sit here and twiddle your thumbs for a bit. We'll send a taxi out to pick you up. Charge it to expenses."

He nodded in Harry's direction. "We've somebody else for your cells. A prisoner."

"Who is he?"

"Name's Harry Fuller, B.R. area manager."

"What's the charge?"

"We haven't figured that out yet."

"Has he been searched?"

"He's clean as a whistle," Dameron said.

The superintendent turned to one of his men. "Handcuffs," he ordered.

The constable fumbled in his pocket, handed them over, and the superintendent tossed the metal bracelets up to Dameron. "Manacle his wrists," he instructed. "Prisoners aren't allowed in patrol cars without being properly constrained. Regulations."

Harry sighed as the handcuffs were snapped in position. Now he really felt like a criminal. Beside him, the little engine driver was watching the affair incredulously.

The commander jerked his head at the open door. "Move."

Holding his arms in front of him, Harry jumped into the night, grunting as his heels thudded into the cindered track. A policeman seized him by the elbow, steering him down the ragged embankment toward the second patrol car. Commander Dameron and his four associates followed briskly, the commander clambering behind the steering wheel. In the rear, one of the detectives chuckled under his breath.

"What's tickling you, sunshine?" Dameron demanded, eyeing him in the rearview mirror.

"Tazelaar. Did you see the look on his face?"

Commander Dameron permitted himself a fleeting grin. "Serves the bastard right. He's too cocky by half."

"I thought he was going to have hysterics."

Harry glanced through the window as Howard McAuley, the South African diplomat, approached through the darkness, escorted by the remaining Special Branch men.

"Shove along a bit and make some room in the back," Dameron ordered.

They fell silent as the rear door opened, and McAuley squeezed in, panting hard on the frosty predawn air. "Quite a night, gentlemen," he said in a cultured voice. "I'm extremely fortunate to have you along."

Dameron slid down the window as the superintendent appeared. "The road's too narrow to turn here," the superintendent pointed out. "There's a field on the left. We'll use the gate to reverse in, and when we're all facing in the right direction, we'll move off in convoy."

"Right," Dameron agreed.

They sat in silence as the lead driver backed his vehicle into the narrow opening, then shifted gear, easing around and drawing to a halt on the opposite side of the road. Dameron started his engine and, pulling forward, gently reversed the car. With an abruptness that startled them all, they found their vehicle suddenly engulfed by a great throng of jostling, buffeting cows. Harry blinked in astonishment. He could see leathery flanks scraping along the patrol car's hull.

"What the bloody hell's going on?" Dameron muttered.

Like an apparition from some extraordinary nightmare, a man materialized among the swirling bodies. Thrusting his head through the open side window, he rammed a pistol against Dameron's temple. Harry recognized the Negro who had escorted him to his meeting with Kate earlier in the day. The man's appearance was so electrifying that for a moment nobody in the car reacted.

Elliot peered at Harry over the commander's head. "Open your door," he snapped.

Harry hesitated, glancing quickly around. Their vehicle was completely surrounded by cattle. Clearly, the police in the roadway had no inkling that anything extraordinary was afoot. Reaching down with his handcuffed wrists, Harry flicked the knob with his finger. The door swung open, and a second Negro lunged in, covering the detectives in the rear with a small snub-nosed Starfire .38.

"McAuley," Elliot growled, jerking his head.

McAuley's face looked ghastly. He glanced at the detectives, but they studiously avoided his gaze, staring bleakly into the night. Chewing his lip, McAuley fumbled with the metal catch and clambered into the darkness. At Harry's side, Dameron looked flushed with anger. The injustice of the moment seemed to push him beyond the boundaries of reason. Harry saw him reaching for the horn, intent on sounding the alarm. Moving swiftly, Harry hooked his handcuffed wrists around Dameron's left palm, dragging it away from the steering wheel, and Elliot, glimpsing the danger, clubbed Dameron across the rear of the skull. Dameron fell forward, banging his head on the top of the steering wheel.

"You'd better come too," Elliot snapped, glaring at Harry fiercely.

Harry didn't need a second invitation. Tumbling into the night, he pushed his way through the frightened, lunging cows, following the second black man, who was dragging McAuley along by his shirt-front, the Starfire thrust against the minister's oily dark hair. Dimly through the darkness, Harry glimpsed a cluster of horses and riders waiting in the center of the field. He recognized Kate, her trim body framed against the starlit sky. Seeing the fugitives emerging, she rode toward them, dragging a trio of spare mounts behind her.

"Harry?" she whispered, her breath steaming on the frosty air.

He nodded, panting hard, scarcely able to speak. She spotted his handcuffed wrists. "Can you mount?"

"I can try," he gasped.

"Get up behind me. The other horses are all accounted for."

Seizing Kate's waistbelt, Harry dragged his stomach across the rear of her prancing mount. Behind him, McAuley, under the threat of the African's gun, was heaving himself into one of the empty saddles. A shout echoed from the roadway, and Harry realized with a chill their flight had been discovered. He struggled hard to retain his balance as Kate tugged on the reins, trying to hold her mare under control. Somehow, he managed to wriggle a leg over the animal's lunging spine and settle himself breathlessly into position. He saw the train etched against the night, spewing out steam from its pressure valves. Framed in the doorway, a thickset figure was crouching forward, arms extended in the classic firing position. Harry felt his senses lurch as he recognized Tazelaar, the South African security man.

Crack-crack. Twin spurts of flame, almost simultaneous, lanced into the night, and Harry heard the shots reverberating above the empty pastureland. The bullets scythed past their heads, making an ominous whistling sound as they sped harmlessly into the darkness.

Tazelaar fired again. This time, by some miracle the bullet ricocheted wildly off a boulder, and Harry, still clinging to Kate's spine, saw McAuley reel in the saddle, hugging his side. Eyes flashing behind its leather blinkers, McAuley's horse reared in terror, and only by the most skillful use of the reins did he prevent it from bolting altogether. As the animal settled, shuffling furiously, Harry glimpsed a scarlet stain spreading across the minister's overcoat.

"McAuley's hit," he croaked.

Kate's face looked white as she glanced in McAuley's direction. His features were twisted in pain, and even in the darkness Harry could see sweat glistening on his pallid cheekbones.

Elliot, sprinting toward them, paused in his tracks to fire blindly at the carriage doorway, and Tazelaar ducked back, flinging himself behind the insulated walls. Elliot ran on and, like an acrobat who had practiced the maneuver a thousand times over, vaulted into the nearmost saddle, and drumming the horse's ribs with his heels, he galloped frenziedly across the rolling pastureland.

With the shouts of their pursuers echoing in their ears, they thundered after him into the darkness.

Seven

The morning sunlight was sharp and chill. It lay across the abandoned train, which still stood mournfully at the top of a grassy embankment. Waldo shivered, thrusting his hands in his overcoat pockets as he watched Palmer receiving the reports of the police superintendent and the officer in charge of the Special Branch contingent. Waldo felt sorry for Palmer. It was hard to believe the thing which had happened, McAuley dragged off his coach in the middle of nowhere. It seemed incredible. You looked for ways in which your credulity might be impaired.

Waldo was not by nature an excitable man. At the U.S. State Department in Washington, he was known for his placid, affable manner, but there were times, he had to admit, he longed desperately to blow his cool, and this was one of those moments. It was not so much the incongruity of the affair as the fact, simple and inescapable, that he had been counting on these talks to put the finishing touches to an otherwise unillustrious career. He had promised his wife, Martha, that once the negotiations had been finalized, he would take six months off and treat her to a European tour. They had spent their honeymoon in Paris, and he knew Martha still longed to return there.

But there was something else, something even Palmer didn't realize, a secret so unthinkable that Waldo shuddered instinctively when he thought of the repercussions McAuley's disappearance might evoke. He didn't relish the job of explaining things to the Secretary of State.

He watched Palmer listening to his subordinates, nodding occasionally in that cool, imperturbable way he had, putting in a word or two when he needed some point clarified. "I want you to contact the Home Secretary in London," Waldo heard him saying, "and ask his permission to get some troops into the field."

"What about you, sir?" the Special Branch man inquired politely.

"I'm going to talk to the Forestry people. You can contact me at their headquarters in Bellingham."

The commander nodded, and Palmer strode toward Waldo, his breath steaming in the chill March morning. It was easy to see he was embarrassed, but he took care not to show it as he glanced around the scene of desolation. "It's a bloody mess," he admitted. "They're gone, all right. Vanished into thin air."

"The ANC?"

"God knows. Could be anyone."

"They can't get far," Waldo insisted. "If you block the roads, you can seal them in."

"I wish it was that simple. They've picked their spot ingeniously. Just over that hill lies the Border Forest, the largest man-made forest in Europe— nearly four hundred square miles of Norway spruce and Sitka spruce, flanked to the east by another two hundred square miles of open hill country. It's an ideal setting for a bunch of fugitives on the run. If they hide among the trees, we can't pick them up from the air, and we can't spot them from the ground. Our only hope is to flood the area with troops."

"Think it'll work?"

"If you want the truth, I think what we need is a bloody miracle."

Palmer paused, eyeing Waldo shrewdly. The wind plucked at the brim of his hat, molding it against his skull, and Waldo saw the firm set of his jaw, the small, almost imperceptible tightening of his facial muscles.

"Mr. Friedman, I want you to be honest with me."

"Honest?"

"I need the truth. I can't operate if I'm fumbling in the dark."

"I don't know what you mean."

"I watched your face when we got the phone call at my club. I watched it again when we found McAuley gone, and I saw something in your eyes which surprised me. Fear."

Waldo felt his cheeks flushing. "You're crazy. I can't tell you more than you already know."

"You must, if you want McAuley back."

Somewhere to the east, a train whistle blew, the sound shrill and discordant in the cold morning air. Waldo sucked in his breath, his mind racing furiously. You couldn't lie to a man like Palmer, he thought. Palmer had lived so long in the milieu of deceit, he could smell it a mile off. Moreover, they needed his cooperation, they needed his expertise. If they couldn't trust Palmer, who in God's name could they trust?

Waldo came to a quick decision. "You're right," he admitted. "There *is* something you haven't been told."

"I thought so."

"There's a clause in the proposed agreement called Option 24."

"Option 24?"

"It would result in immense embarrassment to our mutual governments if the details ever leaked out."

"Why?"

"You've heard of the *Broederbond*, Mr. Palmer?"

"The secret society dedicated to the preservation of the Afrikaaner race?"

"Exactly. A society determined to see its culture survive by whatever means necessary."

Briefly and succinctly, Waldo outlined the details of the controversial clause while Palmer listened in silence, his delicate features impassive. If Waldo had expected some reaction—shock, disbelief, disapproval—he observed nothing. Palmer's eyes remained as inscrutable as ever.

When Waldo had finished, Palmer stubbed at the ground with his toe.

"And the British and Americans, they approved of this?"

"It wasn't a question of approval. It was a question of what was expedient, taking into account the circumstances. You have to give something to get something back."

Palmer glanced at the train, shivering a little in the morning chill.

"And I thought *my* business was unscrupulous."

"We're not acting illegally," Waldo protested.

"I wasn't talking about legality. I was talking about ethics."

"For God's sake, Palmer, the South Africans insisted. They made it a stipulation in any agreement. And viewed in realistic terms, it's a small price to pay when you consider what we stand to gain."

"I wonder if the world will see it that way," Palmer breathed.

"Don't moralize with me, Palmer. And don't try and tell me you've never bent the rules a little to get the job done."

"I wouldn't dream of moralizing," Palmer answered softly.

He paused as the roar of a helicopter reached them in the morning stillness. Waldo squinted into the shimmering sun and saw the chopper framed against the sky, its massive blades thrashing at the chill spring air.

"Looks like our transportation," Palmer said.

Glimpsing the motionless train, the pilot brought his machine to a hover and guided it down expertly in a delicate descent. A sergeant in khaki fatigues helped Waldo on board and fastened him into a bucket seat with a nylon sling. In a smooth, gentle swaying motion, their pilot rose the craft into the air, and Waldo glimpsed the great sweep of the open hills blending into a contourless sprawl of ragged spruce forest which spread as far as Waldo could see, coating summits and valleys alike. As he stared down at the awesome carpet of trees, he realized the dilemma confronting them and felt his spirits sink. Palmer was right, he thought, eyeing the landscape dejectedly. They did need a bloody miracle.

Elliot stood at the side of the logging road and looked back the way they had come. The road slid across the hill slope, ascending steadily in a series of steep switchback bends, carving a ragged tear through

the bristling carpet of foliage. The forest looked like an
intruder, Elliot thought, for though its presence was
inescapable, the trees were too neat and orderly to have
ever been placed there by nature. The landscape, Elliot
knew, represented one of the most remarkable tracts of
countryside in Britain, remarkable because it was
wholly artificial, and because the vast blanket of evergreens cloaking the Northumbrian fells had been carefully sliced and subdivided into a perplexing maze of
firebreaks and service roads, all twisting and inter-
locking in a complex intricate puzzle. For several
hours, they had zigzagged through this bewildering
labyrinth until a terrible truth had imposed itself on
Elliot's consciousness. Though he had worked out his
plan far in advance, had even plotted his route, tortuous though it was, step by meticulous step, the wound-
ing of their captive presented a new and alarming
problem. How long could McAuley survive, jostling
painfully in a constantly moving saddle? In the end,
he had been forced to call a halt, and his companions had tumbled gratefully from their mounts,
their bodies riven with exhaustion. They looked
whacked now, he thought, studying them glumly as
they sprawled about the grassy embankment. Kate was
tending to McAuley, using the team's medical kit to
dress the wound below the minister's rib cage. At
first glance, it appeared strangely innocuous, a small
crimson starburst that barely showed through the
blanket of hair coating McAuley's skin, but the minister's cheeks were pale, and there was a sickly gleam
in his small dark eyes. It had been the devil's luck,
having the minister shot like that, Elliot reflected.
The next few hours could be crucial. If they wished
to remain at large, they would have to stay on the
move, using the forest as a cover, weaving, dodging,

backtracking. He hoped to God McAuley could stand
it.

Several feet away, Malheiro was using his bowie
knife to prize at Harry Fuller's handcuffs. Fuller's
face was smeared with dirt, and he was watching
Kate intently as she cleaned and dressed the minister's wound. Despite himself, Elliot felt a small
twinge of jealousy as Malheiro, with a triumphant
squeal, clicked open the handcuffs and tore them
from Harry's wrists. Did Fuller want her back? Elliot
wondered. Impossible to tell, with a look like that. It
could mean anything, hatred, love, longing, fury.
Elliot turned away, angry and disgusted. You dumb
fool, what does the woman mean to you anyhow? he
thought. You've got a job to do, a difficult and
dangerous job. You've one man wounded and the
rest exhausted. You'll need every scrap of concentration you can muster to get through the next
forty-eight hours. It wasn't easy to ignore Kate's
presence, however. Even sweaty and bedraggled, she
carried a beauty it was impossible to deny. And
something else, Elliot pondered, a natural elegance,
a sense of style. Elliot was not an unworldly man.
He'd known many women during his short and
eventful life, but Kate's demeanor outshone them all.

He walked toward her, his boots scuffling on the
gravel-strewn road surface. "How's he doing?" he
asked, watching her put the dressing in place.

"How do you think he's doing? He's just been
shot, for God's sake."

"Is it good or bad?"

"He needs emergency surgery. The bullet's still
in there somewhere."

"Didn't look too serious to me. I've seen bullet
holes before. That one's little more than a pinprick."

"Shows how little you know about gunshot

wounds. It isn't the bullet that does the damage, it's the shock wave that precedes it and the vacuum which follows. That shot would send a reverberation through Mr. McAuley's internal system, hitting each of his organs in turn. It would suck in pieces of dirt, grass, shreds of clothing, everything in sight. I've cleaned it as well as I can, but if you want my advice, he shouldn't be moved. Too much riding, and there's a serious danger of the bullet piercing his spleen."

Elliot frowned. It was worse than he'd bargained for. He looked down at the sweat coating McAuley's skin. McAuley's eyes were flooded with pain, but there was a glitter of defiance in them as he stared back at Elliot, unafraid. "How do you feel?" Elliot asked.

"Like I'm coming apart at the seams."

"Think you can ride?"

"Are you offering me a choice, young man?"

Elliot shook his head. "Sorry, Minister. Painful or not, we have to keep on the move. The British security forces will soon be flooding this forest like locusts."

McAuley breathed hoarsely as Kate put the finishing touches to his dressing. "May I ask what you hope to achieve by all this?"

"Freedom, ultimately," Elliot stated.

McAuley chuckled. "An interesting word. I've always puzzled about its meaning."

"You wouldn't understand, Minister. But we intend to teach you, in time."

"You young fool, in a single act, you've set back your cause another fifty years, destroyed months of difficult negotiating work."

Elliot smiled sourly. "You're talking about the PAC talks, I take it? The end of apartheid, a noble rallying cry. Well, we're practical people, Minister.

We want an end to apartheid too, but not in twenty years' time. We'll change things in our own way, and when we do, there'll be no bargaining, no compromises."

McAuley blinked. "If you're not interested in the PAC talks, then what in God's name is this all about?"

"We're putting right a terrible injustice," Elliot told him gently. "We're offering your life for the freedom of Joshua Matshoba."

McAuley didn't answer. He lay back on the ground, his eyes closing in the grim rigidity of pain.

"Elliot," Kate said, "unless we get him to a hospital, we won't have anything left to bargain with."

"You know that isn't possible."

"You can't drag him through this forest like a bundle of firewood. He'll die."

"We have no choice, Kate. Our only hope is to keep on the move."

"Listen to me," Kate said soberly. "That bullet is lodged somewhere inside his abdomen. Stick him in a saddle, and it could clip a vital organ. What will we have gained, tell me that, if we end up with a corpse on our hands?"

"You think I like this?" Elliot growled.

"I don't know what you like," Kate cried. "I don't know anything about you. All I know is, we have a wounded man here, and he needs help."

"He's got help," Elliot insisted stubbornly. "You're his help. It may not be much, but you're all he can hope for."

Straightening, he glared at Malheiro. "Fetch the horses," he snapped. "We've rested here long enough."

* * *

The air in the cabinet room was stifling. Despite the coldness of the late March day, the Home Secretary's face seemed clammy as he leaned over the conference table and gazed at the security chiefs gathered in front of him. "The news has just been confirmed," he said. "We're hoping to keep the story out of the press as long as possible. But our editors aren't fools, gentlemen, and this is a democracy we live in. Unless national security is threatened, I have no authority to gag the media, so we'll have to rely on compartmentalization, details relayed on a strictly need-to-know basis. It's tricky, and there's no telling how long we can keep it under wraps, but we've got to try."

The Defense Secretary shifted in his chair. "What happens now, Neville?" he inquired. "The kidnappers couldn't have chosen a better spot. The Border Forest spreads across those hillslopes like a cancer. We could send an army into that wilderness and it'd take months to weed them out."

"We haven't got months," the Home Secretary retorted. "We haven't got days. We have to get McAuley back before the South Africans get wind that he's missing, and before the opposition learns about Option 24."

"Option 24 wasn't our idea," another man stated. "We haven't done anything irregular."

"We condoned it. That makes us culpable."

"For heaven's sake, Neville, we accepted under protest. The South Africans wouldn't budge."

"Try telling that to the electorate."

"Well, they'll have to know sooner or later."

"Better later, when we've got something to crow

about. In the meantime, we must take steps to remedy the situation."

The Home Secretary glanced at General Elsey, who was watching the proceedings with a sense of deepening misgiving. The general flinched when he felt the minister's gaze.

"How long will it take to get the forest surrounded?" the Home Secretary demanded.

"Well, Minister, difficult to say. The army isn't exactly on a war footing."

"What in God's name does that mean?"

"It means simply that the main bulk of our forces are already committed in Northern Ireland and Europe. It will take some time to ferry troops into the area in any reasonable quantity."

The Home Secretary eyed him with exasperation. "Are you telling me that we spend a fortune on defense, and you can't handle a simple emergency on your own doorstep?"

General Elsey looked unhappy. "It's a question of economics, Minister. We deploy troops as and when they're needed. We can't keep the entire army on full-time alert."

"Just give me a straight answer. How long will it take to get men into the Northumbrian forest?"

"In the sense you mean—that is, a blanket operation—ten, twelve days at the soonest."

"Good God," the Home Secretary exclaimed.

"However, I can offer a simple alternative. Units of the Royal Marines are exercising at Otterburn military training camp in the Cheviot Hills. That's within immediate striking of the forest itself. May I suggest a quick reaction group of perhaps a hundred and eighty men, with a further two hundred and fifty as a follow-up in a few hours' time?"

"Do what you can, General. Just get those units moving."

In the pale light of the early morning, the Home Secretary's features looked weary and resigned. He sighed as he rose to his feet. "I suppose I'd better tell the prime minister."

Waldo and Palmer sat in front of the forest officer's desk and watched patiently as a secretary placed coffee mugs in front of them. Sunlight slid through the frosted windows, picking out wallcharts and filing cabinets. The room carried an air of functional austerity which Waldo found strangely quaint and archaic.

The forest officer waited until the girl had left the room, then, taking out his pipe, began to fill it carefully. "It's a big area," he admitted, "but the situation isn't as hopeless as it seems. The Border Forest is probably the only one in the world which was planned and constructed from start to finish entirely by man. It's divided into an elaborate complex of rides and firebreaks, each section meticulously recorded in intricate detail. Your fugitives will have to utilize the open areas as much as possible, and since we know where they entered, and since we can estimate the speed at which they're likely to travel, it shouldn't be too difficult to pinpoint their location."

"We'd appreciate your assistance in that," Palmer said quietly.

"The thing that's worrying me," the forest officer muttered, dropping his match into a nearby ashtray, "is the prospect of conflagration."

"Conflagration?" Waldo echoed.

"In simple terms, Mr. Friedman, the commission's biggest nightmare. Fire."

Waldo frowned. "Is that a possibility?"

"More than just a possibility. We've had red warning flags posted around the plantations for the past two weeks, keeping out members of the public. Spring's always the trickiest time of year. That's when the underbrush is tinder dry, when strong winds can fan the tiniest spark into a raging inferno. But this spring is particularly bad. We've had scarcely any rain since Christmas, and already there've been several small blazes in the outlying areas. I've never seen the forest so volatile. We're sitting on a powder keg, gentlemen, and if those fugitives of yours take it into their heads to start striking matches, we could have something a damned sight more serious than a kidnapping on our hands."

He paused as his secretary looked in. "Mr. Friedman's call to Washington has come through," she said.

Waldo rose to his feet, nodding politely. It was the moment he'd been dreading, the first humiliating point of contact. He hated admitting he'd made a hash of things. Anybody would, he realized, but with Waldo the feeling went deeper and stronger. He wasn't a young man anymore; he'd struggled hard during his early years, learning the intricacies of an intricate business, wheeling and dealing, pressuring and compromising, soothing and mediating, but somehow his inherent ordinariness always managed to get in the way. The things he'd achieved had never been noticed. He hadn't let it faze him, though. "One day," he'd told Martha, "I'll make them sit up and cheer, you'll see." And one day he had. The Vologda Agreement was nothing to be ashamed of. Not many men could have pulled it off. And dealing with the

Chinese had taken a monumental degree of tact. If the PAC talks had succeeded, he might have set the final seal on things, given his sons something to be proud of, shown them the old man wasn't so median, after all. But not now. Never now. Now he was facing vilification and disgrace. No point telling himself he wasn't responsible. Everybody was responsible, everybody who had a finger in the unholy mess. If the details became public, it wouldn't be just the president's neck on the line. It would be the whole damned administration, himself included, and Waldo knew it.

He followed the secretary into the outer office, waiting until she had left the room before picking up the receiver. "Friedman here."

"Waldo?" It was the Secretary of State's voice. "Waldo, is it true?"

Waldo tried hard to keep his voice casual and relaxed. He'd learned that in moments of crisis it helped calm people down. "I'm afraid it is, Dan. They pulled McAuley off a train in the early hours of the morning."

"For Christ's sake, what was the idiot doing? The situation is delicate enough without inviting trouble."

"The Scottish journey was part of a security smokescreen, I understand, in case any reporters spotted McAuley in London."

"Waldo, if anything leaks out, anything at all—"

"No reason why it should."

"You know what I'm talking about, Waldo. Option 24."

"We're well within our rights, Dan," Waldo insisted soothingly.

"Rights have nothing to do with it. This is

politics, and if the public learns about Option 24, we'll have another Watergate on our hands."

"Has the president heard?"

"The president's in California. I haven't had the heart to call him yet."

"Well, if it makes any difference, we seem to have the kidnappers pretty well isolated. They're in a region called the Border Forest. It's a big area, but we're hoping with luck to pinpoint their approximate location."

"How many men have you got covering the job?"

"They're sending in a squadron of Royal Marines. We're waiting for them now."

"Who's handling things?"

"Charles Palmer, head of Britain's Section 4."

"Stay with him, Waldo. Don't let Palmer out of your sight."

"I'll do that, Dan."

"And call me back the minute you have anything new."

"Don't worry, we're doing everything we possibly can."

As Waldo put down the receiver, he heard engines roaring from the road outside. Palmer and the forest officer were standing at the window when he strolled into the inner office. Through the frosted glass, Waldo caught a glimpse of camouflaged truck awnings flapping in the wind.

"The troops have arrived," Palmer said, looking at him encouragingly. "Now maybe we'll start getting somewhere."

Elliot crouched in the underbrush, peering across the tarmac road. The crispness of the early morning had given way to a bright sunny day, and the scent of spruce sap lingered pleasantly in Elliot's nostrils. Behind him, tethered in the trees, he could hear the horses nickering impatiently. Elliot rubbed his mouth with the back of one hand. On the opposite side of the road, nestling on the grassy verge, stood a glass-paned telephone booth, its domed roof beaded with moisture. "I want everyone to remain here," Elliot declared. "If a car comes by, get McAuley into the woods, understand?"

They nodded silently, and Elliot glanced at Harry. "You come with me."

Looking surprised, Harry followed Elliot over the fence and across the open roadway.

"Wait here," Elliot ordered, and stepped inside the booth, closing the door firmly behind him.

Harry knew Elliot was calling the press. He wanted publicity for the movement, publicity for the cause. Stamping his feet in the chill, Harry moved backward and forward along the grassy verge as the wind picked up, stirring the branches above his head. He could feel it slicing through his heavy parka, chilling him to the bone.

After nearly forty minutes, Elliot emerged from the booth and thrust a coin into Harry's hand. Harry looked at him blankly. "What's this for?"

"Call your sister."

"Mildred?" Frowning, Harry picked up the receiver, slipped in the coin, and punched out Mildred's number in Coventry. A voice came on the line, faint but familiar. "Hello?"

"Mildred? It's Harry."

"Harry? You've heard the news?"

"What news?"

"Tim. He's back, Harry. Timmy's back."

A muscle knotted in Harry's chest. He glanced back at Elliot, who was watching him with a crooked grin. There was a scuffling at the end of the line, then Tim's voice echoed in Harry's ear, shrill, high-pitched, filled with excitement. "Dad?"

"Tim, is it you?"

"Hello, Dad, I just got home."

"Are you all right?"

"Terrific. I had a great time, Dad. They gave me a Zulu spear. A real one, with tribal markings on the shaft."

"Tim, are you hurt?"

"Hurt? No, I'm terrific."

"Where have you been, for Christ's sake?"

"I met these people. Friends of Kate's. Kate's back from Africa, Dad."

"Yes, I'm with her now."

"Is she home for good, Dad?"

"We'll see," Harry said. "We'll see. Just tell me what happened."

"They took me to this house, Dad. It was like a school, sort of. They had African dancing and chanting, all that stuff."

"The house, where was it?"

"I don't know. It was dark when we got there. Somewhere near London, I think."

"Listen to me . . ." Harry began as the telephone began to bleep. Cursing, he fumbled in his pocket for change, but he found none. The line went dead.

"Satisfied?" Elliot asked.

Harry nodded silently, and taking the telephone from his hand, Elliot replaced it in position. "There's nothing to keep you here any longer," he said.

"Trying to get rid of me?"

"You're too much of a handicap, Mr. Fuller. I've enough to worry about with McAuley hurt. I'm indebted for your help—we couldn't have done it without you—but you're not one of us."

"I wonder if the police will see it that way."

"The police will understand when they learn about your boy. Things could get rough in the next twenty-four hours. I'd advise you to go while you still have a chance."

Harry stared at Elliot in silence for a moment, his relief at hearing Tim's voice quickly fading. The black man was quite a performer, Harry had to acknowledge that. Could have been an actor, with those looks and all. Elliot had everything—poise, elegance, charm—but he was too transparent. He hadn't fooled Harry a bit.

"Tell the truth, Chamille. I know why you want to get rid of me, and it has nothing to do with McAuley."

Elliot frowned. "What are you talking about?"

"Kate. I've seen you looking at her. I've seen you looking at me. You're jealous, you bastard."

"You're out of your mind, Fuller."

"I lived with that woman for nearly three years. I know what she does to me. D'you think I'm too stupid to see it in somebody else?"

Elliot's face seemed to close in on itself; Harry could think of no other way to describe it. It didn't harden exactly—the features merely constricted, as if somewhere deep inside Elliot was building up barriers, defenses.

"You don't seriously think I'd let personal motives interfere with what we're trying to achieve here."

"You're a human being, like the rest of us."

"A human being with a job to do."

"With feelings and emotions. Nobody's immune from those."

Elliot sighed. "I can't afford to fight with you, Fuller."

"Then stay away from Kate."

"Kate is part of my team. You're the one who's the outsider here. Get out now. Your presence is an embarrassment."

The muscles tightened around Harry's jawline. He knew if Elliot turned him loose, he would lose his chance to hit back. But Elliot had responded to the simplest of all emotional challenges. He was too proud to throw Harry out forcibly.

"You'd better get used to my presence," Harry whispered. "Because like it or not, I'm staying."

Waldo sat in the truck rear and watched the marine lieutenant, a tall young man with a long bony face, discussing the Forestry map with Palmer. Palmer's natural gracefulness had deserted him a little, Waldo noticed, and from time to time elements of tension crept into his modulated voice. Only the lieutenant, trim and austere, appeared at home in the situation, as if, in some curious way, crisis and emergency formed an essential part of his character.

"We can send patrols along the logging roads," the lieutenant suggested, "use the trucks to lace the area up."

"These people are traveling on horseback," Palmer said impatiently. "Stick to the roads' and you'll be wasting your time."

"That underbrush is thicker than porridge. It's difficult enough for a man to move on foot, let alone mounted. They'll use the firebreaks as much as they possibly can. When they shift through the woodland itself, they'll have to cut the fences to get their animals through. That's what we'll look for. Severed wire. If we can find a point where they've entered the trees, we can send in dogs."

Palmer looked at the lieutenant with a new respect. "Of course," he muttered, "I hadn't thought of that."

"We know they're in this western sector," the lieutenant said, circling the map with his pencil. "They can't have traveled farther in the few hours they've been at large, so I suggest we concentrate our efforts in this area."

"One thing I want you to impress on your men, Lieutenant. The forest officer tells me the woods are highly volatile. The slightest spark could set the underbrush alight. Pass the word among the troops. No smoking. No fire lighting. No cooking stoves."

"Right, sir," the lieutenant promised.

He paused as they heard boots crunching on the gravel outside, and a marine popped his head beneath the canvas awning. "Sorry to interrupt, sir. Message from the Forestry office. A man called Wincot's on the line from the *Daily Telegraph*."

Palmer frowned. "What does he want?"

"Wants to know if the story's true, sir. About Mr. McAuley."

Palmer looked at Waldo. "How in God's name could they have found out?"

"The kidnappers probably called them direct," Waldo said. "They'll want maximum publicity for their little escapade."

Palmer glanced back at the young marine. "What else did Wincot say?"

"He mentioned the kidnappers' terms, sir. They're threatening to kill McAuley unless Joshua Matshoba is flown to Angola by noon tomorrow."

Palmer blinked, clearly taken by surprise. He stared at Waldo meaningfully. "So it's not the PAC talks they're trying to disrupt at all. It's Joshua Matshoba they're after."

Waldo nodded, narrowing his eyes. "In the happy timeworn American expression," he said, "I believe this is where the shit hits the fan."

The news burst on the British public at approximately ten-fourteen, when ITN interrupted children's broadcasting with a special bulletin. "Within the last few minutes," the announcer said, "we've received an unconfirmed report that Howard McAuley, chief foreign minister with the South African government, has been kidnapped in Britain by African Nationalist guerrillas. It's understood the minister was snatched from a Glasgow-bound train under the noses of Special Branch detectives and South African security men. At this stage, no details of the kidnapping have been released, and no explanation has been given for Mr. McAuley's presence in this country. We hope to have a full report on our main bulletin at one o'clock."

In Fleet Street, the teleprinters hummed with activity as editors scoured the rolls of copy, struggling to distinguish fact from fiction. At South Africa House, the switchboard operator flicked the lines to neutral, jamming all incoming calls. In Westminster, frenzied reporters barracked MPs scurrying to and from their cars, but the Home Secretary, in the interests of prudence, kept himself shrewdly aloof, refusing to answer queries.

Within a matter of hours, a vast army of media people, reporters, photographers, and TV crews were converging on the forests of north Northumbria. Among the first to arrive were Philip Haskins of the

Daily Express, and his companion, Fleet Street photographer Arty McDonnel. Haskins and McDonnel had flown from Heathrow to Newcastle, rented a station wagon, and driven north through the spectacular Northumbrian countryside. Approaching the first signs of the encroaching fir forest, they spotted a police barrier blocking the road, and Haskins jammed his foot on the brake as a constable came strolling toward them, bending his head to peer through the window. "In a bit of a hurry, aren't we?" the man remarked.

"Sorry, officer, I must've been dreaming. What's going on here?"

"Fire risk. The forest has been placed temporarily out of bounds. You'll have to turn round and go back, I'm afraid."

Haskins fumbled in his pocket for his press card.

"I'm sorry, sir," the constable maintained. "No one's allowed inside the forest area, whatever their authority. My orders are explicit."

Haskins frowned. "What the hell is this? We're on a designated highway, for God's sake."

"Nevertheless, the road is closed until further notice."

Haskins was too old a hand to waste time arguing with the police. Swinging the vehicle around, he drove back quickly the way they had come, pulled to a halt at a wayside pub, and called his editor from the public phone booth.

Haskins' editor, Charlie Meggers, sounded harassed when he came on the line. "It's like the Keystone Cops down here," he moaned. "The whole bloody building's going spare. Where are you?"

Briefly, Haskins poured out his story and heard Meggers mutter at the other end. "Something's up.

They wouldn't go to so much trouble unless the story's genuine."

"Want me to try another way in?"

"No, they're bound to have all the entrance roads blocked."

Meggers thought for a moment. "What about an aircraft? Wasn't there a pilot near Rothbury who helped you on that sheepfarming job?"

"The cropduster?"

"Why not give him a call? They can seal off the highways, but they can't block the air lanes as well."

Haskins felt his pulse racing. "Not unless they're bloody miracle men. Brilliant, Charlie. Hang on to your pants, I'm on my way. I'll call back as soon as I can."

He slammed down the receiver.

Meanwhile, in the middle of the South Atlantic, the news was being received via the BBC's overseas radio service by Captain Hans Eprile of the SS *Arcadia*, thirteen hours out of Cape Town. Sitting in his cabin, he listened incredulously as the commentator outlined the first fragmentary details. The report had barely finished when his cabin curtain was thrust aside and Eprile's first officer, Hendrik Zutphen, stood in the hatchway, clutching a slip of paper. "Message from Cape Town, sir," he announced, thrusting the sheet into Eprile's hand.

The message was signed by Karel Van Brero, head of BOSS, the South African secret police. Eprile scanned the rows or printing quickly, then rose to his feet, grunting under his breath. He was a big man, with a prominent paunch and a round wind-beaten face. "Go back to the bridge," he ordered. "We're changing course."

"How many degrees?" Zutphen inquired.

Eprile ran his fingers through his coarse brown hair, glancing at the paper again. His eyes were dark, somber, reflective. "Turn her around," he said softly. "We're going home."

Eight

Riding at the column rear, Kate saw Mc-
Auley tilt forward in his saddle, and with a
slow, almost delicate motion, topple sideways to the
ground.

"Elliot, stop," she shouted.

Nudging her mount forward, she leapt down,
cradling McAuley's head in her lap. His cheeks were
pale, his eyes riven with pain and exhaustion. Beads
of sweat coated his heavy brow, and there were
yellow flecks in the hollows on each side of his
narrow mouth. It was bound to happen, she told
herself. You couldn't drag an injured man mile after
mile along rugged uneven logging tracks. They'd
scarcely stopped, even for a moment. Elliot seemed
like a man possessed, urging them on when their
bodies and minds screamed out for rest, for sleep, for
replenishment.

She touched the minister's forehead, frowning
worriedly. "He's burning up."

Elliot reined in his mount, studying McAuley
with no expression on his face. "He looks okay to
me."

"He's ill, I tell you. Do you want to kill him?"

Elliot sighed, easing himself from the saddle. He
had lost some of his elegance during the long morning's ride. His skin was coated with grime, his throat

and chin covered with beard stubble. "We'll take a break," he said. "Twenty minutes."

"Twenty minutes isn't enough. He needs surgery, and he needs it quickly. Jostle him about much longer, and that bullet will clip something vital."

Elliot gave no reaction. Calmly, he began to attend to his horse, easing the bridle away from its mouth. His movements were gentle and unhurried. Kate felt her anger mounting. "Listen to me, damn you."

Elliot looked back at her. "There's nothing I can do. We've got to keep on the move until we accomplish what we came for."

"If McAuley dies, we'll accomplish nothing."

"He won't die."

"Look at him, you idiot, he's dying now. That bullet is tearing away his insides. Stick him back in the saddle, and you might as well blow his brains out."

Elliot tethered his pony to a nearby tree and knelt down at McAuley's side. Still mounted, the others sat watching. Kate waited in silence, fighting to control the fury engulfing her. God knew, she wished she'd never gotten into this, could scarcely believe the things which had happened in the last few hours; in the name of the movement, she'd sacrificed her ideals, her convictions, even her loyalty toward the country which had borne her, but she was damned if she would stand by and let Elliot Chamille turn her into a murderer.

"We knew from the beginning," Elliot said reasonably, "our only chance was to twist and turn, use the forest as a smokescreen. Stand still, and the security forces will track us down."

"That was before McAuley got shot. The situation's changed now."

"It hasn't changed for Joshua Matshoba."

"Joshua Matshoba isn't dying, for God's sake."

Elliot sat back on his haunches, peering up at the others with an air of wry disgust. He looked as if Kate's entreaties were pushing his patience to the limit. Rising to his feet, he strolled back to his mount and began to loosen the saddle harness.

Kate watched him, her fury hardening into a cold passionate resolve. There were times Elliot's obstinacy reminded her so much of Harry she wanted to scream. "You didn't tell me this was a murder mission," she snapped. "Why didn't you just finish him off at the train junction, instead of dragging this out like some kind of bizarre Greek tragedy?"

Elliot grunted. "I don't want McAuley to die. What do you take me for?"

"Then get him to a hospital. It's the only thing that'll save his life."

"She's making sense, Chamille," Harry interjected. "The man is sick."

"Keep out of this," Elliot snapped. "You're an intruder here."

Harry's face hardened. There was a look in his eyes Kate recognized and identified. She'd seen it often enough before. Harry was spoiling for a fight.

"When a man's life is at stake, it's everybody's business. McAuley will die without proper treatment."

"What do you want me to do, dial 999?"

"That isn't necessary. There's a little town called Holmkirk barely five miles north of here. Holmkirk has a hospital, built by the Forestry Commission. It's small, and it's functional, but its purpose is to handle emergencies during logging operations. That means it'll probably have a resident surgeon."

Elliot shook his head. "Too risky."

"Not as risky as losing McAuley. If he dies now, this whole operation goes down the drain. Not only that, you'll give the South African government the best propaganda boost it's had in the last twenty years."

Kate saw a flicker of indecision cross Elliot's face. Harry's reasoning had hit home. When Elliot spoke again, his voice was softer, gentler.

"You're a persuasive talker, Fuller."

"In Cumbria, we call it common sense."

Fumbling in his pocket, Elliot took out a tube of tiny capsules and offered them to Harry. "Glucose," he explained. "Good for the energy."

Harry shook his head, and unwrapping one, Elliot popped it into his mouth, tossing the paper casually on the ground. Kate knew he was weighing risks, calculating possibilities. In the end, Elliot came to a decision.

"Okay," he agreed, glancing at Timol and Malheiro. "Get McAuley back on his horse. We're taking him to Holmkirk."

Tazelaar followed the logging road as it dipped and twisted through the spruce forest. Behind him, his little group of followers staggered along wearily in a disorderly line. They were close to exhaustion, Tazelaar knew, tired of trailing, tired of walking. He was tired himself, if it came to that, but something kept him moving remorselessly on. He was a complex man; his neurosis fueled him like a flame. Compulsive by nature, he clung with grim tenacity to objectives others would have discarded in disgust. Outwardly passive—docile almost—his bland face and expressionless eyes belied the turbulence smoldering within. After the stopping of the train, he had refused to withdraw with his men to Carlisle, leading them instead on a grueling pursuit through the baffling labyrinth of forest roads, driven by a kind of hunger.

Could you love those you intended to kill? his mind asked cynically. Of course you could. Love was essential to killing, for only through love could the unspeakable become acceptable. Tazelaar understood such things, for his father's *jambok*, during the long years of his earliest childhood, had scoured his soul in guilt, so that now he could face with a clear conscience actions which others instinctively shrank from. To kill with love in your heart was not a sin, he reflected. It was purifying. Transfiguring. It carried man beyond the levels of mortality; because he made a conscious decision to do the unthinkable, to escape his illusions, he became in a sense a god.

The train journey had sorely tested Tazelaar's patience. The Englishman, the Special Branch officer, Commander Dameron, had set out to be as difficult as possible, but he, Tazelaar, with commendable self-restraint, had refused to be provoked. He regarded that as a victory of sorts—proof, if proof were needed, that he was at last conquering the rages which had plagued him since early boyhood. Now, clad in padded parkas and heavy hiking boots, he and his confederates were in the process of doing what the British had so far failed to do—track down Howard McAuley.

Leroux, his assistant, staggered alongside, gasping heavily. Leroux's bearded face was pale with strain, and spittle ran from the corner of his mouth where fatigue had caused the lips to slacken. "*Menheer*, we are exhausted," he croaked.

"This is no time to rest," Tazelaar said.

"Please, menheer. Our legs are breaking in two."

"*Ja*, mine also. But we cannot let them get away."

"They are already away," Leroux insisted. "They are mounted, menheer. We are on foot."

Tazelaar looked at him with contempt. "That shows how little you know about horses," he said. "Horses have to rest. Men don't. With tenacity, we shall outstrip them."

"In these woods? In the name of God, Taz, we could not find an army in such country. Do we have X-ray eyes to see through the trees?"

Tazelaar didn't answer for a moment. He had noticed that the logging road parted, one branch curving to the left. His eyes detected something lying on the ground, and bending, he picked it up, smoothing it between his fingers. It was, he saw, a sweet wrapper. "You see, already we are on the right path," he said, showing it to Leroux. "They have turned left, toward the north."

Leroux examined the paper dubiously. "A glucose tablet? It could have been dropped by anyone. A Forestry worker, a hiker."

"You have my word for it, they have turned north."

Behind them, Kruger, scouting along the grassy verge, called Tazelaar's name. They turned back, joining Kruger as he crouched over a jagged rock. Kruger's cheeks were flushed, his bearded face lined with fatigue. He nodded at the boulder, and leaning closer in the morning chill, they saw a stain on its upper rim. "Blood," Kruger whispered.

The stain was dark, almost black, but when the sun caught it, the texture turned to crimson. Kruger touched it with his fingertips. "It's fresh. Hasn't even congealed yet."

Tazelaar looked at Leroux, smiling. For once, he allowed his customary composure to slip. His eyes were filled with a mixture of triumph and reproach. "Now do you believe me?" he said.

For more than a hour, the fugitives rode wearily through the dreary corridor of conifers, pausing only once, at Elliot's insistence, to feed the horses from the burlap bags strapped to the saddle of Malheiro's mount; then, toward noon, the forest came to an end, and the logging road filtered into a broad highway, flanked on two sides by ragged strips of moorgrass. From their vantage point on the summit of a gentle hill, they glimpsed the town itself, a small, orderly little community with gray buildings which gleamed cheerlessly in the cold spring sunshine. The streets converged into a central square, its cobbled surface dominated by an ancient courthouse. It looked so peaceful, so incredibly serene, that Kate, watching from above, was shaken by a sense of illusion. Could life go on as normal, as if nothing extraordinary had happened, while only a stone's throw away they roamed the sprawling forest with a wounded man they had snatched at gunpoint?

Elliot crouched in the trees, studying the rooftops in silence for a moment. "That's a town?"

"I didn't say it was Chicago, Illinois," growled Harry.

Elliot glanced around the little clearing, noting the tangled underbrush which would provide excellent cover. "We'll leave the horses here. If we drag them down the main street, somebody's bound to get suspicious. Timol, you look after the animals."

Timol nodded curtly, leading the horses toward a cluster of stunted spruce, and Elliot paused, glancing at Harry. Kate felt her muscles tighten. She wasn't a fool; it was clear the two men couldn't stand the sight of each other. Their antagonism was like a tangible force, and she knew they were just itching for an excuse to tear at each other's throats.

"Stay with him," Elliot commanded.

"I'm not one of your subordinates, Chamille."

"If you want to be part of this team, you'll learn to obey orders. Otherwise, get the hell out. Nobody wants you around anyhow."

Harry's cheeks flushed, and for a moment Kate thought he would take a swing at Elliot, he looked so angry. But the light in his eyes faded after a moment and without a word he turned obediently and joined Timol. Kate's breathing eased. They couldn't afford personal vendettas, she thought. None of them could. They had a wounded man to take care of.

McAuley was holding on to his midsection, his lips twisted in discomfort and pain. Reaching into his pocket, Elliot took out his pistol, and with a casual, almost impudent gesture, leaned one elbow on McAuley's shoulder and pressed the weapon against the side of the South African's neck.

"Mr. McAuley," Elliot said. "We are going to take a stroll into town—you, me, and my friends here. Now since there'll be people in the streets, you might be tempted to call to them for help, but I must warn you, sir, that such a move would be extremely ill-advised. I'm anxious to keep you alive as long as possible, but the minute you cease to be of use to me, the minute there's the slightest danger of your being recognized or recaptured, I intend to shoot you where you stand. Is that understood?"

McAuley looked pale but defiant. "Perfectly, young man. You have an unpleasantly succinct manner."

Elliot nodded, and Kate shivered as he slipped the pistol under his coat. Despite his charm and sex appeal, Elliot could be a cold-blooded bastard when he put his mind to it.

She looked at the minister sympathetically. "How do you feel, Mr. McAuley?"

"A little sickly, my dear. But don't worry on my account. I've got the constitution of a horse. My doctor says so."

His doctor was right, Kate decided. He'd stood up well to the rigors of the long morning's ride, and only a man of exceptional strength could have born himself so uncomplainingly. But it was a crazy idea, whichever way you looked at it, going into the town. The prospect of leaving their forested sanctuary, of exposing themselves to public gaze—particularly the mess they were in, mudstained and bedraggled—filled her with alarm.

She thought about Harry, and her uneasiness strengthened. Something was wrong with Harry, something she couldn't put a name to. He hadn't changed in any discernible way, but you couldn't live with someone for years without sensing a trace of what they were feeling inside. And Harry was angry. Angrier than she'd ever known him. Which, when you came right down to it, she reflected wryly, was no big deal, since Harry was always angry. He was like a jumping jack, exploding wildly in every direction. Only this time it was different, because this time Harry was *controlling* his anger, and that was the thing which worried Kate most.

She walked toward him. In the morning sunlight, with his wild hair and stubbled chin, he looked strangely deranged.

"Harry, why are you doing this?"

"Doing what?"

"You know what. Staying."

He smiled gently. He did it well, she had to give him that, but she'd known him too long to be fooled by such a pose. "You didn't give me much choice," he told her.

"I mean now. Why are you staying now? Tim's been released. You can go anytime you want."

"And leave you?"

"It's *my* funeral, Harry. I got myself into it, walked right in with my eyes wide open. That's no reason for you to be involved."

"I'm not leaving you alone with that Chamille bastard," he said.

"Elliot?"

"He makes my skin crawl."

Same old Harry. He wasn't exactly the jealous type, but he wasn't trusting and naive either. Liked things aboveboard. Issues defined, interests declared. Looked after what was his. He'd always been a bit on the taciturn side, constant to the hilt where his friends were concerned, but hardly what she could call warm and gregarious. "Harry, don't be absurd. Elliot's a good man. He's committed."

"That bloody word again."

"You always were intolerant, Harry."

Which was perfectly true. Intolerant, exasperating, and—paradoxically—kind, passionate, affectionate, loyal, good reasons why she'd always loved him. She felt a funny tightening sensation in her throat as if, suddenly, she couldn't bear to leave. That was the crazy thing about Harry. Even in their wildest moments, he'd always managed to engage her emotions, which naturally made his presence a formidable force. "We'll be back as soon as we can," she promised.

"I'll be waiting," he said.

She understood him so well, she thought, as they started down the gentle embankment. In a sense, it was like turning back the clock, as if the years in-between had scarcely even existed. Was that possible? Could everything that had gone wrong in the past be meaningless in the face of what she felt for him now? She might have fallen happily into Harry's arms, if it hadn't been for Elliot Chamille. Elliot was the one who'd complicated things, because Elliot was a force in himself. Every time he touched her, it was like an electric shock running through her body. She'd heard of situations like that, people who were so physically attuned, their senses exploded almost on contact. Well, Elliot was a very attractive man, there was no getting away from the fact. And she was flesh and blood, for God's sake, she wouldn't have been human if she hadn't responded in some way to Elliot's proximity. But why did everything have to be so confusing?

The streets began to build up around them, trees lining the pavements, dry and dusty in the late March sunshine. Kate spotted a handful of shops, a tobacconist's, a pub. Someone had left a crate of milk bottles at the curbside, and a smear of congealed cream lay among the dirt. They reached the central square where early morning shoppers drifted among the market stalls, examining clothing, pottery, tableware. The hospital stood on the corner, a small functional red-bricked building, flanked by trim lawns and a cindered parking lot. In the lobby, the receptionist smiled at them bleakly. There was no one else in sight.

"Good morning," Elliot said, his voice echoing beneath the marbled ceiling arch. "We have a casualty. He's pretty badly hurt."

The woman glanced at McAuley with no hint of

sympathy in her eyes. "I'm afraid you can't bring him in here."

"Why not? It's a hospital, isn't it?"

"Yes, it is, but it's just a satellite. We handle convalescent cases only."

"This is an emergency, ma'am."

"Then he'll have to be taken to Coldstream. I'll get you an ambulance, if you like."

Elliot sighed. Moving with no particular sign of haste, he reached under his parka and took out the Starfire .38. When she saw the pistol, the woman's eyes bulged in disbelief.

"Who's in charge?" Elliot asked.

The woman swallowed, staring at the pistol mesmerized. "Nobody, at the moment. We're a little understaffed."

"There must be someone around who can make decisions."

"Well, I suppose Sister Johnson is our most senior lady."

"Fetch her," Elliot ordered.

Blinking, the woman pressed a button at the reception desk and spoke into a tiny microphone. Her voice echoed over the internal loudspeaker system. "Will Sister Johnson come to reception immediately, please?"

They heard a door opening along a distant corridor, and footsteps echoed on the linoleum floor. Kate felt her pulses quickening as a white-coated figure appeared. Sister Johnson was a tall angular lady with a mouth like a razor slash. Her eyes, beady and penetrating, swept over the bedraggled group with an intentness that seemed to scour Kate's soul.

"Sister Johnson?" Elliot inquired.

The woman nodded and Elliot showed her the gun. Sister Johnson displayed neither fear nor consternation. She was clearly not a lady who panicked easily.

"What's going on here?"

Elliot nodded toward McAuley. "This man requires immediate surgery. He's been shot."

"Shot?" The sister's eyes narrowed.

"He has a bullet in his abdomen. Unless it's removed quickly, he could very easily die."

"I'm sorry, but the hospital's barely functioning. The wards are empty, and our nurses have been transferred to Carlisle."

"I thought this place was built to handle forestry emergencies?"

"That's true. But we can't keep the building fully staffed twenty-four hours a day, especially in such a thinly populated area. We rely on twice-weekly visits from the doctors in Coldstream."

"You do have an operating theater?"

"Oh yes."

"What about an anesthetist?"

"No one. I told you, the place is temporarily inactive."

"What happens if a forest worker gets hurt?"

"We send him to Coldstream or Carlisle."

"Supposing he's too critical for that? Supposing you have to deal with the injury immediately? How would you put him under?"

The sister hesitated, glancing at the receptionist. "I'd give him a shot of diazepam."

"So, in a pinch, you could make do?"

"Only with a surgeon on the premises."

Elliot looked at Kate and Kate felt her senses jump. "No," she breathed.

"Kate, listen to me."

"No."

"If you don't, McAuley might die."

"I haven't the training."

"You've had the best training in the world. How many doctors can say they've experienced frontline surgery at firsthand?"

"You don't understand what you're talking about. I only assisted, I never handled operations myself. Besides, in a situation like this, diazepam isn't enough. McAuley needs to be ventilated. His stomach wall must be relaxed."

"You can at least take a look, see if it's possible to do a stitch-up job."

"Do you think I want his death on my conscience?"

"Unless you help him, he'll die anyhow. You learned your business the hard way, Kate, by watching, by helping. You're probably a much better bet than the surgeon from Coldstream anyhow. And besides, you're the only hope McAuley's got."

There was an air of resolve in Elliot's eyes which terrified Kate's senses. He gripped her shoulder and she felt the strength radiating from his fingers. He was like an unstoppable force. "You've got everything you need here. Turn your back on him now, and you'll never forgive yourself. At least try, Kate. You must. For McAuley's sake, and for your own."

She felt a sickness spreading through her, but Elliot's face hung in her vision, dogged and determined. She knew there could be no arguing with a face like that.

She sighed helplessly, and looked at Sister Johnson. "Please prepare the operating theater," she said in a toneless voice.

Lying on the trolley, draped in sterile linen, McAuley looked incongruous. Like a mummy, Kate thought, his chest, legs, and midsection completely swathed in white. She was struggling hard to conceal her nervousness. The thought of the operation ahead had thrown her into a state of mental panic. She knew diazepam would put McAuley under, but for deep internal probing he needed to be heavily anesthetized, and that meant ventilating on the anesthetic machine. The chances of penetrating his stomach wall under such light sedation would be stupefyingly slim, but for McAuley's sake, Kate did her best to hide her anxiety as she checked his pulse and temperature.

He smiled up at her, his eyes understanding and sympathetic. "I'm sorry to be such a burden, Miss Whitmore."

"You're no burden, Minister. It's our fault for putting you in this position."

"Nevertheless, my escort had no right to fire so irresponsibly."

"I want you to relax now," Kate said. "Try not to worry. Once the bullet's out, you'll feel a lot better."

She watched Malheiro push the trolley toward the operating bench and strode into the surgeon's room to wash her hands. De Brere was standing in front of the mirror, shaving himself with a tiny scalpel. He looked comical, one side of his chin coated with fluffy soap bubbles, the other scraped clean. "Thought I'd tidy myself up a bit and let you see how attractive I really am." He grinned.

"Get out of here, De Brere," Kate ordered wearily. "I have to get ready."

He picked up a towel, wiping the soap from his face. "I don't blame you for being hostile. That was a stupid trick I pulled back in London. I wish I could turn back the clock."

Kate shrugged. She had neither time nor patience for De Brere's contrition. Her mind was absorbed with the task ahead.

He tossed the towel on to the metal bench. "I've watched you since we hit the train," he said, "and I want you to know I admire the way you've borne up during the last few hours. I admire what you're doing now. You've got guts, Miss Whitmore."

Kate looked at him in surprise. There was an air of honest ingenuousness in De Brere. Perhaps she'd misjudged the man. "You mean that?"

"I wouldn't say it if I didn't."

Kate hesitated, then stuck out her hand. "Why don't we start again? Friends."

"Seriously?"

"Of course."

Whooping, he seized her in his arms and kissed her wildly on the mouth. For a moment, Kate was too incredulous to respond. Angrily, she jammed her palm against De Brere's chin, wrestling herself free. "What the hell do you think you're doing?" she panted.

He blinked. "Starting again."

"Get out of here."

Picking up a jug, she hurled it wildly. It caught the side of De Brere's skull as he backed out of the room, spluttering in confusion.

Kate stood for a moment, filling her lungs with air. Damn the man, she thought. As if she hadn't enough to think about.

Her hands were shaking as she sluiced them under the tap.

Waldo found Palmer sitting on a grassy embankment overlooking the open fields. Palmer's shoulders were huddled against the cold, and in the morning sunlight he looked strangely frail and disconsolate.

"What are you doing here?" Waldo asked.

"Thinking."

Waldo flopped down beside him, fumbling in his overcoat pocket.

"Surprise, surprise," he announced, producing a bottle of whiskey.

Palmer's eyes seemed to focus with an effort. Waldo had the feeling he had withdrawn, tortoise-like, into some defensive emotional shell. Couldn't blame the man for that, he reflected. He felt pretty morose about things himself.

"Where did you get it?" Palmer asked.

"From the Forestry officer. I think he wants us to drown our sorrows."

Palmer took the bottle from Waldo's hand and carefully opened the top. "I seldom drink before lunchtime," he admitted, "but I think this is a special occasion."

Raising the bottle to his lips, he took a long swallow. "That's better," he breathed, handing it back.

Waldo followed suit, grunting as the fiery liquid sent a warm glow surging through his stomach. It was a strange feeling sitting here, knowing he'd screwed up his life, not through inadequacy or carelessness, but through a simple and exasperating twist of luck. Everything came down to luck in the end, he decided. He'd learned that over the years. Napoléon had always understood its value. "Is he lucky?" he'd asked when one of his generals had recommended a promising young officer. Well he, Waldo, had never been particularly strong in the luck department. Of course, he could always go back to Washington and see out his time in second gear.

He could even bring Martha on that European tour, if he wanted to, though he had to admit it wouldn't have the same edge, the same allure. But there was still Option 24 to consider. If the story leaked, if the details became public, he was finished. No question about that, no argument. Himself and the whole administration, kaput. He knew it, the Secretary of State knew it, the president knew it. Unless the British, by some extraordinary miracle, managed to get McAuley back unharmed.

"Any news yet?" he asked.

Palmer shook his head. "The lieutenant's deployed his men. We're concentrating on the northwest sector. Now it's simply a matter of patience."

"I hate that word," Waldo confessed. "It's used by politicians to placate members of the opposition."

In the field across the road, they could see sheep grazing among the foliage. Beyond, the village rooftops glistened in the morning sunlight. Palmer looked moody and depressed; a strange man, Waldo considered, not one who would unburden easily, but he had a feeling, he couldn't say why, that the British security officer desperately wanted to confide.

"I was thinking," Palmer said, staring across the empty pastureland. "If we don't get McAuley back, it could mean the end of my career."

"Why? What happened wasn't your fault."

"Somebody'll have to take the blame, and I'm responsible for McAuley's security."

Palmer took the whiskey bottle from Waldo's hand and raised it to his lips. He'd lost his dapper look a bit, Waldo thought, watching Palmer's Adam's apple furiously bobbing.

"They'll be sympathetic and understanding," Palmer admitted, wiping his mouth with the back of one hand. "Everything will be conducted on a gentlemanly level. That's the way they operate. But I've only a few more years to go. Already, they're looking for replacements. New blood, new attitudes. Early retirement is what they'll suggest. They'll see me all right, no worries on that score. Good pension, index-linked. Generous redundancy bonus."

"You can retire to the country," Waldo said.

"I hate the country."

Waldo pulled a face. This was something he wasn't used to, the role of father confessor. People rarely confided in Waldo, his job saw to that. Associates learned to dodge and weave. They rarely let their guards down.

Palmer glanced at him. "Are you married, Mr. Friedman?"

Waldo nodded. "Twenty-four years in August."

"Children?"

"Two boys. One's at college in Iowa, the other runs a roofing business in Connecticut."

"I have no one. Even my friends are associated with work."

"I'm sorry," Waldo said softly.

"I used to think nothing in the world mattered as much as the department. It offered an identity, a place in the order of things. I was good at my job. I leapfrogged over men who were many years my senior. It's a satisfying feeling, Mr. Friedman, to discover something for which you have a natural and inherent aptitude. What I didn't realize was the department offered an emotional excuse. An excuse for opting out."

He hesitated, staring at the slow-moving river. Tilting back the bottle, he took another copious mouthful, and Waldo waited patiently. He wanted to help, to soothe and commiserate, but didn't know how. It's crazy, he thought, twenty-four years in diplomacy and I can't handle a simple depression case.

"Human relationships have always troubled me," Palmer whispered. "In the service, I'm regarded as a good conversationalist, an agreeable mixer. It's the little things I find difficulty with, the inconsequential human things. I can't seem to relate to people on a personal level."

Waldo heard a horn blaring as a grocery van pulled into the village street. The fields looked peaceful and reassuring in the bright spring sunshine.

"I can talk freely on practically any subject under the sun," Palmer confessed sadly. "Introduce a topic, and I'll give you an opinion. I can be witty, acerbic, or penetrating, depending on the occasion, but I could never in a million years confess to a woman that I found her attractive. It'd be a weakness of sorts, don't you see? Theories and philosophies are coinage to be exchanged and utilized. But revealing one's feelings . . ." He shuddered. "I've tried, there've been moments when I really tried, but it just didn't work. Nor did it matter in any real important sense. I had my work, I had the department."

"Big mistake, building your life around a job," Waldo said gently.

Palmer nodded. "When I look at the future, I get frightened. To tell you the truth, I simply don't know what I'm going to do. If they push me into retirement"—he shrugged—"my life will be over."

Waldo took the whiskey bottle from his grasp and raised it to his lips. The loneliness in Palmer's face disturbed him deeply. "Maybe it'll never happen. Maybe we'll get McAuley back and you'll end up a hero."

Palmer looked unconvinced. He shivered as he

tugged the overcoat around his body. His face, lit by the dappled sun, looked moody and reflective. He hugged his knees, his eyes turned inward, seeing only himself.

"Maybe," he agreed softly.

The light in the theater was startlingly bright. Kate looked at Sister Johnson dressed in smock, hood, and protective face mask. "Is he ready?"

The sister nodded, her eyes hard and unyielding, and Kate sensed her hostility, recognized it, understood. She couldn't blame the sister, she reflected, but God knew, she needed support from somewhere—a hint of sympathy, a nod of encouragement. She glanced at Elliot, who, clad in a green surgical uniform with only his eyes visible, was laying out forceps, scalpels, and catgut strips.

"You understand everything?" she whispered hoarsely.

He nodded without looking at her.

"When I say swab, sponge the incision clean of blood."

"Don't worry," he said.

"Why should I worry?" she asked bitterly. "It's not *my* life at stake here."

She examined McAuley, her eyes sharp and professional. He looked like a man in a coma, which was all to the good, she reflected, since she needed him deeply sedated to relax the muscles of the stomach wall. But twenty milligrams of diazepam was a poor substitute for a full anesthetic, and she'd be lucky, she knew, to achieve anything more than a simple exploratory operation.

Kate eyed the tiny rectangle of exposed skin, coated with scarlet antiseptic, where the blue-rimmed bullet hole stared up at her. It looked so small, so unutterably innocuous.

"What are you waiting for?" Elliot hissed.

She shook herself. He was right, she was procrastinating, putting off the dreaded moment of incision. She couldn't escape it any longer.

She tried to keep her fingers from trembling as she leaned forward and picked up the scalpel.

Nine

De Brere paced restlessly around the hospital lobby, his head still throbbing where Kate had caught him with the jug. He would probably have a splendid bruise before evening, he decided. Bloody woman. What did she have to get so upset about? He'd scarcely laid a finger on her. Kate Whitmore simply didn't understand her own mind. She was extremely attracted to him, De Brere felt certain. He was, after all, an extremely attractive man. Women generally thought so. He'd never had trouble with women before—well, a few, maybe, in the initial stages, but that was only to be expected. Some played hard to get, it was part of their nature, but he never let refusal sway him. He knew deep down the objections were obligatory, designed to salve the lady's feelings. A man who appreciated his value understood such things and accommodated. But Kate Whitmore had him baffled. She'd really looked as though she meant it, he reflected, his footsteps ringing on the marbled floor. Had he at last encountered a woman who was not prepared to wilt beneath the devastating De Brere charm? It was a sobering prospect, for he had never actually failed before. On the other hand, he was forced to admit he had never met a woman quite like Kate before either. Strong, resolute, determined, yet with a strange and elusive vulnerability which contrasted with the more forceful aspects of her personality. He admired a woman like that, admired her deeply. He admired her now, dolled up like a circus clown, prizing lead splinters out of McAuley's innards. No question about it, she was a woman in a million. But he wished to God she would hurry up. It could only be a matter of time before their presence here was discovered. Already there had been three unscheduled visitors at the lobby desk. Under Malheiro's watchful eye, the receptionist had turned the people politely away and stalled all incoming calls; she too, De Brere considered, was handling things remarkably well.

He paused at the window, staring impatiently into the street. Shoppers gathered on the opposite corner, chatting happily outside the post office. It looked like a small town anywhere, De Brere thought, friendly and communicative. Suddenly, his senses froze as a vehicle pulled onto the hospital forecourt. It was an open-topped military scout car, manned by three marines in dark green commando berets. They were each carrying, De Brere noticed, Sterling submachine guns.

The scout car pulled to a halt, and the driver, a heavyset sergeant with a bristling mustache, helped one of his companions to alight. The man was limping painfully, and he leaned his weight on the sergeant's shoulder as they strolled toward the hospital entrance. De Brere hissed warningly at Malheiro and scuttled into the nearby corridor.

The two marines crossed the marbled lobby, the sergeant smiling at the receptionist. "Hi," he said in a friendly voice. "I wonder if somebody could take a look at my mate here. He's done his knee in on one of those barbed wire fences. We've got a first aid kit in the car outside, but I thought I'd better bring him along for a tetanus shot in case the metal proved infected."

De Brere ran back up the passageway and hammered loudly on the operating theater door. Elliot opened it, frowning above his face mask.

"Marines," De Brere gasped. "They're in the reception hall."

Elliot's expression tensed. "How many?"

"Just two. But there's another bastard in the truck outside. They're carrying Sterlings."

"Looking for us?"

"Probably. One of the men's injured his knee. They've come to have it seen to."

"We've got our hands full here. Can't you take care of it?"

"Me?"

"Sure. You're not totally bloody helpless, are you?"

Elliot slammed the door and De Brere hesitated, blinking hard. Jesus, he thought. He plunged into the surgeon's room and tore open the metal wall cabinet. Rummaging through the tunics inside, he selected a long white coat and tugged it brusquely on. Not too bad, he decided, casting a swift glance at himself in the wall mirror. Bit on the short side, but it would have to do.

The marines were still at the reception desk explaining how the accident had occurred when he wandered back into the lobby. "Good morning, gentlemen," De Brere said cheerfully, forcing himself to look relaxed.

The sergeant glanced at him, grinning. "Sorry about this. I hate to disturb you at your work, but we've got a bit of a crisis here."

"Crisis is our specialty," De Brere declared airily.

The sergeant showed him his companion's knee. Blood was seeping through the torn breeches, and there was a worrying smear of dirt around the punctured blue-rimmed skin. "Nasty," De Brere muttered. "It'll need cleaning."

"Can you handle it, Doctor?"

"Of course. This way, please."

Heart thumping, De Brere led the two marines back along the corridor. What in God's name was he going to do now? Not that the injury worried him; he'd handled such things before, dozens of times, but God Almighty, he hadn't a clue where the hospital dressings were kept. "Strangers in the area?" he asked conversationally, keeping his voice carefully neutral.

The sergeant grunted as he helped his companion along the echoing passageway. "We're from 42 Commando Squadron. We've been training in the Cheviot Hills."

"Bit off course, aren't you?"

"They ferried us in to look for that South African, the one who got kidnapped. There's a big flap on at the moment. I'm surprised you haven't heard about it on the radio."

"You mean the foreign minister, Howard McAuley?"

"That's right."

"I should think he'll be miles away by now."

"Not according to our calculations," the sergeant answered. "We believe he's still somewhere in this vicinity. We're sealing off the entire area."

He glanced curiously through the operating theater window, where beyond the inner door they could see Kate, Elliot, and the sister crouched

around the supine figure of the unconscious Mc-
Auley.

"What's going on in there?"

De Brere thought quickly. "Road smash. Casualty case. They brought him in barely an hour ago."

"Bad?"

"Chest cage shattered by the steering column.
He hit a truck coming in the opposite direction."

"Jesus. Head-on?"

De Brere nodded.

"Poor bastard. Is he going to die?"

"Not if we can help it. Fortunately, the truck
driver had a CB radio in his cab. He called the police
direct, and they whisked the casualty straight here,
lights blazing, sirens blaring, the lot. It was like
something out of *Starsky and Hutch*."

"I hope he pulls through," the sergeant said,
following De Brere into the surgeon's room.

De Brere tugged open the wall cabinets. To his
immense relief, he saw a generous supply of gauze
dressings, bandages, liniments, and medicine bottles. Breathing deeply, he forced his muscles to relax.
He was smiling as he laid out antiseptics and cotton
cleansing pads. "Sit your friend in the chair," he said
cheerfully. "Let's see what we can do."

Kate stared down at her first incision. She had
cut transversally, in case the probing needed to be
deep. She nodded at Elliot, and he sponged away
the droplets of blood. Kate changed scalpels, slicing
deeper. She could hear McAuley groaning in his
sleep. A trace of clothing lay in the open wound, and
using the forceps, Kate carefully picked it out.
Though the cloth was infinitesimal, Kate knew it
could set up a dangerous infection later on. The

forceps scraped on the metal bowl. She opened the cut, pausing as Elliot swabbed the incision, then her eyes widened, and a tremor of surprise passed through her body. Embedded in the gray tissue layer which lined the abdominal wall, she discerned a small metallic cylinder. Elliot spotted it at precisely the same moment. "What's that?"

Kate hesitated, her voice drying unaccountably. "It's the bullet."

Elliot frowned at her, his eyes flashing above the face mask. The overhead light seemed to accentuate the tilt of his forehead. "It hasn't even penetrated the muscle wall."

"How could I know?" she cried. "He looked so ill."

"It's nothing but a flesh would. He was never in any danger at all."

."The shot must have spent itself on the ricochet. It was pressing against the diaphragm. That's what caused his pain."

"What about his temperature?"

"Exhaustion probably, coupled with tension. It happens."

"So all this"—Elliot jerked his head around the hospital operating room—"has been for nothing."

She nodded unhappily. "My diagnosis was wrong," she admitted. "His injury was painful, but only superficial. Without an X ray, I simply had no way of telling."

He whistled under his breath. "Do you realize what you've done? There are three marines inside the hospital at this very moment. We've jeopardized the entire operation in coming here."

"I thought he was seriously hurt," she protested tearfully. "I'm not a fool, Elliot. I've watched wounded men die before."

Elliot spread his hands in exasperation. He looked at the ceiling and at Sister Johnson, then he gestured impatiently. "Get the bullet out, and sew up his abdomen. If we leave this hospital in one piece, it'll be a bloody miracle."

Kate chewed bitterly on her lower lip as she leaned forward, gripping the hemostat.

Harry strode up and down the tiny clearing, glancing at his watch as the minutes ticked interminably by. He deeply resented being left behind with the horses. It seemed a declaration of sorts, a gesture of contempt on the part of Elliot Chamille. The wily bastard, Harry thought darkly. He knew damned well what Chamille was up to. Wanted him out of the way. Saw him as an unwanted obstacle in his pursuit of Kate. Well, he, Harry Fuller, had something to say about that. He had other plans for Kate, other plans for both of them. When the moment came, he intended to make them squirm. But he couldn't do it dragging his heels around this stupid clearing. "Where the hell have they got to?" he growled at Timol, who was sitting on a log whittling idly at a piece of wood. "They should have been back half an hour ago."

Timol shrugged, making no comment. He spoke little, Harry noticed, and even when he did, his dialect was so thick Harry had the greatest trouble deciphering what he said.

"I've had enough of this," Harry snapped. "I'm going down there."

Timol looked at him, his yellow eyes glittering. "Major Chamille say for us to stay."

Major Chamille, Harry thought contemptuously. In whose bloody army?

"Major Chamille can go stuff himself. I don't answer to Major Chamille or anybody else. I'm my own man, and I make my own decisions."

He glared challengingly at Timol, who held his gaze for a fraction of a second, then went back to whittling his piece of wood. Harry turned up his hood and, thrusting his hands in his parka pockets, strode down the hillside and into the town.

"That should hold it," De Brere said confidently, putting the finishing touches to the marine's knee dressing. "How does it feel?"

"Stiff," the man said, flexing his leg.

"Bound to be. I'd keep the weight off it for a bit, if I was you. Plenty of rest, that's the ticket."

"Aren't you going to give him a jab?" the sergeant asked.

"Jab?"

"Tetanus."

"Ah, tetanus, of course."

De Brere straightened unhappily. Where the hell was the antitetanus serum? he wondered. "Actually, we tend not to do that anymore. Weakens the body's resistance, you know."

The sergeant's eyes narrowed suspiciously. He had a muscular face, the features broad and prominent. "What are you talking about?"

"It's like antibiotics. Too many injections, and the stuff stops working."

"That's rubbish," the sergeant said emphatically.

"It is?" De Brere's gaze faltered, and he felt panic rising inside his stomach. The bloody sergeant was some kind of medical encyclopedia, for Christ's sake. De Brere forced an embarrassed laugh. "Well, strictly speaking, the practice has been discontinued, but if you're making an issue of the thing"—he turned to the medical cabinet—"a tetanus jab it shall be."

Anxiously, De Brere scanned the rows of bottles and vials. Sweat gathered between his shoulder blades and ran in irritating trickles down the steep curve of his spine. He could feel the marine sergeant's eyes burning into the back of his skull. What in Christ's name am I going to do now? he wondered.

Selecting a syringe, he picked up one of the bottles at random and placed it in the bottom of the sink where the sergeant couldn't see it. Using his back to shield his movements, he turned on the tap and filled an empty cup with water. Taking care to conceal his actions, he dipped the syringe needle into the cup and pulled back the plunger, filling the vial with harmless liquid. "Here we go." He grinned. "Roll up your sleeve, if you please."

De Brere was conscious of the sergeant studying him closely as he pressed the needle into the marine's upper arm. Bloody busybody. Should have been a policeman, he had the nose for it. Suddenly, De Brere felt his senses jump. No wonder the sergeant was examining him so intently. He'd only shaved one half of his chin, for God's sake. He must look like some kind of lunatic. Unhappily, De Brere moistened his lips with his tongue and maneuvered his mouth into a sickly smile. "You're looking at my beard," he said with a strained laugh.

The sergeant didn't answer. His eyes were dark and expressionless, his features stony. Behind the bristling mustache, his face remained uncompromising.

"It's a sort of forfeit," De Brere stammered, fumbling desperately for his words. "Part of a gambling debt. You know what these young interns are. Such a sense of humor. I have to spend the next two weeks shaving only half my face at a time. Childish, really, but"—he chuckled hoarsely—"one has to be tolerant. The follies of youth and all that."

The sergeant's eyes were cold and unflinching. They seemed to glitter beneath his bushy brows. His skin looked pockmarked from some ancient skin disease. "Haven't you forgotten something?" he asked dryly.

"What's that?"

"His arm."

"What about his arm?"

"Antiseptic."

"Oh yes."

Hurriedly, De Brere moistened a cotton wool pad and dabbed at the puncture where the needle had gone. The marine rolled down his sleeve, nodding gratefully.

"That should do it," De Brere declared, tossing the pad into the nearby sink. "A few days' rest, and that knee'll be good as new."

The sergeant grunted as he helped his companion to his feet and shepherded him toward the open door. De Brere stood watching unhappily as they shuffled along the passageway and crossed the lobby to the glass-domed entrance hall.

The third marine sat watching them from the scout car outside. "They didn't chop his leg off, then?" he said cheerfully.

"Shut up," the sergeant snapped. "Get your backside out of that seat and help Wally into the rear."

The marine looked startled by the sergeant's tone. Blinking rapidly, he jumped out, easing the injured man's arm over his shoulder while the sergeant leaned into the driving cab and picked up their radio transmitter. He flicked the switch. "Unit 22 to base," he said. "Sergeant Hoskins here. Are you receiving me, over?"

A voice crackled through the static. "Come in, Unit 22. What's up, Reggie? Pubs not open yet?"

"Sam, listen to me carefully, this is urgent. Get on to the local police, will you? Find out if there's been a road accident around the Holmkirk area within the last two hours."

"What kind of road accident?"

"Head-on collision. The police allegedly rushed a man to hospital under heavy escort."

"Okay, Reg. Hang on a bit. I'll see what I can do."

Sergeant Reggie Hoskins stood fuming impatiently in the hospital parking lot. Something in the doctor's manner had alerted his instincts. He'd looked nervous, apprehensive, ill at ease. Sergeant Hoskins knew the symptoms. He'd witnessed them often enough before, interrogating suspects in the bandit country of Crossmaglen. For whatever reason, the doctor felt guilty, and Sergeant Hoskins intended to find out why.

After several minutes, the radio crackled again, and a voice broke through the static. "Base calling Unit 22. Sergeant Hoskins, are you receiving me, over?"

Hoskins pressed his thumb on the switch. "Hoskins here, Sam."

"Reg, you've drawn a blank, I'm afraid. There's been no record of any accident within the last forty-eight hours."

Hoskins felt his pulse quickening. "You're absolutely sure of that?"

"What do you take me for, an idiot? I spoke to the superintendent myself, for Christ's sake."

"Hold on a minute," Hoskins snapped tersely.

He turned to the marines in the rear. "Tomkins,

duck around the parking lot and guard the side entrance. Wally . . . hop, hobble, or crawl, but get your backside over to that lobby door and keep it covered. Nobody leaves or enters the building without my say-so, understand?"

The marines looked surprised, but impressed by the sergeant's manner, they reached for their submachine guns, scrambling into the dirt.

Sergeant Hoskins was trembling as he picked up the radio receiver. A small knot of tension had tightened in his stomach and refused to be dislodged. "Sam, I'm in the parking lot at Holmkirk Hospital. I want you to put out a call to all units in the immediate vicinity."

He paused, excitement gathering inside him. "I think we've got 'em," he said.

The river shimmered in Waldo's vision. When he half closed his eyes, it seemed to ripple in and out like a strip of india rubber. When he opened them again, it swiveled into focus, its sleekly moving current sending back slivers of refracted sunlight.

Waldo reached for the whiskey bottle and took another drink. "You see before you a ruined man," he declared thickly.

"Ruined?" Palmer echoed, his voice faintly slurred.

"Demolished. Discredited. Done."

"How's that?"

"The PAC talks should have been the pinnacle of my career. Even the president wished me luck. Can you imagine that? The president of the United States came to the airport to see me off. He looked me straight in the eye and said—and I quote—"The hope of the entire free world rests in your hands, Waldo.""

"He called you Waldo?"

"Sure."

"You must be a very important man in Washington."

"Was," Waldo reflected mournfully, passing the bottle back to Palmer. "*Was* important. Past tense. The State Department hates failure even more than I do. If the news about Option 24 leaks out . . ." He twisted his face wryly, leaving the sentence unfinished.

Palmer patted his shoulder sympathetically. Palmer's facial muscles had slackened, giving his features a vaguely rubbery look. One strand of his immaculate hair dangled across his forehead and into his eyes.

"It's an unjust world," he admitted. "Fate doesn't always make the best men presidents."

"Who knows where I might have gone," Waldo mused, "with the PAC talks on my track record? Capitol Hill, the Senate."

"The White House, at least," Palmer insisted.

Waldo looked at him appreciatively. "You're a good friend," he said.

"You really think so?"

"A good, staunch, reliable friend."

"That's funny, nobody ever called me a friend before."

Waldo stuck out his hand. "Put it there, friend."

Palmer choked as he slapped Waldo's palm. He looked strangely overwhelmed. "This is a very moving moment."

Waldo glimpsed the emotion in him, the almost agonizing sense of gratitude. In the harsh spring sunlight, the lines at Palmer's eyes seemed strangely pronounced, and a faint flush appeared above his cheekbones. "Do you mind if I finish off the whiskey?" Palmer asked. "There's only one swallow left."

"Why not? What are friends for, anyhow?"

They heard footsteps on the Forestry Commission parking lot behind them, and a marine came running across the open tarmac, his face gleaming with excitement. "Mr. Palmer," he gasped, slithering to a halt. "They've found them, sir. They're inside Holmkirk Hospital. We've got eighteen units converging on the building now."

Palmer leapt to his feet, his eyes dancing. Waldo noticed all trace of intoxication had drained from his features. He glanced at Waldo, grinning wildly, and together they sprinted toward the radio truck.

Harry wandered discreetly through the marketplace, hiding his stubbled features beneath his parka hood. He was painfully conscious of his unkempt appearance as he stopped a passerby and asked directions to the local hospital. He was glad when the street grew quieter and less congested.

Harry's relief was short-lived, however, for as he approached the hospital parking lot, a queasy sensation crept through his lower stomach. Perched in the entrance and exit doorways sat two marines, machine guns cradled across their bended knees. A camouflaged scout car stood parked in the entrance drive. Harry's step faltered, and a wave of alarm swept through his body. They were trapped, Kate, Chamille, De Brere, all of them. In another few minutes, the building would be swarming with troops.

Harry was shaken by an unexpected emotion. If Chamille reacted stupidly—if, taken by surprise, he decided to make a fight of it, shoot, run, threaten, hide, Kate might get hurt, perhaps even killed. His limbs turned cold when he thought about that. Everything he'd planned—revenge, retaliation— drained from his mind in a single breathless moment. He didn't hate Kate. He'd never hated Kate. She was the one good thing in his life, the only human being, with the exception of his son, who meant more to him than anything in the world.

Harry wasn't the first man in the human race to realize his emotions had been deceiving him. He struggled desperately to think. Kate was in there, helpless and unsuspecting. He had to do something.

He ducked into a news agent's shop and dropped a five-pound note on the counter. "I have to make a telephone call," he said. "Can you give me something smaller?"

The proprietor eyed him balefully. He was a tall man with a crooked eye. "What do you think this is, an amusement arcade? Why don't you buy something?"

Harry swore under his breath and picked up a magazine. "Okay, I'll take this," he said. "Only hurry."

The storekeeper was deliberately meticulous in counting out Harry's change, and Harry watched him, fuming with impatience. Then, snatching up the coins, he made his way to the public telephone booth at the shop rear. He looked up the hospital number in the phone book and dialed it quickly, his pulse throbbing. The voice of the switchboard lady sounded strained but polite. "Holmkirk General Hospital."

"Let me speak to the people holding you," Harry hissed.

There was a pause at the end of the line. "I'm sorry, I don't quite understand."

"Listen," Harry snapped, "I know you're being

held hostage by a group of armed men. I must speak to one of them quickly. It's important."

Another pause. Harry heard a faint scuffling noise, then De Brere's voice came on the line. "Who's this speaking?"

"It's Fuller."

"What's up, soldier?"

"Have you looked out the window lately?"

"You're speaking in riddles, squire. Shouldn't you be watching the horses, like a good little boy?"

"You're trapped, you fool. There are marines guarding the hospital exits. They appear to be waiting for something. Their backup team, I expect."

Harry heard De Brere's sharp intake of breath and waited, glancing across the empty shop.

"Thanks for the tip-off, soldier," De Brere said at last. "I'll have to see what we can do."

There was a click in Harry's ear as De Brere replaced his receiver, and the line went dead.

Elliot watched Kate putting the finishing touches to McAuley's dressing, her movements swift, deft, and sure. His anger faded as he studied her eyes above the surgical face mask. Even with her face obscured, you could see the beauty in those eyes. It wasn't her fault McAuley's wound had been superficial. She'd simply been doing her job, and Elliot had to admit he admired the way she'd handled things. No fussing, no panic. Just that quiet determined strength, that singular dedication. The fact that the operation had proved simple and straightforward didn't matter. Kate's essential resilience had come shining through.

Kate nodded at the sister, who began to cover McAuley up. Tearing off her cap and face mask, she shook her hair to untangle it. Without realizing what he was doing, Elliot took her in his arms and pressed her face gently against his chest. He could feel her limbs trembling under his touch, and patted her shoulder reassuringly. "Shhhh," he whispered. "It's over now. Everything's okay."

"I thought the bullet hole was deep," she whimpered. "I thought we were saving his life."

"Forget it. I was sounding off because I was agitated, that's all."

He was suddenly conscious of the softness of her body, and the mucus in his mouth seemed to dry unaccountably. The fragrance of her perfume lingered in his nostrils as she gently disengaged herself. "I don't know what you must think of me," she said, wiping her cheeks with her sleeve. "I'm not usually so emotional."

"You've been through a lot in the last twenty-four hours. You must be pretty close to exhaustion."

"I think we could all do with a rest," she agreed.

He took her arm, waving the sister through the door in front of them.

"First, we get McAuley out of here, then we rest."

"That won't be easy. He'll be groggy for another hour at least."

Elliot grunted. "Let's hope our luck lasts that long."

He frowned as he saw De Brere hurrying toward them along the corridor. Something in De Brere's manner carried a hint of imminent calamity.

"We're trapped," he breathed. "Those marines must've spotted something. They've got the exit blocked."

Elliot moved to the window and drew back the heavy curtain. He could see uniformed figures crouched in the parking lot outside. The sunlight glittered on the barrels of their submachine guns.

His lips tightened and he glanced at the sister. "Is there another way out of here?"

"There's an emergency exit at the side of the building," she said.

"They've got that plugged too." De Brere muttered.

"How many men?"

"Just one."

Elliot considered quickly. "Take Malheiro and get McAuley onto a cart. Bring his clothes and parka."

"Which way are we going?"

"Out the side. It's the weakest point of resistance."

Elliot looked at the sister, his eyes dark and penetrating. There was an air of savage determination on his handsome black face. "You make a good substitute anesthetist," he admitted softly. "I just hope you can act as well."

Marine Lester Tomkins, crouched on the lawn at the hospital's rim, started when he saw the sister appear in the open doorway. "Hurry," she screamed, gesturing fiercely. "They're bleeding to death in here."

Without pausing to think, Tomkins leapt to his feet and hurtled headlong into the narrow entrance hall. Realizing his mistake in an instant, he slithered desperately to a halt, but he was already too late. The blunt nose of a heavy service revolver thrust itself against his rib cage and he felt his cheeks turn pale as a man stepped through the adjoining door and gently prized the machine gun from his fingers. The man was tall, wild, unkempt-looking, and—Marine Tomkins registered this fact with an air of absent incredulity—one side of his chin was covered in beard stubble, the other shaved clean. It gave him, Tomkins thought, a vaguely unhinged look.

"Sorry, soldier," De Brere said, smiling. "This just isn't your day."

Harry stepped out of the news agent's shop and turned back toward the market square, walking swiftly. Someone had to stay loose, weigh up strategies, possibilities. If Chamille broke out, there would be no time for dithering. It would be cut and run, win or lose.

He felt the tension knotting in his stomach. He'd thought he'd hated Kate, thought he'd wanted nothing more than reprisal and revenge, but he'd been wrong. She was the only thing in his life that had ever been worth a damn, and he couldn't bear to lose her now. Please, God, don't let anything happen to her, he thought. Not just when he'd found her again.

He neared the marketplace. With lunchtime approaching, the square was growing busier. A group of unshaven men pushed through the throng toward him, and something in their appearance made Harry hesitate. Alarm filled him as he recognized Tazelaar, the South African security agent. Tazelaar spotted Harry at precisely the same instant and his placid eyes came suddenly alert. He muttered something under his breath, but Harry didn't wait to see his companions' reaction. Spinning on his heel, he sprinted back the way he had come.

With cries of consternation and alarm, the South Africans set off in hot pursuit.

* * *

Kate watched Elliot and De Brere wheeling McAuley along the narrow passageway. They had locked Sister Johnson, together with the receptionist and the captured Royal Marine, in a secluded broom cupboard under the ornate staircase and, with McAuley muffled inside his padded parka, were heading swiftly toward the hospital's side exit.

She felt her tension mounting as McAuley snored peacefully on, oblivious to the panic and commotion occurring on his behalf. Elliot's face looked tense as he gave her a nod. "Hold back the door," he ordered.

She seized the handle, swinging it open as a clatter of engines echoed on the road outside. Frozen with disbelief, Kate watched a convoy of camouflaged trucks thunder into the hospital parking lot. Marines leapt from the slow-moving vehicles, fanning out across the open forecourt. Dismay swept through her, chilling her limbs, stunning her senses. It seemed cruel, cruel for the troops to arrive when they had come so far, achieved so much.

Overwhelmed by the injustice of the moment, she pounded the wall with her fist. "We're too late," she cried angrily. "We're too bloody late."

Harry spotted the troops as he galloped furiously along the main street. They were forming a massive cordon around the hospital, deploying themselves in an elaborate starburst formation which effectively sealed off the building in every direction. A young lieutenant was bellowing orders from a scout car as his men scurried into position.

Harry slithered to a halt, peering furiously

around. A narrow lane slanted to the left, curving
back toward the market square. He scuttled along it,
his feet pounding the shiny cobbles, and, bellowing
furiously, the South Africans followed in his wake.

Standing up in the scout car, Lieutenant Canby
recognized the distinctive cadence of South African
voices and blinked in puzzlement. Glancing over his
shoulder, he glimpsed a cluster of disheveled men
sprinting toward a nearby lane. Their language was
unmistakable. Lieutenant Canby had spent three
years in Zimbabwe and would, he knew, recognize it
anywhere. Afrikaans. My God, he thought, the bastards have broken out through the rear.

He waved his arm at the startled marines, his
cheeks flushed with urgency and decision. "Round
up those men," he bellowed.

Huddled in the hospital doorway, Kate watched
the marines scattering up the narrow roadway. Only
a handful of men remained, grouped around the
lawn at the opposite corner of the building. Because
of the hospital's angle, she and her companions were
momentarily hidden from sight. Elliot was quick to
spot the advantage. He glanced at Malheiro and De
Brere, his eyes flashing wildly. "Move," he bellowed.

And pushing McAuley's cart in front of them,
they rattled into the deserted parking lot.

Harry's lungs felt close to bursting. At the end of
the lane he paused and glanced back over his shoulder. Tazelaar and his companions were completely
surrounded by Royal Marines. Red-faced with em-

barrassment, they were struggling to explain their
identity, but the troops pushed them brusquely
against a nearby wall.

Leaning forward, Harry began to laugh. He was
still laughing as he ducked around the corner and
shuffled toward the bustling marketplace.

It was a wild, disorderly scramble, propelling
McAuley's unconscious body through the seething
shopping crowds. The onlookers followed their progress with open-mouthed astonishment, engrossed by
the sight of white-coated orderlies careering through
the square with a runaway hospital cart.

When they reached the town outskirts, they
lifted McAuley as delicately as they could and
carried him up the hill to the cover of the trees.
Timol hurried forward to help, and as they laid the
minister's motionless body down, Kate saw him
gently blink his eyes. "He's coming round," she said.

McAuley looked confused, like a man who
found himself in some strange and inexplicable
environment. Groaning under his breath, he moved
his hand to the padded dressing on his lower abdomen.

Kate caught his wrist. "Leave it," she said.
"You'll start the wound bleeding again."

McAuley's eyes swiveled into focus, settling on
her face questioningly. His expression lost its bewildered air and she saw sense and awareness enter his
features.

"The bullet's out," she told him. "You'll be a bit
sore for a day or two, but once the incision heals, you
should be right as rain."

McAuley gave no answer. His cheeks looked
suddenly stricken and he gulped furiously at the air.

Then, rolling onto his side, he began to vomit into the spruce needles. Kate glanced at the others with embarrassment. "It's just the aftereffects," she explained.

Elliot grunted and walked back to the horses. She knew he was impatient to be on his way.

"There's a man coming," Timol called softly, watching the slope below.

Kate rose to her feet, her senses quickening. She saw Elliot gesture briskly to the others and reach for his pistol. Kate ducked under the nearest spruce boughs, keeping the trunk between her and the gently sloping embankment. Her spirits soared as she spotted a familiar figure striding up the incline toward them. There was no way in the world she could mistake that shambling frame or that tousled hair. A feeling of exaltation filled her. "It's Harry," she cried.

Elliot thrust the pistol back under his jacket and strolled into the open, watching Harry's approach with a sour smile. "Like a bad penny," he said, "you keep turning up."

Harry grunted. "I told you before, I'm not an easy man to get rid of."

"I suppose you think you're a hero now?"

Harry considered for a moment. "Yes," he admitted modestly.

"Well, you're not. You disobeyed orders."

"If I hadn't, you'd be on your way to jail."

"Just the same, once is enough. Try that again, and you're out. No arguments, no back talk. Understood?"

"Perfectly."

"Good."

Elliot glanced at the others. "Get McAuley into the saddle. We've hung about here long enough."

* * *

The radio operator looked embarrassed as he took off the headset. He was a pale young man with a smattering of freckles which gave him a curiously unformed innocent look. Crouched in the truck rear, Waldo and Palmer stared at him expectantly.

"Well?" Palmer demanded.

The operator hesitated. It was clear he didn't know how to phrase his reply. "They got away, sir."

"Away?" There was a hint of anger and disbelief in Palmer's voice.

"Lieutenant Canby arrested a group of South African security men by mistake."

Palmer glanced at Waldo, frowning. "Tazelaar," he breathed.

The radio operator ran his fingers through his short-cropped hair. The earphones had left a smear of dirt on his upper cheek, and in some strange way it made him seem more youthful than ever. "The kidnappers smuggled McAuley out in the confusion. He appears to be injured, sir. Several witnesses saw them pushing a hospital cart into the woods on the edge of town. They thought it was some kind of student prank."

"And the South Africans?"

"They've been released." The young man paused. He was conscious of the nature of his message and the dismay it would cause, wanted desperately to offer some encouragement. "Lieutenant Canby extends his apologies, sir. He says he's sorry about the mix-up, but at least we now have detailed descriptions of the people we're looking for. He's deploying his men along the Forestry roads in an attempt to seal them off."

Palmer nodded. To Waldo's surprise, he looked

unperturbed, as if he saw the fugitives' escape as little more than a temporary setback. "They can't get far," Palmer declared. "On foot or on horseback, we know where they are now. Contact RAF Kinloss and get a squadron of helicopters over the area immediately."

"Right, sir," the radio operator said.

Waldo grimaced at Palmer as they clambered from the truck rear. "Tough luck, Charles. You almost had them in the net."

Palmer shivered as the chill wind bit through his overcoat. He coughed under his breath, hunching his shoulders. "We'll get them," he promised. "Now that we have a location, it's only a matter of time. What's worrying me is Tazelaar and his bunch."

"The South Africans?"

Palmer nodded, glancing at Waldo questioningly. "They have no right to go stampeding around the British countryside without proper authorization. What the hell do they think they're playing at?" he said.

Ten

The atmosphere in the seething pressroom seemed strangely electric as the Home Secretary, seated on a small platform and flanked on each side by his closest advisers, commenced his statement under a barrage of popping flashbulbs. The statement was stark, dry, noncommital. It conveyed the facts coldly and precisely. "In the early hours of this morning, Mr. Howard McAuley, minister for foreign affairs with the government of the South African republic, was kidnapped from a train near Carlisle by persons unknown. Several hours later, Holmkirk Hospital on the Northumbrian Scottish border was taken over by a group of armed men, and the nursing sister there was forced at gunpoint to assist in an operation to remove a bullet from a patient's abdomen. It is not known at this stage whether the patient was Mr. McAuley or one of the kidnappers. A massive security operation is under way in the Border Forest area, and we expect an arrest to follow shortly."

As the Home Secretary paused for breath, a flood of questions burst from the impatient newspeople. Unabashed by the barrage, the minister answered the queries fluently and professionally.

"What about the suggestion that the Royal Marines arrested the wrong people?" one man shouted.

"Well, there was an understandable amount of confusion at the time. I gather some members of the South African police force were inadvertently caught in the security net."

"What will be Britain's position if the South Africans refuse to release Joshua Matshoba?"

"That decision rests entirely with the Pretoria government. Our principal concern is to ensure Mr. McAuley is returned unharmed and the terrorists are brought to justice."

"How would you answer accusations that the security operation has been bungled from start to finish?"

"Mr. McAuley was afforded the most stringent protection from the moment of his arrival in this country. However, one cannot always prepare for the unexpected. In this particular case, a series of unconnected incidents paved the way for the kidnapping."

"Is there any truth to the rumor that the real purpose of McAuley's visit was to carry out exploratory talks with British and American mediators?"

"Mr. McAuley was paying a personal visit to his ancestral home in Ayrshire, Scotland. We can't speculate at this stage on any secondary motives he may have had in mind."

The questions, shrewd and penetrating, were designed to put the Home Secretary on his mettle, but he was an old hand at conducting such affairs and fenced them off with seasoned dexterity. No one was prepared, however, least of all the Home Secretary himself, for the query which came after twenty minutes of frenzied questions. "Can you explain to us, Minister," a small nondescript man asked, "the meaning of Option 24?"

The Home Secretary froze in his chair, moistening his lips with his tongue. In the crowded conference room, the hubbub abruptly faded. Glimpsing the minister's discomfort, the reporters waited breathlessly for him to continue.

"I ask you again, Minister, what is the meaning of Option 24?"

Flustered, the Home Secretary glanced at his two companions, then gathering his papers together and rose to his feet. The journalists watched unbelievingly. It was the first time they had seen the minister lose his composure.

"I'm sorry, I can answer no further questions at this point," the Home Secretary announced. "We'll issue another statement as soon as we have something definite to report."

Pandemonium erupted as the minister scuttled for the door. Reporters rushed to cut off his retreat but a cordon of policeman held them doggedly back, and the frustrated newspeople milled about in confusion while the Home Secretary and his two advisers escaped into the sanctuary of the empty corridor.

"How could they possibly know about Option 24?" the Home Secretary muttered as they scurried back to his private office.

"The man's a plant. Got to be."

"That's no comfort," the minister remarked dryly. "If the story hits the headlines, somebody in this government's going to have to resign."

Four thousand miles away in Washington, D.C., the president of the United States called a meeting of his special advisers in the Cabinet Room on the second floor of the White House. The room had once been a study for presidents Franklin D. Roosevelt, Truman, and Eisenhower, and the walls were hung with ship prints and antique photographs. Above the mantelpiece hung Rembrandt Peale's famous portrait of George Washington.

"Looked at realistically," the president said, "what are the chances of the details leaking?"

"That shouldn't be a problem," the Secretary of State told him. "If the British get McAuley back, they can hold on to their original claim that he was visiting the home of his ancestors. If, on the other hand, something does get out, there's no reason at all why it should compromise this administration. We can't be condemned for trying to destroy apartheid."

"Tell that to the press."

"Option 24 is South Africa's creation, not ours. We'll state our case before the people, make it plain that we deplored the clause's inclusion but felt, in view of what might be gained, its acceptance seemed justified."

"Dan, you're dumber than I figured if you imagine that'll satisfy the American public. Option 24 may be legal—and to some extent even defensible—but if the details leak, we'll be lucky to survive impeachment."

The president sat back in his chair, rubbing his thumbnail down the side of his jaw. His eyes looked unnaturally bright, like those of a man in a fever. "For all our sakes, let's hope the British get McAuley back soon."

Kate guided her chestnut down the steep tufted firebreak. Ahead, she could see the winding course of a narrow stream, then more forest rippling drearily over the tops of the nearby hills. Flies rose humming in a suffocating shroud. The woods seemed like a living force, bent on their destruction.

Trees hung everywhere, crouching in gullies, hovering on hillslopes, surrounding them like an inescapable enemy.

Her body ached from the long day's ride. She simply wasn't used to this, hour after hour in the saddle, the landscape repeating itself again and again. She scarcely knew how McAuley stood it, with that wound of his. She'd changed his dressing several times during brief rest halts among the underbrush, and despite the stitches she'd put in, it was clear the incision was bleeding profusely. There was no denying the minister's courage, and no denying, either, the quiet intensity of Elliot Chamille, whose singular passion kept them moving forward when every muscle in their spent bodies cried out for sleep. Even Timol and Malheiro had stopped their customary banter and were riding with their shoulders stooped in weariness.

Kate could feel Harry's body pressed against her in the saddle. It was a disturbing sensation, arousing emotions she found difficult to comprehend. Her heart had leapt when she'd seen Harry climbing the hillslope above Holmkirk. She could feel it starting again, the old excitement, the old misery, the old breathtaking dilemma.

De Brere nudged his mount alongside her own, grinning. He looked ridiculous with one side of his chin bearded, the other side shaved. Unclipping his canteen, he pulled out the stopper and took a long drink, his Adam's apple bobbing. "You'll have to tell me your secret, soldier," he said to Harry, wiping his lips with the back of one hand. "Miss Whitmore here seems to find me eminently resistible, whereas the minute you appear, she goes all weak at the knees."

"Get stuffed," Harry answered sweetly, and De Brere chuckled.

"I see you both graduated from the same charm school. You deserve each other, you two."

Ahead, Elliot reined in his mount, lifting one arm to bring the little cavalcade to a halt. Kate sat peering over her horse's mane, flies buzzing around her cheeks and throat. Below, the firebreak narrowed, and they could see a little clearing in the woods. "We'll rest here," Elliot announced. "Give the horses a break. Eat if you want to, but save the iron rations for later. We may need them."

With thankful groans, they guided the horses into a cluster of underbrush and clambered wearily from the saddles.

The clearing they had chosen was ragged but secluded. It offered a haven of sorts, a place to rest, recuperate, bolster their sagging senses—for Elliot Chamille, an opportunity to rethink, consider their position in the light of changing circumstances. So many things had gone wrong since the stopping of the train—McAuley shot, their escape from the hospital, and now Harry Fuller. Fuller was not a problem in the strategical sense, the military sense, but in terms of Elliot's personal aspirations, the man was a destabilizing presence. Elliot wasn't a fool. He'd seen the look in Kate's eyes when she'd spotted Harry approaching up the hillslope above Holmkirk. She loved the bastard, that much was clear. He couldn't hope to compete with the intensity of that love, but with deviousness and luck, he might just manage to divert the course of her affections.

Elliot couldn't understand why Kate's feelings for Harry should bring him so much pain. He scarcely even knew the woman, when you came right down to it. Did he care, he asked himself, truly care if he never saw Kate again? But the answer, cold and clear in his mind, inescapable and unmistakable, was yes, yes, by God, he did care. He wanted her. Wanted her badly. Wanted her more even than victory. You loved someone who fulfilled a need within you, he thought, and you loved according to the intensity of that need. It was a human thing, an inchoate, indefinable yearning which went far beyond the physical. She was everything he'd ever dreamed of in a woman, intelligent, sophisticated, refined. But he would have to move quickly, make his approach before Fuller had a chance to interfere.

Elliot waited until Kate had finished dressing McAuley's stitches, then, taking her by the arm, drew her toward the adjacent trees. Kate looked on the brink of mental and physical exhaustion. "How is he?" Elliot asked.

"Still bleeding. What do you expect, the way we're jostling him about?"

"Is it dangerous?"

She shook her head. "Stitching's holding firm. As long as we keep the cut clean, there should be little to worry about."

"What about Fuller?"

"Harry?" Kate looked puzzled.

"He doesn't belong here, he's not one of us. Think we should turn him loose?"

"He won't go. I tried."

"He'll have no choice if we dump him at the roadside."

"You don't know Harry. He's a very stubborn man."

Something in the way she said it, an air of pride, approval, made Elliot flinch. He plucked at a tree twig, twisting it around his middle finger. "I know what you're thinking," he said. "You're wondering if you'd handle things better a second time around, you and Fuller."

Kate glanced at him with surprise, and Elliot smiled gently. "Don't. It would be a terrible mistake. Life's a progressive thing. You keep moving, or you stagnate and die. Everything changes, that's nature."

"What makes you so wise and knowing all of a sudden?"

"Instinct. I get feelings about these things. Besides . . ." he paused, tossing the twig on the ground, "I've got a stake in this too."

"What kind of stake?"

"You," he said.

Kate blinked. "You're not serious."

"Try me."

"Here we are stuck in the middle of the biggest forest in Europe, and you start getting romantic?"

"Not romantic, that's not my style. I just like things in the open, no lies, no subterfuge. I want you to think about it."

"Think about it?"

"About us."

She brushed back her hair bewilderedly. "Are you always so damned sure of yourself?"

He smiled, and Kate felt a sudden constricting pain around her middle.

"When it comes to something I really want," he said. "Always."

Twenty feet away, Harry watched the exchange worriedly. Something in Elliot's face told him it was more than just a casual inquiry. Elliot looked as if he was putting his whole life on the line. Harry felt something stirring inside him. Jealousy. He was such a handsome bastard, Elliot Chamille. More disturbing still, he was everything Harry was not—idealistic, dedicated, the kind of man Kate would instinctively admire. She'd appreciate his virtues, respect his integrity; not like Harry, who always brought out the worst in her.

Harry threw aside what was left of his sandwich and rose to his feet. A warning bell sounded deep within his consciousness, but he ignored it as he strolled across the clearing. "What's going on?" he demanded.

Kate looked at him with surprise. "We're having a private discussion," she said. "It has nothing to do with you."

"Everything this bastard says has something to do with me. He took my boy, he ruined my career. I'll probably go to prison, have you considered that?"

"Just keep out of this, Fuller," Elliot told him warningly.

Harry felt a strange recklessness taking hold of him. His weariness vanished as his pulse quickened. "I'm getting sick and tired of your orders, Chamille."

"If you don't like them, get out."

"That's what you want, isn't it? You want me to leave you alone with her."

"Harry, you're talking like an idiot."

Harry looked at her fiercely. "Tell me what he was saying."

"You're making a fool of yourself, Harry."

"Did he ask you to go off with him? Somewhere nice and cozy where you can both find happiness exchanging platitudes on the great revolutionary struggle?"

"This has gone far enough, Harry."

"He talks in slogans, can't you see that? He's not a human being at all, he's just a collection of attitudes."

"Cut it out, Fuller," Elliot warned.

"What's wrong?" Harry asked. "Did I just destroy the emperor's new clothes?"

"Goddamn you, I said cut it out."

But Harry seemed unable to stop. He was caught in a madness of his own making. For a moment he struggled to control the wildness engulfing him, but it was too strong, too powerful to resist, and with a hoarse cry he hit Elliot between the eyes, sending him sprawling into the underbrush.

De Brere and Malheiro leapt up, seizing Harry's arms, and Harry made no attempt to throw them off. On the ground, Elliot peered up at him with a look of undisguised hatred, blood pouring from his nostrils.

"Let him go," he ordered softly.

"Easy, soldier," De Brere warned. "We've enough on our hands without fighting among ourselves."

"I said let him go."

De Brere glanced at Malheiro, nodded, and they stepped back warily. Keeping his gaze locked firmly on Harry's face, Elliot clambered to his feet, his eyes smoldering. Harry felt his muscles tighten.

"Elliot?" Kate whispered in a frightened voice.

Elliot hushed her with a jerk of his hand. It was clear he was beyond human restraint. "Okay," he breathed, his chest rising and falling, "let's settle this once and for all."

Harry grunted. "Any way you like."

Elliot moved in fast. There was no warning to his attack. He dove forward, head down, and Harry felt the breath explode from his body as Elliot's head slammed like a battering ram into the center of his abdomen. His trunk seemed stricken by a strange debilitating numbness, and for some reason he couldn't immediately explain, he found himself rolling over the ground, Elliot's forearm locked across his windpipe. Harry's eyes bulged as he struggled desperately for air. He could smell Elliot's sweat as they kicked and thrashed around the cluttered clearing, squeezing, punching, twisting, straining.

Harry lashed out with his fist, heard Elliot hiss, and thought, got you, you, bastard. But, trim and wiry, Elliot shifted position, straddling Harry's chest, his strong hands seizing Harry's throat, shutting off his oxygen. Harry's lungs labored, and his brain drifted dangerously. He was losing consciousness, he realized.

Jamming his elbows against the ground, he arched his stomach into the air, and a wave of relief flooded his body as he felt Elliot topple sideways. Choking hoarsely, Harry scrambled to his feet. Elliot was only a fraction behind him, moving in for the kill, inching forward this time, balancing his weight on the balls of his feet. Sunlight lit his eyes, and the blood from his nostrils spread along the thin line of his mouth, coating his white, evenly spaced teeth. He moved suddenly, lashing out with his left foot, and Harry danced to the side as the boot grazed his stomach wall.

Without giving Elliot a chance to recover balance, Harry stepped in smoothly, landed a short jab on Elliot's left temple, then smashed his fist to the side of Elliot's jaw. Elliot slammed into a tree trunk with stupefying force, and Harry went to work on his stomach, picking his targets with ruthless deliberation.

He could see the pain and confusion in Elliot's eyes, he could see the swelling on Elliot's jawline. Then something bewildering happened. He heard a sound like a roll of distant thunder, swelling, rising, deadening his senses, filling his ears and head and brain. Stepping back, he saw a helicopter gliding

above them over the gently swaying treetops.
Alarmed by the din, their animals began to buck and
lunge.

Elliot thrust himself up from the spruce trunk,
his face swelling ludicrously. His anger faded in the
urgency of the moment. Ignoring Harry, he glared at
the others wildly. "Get mounted," he bellowed.
"Move those horses into the cover of the woods."

Flight Lieutenant Holland checked his altimeter
and glanced down at the woodland. Wisps of mist
traced the trees in the narrow gullies, and cloud
wreathed the summits like regal lace. Holland's
hands froze at the controls as he glimpsed a group of
matchlike figures scattering wildly through the timber, their hair and clothing whipped by the down-
draft from his rotor blades. He felt a shiver of
triumph and excitement. For a moment he sat staring
down at the scurrying figures, struggling to bring his
brain into focus. Then, senses racing, he flicked his
radio switch and spoke into his headset microphone.

"Wessex 2 calling control, Wessex 2 calling
control. Runaways spotted directly below. Position
Section 16, seven miles south of Holmkirk. Subjects
mounted and heading in a westerly direction. Request instructions. Over."

The drone of the aircraft seemed strangely sopo-
rific, and Haskins and McDonnel had to struggle to
keep themselves awake. Barely an hour had passed
since the two *Daily Express* men had taken off in the
tiny cropduster four-seater in an attempt to breach
the police cordon by air, and Philip Haskins was
finding the strain of the chase curiously fatiguing.

Beside him in the passenger seat, Arty, his photographer, looked peacefully benign. Arty McDonnel was one of those placid people who never got excited by life, and Haskins envied him his calmness, his assurance, his intrinsic sense of his place in the order of things. He, Haskins, was a born worrier, a perfect candidate for sprouting ulcers and hardening arteries.

He glanced down at the forest. Viewed from on high, the furred hillslopes seemed to lose their density, blending into a contourless sprawl which was strangely drained of perspective. If there were men down there, they could vanish like wraiths in such a desolate wasteland, Haskins thought. He did not envy the security forces the task of smoking them out.

His eyes narrowed as he glimpsed, moving toward them at incredible speed, a strange bulbous object with a metal hull. A feeling of disbelief rose inside him, and he felt the blood drain from his face.

Jesus God, it's a helicopter, he thought.

Flight Lieutenant Holland banked steeply, glancing down through his Plexiglas nose cone at the fugitives fleeing below. They were galloping through the trees, following the bank of a twisting river, the horses, panicked by his rotor blades, hurtling along at breakneck speed. Watching from above, Holland was filled with a fierce and impossible-to-ignore excitement. Hunter's instinct, he told himself elatedly, the thrill of watching a quarry on the run. There was no sensation in the world to match it.

He swung his machine into a sharp curve, doubling back on his vapor trail. He would make another pass and keep the animals moving. If they wore themselves out, it would make things easier when the backup team arrived.

The sun shimmered in Holland's eyes, momentarily blinding him, and he blinked as a blip appeared on his radar screen, flickering warningly beneath his nose. Puzzled, he squinted through the windshield. His muscles knotted as he saw, directly in front, a machine framed against the shimmering sky. It was a tiny biplane, its outstretched wings catching the savage glare of the sun. A chill of horror ran through Holland's chest and he felt his stomach cringe. Sweet suffering Jesus, he thought.

And hauling hard on the controls, he sent his helicopter into a wild despairing arc.

Galloping through the brush, Kate watched the helicopter pilot battling for altitude, knowing he would never make it, knowing too that the collision, when it came, would be tumultuous and devastating. At the last minute, the biplane seemed to spin to starboard, its pilot, glimpsing the danger, tilting his wingspan in a frenzied effort to bank. For a moment, it seemed the two machines might actually pass unscathed; then, with a dry toneless cracking sound, the aircraft's wingtip caught the spinning rotor blades and whirled sharply on its own axis. The plane executed a toplike twist, colliding with the chopper's fuselage, and the twin hulls erupted into a blinding starburst of smoke and flame. Kate flinched under the brain-shuddering explosion, and splinters of twisted metal showered the trees in all directions. She watched the wreckage hit the ground, filling the air with the shriek of tortured timber as the great fireball plowed remorselessly through the tinder-dry underbrush, disintegrating as it went, scattering blazing fragments in an awesome corridor of devastation.

Flying Officer Seton, coming in fast from the south, glimpsed the flames as he guided his helicopter over the bristling carpet of spruce. He saw the smoke churning skyward, and the flickering nest of crimson where the fire danced among the stricken tree trunks, leaping, scorching, devouring.

Cursing softly under his breath, he switched on his radio microphone.

Waldo was sitting in the radio truck when the message came through. His mouth went dry as he watched Palmer scribbling down the details. "I think we can forget McAuley for the moment, Charles," he whispered.

Palmer looked at him. "What are you talking about?"

"Ever seen a forest fire before?"

"This is England, Waldo. Our problems are generally of a moister variety."

"Well, I have, and I never want to see another. A fire like that can travel twenty miles in a single night, if the conditions are right."

Palmer frowned. "Are you saying McAuley could be in serious danger?"

"I'm saying we've entered a new dimension here."

He leaned forward, his face earnest and intent. "Listen to me, Charles, I know I haven't any authority in this, but I've seen forest fires in the Appalachian foothills and the mountains of Colorado. I've seen wind-driven flames creating their own air currents and carrying sparks farther and farther afield. If that blaze isn't contained, you could have a disaster on your hands that'll make the London blitz look like Chinese firecracker night."

Palmer studied him in silence for a moment, pursing his lips, his cheeks a blur in the fading sunlight. He scribbled something on a slip of paper and handed it to one of the marines. "Get this to the Forestry officer immediately," he ordered.

Tazelaar and the South Africans watched the fire taking hold. It was an awesome sight, leaping and roaring among the tree trunks, the sparks flinging themselves frenziedly skyward. Tazelaar had never seen such energy in his life. The wind tugged at his clothing as oxygen was sucked into the writhing maelstrom. It seemed almost as if the fire were alive, a hungry monster consuming everything in its path.

"Almighty Father," Tazelaar muttered compulsively, "Everlasting God, in whose hands we are, in life as in death . . ."

The fire seemed a signal of sorts, a sign from some unearthly power that he was not alone in his sacred quest. True, things had gone a little topsy-turvy. He still hadn't gotten over the way he'd made a fool of himself with the British Royal Marines. It had taken all Tazelaar's persuasive powers to convince them he was a legitimate part of their security operation. But he was on the right track now, no question about it. In his hand he clutched a small paper wrapper, its greased surface mudstained and bedraggled. It came from a glucose tablet, simple proof—if proof were needed—that their quarry had passed this way recently. But the sprawling valleys and wood-cluttered hillslopes were too empty, too desolate; they presented a baffling wilderness in which a man could lose himself for days, weeks, maybe even months at a time.

Now, as he watched the flames licking their way through the topmost branches, crawling higher and higher, setting the spruce tips in stark relief, a startling thought occurred to Tazelaar. If they could keep the fire moving, spread it out, start individual blazes of their own, they could create a living barrier, slicing off the entire valley. The concept made his senses swim. A firestorm, like an earthquake, was beyond the capacity or control of man. Flames, carried on air currents created by their own vortex, could leap across clearings and firebreaks alike. They would sweep everything before them. "Set the underbrush alight," Tazelaar commanded crisply.

Leroux looked at him with disbelief. "Menheer?"

Tazelaar knew Leroux was afraid of him; they all were. He regarded it as a failure of sorts, the way he generated fear among his subordinates. He forced his lips into an encouraging smile. "It will be like the wrath of God Himself," he whispered. "We will spread the fire and consume our quarry in the searing flames of hell."

Eleven

The fire engine roared along the narrow logging road, its scarlet flanks strangely incongruous amid the encroaching evergreens. Squinting through the windshield, Maurice Southwick, duty fire forester, struggled to see into the breathless curtain of gloom. The odor of smoke, harsh, pungent, and familiar, hovered menacingly in his nostrils, and he felt his genitals move in an involuntary spasm as the road topped a gentle hillock and he glimpsed the blaze roaring frenziedly ahead. A forest fire was frightening enough when you saw it by day, he reflected, but witnessed at night it took on new and terrifying dimensions. The bed of the fire was a searing torrent of flame. Only at its fringes, where sparks, fanned by the wind, danced voraciously into the surrounding foliage, did the holocaust assume definition. Southwick could see the deadly crimson flames spiraling among the branches. Black smoke belched into the air, creating a billowing column which blotted out the stars completely.

Maurice Southwick was an experienced Forestry officer. His job, he knew, was to halt the conflagration's advance if possible, call for reinforcements from the neighboring fire departments if the situation appeared out of control. His tender carried barely two hundred gallons of water, a fractional amount against the intensity of the inferno ahead, but he reasoned if he could hold the blaze at a natural break, the logging road itself, he might be able to contain it without calling on resources badly needed by the nearby towns.

Southwick's team went into action with the calm precision of seasoned professionals. They moved in harmony, no panic, no expressions of alarm, each man coordinating his efforts with the next. Hoses were unrolled and clipped to the tender at the fire truck's rear. The hoses had been punctured with holes to produce a pepperpot effect, spraying water into the air to present a solid barrier of liquid between the advancing flames and the untouched woodlands beyond. For twenty minutes, Southwick and his companions watched the fire's insidious approach. Scorched by the white-hot wind currents, they waited in silence, hoping and praying the watery rampart would halt the furnace in its tracks. For a while, it looked as though their strategy might succeed. Like an animal faced with some strange and bewildering obstacle, the fire seemed to pause, falling back on itself, spreading outward in different directions. And then, with a furious full-throated roar, it leapt over the cascading water, leapfrogging the open safety lane and pouncing hungrily among the foliage at the opposite side.

Southwick felt his spirits blanch. He groaned. "The flames are crowning."

Running back to the vehicle, he pulled out the radio and flicked the transmitter switch. "Section 16 to fire control center," he bellowed, "Section 16 to fire control center."

"Is that you, Maurice?" a voice asked, breaking through the static.

"Hal, the blaze is running out of control. Contact the Bellingham brigade, then get on to Newcastle and Carlisle. We need clearage crews, fire teams, water tenders, any and everything you can get. If we don't get this conflagration stopped, the whole bloody forest could go up in flames."

Sitting in the control center, Waldo watched sympathetically as Palmer listened to the Forestry officer's report. The man was trying hard to appear controlled, but Waldo could see the anxiety in his features. "Everything's against us," the officer explained. "Especially the weather. We've had a high-pressure system for nearly three months, a mass of dry air stalled over the northern Pennines, blocking rain systems coming in from the west. The underbrush is as dry as kindling, and the moisture content of the trees themselves is exceptionally low. On top of that, there's now a low-pressure system moving down from the north, bringing winds of thirty miles an hour. When they reach the blaze and their oxygen is sucked in to feed the flames, they could reach eighty miles an hour. They'll fan the fire, keep it moving. Ordinarily, conflagrations like this only happen in the smaller plantations. Once trees reach a height of ten or fifteen feet, the lack of underbrush diminishes the fire hazard to some extent, but what's happened here is that flames have entered the topmost branches and are leaping across clearings and firebreaks alike. The process is known as crowning. A fire which crowns is almost impossible to contain. According to our reports, it's already advancing faster than a man can trot."

"What will you do?" Palmer asked gently.

"First, I've called in reinforcements from Carlisle and Newcastle. Next, I'm going to evacuate all the villages in the immediate area. We've never had a major bush fire in this country, but the Sundance Fire of northwest Idaho covered sixteen miles in nine hours, and I don't plan on taking any chances. I'd rather overreact a bit than live to regret it afterward."

"I understand," Palmer said sympathetically.

The Forestry officer hesitated, toying feverishly with the corner of his blotting pad. "There's something else. We need men to widen the firebreaks, clear out the scrub and dead foliage. If this blaze gets out of hand, we could face disaster on a level never before witnessed in this country."

"You want to use some of my troops?"

"I'm sorry, Mr. Palmer. I do appreciate your position, but this is a war we're fighting."

"Quite. Take what you require."

"I need helicopters too."

"Helicopters?"

"Partly for reconnaissance, partly for dropping anti-incendiary foam on plantations lying in the fire's path. It could help slow the flames down a bit."

Palmer sighed. "Very well. Anything you wish."

He paused as the door opened and a secretary looked in. "There are some people in reception who'd like to speak to you," she said.

"What kind of people?" Palmer asked.

"Reporters and TV crews."

Palmer glanced at Waldo, exasperated. "Just like the bloody thing. I thought we had the approach roads sealed. They must have managed to wriggle their way through."

"Be careful what you say, Charles," Waldo warned. "We don't even know if McAuley's still alive."

Palmer nodded as he rose to his feet. His cheeks looked pallid, his eyes somber and resigned. "God help the poor bastard if he's still out there," he said.

Kate moved through the darkness, her mind in a torpor. She seemed beyond the realm of conscious thought. She had scarcely noticed darkness falling—not gently, as was customary in the English countryside, but with the abrupt and breathless hush of Africa, the shadows rising out of the hollows and timber stands, blending to form a wall of impenetrable gray.

Smoke drifted into her nostrils, and even at that distance she could hear the ominous crackle and sizzle of flames. The helicopter crash still hung in her senses like some strange and haunting fantasy. No one could have survived such an inferno, she thought. When she glanced back, the night sky seemed ablaze with light. Hard to believe the fire could spread so rapidly. It was a terrifying spectacle, carrying death and devastation in its wake. The horses sensed its nearness and were nervous and rebellious, difficult to control. Elliot had ordered the team to dismount, and now they were picking their way on foot, leading their mounts along the line of a narrow riverbed.

Behind her, Kate could hear Harry panting wearily. Damn fool, Harry, attacking Elliot back there. Awful, it had been, watching the two of them savaging each other. That was the trouble with Harry. He thought he could tackle every problem with a sledgehammer.

She was not the only one riven with exhaustion, however. The others were stunned to a man, their nerves ragged, their bodies spent. Elliot alone kept them moving forward. He was an admirable man, and no mistake. Despite the strenuousness of their retreat, despite his crazy encounter with Harry, he had never lost his sense of style. He looked graceful still, picking his way through the trees at the head of the column, his head poised warily as he listened for any sound which might signify the presence of another human being. Kate felt flattered by Elliot's approaches in the clearing. Elliot was no ordinary man, she felt. He was warm and sensitive, passionate and proud. Easy to love—or would have been, if it hadn't been for Harry. Mad, stubborn, exasperating Harry. She rued the day she'd ever set eyes on him, the bastard. He made everything so complicated, simply by being there.

The trees parted and Kate saw Elliot draw to a halt, muffling his horse's nostrils with his fingers. Below, a sprawl of open fields surrounded a stone farmhouse perched at the side of the river. Lights shone in the curtained windows, and dimly in the moonlight Kate spotted the slender thread of a road sliding eastward into the night.

"People," she whispered.

Elliot nodded, his eyes gleaming in the starlight.

"You're planning to go down there?"

"We have to. It'll give us a base, a place to regroup. Sleep too, that's important."

"Shouldn't we detour? Could be dangerous."

"We've run long enough. We must have rest before we collapse from exhaustion. And McAuley's at the end of his tether. That stitching's giving him a lot of pain."

He glanced at the others. "They could have shotguns on the premises, so be careful. Don't shoot unless you have to, and keep the horses quiet as we approach."

It took them nearly twenty minutes to steer their mounts across the open pastureland, cutting the fence wires as they went. By the time they reached the farm itself, Kate's nerves were stretched to the breaking point, and she was filled with a sense of dire foreboding, as if calamity lay just around the corner.

Elliot tied his mount to the door of the nearby barn. In the darkness, his swollen face looked curiously out of alignment; blood, dry and crusted, stained his lips and the tip of his chin.

Taking out his pistol, he checked to see if it was loaded and nodded to De Brere. Without a word, De Brere made his way to the house rear, his lithe body vanishing into the gloom. Elliot crossed the forecourt, his boots crunching on the scattered gravel. Somewhere, a dog began to growl.

Elliot hammered on the door with his fist. It was opened a moment later by a man with a thatch of unruly red hair. There were deep creases at the corners of the man's eyes, and his cheeks were cratered, giving him a battered weatherbeaten look. He stood blinking at Elliot standing on the threshold step, and then his eyes widened in astonishment as Elliot thrust the pistol hard against his breastbone. "Don't speak," Elliot warned softly. "Don't say a word. Just keep your hands where we can see them and move inside, slowly and gently."

The man obeyed without a word, his bony face taut with tension. The others followed in single file, shuffling along the narrow passageway. The farmhouse walls were papered with some lurid floral design which, over the years, had lost its initial coloring so that now it looked listless and dispiriting. A potted plant stood on the windowsill at the rear.

In the kitchen, they found De Brere covering the farmer's wife with his pistol. She was a plump ruddy-cheeked lady in her early fifties, and she looked terrified out of her wits at the sight of so many armed invaders. Feeling sorry for her, Kate said, "Please don't worry, nobody is going to get hurt."

Elliot eyed the farmer shrewdly. Now that his initial surprise had passed, a sullen anger lingered in the man's dark eyes.

"Who else lives here?" Elliot demanded.

"Naebody," the farmer answered.

"You're lying. You couldn't work this land alone. Not without help."

"I divent work the land at all," the man answered sullenly. "This is a sheep farm. I tend the flock."

"You and who else?"

"Naebody," the farmer told him stubbornly.

Elliot pressed his pistol under the man's chin, and the man glared defiantly back. He was no shrinking violet, Kate thought, not one to be intimidated easily. It was the woman who broke first. Whimpering deep in her throat, she said, "We've got two boys. Malcolm and Les. They're doon in Hexham for the sheepdog trials."

"When are you expecting them back?"

"The morra neet at the earliest."

Elliot nodded. He peered around the room, his eyes noting the rough ceiling beams, the stone flags, the wooden wall cabinets. "Any shotguns in the house?"

The man shook his head. "Divent believe in such things. Too many accidents wi' shotguns around."

His wife sighed resignedly. "There's a twelve-bore in the cupboard upstairs. Malcolm uses it for hunting rabbits."

Elliot smiled. "I'm glad to see you are being sensible. We have no desire to hurt you. We need sleep, a chance to rest and recuperate. We'll take nothing from your home except maybe a pot of coffee if one's going. When we depart, you'll be left behind unharmed. Until then, however, I'd be grateful if you would remain inside this kitchen, unless escorted by one of my men."

The farmer and his wife nodded silently, and lowering the pistol, Elliot thrust it into the holster under his padded parka, his handsome face stricken with exhaustion. Somewhere outside, a dog began to bark as its nostrils caught the odor of drifting woodsmoke. The sound was harsh and discordant on the chill night air.

"Well," Elliot said, sighing wearily, "who takes first watch?"

Kate finished changing the dressing on McAuley's abdomen, then wandered thankfully into the darkness. She needed air, she told herself, room to think, room to breathe. She was facing an emotional crisis, one she sensed but scarcely knew how to accommodate. She was not the first woman to be torn between two suitors, but Kate's dilemma was intensified to some degree by the circumstances in which she found herself. Unreal, unnatural, she seemed caught in a world of her own making where reality itself had come dangerously askew; in such surroundings, conscious thought became suspect, feelings and emotions transitory. She loved Harry, she'd never doubted that fact. But suddenly and inexplicably, she loved Elliot too. How could you

love a man you'd known only a few bare days? she
wondered. And yet, love him she did. Mindlessly.
Unreservedly. She loved him for his sensitivity, for
his gentle and compassionate nature, for the fierce
physical awareness he aroused in her at the merest
touch. You couldn't compete with that. You couldn't
ignore it. And there lay the problem, for she was
caught in a quandary of the senses, a confusion of
tenderness, futility, passion, and fury, bolstered and
constrained by the bizarre experiences of the past
few hours. The memory of the helicopter crash hung
vividly in her mind. She saw it as a series of still
frames, each connected jerkily to the other—the
biplane homing in, the pilot banking, the sickening
moment of impact. Recalling the horror, she shuddered. It had seemed so simple in the beginning—
grab McAuley, vanish into the Northumbrian forest—a
piece of cake, Harry would have said in his blunt
inimitable way. But nothing so far had been a piece of
cake. And with the predicament now confronting her,
the situation was becoming even trickier.

She paused, filling her lungs with cold night air.
The odor of smoke was definitely strengthening, she
thought worriedly. The fire was something else they
hadn't bargained for, but at least, looking at things in
the positive sense, it might prove a bonus in their
favor. The fire would keep the soldiers occupied, if
luck held out.

A movement caught her attention near the
building's corner, and she spotted Elliot leaning
against the dark stone wall. He was smoking a
cigarette, and something in his face made Kate
frown. He looked as if he were trapped in some
airless cavern, fighting for breath. He was staring at
the glow in the distant sky, his chest rising and

falling erratically. He's afraid, she thought. You couldn't mistake the sight of naked fear, it carried an aura all its own. And Elliot's was more than mere physical fear. His eyes gleamed with an almost superstitious dread.

Puzzled, Kate walked toward him, thrusting her hands into her parka pockets. "Anything wrong?"

"The fire," he whispered. "It's getting stronger."

"It's miles off yet."

He looked at her strangely, and she noticed his hands were trembling.

"I hate fire."

"Well, I'm not exactly wild about it myself, but look on the bright side. It'll help cover our retreat, keep the soldiers busy."

A hint of embarrassment entered his eyes. Drawing hard on the cigarette, he injected a jaunty note into his voice, deliberately changing the subject. "How's McAuley?"

"Tired, like everyone else."

"And his stomach?"

"Bearing up. The incision's still bleeding, but the stitching's holding firm."

"Good. We'll stay here as long as we can, rest up, recuperate. We're human beings, not machines. Without sleep, we'll fall to bits."

"Oughtn't we to cut the telephone wire? This farm's just the sort of place the police might check."

"Better leave it. They're more likely to get suspicious if the line's out of order."

She stared at the trees smothered in their thin white haze, her nostrils picking up the pungent odor of woodsmoke. "It's a desperate mess, isn't it? Everything's getting out of hand."

"I wouldn't say that. We got what we came for.

And twelve more hours is all we need. By then, Joshua Matshoba will be in Angola."

"I'd almost forgotten Matshoba," she admitted wryly. "I'd almost forgotten what we're doing here. I feel as though I've been trapped in this forest for a million years."

A livid bruise marked Elliot's jawline, making his face oddly lopsided, and Kate felt her features soften. "I'm sorry about Harry."

"That's okay. It was bound to happen sooner or later."

"I should have warned you he's rather volatile."

Elliot grinned ruefully. "I found that out the hard way. Anyhow, it wasn't completely his fault. I blew my stack a bit myself."

He paused, peering at his cigarette. "Did you think over what I said today?"

She smiled. "You're a very persistent man."

"I have to be. I'm not the only one in the market."

She crossed her arms, massaging her shoulders with her fingertips. "Why don't we think about the future after Matshoba's free? Let's get the job done first." She glanced at him curiously. "What will you do when it's over?"

"Go on fighting, I guess."

"Never think about returning home? Back to Detroit? You must have family there. Friends."

He grinned painfully. "I'm sort of the prodigal son. My father and I didn't see eye to eye. What you might call a crisis of philosophy. When I joined the movement, he cut me off without a cent."

"Is he awesomely rich?"

"Sure, richer than Croesus." He grimaced. "And I wasn't a gawky boy from the boondocks, you understand. I'd learned to appreciate the finer things of life. Suddenly, I found myself struggling to survive."

"Most people do it automatically."

"True, but then I'm not most people."

He glanced at his cigarette, as if faintly surprised to discover he was still holding it. Dropping it on the ground, he stubbed it out with his toe. His humor was gone now, replaced by something she found difficult to define, a kind of reluctant irony.

"I was like you once, full of purity and high ideals. I was going to save the whole black race single-handed. I was pretty naive, I guess. I learned the truth the hard way. The power struggles going on among our own people are just as savage and unremitting as the struggle for freedom."

In the diluted light, the bruise on his jawline seemed to blend into the ebony hue of his stubbled chin. "Besides," he added, "I discovered I have extremely expensive tastes. They've been bred into me from the cradle. Tastes like that have to be catered for. In our family, personal achievement was considered the highest of all social graces. The pursuit of riches, of material success. I'm a modest man. I want only two things from life. Money and power."

She frowned. "Is that what the movement means to you?"

"What else?" he asked.

"How about justice? Equality?"

He laughed. "Nothing but words. South Africa's one of the richest countries in the world, and I want a share in those riches. I'm sorry if my grossness offends you, but you wanted the truth and now you've got it. I'm in this for me, not some weird notion of brotherly love. Whatever I do, I do for Elliot Chamille."

She frowned in the darkness. "Why are you telling me this?"

"Because I want there to be no deception between us. To you, our cause is a sacred thing. To me, it's a means of getting back an existence I grew uncomfortably used to."

She shook her head wonderingly. "I believe I'm seeing you for the very first time."

He looked as if the moment of disclosure had been a purifying experience, a ritual unburdening in which everything—the ugly, the sad, the secret, the contemptible—had been exposed in one cauterizing outpour.

"Now at last, maybe we're beginning to get somewhere," he said.

Sitting at McAuley's bedside, Harry heard the murmur of voices from the room downstairs. It was the farmer and his wife eating supper under the watchful eye of Timol and Malheiro. Beside him, McAuley lay on top of the fluffy eiderdown, his body wrapped in a thick wool blanket. McAuley's cheeks were gray and there were dark shadows under his deeply sunken eyes. Though no murmur of complaint passed his lips, Harry knew he had found the long day's ride excruciating. Harry had to admit he admired McAuley. Despite the pain he'd suffered, the little South African had maintained an air of quiet defiance. Not once had he fallen behind, though Harry was willing to bet that without the injury, they would have found him quite a handful. McAuley was nobody's weakling, tough as stamped steel.

McAuley shifted under the blanket, and his tongue crept out to moisten his narrow lips. "Can you smell something?" he murmured in a hoarse voice.

Harry frowned and breathed in deeply. "Smoke."

"Outside or inside?"

"It's coming from the hills. It's the forest fire."

McAuley grunted. "Must be getting closer."

He lay for a moment, staring at the ceiling rafters, his pale face glistening with sweat. "I was in a bush fire once, in Natal. I never want to be in another."

"Don't worry, it's not like Africa here. This forest has been built from scratch. Firebreaks, water tanks. They'll get things under control."

McAuley laughed dryly. "You know what wind does to blazing timber? Spreads it everywhere. Your firebreaks won't do a damned bit of good. The flames will simply leap across."

"At least it'll give the army something to think about."

"A forest fire takes no sides," McAuley whispered. "When the land's ablaze, there's only one enemy, and it kills and maims indiscriminately."

"Why don't you tell that to Elliot Chamille? I didn't start this madness."

McAuley looked at him, frowning. "I was wondering what you were doing here, Mr. Fuller. You're not like the others. You're more . . ." He paused.

"Selfish?" Harry prompted.

"I was going to say sensible."

Harry laughed humorlessly. "Well, they forced me into it, kidnapped my boy."

"I see."

"That's not strictly true," Harry admitted after a moment. "I do have a personal interest."

"The lady?" McAuley chuckled. "I'm not blind,

Mr. Fuller. I've seen the way you two look at each other. I also watched you attack Mr. Chamille today. You were jealous. I believe you are jealous still."

"Kate and I used to live together. A long time ago. It wasn't exactly an overwhelming success."

"What happened?"

"We couldn't get along. Different personalities, I suppose. Kate was into everything in sight, any cause—you name it—she'd be out there, marching, demonstrating."

"And you?"

Harry shrugged. "Life's too short. I'm damned if I'll walk around in sackcloth and ashes because of injustices that had nothing to do with me in the first place."

"You don't believe, then, in getting involved?"

"Absolutely not."

McAuley was silent for a moment. Some of the anguish had gone from his cheeks. In the light from the little bedside lamp, his face looked calmer, steadier. "I believe she's still in love with you," he said at last.

"I doubt that. She needs somebody far more exciting. I'm stuck in a rut, about as interesting as a block of wood. I find things like railways romantic. Do you know anything about railways, Mr. McAuley?"

McAuley shook his head, watching Harry intently.

"When I was a boy, I thought there was nothing in the world as captivating as a railway. Of course, they were different then. No diesels, no electrics. Nothing but steam."

Harry peered at the ceiling, where cobwebs, cluttering the rafters, picked up nuances of refracted light. "What a sight they made, those old locomo-

tives. You can't imagine what it was like to watch the
West Coast Postal Special thundering through Carlisle at sundown, or the Caledonian Express hitting
the northbound ascent of Grayrigg Bank. I can remember, like it was yesterday, the Royal Train, with
two Class 5's, one behind the other, crossing Hugh's
Crag viaduct, sixty feet above the River Lowther. It's
a different world now. A different age."

"And Miss Whitmore couldn't understand that?"

"I believe she thought I was crazy."

"But you must have had something in common."

"Well, we liked music." Harry hesitated, looking
embarrassed. "I play the cello," he added.

McAuley looked surprised. "Really?"

"I realize I don't exactly look the type, but it's a
funny thing; when I'm feeling bad, when I've done
something I know I shouldn't, I pick up that instrument and it washes me clean like water."

"You're a lucky man, Mr. Fuller. You're not like
a block of wood at all."

Harry stared at the opposite wall. "Last night, I
hated Kate. I felt she'd committed the unpardonable
sin, threatened the most important thing in my life. I
wanted revenge more than anything in the world.
Then . . ." He pulled a face. "I saw the marines at
the hospital, and for one terrible moment, the idea
hit me that she might actually get killed. That's what
I realized. It wasn't hate I felt at all."

"Emotion can be the damnedest thing. No sense
or reason to it. No logic, either," McAuley said.
"However, I'd watch out for that black man, if I were
you. A most unusual fellow, Elliot Chamille. American, isn't he?"

"I wouldn't know."

"He's not from the Homelands, certainly. I wonder why he's fighting for the ANC? His color, do you think?"

"Good a reason as any."

"In which case, he's a fool. He's destroyed the greatest chance his people have had since the declaration of South African independence."

Harry frowned. Something in McAuley's reasoning irritated him. "Maybe he doesn't see it that way. You're offering to dismantle apartheid, but you're insisting on doing it on your own terms. Men like Chamille, they're not prepared to wait. They want their freedom now. Not next year, not next month, not next week. Now."

McAuley sighed. "Have you ever tried reasoning with the South African *Broederbond*, Mr. Fuller? It's taken me years to get my proposals accepted, and just when I'm on the brink of success, the entire project is jeopardized by a bunch of idiots who imagine they're acting in the interest of African nationalism."

"Maybe they think you're planning to sell them down the river," Harry said.

"With compromise? With civilized debate? Is that your concept of treachery, Mr. Fuller? Look at the alternative, man. Revolution and bloodshed."

"Maybe it's too late to talk about compromise and civilized debate. Maybe after centuries of exploitation and genocide, there's only one answer left. Elliot Chamille doesn't give a damn about your talks. He sees them as a desperate attempt to gain time when you know bloody well time has already run out. You can't fight the people, McAuley. What's happening in South Africa is like that fire raging out there. It's getting bigger, hotter, wilder. One day it'll consume you all."

In the room downstairs, somebody turned on a television set. They heard the introductory music to the ITN news. "It seems to me," McAuley said gently, "that for a man who doesn't believe in getting involved, you display an extraordinary degree of righteous indignation."

Harry didn't answer for a moment. He was thinking precisely the same thing himself.

Twelve

Something woke Kate in the early hours of morning. Smoke, harsh, pungent, nostril-prickling, filled the room like a suffocating vapor. Rising to her feet, she tugged open the farmhouse window, her heart thumping as she glimpsed, beyond the nearby hill, a coppery glow illuminating the western sky. Flashes lit the shadowy cloud formations, turning them into a fluctuation of light and shade. It was like watching a battle on some distant continent.

Hurriedly, Kate tugged on her parka and ran into the next room. Elliot and De Brere lay draped on separate beds, sleeping peacefully. She switched on the electric light and shook Elliot by the shoulder.

"We've got to get out of here," she snapped. "The fire's practically at the door."

He blinked, struggling to fix his gaze and focus, then into his face crept the same strange aura of fear she had witnessed the evening before.

It was De Brere who recovered first. Struggling to his feet, he flung open the bedroom window and peered at the blazing sky. "Jesus," he muttered.

"We must escape now," Kate said, "before the flames reach the farmhouse."

Picking up his watch, Elliot strapped it to his

wrist, sweat beading his skin. "Where are Malheiro and Timol?"

"Standing guard."

"And the farmer?"

"Sleeping, I think. He's in the parlor, with his wife."

They clattered downstairs, flinging open the parlor door. The farm couple lay on separate sofas, Malheiro and Timol in armchairs nearby. At Elliot's appearance, everyone sat up.

"Fire's gaining," Elliot announced. "We have to get out of here. Is there a car in the garage?"

The farmer nodded.

"Take your wife and drive clear of the timber. Don't stop until you reach the nearest village."

"And us?" Kate asked.

"We'll use the horses."

Kate hesitated. "Is that wise?"

"God knows, but we'll have to risk it. Fire or no fire, the trees are the only cover we've got."

Fifteen minutes later, the first slivers of gray flickered across the morning sky as, picking their way in single file, they guided their horses into the encroaching woodland.

Maurice Southwick, duty fire forester, paused in his digging and stared at the blinding wall confronting him. In a few short hours, the blaze had stampeded across the timbered hillslopes with a speed and ferocity he would never have believed possible. The roar of crackling woodland, the screech of tumbling tree trunks, the frenzied explosions as the flames leapt into fresh stands of foliage was like a continuous barrage, stultifying his senses. The wind roared around his head, swirling into a dizzy vortex as oxygen was sucked into the furnace's heart. Great globs of soot-blackened earth had begun to show in the middle of the holocaust where the fire, having consumed every living thing in sight, was spreading outward in its furious search for fresh fuel. Clad in protective clothing and headgear, Southwick's men labored hand in hand with the fire brigades and the Royal Marines, hacking at the earth, clearing out the underbrush, using bulldozers and power saws to open up the firebreaks. But through the long spring night the fire raged inexorably on, feeding relentlessly on its own fury, maiming the landscape, scorching the topsoil, incinerating everything in sight. Like a crimson stain, it trickled across the helpless countryside, sometimes curling back on itself, picking up the slack as it rediscovered fresh areas of sustenance and nourishment. A blanketing pall of smoke hovered eerily above, blotting out the night sky.

Helicopter pilots, braving the hazards of the flames, used the glow to guide them as they homed in over the surrounding plantations, dropping tank-loads of anti-incendiary foam. Fire teams, smoke-grimed and sweating, toiled through the long hours of darkness, hacking out gaps across the hillslopes and bombarding the blaze with water jets. But still the fire, like a writhing, scavenging army, pushed them steadily backward, consuming everything which lay in its path.

In the early hours of the morning, Maurice Southwick, wiping a forearm across his sweaty cheeks, watched dismayed as the flames scuttled up a narrow gully, taking hold on a fresh stand of timber. He groaned. "We've lost it again. Call control and tell them the fire's broken loose. It's out of Section 16 and stampeding south toward Burnt Tom

and Muckle Knowe. Ask for more men, more tenders, more bulldozers, more water. We'll need all the
support we can get if we hope to hold it at the river."

Kate straightened angrily in the saddle. She'd
almost fallen asleep, she realized, would have if her
horse hadn't stumbled. How humiliating it would
have been if she'd tumbled inelegantly into the dust.
Malheiro rode at their head, spruce boughs brushing
his shoulders, sprinkling his parka with tiny needles. Above, the sun was lifting rapidly, but amid the
tree rows the gloom still lingered. They were all
tired, drained to the point of exhaustion, and no
wonder; the long hours of flight, the fevered knowledge that at their rear the fire was slowly, ruthlessly
advancing, had had a debilitating effect on their
senses. She glimpsed something gleaming through
the darkness and frowned, narrowing her eyes. A
river. A cry of thankfulness broke from Kate's lips as
her chestnut, scenting the moisture ahead, scuttled
unbidden down the steep clay bank and into the
cool, life-imbibing water, plunging its nose beneath
the rippling surface. Kate eased herself out of the
stirrups, scarcely caring as the chill liquid filled her
boots, rising above her knees. She leaned forward,
splashing it over her face and neck.

The others were all around her, wallowing with
unrestrained gratitude and delight. Malheiro had sat
down, fully clothed, and was leaning back, gasping,
the current swirling around his ears.

Elliot knelt in the shallows, filling his empty
canteen. His heavy parka was stained with mud, and
at a point where a spruce bough had ripped away the
pocket, wads of padding material poked inelegantly
through. Face swollen, chin stubbled, Elliot was

practically unrecognizable as the handsome black man who had brought them from Mozambique.

His eyes flickered in the glow of the approaching flames as he studied his companions shrewdly. "We'd better rest. The horses are finished, and so are we. It'll be hours before the fire can reach us here. We'll take it in turns to grab some sleep."

Kate felt a flood of relief. She seemed in some kind of stupor, as if her body and mind had separated, taking on identities of their own. Even the chill of the water failed to infuse her with any true sense of life.

De Brere grunted. "This place reminds me of somewhere. The reformatory where I grew up, there was a river like this. We used to swim there on summer evenings."

Harry leaned back against a rock, his features slack with weariness.

"It's called Blood River," he said. "There was a battle here once, in the 1500s. Scots and English."

"Who won?"

"English, I think. They say the waters ran crimson with blood."

"How come you know so much?" demanded De Brere.

"I fish here sometimes, in the summer."

Elliot eyed him curiously. "Did you say Blood River?"

Harry nodded, and Elliot's lips twisted into a humorless grin.

"What's so funny?" Harry queried.

"Ask McAuley."

Hunched on a rock, McAuley looked devastated. His cheeks had sunken during the night, accentuating the hollows of his skull.

"Tell them, McAuley," Elliot prompted. "Tell them about Blood River."

"There's a Blood River in South Africa too," McAuley said with a sigh. "It was also the site of a great battle. Three thousand Zulus died on its banks, slaughtered by the Voortrekkers. It marked the birth of the Afrikaaner consciousness, the most sacred event in their history. Every year, on December sixteenth, on what is now called the Day of the Covenant, the faithful gather to give thanks for their conquest over the black man. You might say Blood River has become a symbol of Afrikaanerdom."

"That's history, McAuley," Elliot said, tugging off his boots and dipping his feet into the river. "I'm talking about the present. Tell them what Blood River means today. Tell them about Option 24."

Kate saw McAuley flinch. She frowned, sensing something she didn't understand.

Elliot chuckled deep in his throat. "Did you think I didn't know? My dear minister, Matshoba's imprisonment is not the only injustice we're fighting here."

"I haven't the faintest idea of what you're talking about."

"What *is* Option 24?" Kate demanded, puzzled.

"It's a little clause which Mr. McAuley and his friends dreamed up. An integral part of the PAC talk negotiations. Quite ingenious, really. They intend to establish a new settlement on the island of Ulithi in the South Atlantic, a settlement which will one day become a city, the city of Blood River. It's all been mapped out, schools, hospitals, waterworks, apartment blocks, even a railroad. It'll be a new Brasília, all done with the full knowledge and cooperation of the British and U.S. governments."

Kate felt her puzzlement deepening. She could

see by McAuley's face the disclosure had some major significance, but she couldn't for the life of her distinguish why. "What will be the purpose of this new city?" she asked.

"It will be a center for Afrikaanerdom, based on the sacred principles of the *Broederbond*," McAuley explained. "You must understand that fear of the black is rooted in the deepest corner of the Afrikaaner's psyche. It dates back to the days when Dingane's Zulus slaughtered the party of Piet Retief, men, women, and children alike, in the Drakensberg foothills. Since then, the Afrikaaner has been obsessed with the belief that one day he will be overrun by black people. What we are doing is offering a bolt-hole to those who wish to leave, a new society, a sacred sanctuary in which their culture may be preserved."

Elliot laughed sourly. "You're quite a talker, McAuley. Very persuasive. I can see how convincing you must be at the conference table. Now tell them the true purpose of Blood River. Tell them how the city will be financed."

McAuley's lips tightened and he stared silently into the slithering current.

"What lies at the heart of South Africa's life-blood?" Elliot demanded. "What is the one thing that's kept her stable all these years? Despite sanctions, despite international condemnation, what gives the rand its credibility, ensures South Africa's economic survival?"

"Gold?" Kate suggested.

"Precisely. Gold. Gold extracted from the Witwatersrand Basin. Gold has provided a financial bulwark for generations, sustaining economic confidence in the fluctuating money markets. South Africa produces more gold than any country on earth.

Its goldfields extend over four hundred and eighty kilometers in the Transvaal and Orange Free State. In 1970, at the height of its output capacity, the country mined nearly thirty-six million ounces, compared with a paltry seven million weighed in by its nearest rival, the Soviet Union."

Elliot shuffled up the riverbank and sat rubbing his feet vigorously. His eyes gleamed in the early morning. "South Africa's bullion stocks are kept in high-security vaults near Johannesburg," he said. "The men responsible for its welfare are members of the *Broederbond*. They intend using those bullion stocks to finance the new Afrikaner settlement. And that's not all. During the next few years, while apartheid is gradually phased out of existence, they intend smuggling out steady consignments of bullion and transporting them to a new depository to be built at Blood River. By the time a real transfer of power becomes a viable possibility, a large proportion of South Africa's gold supplies will lie firmly in *Broederbond* hands."

They stared at him in silence, struggling to make sense of the disclosure. He looked at them with exasperation. "You still don't see it, do you? Since the beginning of time, gold has fascinated mankind. That shiny metal has attracted artists from every civilization in history. Examples of gold workmanship have been discovered on ancient Egyptian, Minoan, Assyrian, and Etruscan archaeological sites. The craft of chemistry came into being because alchemists in the Middle Ages tried to convert other metals into gold. Practically all the gold ever mined is still in circulation today, and that's what makes its value so mercurial. If the *Broederbond* can salt away enough, they can affect gold prices throughout the world by simply withholding their stocks or flooding the market."

"Why would they do that?" Kate asked.

"Because it won't matter a damn who takes over power in South Africa. Since it's gold which underpins the country's economy, the *Broederbond* will still be in a position to influence government policies by exerting economic pressures South Africa will be unable to resist."

Kate felt the air whistle from her lungs. The audacity of the idea stunned her.

"He's making it sound like some kind of crime," McAuley said. "There's nothing dishonest about it at all. It's simple common sense. No one's suggesting government decision-making could be impeded in any material sense, but at least white South Africans would have an option, a lever, and what's wrong with that? They've poured their blood into that country, and they deserve some kind of safeguard, some kind of insurance. Besides, if they knew there was a powerful pressure group representing their interests, they might be more sympathetic to the concept of democracy."

"But that gold belongs to the African people," Kate breathed.

McAuley gave an impatient gesture. "The gold itself is unimportant. What matters is the power it wields. And the black man will still have what he's always asked for. Equality."

Kate felt her temper rising. The insidiousness of the scheme outraged her. Nothing changed, she thought. Governments, people, it all came down to the same thing in the end. Power and self-interest.

She rose to her feet, balancing herself against the rippling current.

"Listen to that fire, McAuley," she whispered.

"Listen to it crackling and snapping. It's feeding on itself, gathering strength and momentum with every minute that passes. We can't stop it, because it's unstoppable. It's creeping up like some kind of insatiable beast. The struggle for democracy is like that. No matter what you do, it'll sweep you off and carry you away. Your little scheme will never work, because we're going to tell the world about Option 24, and perhaps in time, when Joshua Matshoba has been released, this Blood River will become a symbol too. Of a new South African consciousness, a new culture." Her eyes glittered in the lifting sunlight. "A culture of freedom," she breathed fiercely. "A culture of the people."

Thirteen

Karel Van Brero stood in the corridor, outside Cape Town's House of Assembly and waited impatiently for the South African president's appearance. The meeting had lasted for over two hours, which Van Brero considered a bad sign, since it showed the delegates were undecided, whereas Van Brero had hoped—counted—on the fact that no self-respecting Parliamentary member would countenance the proposal the president was offering. The news of McAuley's kidnapping had sent a shock wave through the party's elite, since apart from the president himself and a handful of trusted confidantes, few had any idea the PAC talk negotiations were even in progress. Van Brero had hoped their exposure might bring the matter to a head, but he regarded the protracted conference as an ominous sign, for it showed the delicate balance of argument and debate was afoot.

Van Brero straightened as the cabinet room door opened suddenly and the MPs came strolling out. He eyed them worriedly, but it was impossible to judge from their expressions which way the meeting had gone, and he had to wait until the president appeared, his eyes filled with the exhausted look of a man who had pushed himself to the limit to defend, or justify, some dangerous but necessary course of áction. Van Brero moved toward him, tension knotting in his stomach. "How did it go, *menheer*?"

The president took his arm, shepherding him along the narrow corridor, his manner friendly, almost paternal. "We have decided, in view of the circumstances, to release Joshua Matshoba."

The walls seemed to ripple in Van Brero's vision. He was shaken by a sense of anger and disbelief. "You can't be serious! Joshua Matshoba is a dangerous revolutionary."

"At sixty-eight? I doubt that. In the name of humanity, we should allow him to spend the rest of his days with his family. A small concession, Karel, setting free one helpless old man."

"You are making a terrible mistake, *menheer*. You simply cannot negotiate with these people."

"We must try to learn. I've told you before, the old ways are over."

"But how do we know McAuley is still alive? We are dealing with terrorists, fanatics. Release Matshoba, and you could be signing McAuley's death warrant."

"That's possible, but unlikely. By murdering McAuley, the ANC would destroy their credibility before the entire world. On the other hand, if we release Matshoba, we'll be making a gesture—a small one perhaps, but a gesture at least—of our willingness to compromise."

"The ANC isn't interested in compromise," Van Brero insisted. "They want total and absolute power."

The minister patted him gently on the arm. "What we're doing is right, Karel. Right for South Africa, right for humanity. One day you'll understand that."

He paused as they stepped through the door to

the open terrace. At the foot of the steps, a small party of security men, members of Van Brero's diplomatic department, hovered near the president's limousine.

"Menheer," Van Brero said, "what about the SS *Arcadia*?"

The president frowned. "The *Arcadia*?"

"She's still at sea, and without a military escort. Shouldn't she return to harbor? As long as McAuley's a prisoner, she's in considerable danger."

"I doubt that. Besides, if everything goes according to plan, I want the PAC talks to proceed as arranged."

"But if things *don't* go according to plan, if the kidnappers execute their prisoner, what then?"

The president looked at him remonstratively. "You have no faith in human nature, Karel."

"I am a policeman, menheer. I have learned from bitter experience to anticipate the unexpected. I took the precaution of recalling the *Arcadia* the minute we received the news from England. She is standing offshore at this moment, awaiting permission to reenter port."

The president's face darkened. He glared at Van Brero with a mixture of anger and indignation. "You had no right to issue such an order."

"Exceptional circumstances demand exceptional measures. As head of security, I had to exercise my own judgment."

"You've overexceeded your authority, Karel. The *Arcadia* must continue to her destination at once."

"Menheer, if anything happens to McAuley, we'll find ourselves in an untenable position. The ship should be held in tight security until the crisis has been resolved."

The president's eyes flashed dangerously, and his skin looked mottled beneath its carefully toned suntan. Rarely had the police chief seen him so enraged.

"If McAuley dies, then—and only then—you may recall the *Arcadia*. Until that happens, she is to continue her voyage undisturbed, is that understood?"

Van Brero bowed his head in acknowledgment as the president strode down the staircase and climbed into the waiting car.

Through the long hours of darkness and into the grayness of the early dawn, the great fire raged on relentlessly. Though the teams battled to halt its advance, the flames, with each fragmentary success, pulsed off in different directions, and by daylight the fire crews, drained, weary, physically exhausted, were beginning to concede defeat was staring them in the face. The forest, which had been regarded as among the safest in Europe, carefully laid and administrated to keep the risk of conflagration to a minimum, had proved, through a series of bizarre circumstances, to be a seething holocaust when the unthinkable happened. RAF helicopters roared through the chill spring night, spraying the foliage with fire-retardant chemicals, but as morning approached, the wind began to intensify, accelerating the blaze's progress until at last the crews were ordered to beat a hasty retreat. As dawn broke, the fire began to race uphill, creating its own updraft and consuming gullies and toplands alike. While the fire crews, using powerful bulldozers, labored desperately to widen the break gaps, the flame-induced winds reached hurricane proportions, ripping out entire plantations of spruce, and blazing brands, sucked into the air, danced on the searing convection currents, leaping across the open spaces. In the first gray light of day, the fire front, now several miles wide and accompanied by tumultuous whirlwinds, was hurtling across the summits of Stower Hill and Jock's Pike. It was impossible to estimate how many acres of woodland had been decimated, for above the entire area black smoke had formed a breathless canopy, shutting out the sun. But first reports put the figure at nearly fifteen thousand.

As the morning lengthened and the sun climbed higher, fire chiefs used helicopters to hover over the blaze and map out possible areas of advancement. They decided to bomb the flames directly from the air. "Bambi-buckets" were used, large plastic containers slung on chains beneath the helicopter fuselages; trailing the buckets below them, they skimmed over the surface of Kielder Reservoir (weighted with lead, the buckets tilted forward, scooping up water as they progressed) then the pilots braved the hurricane-force winds, ferrying their hundred-gallon water bombs into the fire's heart and discharging them by releasing the electronic suction valves. The maneuver proved hazardous in the extreme, for not only were the rotor blades dangerously susceptible to the strong updrafts of heated air, but the swirling smoke made visibility practically nonexistent. Just before ten, a pilot, disoriented by the fumes, lost control as he hovered close to the burning hillside, and horrified spectators saw his machine spin to starboard, crashing headlong into the blazing timber. Miraculously, the man survived, plucked into the air by a companion helicopter, its copilot dangling on a cable from the aircraft's hatchway. However, fire chiefs decided to call a halt to the water-bombing technique, and by eleven o'clock that morning the great column of smoke, now nearly twenty thousand feet high, could be seen as far away as Edinburgh, Newcastle, and Carlisle as, tireless and insatiable, the fire continued its inexorable rampage southward.

The village looked strange in the drifting woodsmoke. It was hardly a pretty place, Kate thought vaguely. The houses, squatting in rows around a central, neatly mowed green, looked too austere, too functional to be classed as visually appealing, but it was not the grimness which puzzled her, it was the utter lack of people.

The fugitives came out of the trees, leading their horses wearily, the animals on the brink of exhaustion. At first, the scent of the fumes had driven them half crazy with terror, but that too had passed, and now, bodies limp and submissive, they clattered along in a passive convoy, happy to be free of their burdens at last.

Kate still hadn't got over Elliot's revelation in the forest. The sheer deviousness of Option 24 made their own petty crusade seem somehow pointless and trivial. What was one man's freedom against the future of an entire race? she thought. The South African *Broederbond* had outwitted them every step of the way.

As they neared the village, the little group of fugitives peered in puzzlement at the silent implacable house fronts. The village store loomed out of the fog, and Elliot, frowning, handed his reins to De Brere and tugged gently at the door. It was locked. "What time is it?" he asked.

"Nearly ten-thirty."

"Should be open by now."

He rattled loudly on the glass panel. There was no response. Suddenly Kate understood. "The village has been evacuated. It's the fire."

They stared about them, noting the sealed windows, the lack of movement or activity. It was like some kind of nightmare, Kate thought, the air of fantasy emphasized by drifting spirals of woodsmoke.

Elliot rubbed his face with his hands. He looked almost at the end of his tether. "Turn loose the horses."

"What're we going to do for transport, soldier?" De Brere wondered.

"Nothing. We're finished with running."

Kate frowned. "We're staying here?"

"Good a place as any."

"You realize the village is an obvious landmark? The security forces are bound to check it sooner or later."

"We're dead on our feet. The animals too. We can't move another step."

Staring into his face, Kate longed to put her arms around him, draw him close, offer him comfort and assurance. "Oh, Elliot," she breathed, "I'm sorry."

"What the hell, we gave them a good run for their money."

"Maybe they'll free Matshoba anyhow. Maybe, when they see the strength of world opinion, they'll have a change of heart."

He smiled, ruffling her hair with his fingers.

"You don't really believe that."

She shook her head, choking.

"I want you to look after McAuley. Break into one of the houses and make him as comfortable as you can."

"What about you?" she asked.

"We'll stay here. We've got things to do. Prepare."

Something in Elliot's manner disturbed her. She felt a sudden surge of alarm. "You're not planning to fight?"

There was no change in Elliot's features, nothing she could put a name to, but watching him at that moment, she knew—knew beyond any shadow of doubt—that her intuition had been correct.

"They've seen enough of our backs," he told her calmly. "I thought we might show them our faces for a change."

Panic swept her. "You can't take on the whole British army, you idiot. They'll wipe you out to a man."

She couldn't believe what was happening here, she couldn't believe the senseless stupidity of it all, the asinine waste.

Elliot reached out, holding her gently by the shoulders. He could do that, dominate her by simple physical contact. She recalled his power at the hospital, the way his touch had infused her with new vitality, new strength.

"You'll be safe in one of the houses," he said. "Take Fuller with you. He doesn't belong here. You can come out after it's over."

Tears sprang to Kate's eyes, rolling down the steep curve of her cheeks. He looked so handsome suddenly, despite his bruised jaw, despite his tired eyes. And she loved him. Loved him for what he was. "What are you trying to prove, that you're not afraid to die? Will it help Joshua Matshoba, throwing your lives away?"

"It'll show the world how much we're prepared to sacrifice in the name of freedom," Elliot told her softly.

"Freedom," she sobbed. "Freedom's nothing but a word. You wouldn't recognize freedom if you saw it walking down the street."

Suddenly it came flooding out of her. She couldn't stop herself. It was as if she had reached a point where time hung suspended, where only truth remained—an ugly truth, sad, tawdry, contemptible. "It doesn't exist," she shouted. "Can't you understand that? There is no freedom. There's only power, greed, corruption, that's what keeps the human race going. Self-interest is the real motivating force, not great causes and noble sacrifices."

She scarcely knew what she was saying anymore. All she could think about was this fine compassionate man throwing his life away on some futile heroic gesture. It brought a chill to her heart, a sickness to her stomach.

Oh Elliot, she thought. She hadn't realized how strongly she felt about him, had been confused by the demands of the moment, and, of course, by the presence of Harry—dear, lovable, prickly Harry. "Don't do it," she choked. "Please don't."

Reaching out, Elliot ran his fingers gently down her cheek. "Look after McAuley. He's beginning to wilt."

It was clear nothing in the world would change Elliot's mind. He was as stubborn as Harry when he had a mind to be. Some things you couldn't stop, she thought, no matter how hard you tried. Things people did. You just had to go along, accept, compromise. Especially with a man like Elliot.

Whimpering, she took McAuley's arm, shepherding him toward the empty housefronts, Harry following at her heels. It seemed such a tragic, indefensible waste. If Elliot died, what would the movement gain? Another forgotten martyr, another

name on the roll of death, while the world would
have lost an extraordinary and remarkable man.

They reached the buildings and Harry smashed
one of the windows, reaching in to slip off the catch.
The house was small, nicely furnished, pleasantly
maintained. Harry helped McAuley into an armchair
while Kate opened her medical kit and rummaged
tearfully inside. When she removed the minister's
dressing, she saw that constant friction had caused
the bleeding to start again. The surgical pads were
coated with a thin yellowish pus, while McAuley
himself seemed almost beyond awareness; he lay
with his head against the seat cushions, his cheeks
molded macabrely around the contours of his skull.
She redressed the wound as skillfully as she could,
Harry watching, his smoke-grimed face etched with
fatigue. "He's quite a character, that black man of
yours," he said.

"He's a fool," she growled. "He's making a
gesture, that's all. A stupid and irresponsible one."

"He's doing it for the cause, isn't he? Justice,
equality, all that rubbish."

"It has nothing to do with the cause. It's pointless and irrational. Life is real, it's precious. It's not
something you throw away for the sake of some
tinpot idea dreamed up by politicians."

Harry's lips twisted into a crooked grin. "At last
you're beginning to understand."

"I always did understand," she snapped fiercely.
"It's not me who's doing the dying. Now shut up,
damn you, I don't want to discuss it anymore."

Rising to her feet, she switched on the radio. She
wanted to stop the argument, stop everything, including the workings of her own mind. The voice of
the newscaster filled the room. ". . . according to
the Forestry Commission, cattle and livestock are

being evacuated as a precautionary measure. Official sources say the fire is causing damage estimated at billions of pounds.

"Meanwhile, the search continues for Howard McAuley, the kidnapped South African foreign minister believed to be somewhere within the forest area. And within the last few minutes, we've received an unconfirmed report from our correspondent in Pretoria that South Africa has agreed to the kidnappers' demands for the release of Joshua Matshoba. At noon today, he's being transferred from Robben Island prison near Cape Town and flown by special plane to Lusaka, Angola."

Kate stared at the set, a sudden breathlessness gathering in her diaphragm. She looked at Harry wildly. "Did you hear that?"

Harry nodded. "You've won."

"Not yet," she breathed, elation driving away the tiredness inside her. "We haven't won yet, but by God we're going to. Come on, give me a hand with McAuley."

Wrestling the minister between them, they steered him into the crisp morning air. Kate spotted Elliot and De Brere crouching with the two Africans behind a dry-stone wall. "They're turning Matshoba loose," she cried. "We just heard it on the radio. They're flying him to Angola at noon today."

Silence. Shouldn't Elliot be delirious at that? Kate thought. For God's sake, why didn't he react?

De Brere grinned, his eyes suddenly bright and alert. "Hey soldier, if we can keep McAuley loose for a few hours longer, we'll have done it."

Elliot stared at him with no expression on his face.

"What happened to the horses?" Kate asked.

"We let them go," De Brere told her. "But don't worry, we can still ride out in style."

He ran to a parked truck and, throwing back the hood, leaned forward to connect the leads. Kate heard a splutter as the engine roared into life. Still, Elliot made no move. His features looked unnaturally tense, his skin stretched taut across the bony prominences of his cheeks. Suddenly he reached beneath his jacket, tugging his pistol from its leather holster. Kate stared at him in astonishment. "What are you doing?"

Moving with an almost casual grace, Elliot trained his weapon on Timol and Malheiro. "Drop your guns on the ground," he ordered.

Neither man moved. They stared back at Elliot in bewilderment. Elliot fired at the pavement, the bullet ricocheting upward among the eddying smoke, and without a word the two Africans drew out their pistols, throwing them obediently into the gutter.

De Brere, startled by the shot, groped under his combat jacket, but aiming his pistol directly at the Englishman's throat, Elliot said in a calm, clear voice, "Touch it and you're dead meat."

De Brere hesitated.

"Drop it with the others."

De Brere did as he was ordered, staring into Elliot's face. Kate felt as if the world were tilting out of alignment, plunging them into a vacuum where everything familiar had become distorted and unrecognizable. De Brere was smiling, she noticed, a bleak, bitter smile, filled with a strange, ironic awareness.

"De Brere, what's going on?" she stammered.

"Can't you figure it out? Our friend Major Chamille here is a BOSS agent."

A shock ran through Kate's limbs. She stared at De Brere, thunderstruck. "You're insane."

"Look at his face, for Christ's sake."

Elliot's features had become a stone wall, cold and implacable. Gone was the handsome young black man Kate had worshiped and admired.

"It was Major bloody Chamille who brought us the PAC documents in the first place," De Brere declared, spitting on the ground. "He probably got them direct from Karel Van Brero."

"No," she croaked. "It isn't true. Tell me it isn't true."

Silence.

"Tell me," she shouted.

Elliot sighed. "I didn't promise you a hero. I warned you what I really am."

Oh God, what a fool she'd been. What a stupid, unreasoning fool. She felt hollowed out inside, conscious of a strange and bitter anger directed not so much at Elliot as at her own naïveté.

"Why?" she whispered. "Why, why, why?"

De Brere grunted. "He's trying to sabotage the PAC talks. Karel Van Brero would do his damnedest to stop any negotiations on the future of apartheid."

"Even to the extent of kidnapping his own foreign minister?"

"If McAuley dies, it'll prove to any would-be moderates in South Africa the ANC is not to be trusted. It'll also prove to the rest of the world the movement is nothing more than a ruthless terrorist organization. Van Brero gets two bites at the cherry. He ruins the talks and discredits the ANC."

A chill gathered in Kate's stomach and she felt her legs turn rubbery. Why was she always staggered by the treachery of others? She could have taken anything where Elliot was concerned, but not this.

His deception had turned her ideals into a mockery.

If Elliot was conscious of her outrage, he gave no indication. His face looked savage and uncompromising. "Move over to the truck," he ordered.

Gathering in a group, they glared back sullenly, willing him to lower the pistol, capitulate, admit this bizarre confrontation had been nothing more than a tasteless joke. But Elliot didn't capitulate. His eyes watched their every move like chinks of frosted glass.

"Sit on the ground."

They obeyed in silence, leaning against the truck's vibrating hull.

"What happens now?" Kate asked, her senses reeling.

Elliot settled himself against the dry-stone wall, the pistol resting across his folded forearm, his face cool and expressionless.

"We wait," he said softly. "We just wait, that's all."

The roar of the helicopter echoed in Waldo's eardrums. From his position strapped against the bulkwark, it was just possible to discern dancing columns of flame twisting and cavorting among the foliage below, but the true extent of the fire was difficult to conceive from the air, for the entire area had been obliterated by the awesome smoke canopy.

The pilot banked, swinging southward, and Waldo gave a gasp as he glimpsed the devastation stretching across the skyline. In the fire's wake, a desert of ash and cinder littered the landscape as far as the eye could see.

Waldo felt the helicopter jolt as the pilot brought his machine to a hover and slowly, delicately settled in a clearing at the side of the logging road. Tugging at his seat belt, Palmer ducked through the hatch into the open air, and Waldo followed, blinking as the fierce heat stung his eyes, making them water.

On a narrow loading bay, fire engines had been drawn into a haphazard circle, protective sheets stretched between them, forming a makeshift tent from which the fire chief, like a military general, could coordinate his troops. The man was snapping out commands as Waldo and Palmer entered, his dirty face displaying the harrowing truth of his nightlong conflict.

Palmer introduced himself, and the fire chief— relieved, Waldo guessed, to have someone of authority to unburden to—outlined graphically the fire's progress and his crews' attempts to bring it under control. "We've got one chance," he explained. "The wind's changing direction, and according to the Met office is scheduled to drop in an hour or two. We failed to hold the fire at Blood River, but just south of there lies Blackcleugh Sill, a natural fault in the earth's crust. It's a line of high cliffs tracing the rim of Saughtree Lake. If we can turn the fire toward the clifftop, it'll have nowhere else to go. Without the wind, it'll be impossible for the flames to crown, and even if the sparks are carried on their own air currents, they'll have to jump the full width of the lake to reach fresh foliage."

"How will you do it?" Palmer asked.

The fire chief hesitated. He seemed faintly embarrassed, as if the idea was too preposterous for words. "We're going to set the woodland ablaze, and hope the wind currents carry the flames toward the clifftop. If they do, we'll link up our own conflagration with the main fire."

Taking off his helmet, he wiped one hand across

his sweaty forehead; the movement left a smear of dirt against his smoke-grimed skin. He looked like a man to whom optimism seemed an undreamed-of luxury. "It's a chance in a million, I know, and everything depends upon the Met boys getting their calculations right, but if we can back the fire on to Blackcleugh Sill, maybe we can just sit tight and wait until it burns itself out."

Fourteen

Tazelaar saw the village emerging through the smoke. The silent buildings carried an air of abandonment and desolation, and suddenly he guessed the reason. Evacuation. The inhabitants had been moved out, the fire was drawing too close.

He was beginning to regret his impetuousness in spreading the blaze. It had been a momentary inspiration, wrought by the need of the moment. He had seen the fire as an ally, shutting off the escape route to his rear. Now it seemed like some predator creeping remorselessly at their heels. He felt ready to drop from exhaustion and fatigue. The endless hours without sleep were causing his brain to hallucinate. That was what happened, they said, when the body was deprived of slumber—the mind turned in on itself, producing illusory images to replace the awful truth of reality. He stumbled down the steep embankment, scarcely caring where he was going anymore, and behind him the others followed dutifully, their bodies racked with weariness.

The heavy pall of woodsmoke stung Tazelaar's eyes, dried his throat, made his nostrils prickle. He grunted as he spotted something shiny lying among the underbrush—a glucose wrapping. Ahead, the field dipped into the village square where rows of Forestry cottages bordered a neatly trimmed green. A truck stood parked at the roadside, its engine running. Sprawled in its shade, he glimpsed a group of bedraggled figures staring dumbly at a solitary Negro who stood aiming a pistol at their heads. The Negro looked grim and determined, and a hoarse chuckle burst from Tazelaar's throat. He wanted to laugh at the incongruity of it. It seemed so priceless—now—with defeat staring them in the face, to find their quarry helpless and waiting.

"Looks like the *bobbejaan* is dependable after all," he muttered to his companions.

He went on laughing as they stumbled down the hillslope, struggling to infuse some semblance of life into their aching limbs. The Negro showed no sign of surprise at their approach. He continued scrutinizing his captives with an air of steely absportion, and Tazelaar eyed him with amusement. Nothing like a Bantu for taking himself seriously, he thought. This one looked brighter than the rest—some of the harshness had been planed away—but under the surface, they were all the same, these people.

"You've led us on a merry dance, boy," Tazelaar said. "What happened to the route you were supposed to follow?"

Elliot eyed Tazelaar calmly. "McAuley got shot. I had to improvise."

"You damned fool, it's a miracle we managed to trail you here at all."

"I did as we planned, left the appropriate signs."

"Glucose wrappings? They were for emergencies only."

"I had no choice. We had to take McAuley to Holmkirk."

Tazelaar glanced at the foreign minister, who was lying almost unconscious against the massive truck wheel. "Who did it? Marines?"

"You. Back at the train."

Tazelaar pursed his lips as he studied the prisoners thoughtfully. They were in a bad way, all of them. Like his own men, worn to a frazzle. A miracle, it had been, finding them like this. But there was no time to celebrate. No self-congratulatory accolades, no patting himself on the back. He had a job to do, a vital but unpleasant job. His justice must be swift, sharp, merciful. Tazelaar struggled to infuse his mind with love. Love conquered all, he thought. Under its balm, even the unspeakable could be absolved.

"Why is McAuley still alive?" he whispered.

"He was shot by a bullet from your gun. You want the British police to discover that?"

Tazelaar felt a twinge of uneasiness. "What difference does it make?"

"A big difference. It won't be the ANC who'll get blamed for the minister's death."

Tazelaar hesitated. The bastard was too cocky for his own good, but there was an irrefutable logic to his argument. Everything had to go like clockwork. He'd learned, over the years, to leave nothing to chance. Too often he'd seen months of work ruined because of somebody's carelessness, a simple and impetuous act.

Elliot jerked his head at the village shop. "The phones are still working. Call your contact in London. We must have confirmation before we go ahead."

Frowning, Tazelaar studied Elliot suspiciously. It wasn't Elliot's reasoning which troubled him, it was simply the fact that Tazelaar disliked taking orders from a black.

"Check, Tazelaar," Elliot said coldly. "Better make sure it's what Van Brero wants."

Tazelaar scowled. The *bobbejaan's* words made sense after all, he realized, but once this was over, he was going to slap some sense into that woolly black head. That was the trouble with these people. Give them a little responsibility, and in no time at all they thought they were superior beings. He would demonstrate to the Kaffir his real place in the order of things.

The shop door was locked, but Tazelaar jimmied it easily and found the telephone at the counter end. He dialed a number in London and waited as the line buzzed in his ear. After a moment, a man's voice said crisply, "Schoeman speaking."

"This is Tazelaar."

There was a slight pause. "Has the delivery arrived yet?"

"Just."

"And are the contents satisfactory?"

"Not quite. The package has been damaged in transit. We wondered if you'd prefer the goods returned?"

"Negative," the voice declared. "The package must be destroyed at once."

There was a slight pause. Tazelaar heard the man's breathing at the end of the line. "All the goods," the voice repeated. "Do you read me? *All* the goods must be destroyed. We have our reputations to consider."

Tazelaar nodded, glancing through the window at the group outside.

"*Ja*, I understand," he said. "I will see to it myself."

Karel Van Brero heard the telephone ringing and jerked impulsively, opening his eyes. He was lying on the conservatory sofa, sunlight streaming through the overhead window. Blinking, he reached out, fumbling for the receiver. "Who is it?" he slurred, his voice heavy with sleep.

Menheer? He recognized Peter Hoosen, his chief security aide. "We have a call from London, England, *Menheer.* Erik Schoeman. You said to contact you day or night if he telephoned."

Van Brero sat up on the sofa, his brain suddenly bright and alert.

"Put the call through," he ordered.

There was a momentary pause, then a voice said, "Schoeman here."

"This is Van Brero. Do you have any news?"

"We have heard from Tazelaar."

"And?"

"The package has arrived."

Van Brero took a deep breath. Somewhere outside, a dog was howling mournfully. He heard the rhythmic ticking of the clock. "The goods?"

"They are being dealt with at this moment," came the reply.

"Thank you," Van Brero said.

He put down the receiver and sat staring through the conservatory window, sunlight shading the hollows under his eyes. He looked taut with excitement, his cheeks flushed and alive. He waited barely a moment, then, leaning forward, picked up the telephone and began to dial again.

Hans Eprile, captain of the SS *Arcadia*, sat in his cabin and studied the wall charts moodily. He was in a vulnerable position, he reflected. For four hours, he'd been standing off the west African coast, awaiting orders from Pretoria, and already three merchant vessels had passed within a hundred yards of his bow, imagining him in some kind of distress. It had taken all Eprile's persuasive powers to convince them he was simply carrying out repairs, and in no need of assistance.

When he thought about the cargo in his hold, Captain Eprile's spirits blanched. He couldn't sit here forever, he considered; though he was outside the two-mile limit, it was only a matter of time before some nosy patrol boat decided to investigate.

He was considering this unpalatable thought when Hendrik Zutphen, his first officer, stamped through the cabin doorway, clutching a hastily scribbled radio message. "The order's just come through, menheer. We're to proceed at once to Cape Town. There'll be a military convoy waiting to escort us in. We have special clearance to discharge the cargo immediately."

Captain Eprile breathed deeply, filling his lungs with air. The tension of the last few hours had pushed his nerves to the breaking point. "Thank God," he declared, his plump face creased with relief. "I thought they had forgotten we were here."

Sprawled against the truck wheel, Kate watched Tazelaar strolling toward them, his shoulders hunched against the morning chill. It was impossible to tell what the man was thinking, for his face, square, blunt, studiously impassive, looked as though nothing in the world would induce it to betray emotion. He fumbled in his pocket and took out a packet of small cheroots. Crouching down, he offered them to Timol and Malheiro, who took one apiece.

Tazelaar smiled at De Brere. "You looked tired, *kêrel*. It has been a long haul."

"Up yours, you rednecked bastard," De Brere answered amiably.

Tazelaar showed no sign of anger. He turned toward Kate, his face surprisingly gentle. "You must be Miss Whitmore. They told me there would be a woman with the team."

"What are you going to do with us?" she demanded.

"I wish you no harm, Miss Whitmore. I want you to know I feel nothing toward you but love in my heart."

And she might have believed him, might almost have accepted that avuncular stare, except that something in his eyes made Kate's skin crawl; it was nothing she could put her finger on, but Tazelaar looked strangely depraved, as if just by being in close proximity, he had the power to contaminate everything around him.

He leaned over to light Timol and Malheiro's cigars, then rose to his feet and turned toward Elliot. Though he lowered his voice, Kate heard his words distinctly. "You must kill them," he whispered. "That is the order."

Kate sat rigid with shock, her heart hammering wildly against her rib cage. She could scarcely believe the horror of what Tazelaar was saying.

Elliot didn't answer. He stood staring at the captives, and it was difficult to tell whether he was listening to Tazelaar or not.

Tazelaar eyed him sharply. "Did you hear me, boy? I gave you an order."

Still, Elliot didn't move.

Tazelaar studied him, frowning, as if he regarded Elliot's lack of response as some kind of

personal affront. Smoke drifted around Elliot's head,
blurring his wiry hair into a featureless smudge.
Tazelaar turned to one of his companions. "Leroux,"
he snapped in a crisp voice. "Shoot Mr. McAuley."

Leroux displayed no sign of emotion, that was
the awful thing. Tazelaar might have said, "Give him
a light" or "Button his coat," for all the responsive-
ness Leroux showed. Raising his pistol, he balanced
it across his folded forearm, while Kate watched the
scene in horror and disbelief. He seemed so casual,
so incredibly matter-of-fact, she could scarcely believe it was happening. Her eyes focused on the
barrel's opening.

Kerrr-aaacckkk. The shot was like a racking
cough, hoarse, toneless, brain-numbing. Kate saw
Leroux's left eye vanish in a spurt of blood, and he
spun dizzily, crashing into the roadway, his pistol
clattering across the empty pavement. She blinked,
her pulse quickening. A wisp of cordite drifted from
Elliot's automatic. He had fired without turning his
head, tilting his pistol slightly to the left. For a
moment, the shock of Leroux's death froze them into
a silent tableau, then De Brere, moving with an
alacrity that astonished Kate, hurled himself sideways, scrambling along the gutter toward Leroux's
still spinning revolver. He snatched it up, rolling
wildly, and, firing almost by reflex, sent a bullet
soaring upward through the chin of the nearest
South African, splitting his skull like a ruptured
pumpkin. Tazelaar fired twice, not bothering to aim,
releasing his shots with a blind impassioned fervor
which proved tragically and devastatingly accurate.
Kate sucked in her breath as she saw De Brere's face
crumple inward, the features disintegrating into a
ragged crater as his body gave one violent involun-

tary shudder and settled hopelessly into the rigid abandonment of death.

Elliot swung his arm in a vicious arc, hitting Tazelaar across the back of the skull. The brutish body flopped to the ground as the two remaining South Africans scuttled for the cover of the dry-stone wall.

"Up," Harry bellowed. "Get McAuley into the truck."

He tore at the driver's cab door, dragging himself behind the steering wheel. "Inside," he yelled at Kate, his muscular face writhing.

Kate glanced at Timol and Malheiro, who were pushing McAuley's supine body into the canvas-roofed rear, then she scrambled into the passenger seat, her senses racing wildly.

Elliot stood watching them in silence, his face as implacable as ever. Harry glared at him. "Well, make up your bloody mind. Whose side are you on, theirs or ours?"

Elliot hesitated barely a moment. He glanced down at Tazelaar, who was stirring painfully on the ground, then he ran to the truck and tumbled in. The engine roared as Harry pressed his foot on the accelerator, and they thundered off into the billowing smoke.

Tazelaar felt rough hands dragging him to his feet. He stood swaying in the roadway, fighting for balance as a dull throbbing pain pounded through his skull. "Where's McAuley?"

"In the truck," Kruger said.

"You let them drive away?"

"They were armed, Taz. And the blackie was

helping them too. Look at Jan and Leroux. They're both dead."

Tazelaar grunted. He hadn't cared for Erik much, he reflected. Too full of himself. Flashy and conceited. But Leroux had been loyal, obedient, and dependable.

Tazelaar's was a face which seldom changed expression. Now, to his companions' surprise, he seemed almost beside himself with rage. Peering around, his lips twisted hysterically. "Find something," he croaked. "Some kind of transport. Anything."

Impressed by their leader's intensity, they scuttled about the village, searching garages, drives, parking lots, but every vehicle had been commandeered for the great trek southward. It was Kruger who found the motorcycle. He wheeled it into the open, an old-fashioned Norton with a battered mud-stained sidecar. The others eyed it uncertainly.

"Are you sure it works?" Tazelaar muttered.

"We can try, Taz."

"What about gas?"

"There'll be enough to get us where we're going."

Kruger slammed his foot on the starter pedal and the engine roared into life. "Good man," Tazelaar said. "You know how to operate this thing?"

Kruger grinned mirthlessly. "What do you think I did with my misspent youth?"

Tazelaar jerked his head at Rautenbach. "Get in the sidecar. I will sit on the pillion saddle."

There was a deafening roar as Kruger opened up the throttle, and they thundered off along the highway to the south.

*   *   *

Hans Eprile, captain of the SS *Arcadia*, was standing on the bridge when he heard a shout from the deck below. Peering worriedly through the port-hole, he saw breakers crashing against the rugged west African shoreline. Slightly to starboard, he glimpsed a small open fishing boat, the type used by villagers from the Namibian coast. The craft was dancing on the swell, and Eprile felt his stomach tighten as he discerned, shackled to the vessel's mast, the haggard outline of a solitary white man, his clothes tattered, his cheeks ravaged, his body glistening with spray. The man's skin had been scorched red by the sun, and Eprile saw blood trickling from his lower rib cage.

A feeling of uneasiness arose inside him. Shouting with excitement, his crew members were struggling to bring the vessel alongside. Captain Eprile left the bridge and climbed down the companionway ladder. Spray leapt into his face, stinging his cheeks and eyes, and his nostrils caught, like some forgotten fragrance, the odor of land half a mile off *Arcadia*'s bow.

Eprile heard the fishing boat clanging against the freighter's hull, and saw the white man, arms pinioned along the cross spars of the mast, peering up at them dementedly. He looked insane, Eprile thought. Poor devil, he was probably crazed by sun and thirst.

A heavy tarpaulin covered the fishing boat's deck, and as Eprile watched unbelievingly, the sheet was thrust abruptly aside and figures rose, shouting, their eyes blazing with excitement. Eprile saw black faces, speckled combat jackets, the blunt outline of Uzi submachine guns. Something sailed through the air, a grappling hook. Its steel tip bit into the *Arcadia*'s gunwale, holding firm, and a man began to scramble up the still writhing rope. Suddenly the air was filled with grappling hooks, and Eprile watched in horror, the hairs puckering on his neck, as the invaders, yelling insanely, swarmed like rats over the *Arcadia*'s side.

"You're a fine bundle of tricks," Harry said grudgingly, keeping his eyes on the road ahead. "What happened to all that claptrap about black brotherhood?"

"It wasn't claptrap," Elliot told him. "But I have certain needs which have to be taken into consideration. I've been taught to appreciate the finer things of life, and I was deeply gratified when the South African secret police offered me money—a great deal of money—to infiltrate the ANC. It seemed to me eminently poetic, using apartheid's death throes to line my own pockets."

"How could you deceive your own race?" Kate asked bitterly.

Elliot looked mild. "It wasn't the movement I deceived. It was the men from BOSS."

Harry grunted. "So you're a double agent?"

"I guess that's the popular term."

Kate shook her head disbelievingly. "But why go through that ridiculous charade?"

Sunlight slid through the dusty windshield, lighting Elliot's face. It was still a noble face, handsome and appealing, despite the bruising on the jawline, but that didn't make things easier, she thought, the knowledge that she'd been fooled. Elliot seemed unmoved by what had happened, as if the episode in the village had been little more than an interlude in some elaborate melodrama.

"It was the only way to get the job done," he said.

"Matshoba's release?"

"That isn't at issue here. Oh, we'd like it all right. Matshoba's a symbol, and we'd like him freed sooner or later. But at this moment, there's something far more important at stake."

"Gold," Harry said crisply.

"Correct, Seven million dollars' worth of gold, on its way to the *Broederbond* settlement on Ulithi island. It's in the hold of a freighter called the SS *Arcadia*. Unfortunately, by the time I discovered its existence, the ship had already left Cape Town. We had to find a way of bringing her back."

"By kidnapping McAuley?"

"The kidnapping was Karel Van Brero's idea. He's been against the PAC talks from the beginning. When he decided to sabotage the negotations, he presented us with the perfect diversion. We wanted the *Arcadia's* return, and we reasoned he would authorize that, if everything went according to plan."

Kate blinked in puzzlement. Things were moving too fast for her poor brain to keep pace. Only Harry seemed totally at home, understanding, assimilating. He was driving with a tricky little grin on his lips, as if Elliot's word imbued him with a reluctant admiration. "But why did you betray us to the bloody South Africans?"

"I had to. Van Brero's a powerful man, but we knew he wouldn't dare order the *Arcadia* into Cape Town, without being secure in his own mind that McAuley was already dead, murdered by the ANC."

"So you were supposed to kill him?"

"Exactly."

"I can't believe what I'm hearing here," Kate cried.

This was an Elliot she scarcely knew, beyond her experience, beyond her conception. Had he always been so brutal? They said those who loved were blind, but nobody ever mentioned stupidity. How naive she'd been.

"McAuley's death was a necessary unpleasantness," Elliot told her. "We didn't want to kill him, but he had to be sacrificed for the sake of the movement. Besides, he was the representative of a hated regime."

"And white," she accused.

"That's right," Elliot agreed mildly. "McAuley was white. And our people know all too well what to expect from the white man. He destroyed our culture, he told us we were primitive and barbaric. But like that fire out there, we've set South Africa burning. McAuley's death would have helped keep it alight."

Kate felt slightly nauseated. "I was wrong about you, wrong from the beginning. You're like every other terrorist; ruthless, barbaric, and fanatical."

"Barbaric?" Elliot echoed. "How many children will be shot on the streets of Sharpville, Soweto, Brandfort, before our people achieve freedom? You expect me to worry about the life of one individual? When a man turns his back on tyranny, when he refuses to act, when he claims the battle isn't his and leaves it to somebody else, that man is guilty of complicity. Guilty by default. It isn't only our children who are dying in the townships of South Africa. They belong to us all."

Harry reached down, operating the gear lever. "That's quite a speech, but you haven't explained why McAuley's still alive."

Elliot hesitated. Some of the fight seemed to drain out of him as he sat back against the seat cushions. "I was supposed to shoot McAuley and let Tazelaar telephone confirmation of the kill. I couldn't do it. I thought I could, but when the moment came . . ." He shrugged, staring glumly through the windshield at the road ahead.

"I had to find another way. I had to bluff Tazelaar into making the call with McAuley still alive. He was the only one who knew the identity and phone number of the BOSS intelligence agent in London."

"Hell of a gamble."

Elliot nodded. "However, if the agent passes the news to Van Brero, he'll order the *Arcadia* to return to port. When she does, our people will be waiting to intercept her."

Harry chuckled dryly. "You know, for a man who cares only about number one, you do a pretty good imitation of a dedicated Joan of Arc."

"I *am* dedicated," Elliot said. "Especially to luxurious living. Whatever the movement gets from the *Arcadia*'s cargo, I'm on two percent commission."

Harry laughed out loud, hammering the steering wheel with his fist.

"By God," he exclaimed. "You're a bigger bastard than I took you for."

Kate felt benumbed, helpless. How could she take it all in, the things she was listening to here? Just when she'd realized how much she loved Elliot, he'd turned the world upside down, thrown her affection back in her face, demeaned her emotions. And now, before she'd had a chance to comprehend that fact, here he was switching everything back again. It was a crazy story, whichever way you looked at it, and only a crazy man like Harry would have embraced it so completely.

Suddenly Harry shot up straight, jamming his foot on the brake, and Kate felt her skin turn cold as he brought the truck to a slithering halt. Cruising up the road toward them, she spotted a military convoy. She recognized the scarlet berets and speckled combat jackets of the Parachute Regiment.

"Think they've seen us?" she breathed.

"Of course they've seen us. We're sitting in the middle of the road, for Christ's sake."

"We're finished," she breathed.

To her surprise, Harry's face was blazing with anger. "They haven't copped us yet, have they?"

"Harry, we've no place left to go. If we back up, we'll run into the South Africans."

"I suppose you think we should give ourselves up."

"We have no choice, Harry. They've bloody won, can't you see that?"

"D'you think I've gone through all this, galloped around this stinking thicket, to pack it now without a murmur?"

She stared at him, blinking. "But you said . . . everything I've ever done, you've ridiculed."

"I've ridiculed people who place ideas about human beings. But what could be more human than an old man who's spent twenty-five years of his life in a stinking South African jail? We set out to rescue Joshua Matshoba, and by Christ that's what we're going to do."

Kate had never seen Harry so angry before. His entire body emanated indignant fury. Slamming the truck in reverse, he propelled them backward along the narrow road. Kate, peering in the rearview mir-

ror, felt her heart sink as she glimpsed a motorcycle
hurtling toward them from the direction of the
village. "We're trapped," she cried.

"Like hell," Harry said grimly.

He spun the wheel, turning the truck along a
narrow logging road which arced diagonally into the
encroaching forest.

"Where are you going?" Kate yelled.

"The only place they'll never dare follow,"
Harry told her determinedly. "Into the fire."

Perched on the pillion saddle, his eyes watering
in the buffeting slipstream, Tazelaar watched the
truck skid into the logging road opening and hammered Kruger's shoulder with his fist. Kruger nodded to show that he understood. As they neared the
turnoff, they glimpsed a convoy of military vehicles
approaching along the highway from the south. It
was clear the truck's unorthodox maneuver had
alerted the convoy commander's suspicions because
a small khaki-colored staff car was speeding ahead of
the main column, ostensibly to investigate. Tazelaar
hammered Kruger's shoulder again. "Faster," he bellowed. "Faster."

The engine roared as Kruger opened up the
throttle and Tazelaar felt the incredible surge of
power vibrating between his thighs. He had lost his
composure completely, years of meticulous self-
discipline vanishing in the twinkling of an eye. He
was conscious only that the fugitives were escaping.

Tazelaar was not a rational man. Though he
conveyed an outward facade of imperturbability,
sinister forces bubbled constantly beneath the surface. Now rage consumed him, a violent, incoherent,

unthinking rage which stunned his brain and paralyzed his senses.

At his knee, Rautenbach's head began to bob in
the shuddering sidecar, and tears streamed down
Tazelaar's cheeks as he fought to see through the
suffocating wind currents pounding his face and
throat.

The staff car drew closer, the driver spotting
them now, wavering slightly as he realized the
motorcycle had no intention of giving way. Tazelaar
hooked his arm around Kruger's body, gritting his
teeth, cursing under his breath in a stream of rapid
ingenious profanity. At the last moment, the staff car
swung to one side, mounting the grassy verge, and
Tazelaar glimpsed the occupants' startled faces as
Kruger spun off the highway and roared frenziedly
up the logging road in Harry's wake.

Kate held hard to the shuddering dashboard,
struggling to see through the blanket of smoke which
billowed against their windshield. Its acrid fumes
filled the driving cab, prickling her nostrils, stinging
her eyes. She could hear the roar of the flames ahead
and feel—or imagined she could feel—the stunning
heat which preceded their ravenous advance. Harry
had gone mad, she felt certain. There was nothing up
front but desolation and destruction. But Harry had
that look in his eye, the gleam she had come to
recognize over the long years of living and loving
and quarreling. His mind was set. Nothing would
change it. He was like a tank when the mood took
him.

"Harry, this is crazy," she yelled. "Nobody can
survive up there. Nobody."

"We're not bloody quitting now," he snapped.

Kate sighed. He'd been against them from the beginning, had tried to scotch their chances if the truth were known. Now, with typical Harrylike perversity, he was the one element holding them together.

Beside her in the passenger seat, Elliot Chamille looked stricken. Never in her life had she seen such terror in the face of a human being. Fire seemed to unnerve him completely, arousing specters she could scarcely begin to understand.

"We've got to go back," Elliot insisted.

"No," Harry bellowed.

"Let me out, damn you. Let me out now."

"Hold on to your socks," Harry yelled.

Ahead, the smoke seemed to lift, not vanishing exactly, merely rising above them like a theater cloth unfolding on some grotesque and impossible-to-believe stage, and Kate gasped as she caught her first glimpse of the spiraling flames. It was like staring into the gates of hell, she thought, a world without substance, an incredible furnace swirling across the entire realm of her vision, a white-hot barricade carrying every living thing in front of it, leaping and cavorting, wriggling and twisting, darting out tormentingly in fiery little sorties to set new timber stands alight. Its brilliance was dazzling. It stung her eyes with its sheer intensity. Its roar thundered in her eardrums. Then the smoke dropped back and in one breathless second the inferno was blotted from her gaze, lost in the swirling fumes drifting around their driving cab.

"Did you see it?" she croaked.

Harry didn't answer. He was leaning forward, his grimed face savagely intent, fighting to see through the windshield.

"Did you see it?" she screamed in a hysterical voice.

"Shut up," he snapped. "Shut up, damn you."

"What are you trying to do, kill us all?"

Harry didn't answer. They were drawing closer to the fire wall now. On each side of the road, clumps of blazing foliage soared through the air, and she could see fresh flames leaping between the trunks, roaring and multiplying with stupefying ferocity. She watched in awe as the fire danced skyward, crawling higher and higher, forming a grotesque backdrop which set the spruce tips in stark relief. With a howl of discovery, the flames found a fresh trunk, then another, gobbling them up with furious voracity, turning the skyline into a billowing rampart of orange and red.

"You've got to turn back," she yelled. "This is madness, nothing but madness."

"It's the only place they'll never catch us."

"What good will that do if we're all dead?"

"Nobody's going to die. Nobody."

Kate shook her head in bewilderment. How could you understand a man like Harry? He didn't follow any predictable pattern. He went his own way, no matter what. But God knew, she wished he wasn't so vehement. You just couldn't stop him when he put his mind to something.

The heat was almost unbearable now, and beyond the driving cab, she felt the air lurch as oxygen was drawn remorselessly into the heart of the inferno. Their left tire exploded with a deafening bang, and the truck lurched violently to one side, slewing across the road. Almost simultaneously, the second tire went, and they came to a rest with their front wheels perched above the ditch.

"Out," Harry croaked. "Everybody out. Get McAuley from the rear."

"You're crazy," Elliot protested, his features riven with panic. "We'll incinerate out there."

Harry's face, soot-stained, sweaty, looked strangely demoniacal.

"We're going through the fire," he bellowed. "We're taking McAuley with us."

"How?" Kate yelled. "How, damn you? How do you expect us to survive?"

"Blood River. We'll use Blood River as an escape valve. The water will give us protection. Now move, you little fool, before the fire cuts us off completely."

Sobbing deep in her throat, Kate followed Elliot into the flame-scorched air. The buffeting wind currents lashed her face, drying the moisture from her eyeballs. She could scarcely believe the intensity of the heat flurries. They came at her from all directions, searing, smoldering, singeing, burning. She saw Malheiro and Timol wrestling McAuley over the truck's flapping tailgate. The minister seemed beyond the realm of conscious awareness, his head bobbing helplessly above his narrow shoulders. Shuddering with terror, Elliot scampered in to help, hooking one of McAuley's arms across the back of his muscular neck.

"This way," Harry yelled, shuffling down the grassy embankment.

And strung out in a ragged line, they followed him into the holocaust.

Tazelaar saw the truck in the road ahead and hammered hard on Kruger's shoulder. "Stop," he hollered.

Kruger jammed on his brakes, bringing the mo-

torcycle to a screeching halt. The air surged and
lunged around them, plucking at their clothes and
hair, a white-hot furnace of air which bit voraciously
into their cringing flesh. Its strength was stultifying,
and Tazelaar's ears filled with a strange and eerie
wailing sound which mingled macabrely with the
deafening clamor of crackling flames.

"They've gone into the fire," he shouted.

"They'll be baked to a cinder," Kruger bellowed.

"We've got to catch up."

Kruger's face registered incredulousness and
fear. "Are you out of your mind? We'll roast alive in
there."

"We are going after them," Tazelaar roared,
reaching for his pistol.

"The hell we are."

Kruger stabbed his foot on the pedal, sending
the engine thundering into life, and without hesitating, Tazelaar fired at the motorcycle's front tire. It
exploded with a deafening bang.

"You fool," Kruger screamed. "You bloody crazy
insane fool."

Grimly, determinedly, Tazelaar aimed his pistol
at the fuel tank.

"Jump," he bellowed. "Jump, damn you."

Faces stricken with terror, Kruger and Rautenbach scrambled from the crippled machine. Tazelaar
fired again, and with an ear-splitting roar the gas
tank, already over-hot from the encroaching blaze,
exploded outward in a burst of smoke and flame.

Kruger stared incredulously at the twisted heap
of charred, smoldering wreckage at the roadside.
"Look what you've done," he shrieked. "How the
hell will we get out of here?"

"We are not getting out of here, we are going

after them," Tazelaar repeated grimly, covering his companions with the pistol. "Now move or die."

Muttering in terror, they shuffled down the ragged embankment and followed despairingly in Harry's wake.

Kate ran like a woman in a daze. The world seemed to have lost substance, perspective, tangibility. She was lost in the labyrinths of her mind, caught in a reverie which had no shape or meaning but which seemed, demonlike, to consume her very soul, as if she had actually died back there—was dead now—sprinting insanely through the unspeakable hinterlands of hell.

The air lurched and twitched around her head as she pounded toward the great sheet of swirling destructiveness. The tender mucus-coated surfaces of her throat and nostrils seemed baked dry like slabs of ancient leather, and her skin felt flayed, as if, paintlike, it was peeling from her body, leaving her flesh and arteries vulnerable and exposed.

The flames began to bite, licking hotly at her thighs and calves, stinging her skin with fingers of excruciating pain. She saw something gleaming through the twisting smoke tendrils ahead and turned toward it, sprinting impulsively now, half crazed with agony and fear. Reaching the bluffs, she slipped down the grassy bank and, without hesitating, plunged into the river's shallows, lunging and wallowing until she'd reached the central current. She sank back thankfully, letting the icy water bathe her fevered skin. The others followed in a disorderly tangle, staggering through the fiery timber, Harry leading, his hair trailing out smoke on the furnace-hot air. Tottering into the river, he threw himself full-length, plunging his head beneath its rippling current.

The others entered the shallows, steering McAuley between them, battling for balance as they maneuvered him bodily into the waist-deep water. They were like strange monsters from some mystic vision. The whole world was a nightmare, and Kate felt sick with strain and fear. There was no way out, no escape, no deliverance. They'd run themselves into a death trap. Harry had stampeded them into it in his mad impassioned way. Unthinking, unreasoning. And now they were done for. Harry himself looked practically unrecognizable. His head, glistening with water, shimmered in the coppery glow.

"We've got to keep moving," he shouted. "If we stay here, we'll fry. Come on."

Dazedly, Kate followed the center of the boulder-strewn riverbed, the icy torrent eddying around her hips and rib cage. Oh, he was an excellent strategist and no mistake. Down or out, win or lose, you couldn't knock Harry back. He kept on going, it was the only thing he knew. They were in the middle of a fiery tunnel, hemmed in by twisting tendrils of flame. The wind buffeted them unmercifully, scorching their bodies with its searing touch. Elliot looked practically demented, his features writhing out of control. He seemed caught on a rack of his own making, petrified by forces the others couldn't comprehend.

Sometimes the smoke belched blindingly around them, shutting out the entire world. It filled their lungs, stung their eyes, smothered their senses, but dazed and desperate, they battled their way up the uneven riverbed, the air screeching in their ears. The scene seemed frozen into Kate's mind like some macabre tableau—the five men, scarcely recognizable as human beings, their

faces black, their clothes smoldering, fighting remorselessly through the bubbling torrent, mist hissing from
the water's surface, mingling with the suffocating
smoke canopy above them, and the fire dancing, slithering, mocking, enveloping them all in a frenzied
vortex of sound. The flames were the only reality. She
could feel their touch on her cheeks and shoulders. A
freak wind current sent a white-hot beacon directly
across the river's surface and they crouched back in
their tracks, watching the tenacious fire talon until it
had flickered and died, then stumbling on into the
stupefying heat. Kate saw her parka sleeve turning a
dull russet brown, as if a smoothing iron had been laid
unaccountably upon it; smoke drifted around her elbow, and she felt an agonizing barb lancing into her
forearm. With a scream, she flopped into the water,
letting the blessed coolness neutralize the anguish of
her ravaged skin.

A strange hissing sound reverberated across the
stricken woodland, and glancing up, Kate felt horror
engulf her as she glimpsed, sweeping toward them
like a giant tidal wave, a great whorl of blazing
firebrands whipped into a vortex by hurricane-force
winds and bearing down on them in a solid bulwark
of shimmering flame. It was an awesome sight, a
huge barrier of fire rearing into the sky like the prow
of some incredible galleon.

"Duck," Harry bellowed.

Kate threw herself forward, plunging desperately under the water's surface. She pressed herself
against the pebbly river bottom as the flames hit the
frothy current with the impact of an artillery barrage,
and Kate felt the water dancing around her shoulders. Her body seemed to shed its substance, lost in
a strange delirium which carried no semblance of

reason or reality. She struggled for breath, her chest creaking and straining; then, raising her head cautiously, she peeked above the rippling surface to find the fireball had passed, leaving them drained and gasping, yet incredibly, alive.

Tazelaar scarcely knew where he was going. Thick smoke rushed at him from all directions, blinding his vision, suffocating his lungs. Black and acrid, it seemed almost tangible, a shifting, living force, intent on his destruction, and he was conscious of a strange absence of awareness. Madness, it had been, coming here. There was no sign of the fugitives anymore. He had let his rages rule him. After all these years of careful constraint, he'd led his comrades into this conflagration, through impatience, through stupidity.

The fire was all around them, licking and teasing, hurtling between the spruce trunks to ram them headlong, sneaking around the rear to snatch at them from behind. Around their heads, the air seemed to lurch as oxygen was sucked into the maelstrom. The pistol burned his hand, and with a stab of alarm he hurled it into the flames as the shells exploded in a series of sharp discordant cracks. The smoke came in again, blotting out the world, filling his throat and lungs till he gasped despairingly for breath. Nothing to see in this deafening, buffeting clamor. Nothing to feel but the monstrous heat of hellfire. It seemed like a scourge for the sins of his past, cleansing and cauterizing. He could see Kruger directly in front, his eyes bulging with fear. "We've got to go back," Kruger screamed. "It's crazy to push any farther."

Tazelaar nodded to show that he understood.

Kruger was right. The fire was an overpowering force, impossible to resist, impossible to penetrate.

"This way," he yelled, desperately retreating.

They followed him blindly, crying out as the dancing flame gusts bit into their their tortured flesh. Tazelaar felt his hair taking fire. There was no warning. They had been pounded by white-hot gusts for so long, he'd thought the flames had no surprises left, but suddenly terror gripped him as he felt his skull being flayed alive. Oh my God, I am heartily sorry for having offended Thee, Thou who are worthy of all my love . . . Contrition came like a childhood dream, hauntingly familiar. He could lose himself in the labyrinths of memory, retreat cowardlike into the dimmest recesses of his mind.

Then suddenly Rautenbach's clothing spontaneously ignited, and in front of Tazelaar's horrified eyes the fire transformed him into a wriggling living torch. It was impossible to see Rautenbach as a human being anymore. At the heart of the blaze something moved, but it was little more than a kernel, a blurred mass, indefinable amid the flickering yellow and crimson tongues. Almost simultaneously, Kruger too burst into flame, and Tazelaar's stomach cringed as he watched the human flares darting and careering among the blazing tree trunks. Horror was debilitating when it came without warning, he thought; the mind balked at it, backed off, capitulated. Wrapped in flames, his companions were dancing out their lives in a frenzied ritual of anguish and pain.

He was shivering from head to foot, his limbs no longer part of his body. Despite the need for speed, he moved with agonizing slowness, sucking at the smoke in short erratic bursts. Fighting for breath, fighting for balance, he stumbled through the fiery woodland, battered, dazed, bewildered, his frame a blackened, crusted shell.

Something loomed in his path, a metal canister, one of the water tanks built by the Forestry Commission at strategic points in the sprawling timberland. Whimpering helplessly, Tazelaar turned toward it. The metal lid burned his fingers; it was red hot. As he stared into the tank's interior, Tazelaar felt his spirits sink. The water was already boiling, its surface dancing and bubbling merrily. He ducked back, clenching his teeth, trying to squeeze beneath the base of the metal hull. The smoke parted, and he saw the fire rearing above him, not fragmented any longer, but a solid rampart of living flame, bearing down with stupefying force. He saw the tongues reaching out, licking his cheeks, shriveling his eyelashes. He saw the sparks lashing across the foliage in wild spiraling jets.

Then the fire took him, and his vision vanished in a blinding paroxysm of pain.

Waldo heard the roar of truck engines and, pulling back the tent flap, spotted a convoy of military vehicles lurching toward them up the logging road, led by a staff car with camouflaged bodywork.

"Looks like reinforcements," he said to Palmer. "Men from the Parachute Regiment."

Palmer strode out to meet them. As the staff car drew to a halt, a man in a major's uniform clambered out, saluted smartly, and spoke to Palmer in low, earnest tones.

Waldo frowned as Palmer came hurrying back. "What's happened?"

"I have to use the radio. They've spotted people on the road back there."

"McAuley?"

"Got to be. As soon as they got their eyes on the convoy, they scampered into the woodland. I'm ordering helicopters over the area immediately."

Fifteen

The South African sun cast elongated shadows across the giant syringa trees flanking Cape Town's international airport, and Van Brero watched sullenly as the cavalcade of police cars pulled onto the concrete concourse. In the convoy's center, the prison truck looked strangely out of place, its narrow wire-bracketed slits contrasting incongruously with the broad windshields of the sun-visored limousines.

Van Brero felt frustration gathering inside him. Hours, it had been, since he'd received the phone call from England, but why nothing since? There should have been confirmation, a final assurance that the issue was settled. He needed that, some kind of proof, some kind of testimony. He'd done his bit, God knew. Recalled the *Arcadia*. Nothing to reproach himself for. Everything he'd planned had been for the sake of his country. In his mind, there had been no confusion of loyalties. He was, first and foremost, an Afrikaaner, a product of the Voortrekkers—a patriot who demanded life for his people instead of death, dignity instead of defeat.

He felt fury smoldering inside him as the motorcade drew to a halt at the side of the waiting aircraft, the guards fanning out, surrounding the prison van warily. The door creaked open, and into the sunlight stumbled Joshua Matshoba, frail, bewildered, dazed, his left wrist handcuffed to a uniformed police officer. He gazed about him, his shoulders stooped, his crinkly hair grayer than Van Brero remembered. At the aircraft steps, the policeman took out a key, carefully unlocked the metal manacles, and Matshoba rubbed his wrists, blinking in confusion. He was still dressed in his prison uniform, a shabby boiler suit of unrelieved gray. Van Brero sighed. It seemed wrong, wrong, that at the moment of victory, his most celebrated political prisoner should be spirited out from under his very nose. He'd tried, God knew how he'd tried. Done his damnedest to halt the winds of change. Risked his career, his entire reputation. Now it looked as though he was being rewarded in the most ungrateful manner.

Van Brero strode into the airport office. "I have to use your phone," he snapped at the girl behind the counter.

She withdrew without a word, closing the door behind her, and Van Brero dialed his office in Roeland Street, Cape Town. His assistant, Piet, came on the line. "Any news from Tazelaar or Chamille?" Van Brero demanded.

"Nothing, *menheer*. But we have just received word from our coast guard people."

He hesitated, and something in his voice made Van Brero's spine tingle.

"Out with it, Piet. What's happened."

"The SS *Arcadia, menheer*, it's . . ."

Van Brero felt a sickly sensation spreading through his lower stomach.

"The *Arcadia*?" he echoed.

"It has been hijacked, *menheer*. It is already docking at Lobito in Angola. We understand the terrorists have asked the Angolan government for asylum."

Van Brero passed his hand weakly across his forehead. In his vision, the walls seemed to be rippling in and out. "And the gold?"

Piet sounded desperately unhappy. "In the hands of the ANC."

The roar of the aircraft brought Van Brero back to his senses. Slamming down the receiver, he sprinted into the open air. "Stop that plane," he shouted.

But he was already too late. The glistening fuselage thundered down the narrow runway, then slowly, gently banked skyward, skimming over the lush green scrublands of Smitswinkel Flats before turning north toward the misty line of the distant hills.

Van Brero saw two men scrambling from a police jeep and recognized Hans Eprile, captain of the SS *Arcadia*. Eprile's head was bandaged, and his left arm dangled in a sling suspended from his neck. Even at that distance, Van Brero could see the pallor of defeat in Captain Eprile's eyes.

Somewhere far off, he heard a hypnotic throbbing sound. It started gently at first, drifting on the air like an incoming tide, swelling, strengthening until it filled Van Brero's senses. His spirits blanched as he recognized its cadence.

It was the unmistakable rhythm of a tribal victory chant.

Time had little meaning for Kate, struggling along the twisting riverbed. The minutes seemed to run into each other, as if she had reached a point in space where everything hung suspended. They appeared to have been clambering for hours now, their outlines scarcely human anymore, their hair and clothing singed to a frazzle as they stumbled over fallen tree trunks, wriggled between rocks and smoldering underbrush, immersing themselves every few yards or so when the fire's intensity became too great to bear. In sections where the river ran shallow, they scampered briskly through the ankle-deep water, or crawled belly-flat among the silt.

The blaze was all around them, no longer dancing, but blending into an impossible-to-imagine incandescent glare.

Kate's flesh felt like a block of fudge. There was no pain. She was conscious only of a disturbing numbness, as if her body had lost its capacity to respond in natural human terms. She willed herself to keep moving, her mouth a hole through which she sucked plaintively at the searing oxygen-starved air. The smoke fumes, she knew, with their carbon monoxide concentration, could easily prove lethal.

"How much farther?" she gasped at Harry.

"Christ knows."

"My legs are wilting. I can't even feel my skin anymore."

His face, barely identifiable, squinted at her through the smoke.

"Don't think. Just keep moving, that's all."

They shuffled through a world alive with color, a world of brilliance, of sparkling phosphorescence, but there was little beauty in the spectacle. It hemmed them in from every corner, roaring and howling, shattering their senses, lashing their bodies with showers of flaming ash.

Kate felt her spirits flounder as she glimpsed, directly in their path, a cluster of fallen tree trunks sprawled across the riverbed. It was too dangerous, she realized, to clamber over their still-smoldering boughs—that would expose them momentarily to the hazard of burning. They would have to duck under, pick their way through the maze of splintered branches which formed a baffling tangle against the river floor.

"We could drown under there," she protested. "What if we get stuck in the branches?"

"We won't," Harry said reassuringly. "We'll force our way through."

She felt panic engulfing her. "For God's sake, the fire's bad enough. I can't stand the thought of being suffocated."

He gripped her shoulder comfortingly. He was no longer recognizable as Harry, only a shapeless, smoke-blackened creature dredged from some bizarre fantasy. "Trust me. Okay?"

"What do you think I've been doing for the past hour?"

Harry went first. Ducking beneath the bubbling current, he began to wriggle through the complex infrastructure of twisted undergrowth.

Kate held her breath, lowering her body into the water as she waited for Harry's reappearance. Thirty seconds, she counted. Forty. Forty-two. Then, with a wave of relief, she saw him emerge, coughing and spluttering, at the other side of the smoldering timber dam.

The two Africans went next, supporting McAuley between them. They took almost a minute—probably, Kate guessed, because the strain of moving in unison had made the narrow apertures difficult to negotiate.

Now it was her turn. A spasm of fear shot through her. What if she got jammed in a tree branch? She felt someone seize her elbow. It was

Elliot Chamille. The terror was still evident in his features, but—probably for her sake, she realized—he was holding on to his nerve with a deliberate effort. "Ready?" he asked.

"I'm frightened."

"We'll make it all right. Just go when I say, okay?"

She nodded. He jerked his head downward, and taking a deep breath, she plunged herself under. Elliot's fingers tightened on her arm. She felt grateful for his presence. She couldn't have stood it, picking her way through the suffocating spruce boughs alone. She'd have lost her head. Frozen. Elliot's nearness was comforting. Just the same, she could sense the terror in his fingers, understood in some curious way the ordeal he was going through. For the rest of them, there was the fear of pain, the fear of extinction, but with Elliot, the ordinary simple human things which molded his entire personality appeared to have aborted, as if he had become a different creature, blinded by panic and mortal apprehension.

The branches gathered around her, blocking her passage at every turn. She felt trapped, smothered, suffocated. Silt, kicked up from the river bottom, made it impossible to see through the eddying current. I'll never get out of here, she thought, the air straining in her chest. Elliot's hand tugged at her arm, dragging her relentlessly along the shaly bottom. Suddenly she felt him hauling her upward, and her head broke the surface, the air white-hot, drying the moisture from her skin as she sucked smoke into her tortured lungs.

"Come on," Harry yelled. "We've got to keep moving."

"Give her a minute," Elliot protested. "She's half drowned, for God's sake."

"We haven't got a minute," Harry snapped. "We must break through to Saughtree Lake."

On they trundled, flinching and ducking as the flames pounded their progress with agonizing persistence. Kate lost count of the number of times they had to plunge beneath the water. She was conscious only of a strange delirium, as if reality itself had somehow swiveled askew. The fire formed a blazing arch which hovered menacingly above their heads. Its strength was unassailable. There was nothing to see but smoke and flame, nothing to hear but the thunderous roar of each stampeding assault.

She was filled with a terrible premonition. What chance did they have, stuck in their macabre corridor, the inferno raging around them? It was like a monstrous eruption heaved up from the bowels of the earth. She heard a screeching splintering sound, and terror lanced her insides as she glimpsed a blazing tree trunk swaying, toppling, crashing down from the cataclysm above.

"Harry," she screamed.

Harry saw the danger at the last moment and turned back, wallowing desperately against the buffeting current. The tree tore down, gathering speed as its angle lessened, its branches blazing, trailing smoke through the fiery air, hitting the water in a dazzling welter of spiraling steam and cascading spray. "Are you all right?" Kate gasped.

Harry nodded, splashing water over his smoldering hair.

Ahead, the trees seemed to open, not parting exactly, but losing some of their density, smoke pulsing between their crackling trunks. Kate wiped

her cheeks with her hands. Something was out there,
something different.

They scrambled forward, picking their way over
the fractured boulder bed. A narrow chasm confronted them, dipping sharply into the churning
maelstrom below. The chasm's walls were roughly
thirty feet across, and spanning this perilous gap, a
slender water trough, supported on metal stilts,
formed a precarious bridge to the opposite side. A
tree, torn loose by its roots, had crashed across the
canyon rim, hitting the trough directly in its center,
buckling it dangerously to the left. The tree, still
blazing, lay propped against the metal gutter, bearing
down with breathtaking intensity.

They stood gasping, staring at the route ahead.
"What is it?" Kate croaked.

"Saughtree Aqueduct," Harry said. "The Forestry Commission built it in the early fifties. The
river used to run into the ravine down there, but they
funneled it across so they could float logs over the
summit of the crags opposite and into the lake at the
other side. That was before they were properly
mechanized. If we can cross this gully, we're home
and dry."

They looked dubiously at the charred superstructure. Already several of the support struts had
begun to bend ominously, and the chute itself was
creaking and swaying in the wind. Beneath, the gully
floor looked like a blazing gridiron, its entire bed a
sheet of flame from wall to wall.

"We'll never do it," Elliot breathed.

"Well, we can't go down," Harry said, "and we
can't detour either."

"If that trellis gives way, we'll bake to a cinder."

"We'll take it in twos. Keep the weight down a
bit."

Elliot compressed his lips, gazing into the roaring inferno. It was back again, Kate saw it in his face, that crazy terror that had no sense or meaning. Harry spotted it too. He frowned as he glimpsed the panic in Elliot's features. Then he wiped his lips with his sleeve and nodded at Timol. "Take McAuley. And no risks, understand? If you feel the gutter giving way, get back fast."

Timol nodded, his black face showing no emotion. He helped McAuley into the metal channel and followed gingerly. Kate watched, scarcely daring to breathe. The thought of venturing along that slender precarious ribbon filled her brain with dread.

Timol hooked McAuley's arms around his neck, dragging him piggyback fashion as he eased into the conduit's mouth, inching along on his elbows. It was a slow and difficult maneuver. The river pulsed around him, streaming into the narrow funnel, but at the point where the tree had struck it, Kate saw water flowing over the metal rim, teeming into the flames below. She held her breath, watching Timol's agonizing progress. With McAuley hampering his movements, he had to depend on slow, painful worming motions, the trestle creaking and swaying with the strain. He reached the point where the fallen tree had pierced the channel wall and, wriggling to the side, somehow negotiated the delicate obstacle, dragging McAuley behind him. Ignoring the ominously teetering superstructure, he fought his way to the opposite wall.

Kate felt relief flood her as they watched Timol waving at them through the smoke fumes. Thank God, she thought. Elliot studied the water chute, his eyes still rolling wildly. "Those support posts can't stand much more of this."

"Get moving, then," Harry said. "Take Kate with you."

"I can't," Elliot stammered.

"What's wrong, for Christ's sake? You're acting like a crazy man."

"You don't understand. Fire destroys everything. Body, soul, everything."

Harry's face twisted furiously. "We haven't time for this. That aqueduct is ready to drop at any second. Now take Kate and get moving before we're all bloody killed. I'll follow with Malheiro."

Elliot swallowed, moistening his lips with his tongue. He was trying hard to pull himself together, and Kate felt her muscles tighten as she glimpsed the struggle taking place in his face. How could a man get so scared? she wondered. Not just simple scared like the rest of them—scared of pain, scared of dying—but supernatural scared, the way a man might be when faced with some kind of incalculable demon. Glancing at Kate, Elliot clambered into the water chute and lowered his body nervously into the stream. Kate watched him, a faint queasiness gathering in her stomach. She didn't want to go, she realized. The aqueduct looked too unstable, too precarious. But Elliot was inching warily along the conduit's bottom, his dark cheeks livid with panic, and gritting her teeth, Kate followed, scarcely noticing the cold water rushing around her throat and neck. Smoke belched into her face, shutting off the flames below, and steam rose from the rippling surface where the metal chute, heated by the blaze, came into contact with the icy current. She could feel the chute dipping and shuddering beneath them, and her heart jumped. Don't think about it, she told herself grimly. Don't think at all. No memory, no imagination. Mind blank, that was the answer.

Numb and breathless, she followed gingerly in Elliot's wake.

Elliot fought to stave off his panic, concentrating instead on the awful task of shuffling forward. On the periphery of his vision, he was conscious of a sea of flame beneath and realized the fire, like a nemesis, had returned to consume him, just as one day he'd always known it would. He could see Modipane's image writhing helplessly among the embers, hear his voice calling Elliot's name. Stop that, he told himself angrily, and, wriggling and squirming, slithered breathlessly toward the refuge of the opposite cliff.

The smoke grew thicker, wafting ominously into Kate's eyes. She could scarcely see Elliot anymore, for nothing seemed to exist beyond the few square feet in which she moved, and she was beginning to shiver now, not from cold, but from the sheer unspeakable strain of exposure. The chute was old, rusty, derelict. The fallen tree had weakened its structure, and sooner or later it was bound to crumble. A sprung rivet, a buckling trestle, then everything would go. She turned her mind from that, steeling herself consciously as she might shut out a sinful temptation.

She saw something looming out of the fumes ahead. Branches. She had reached the aqueduct center where the toppled tree lay sprawled across it. She could see flames licking along its ravaged trunk, and easing herself to one side, she inched forward, feeling the aqueduct swaying. Not too far, she thought, mustn't unbalance the chute. Wriggling and squirming, she ducked her head beneath the prickly spruce branches. If she hesitated, even for a moment, she knew her courage would desert her.

Creee-aaacccckkkkk. The trestle moved. No doubt about it, the chute was shifting. Water spumed over the rim, and she felt the conduit bending, buckling, tottering. Dear God in heaven, she thought, I'm going over.

The swirl of the current took her, driving her bodily against the chute wall, and she clutched at the parapet, wincing as the hot metal stung her unprotected fingers. Her legs slithered over the edge. She had a sense of falling and hung on desperately, her stomach dissolving. She felt the blast of heat from the gully bed below, glimpsed with a quaking heart the terrible caldron of flame which seethed and rippled beneath her, and something seemed to lock inside her head. She was dangling in midair, holding fast to the tilting water trough while the flames, like a pack of scavenging wolves, waited hungrily for their prey.

Elliot heard Kate's involuntary cry and, paralyzed with terror, tensed himself for the moment the buckling chute would pitch them both into the furnace beneath. The aqueduct groaned and creaked as Kate's desperate movements pitched it farther and farther to the left, and something exploded in Elliot's mind—not terror any longer, but a fierce and bewildering urgency. He forgot his panic in the gravity of the moment, forgot everything except the riveting realization that Kate needed him, she was in danger.

Thrusting his elbows against the chute bottom, he inched backward, wriggling and twisting desperately as he struggled to retrace his route.

* * *

Squinting hard, Kate saw Elliot reaching down toward her, his eyes blazing through the drifting fumes. "Give me your hand."

She couldn't move. She seemed caught in a state of abject terror, scarcely able to believe the intensity of the heat beneath. It was like hovering over the mouth of some dreadful incinerator. Smoke belched around her face and limbs, and the metalwork squeaked as the trough sagged lower.

"Come on, for Christ's sake," Elliot snapped. "Do you want to go over?"

Fear transmitted itself into movement. She reached up, seizing Elliot's hand, and he hauled hard, grasping her shoulder with his other fist. Sobbing, she hooked one elbow over the aqueduct's rim, thrusting with her feet against the buckling trestlework beneath. Somehow, kicking and scrabbling, she worked her way back into the shallow gutter and lay gasping, fighting hard to keep herself from throwing up.

Elliot glared at her. "Don't just sit there. D'you want this thing to collapse? Come on."

Whimpering, she followed his blurred outline, moving by reflex now, her brain dulled, her perception blunted. The wind, white-hot and searing, tore at her hair, screeched in her ears. Nothing had any meaning, except the will to keep going. The aqueduct broadened, and eyes blinded by tears, she glimpsed gorse bushes rearing out of rock-studded peat. A wave of relief flooded through her as she realized they had reached the opposite clifftop. We've done it, she thought. Sweet God in heaven, we've done it.

*   *   *

Elliot's legs felt wobbly as he rose to his feet and shuffled to the precipice edge. He was trembling all over. Even his goddamn teeth were chattering, he realized. He couldn't believe he had made it, actually crawled above that writhing maelstrom and come through intact. Not even a scorch mark, he was willing to bet. The act of rescuing Kate had taken away his fear, obliterated for a few vital seconds the tremors threatening to engulf him. He felt delirious with relief as he waved his arms vigorously in the air. "Okay, Fuller," he yelled. "It's your show now."

Harry felt his senses tighten. He could see Elliot clearly above the eddying smoke. He'd done it, they both had—he had Kate together. Harry felt a wave of thankfulness at the realization that Kate was safe. For one dreadful moment back there, he'd thought his world about to disintegrate, but Elliot had dragged her back into the chute, and he, Harry Fuller, would never forget him for that.

Skin crawling, Harry eased into the shuddering aqueduct, Malheiro following close behind. Ahead, the trough rippled in and out like a strip of india rubber. Musn't let them see he was frightened, he thought. Not after the way Elliot Chamille had just behaved. Bloody hero, temperament of a lion. Not like Harry, who was scared stiff, it the truth were known. Well, no point worrying about it now, no point worrying about anything at all, except the need to keep going.

Sucking in his breath, Harry wriggled shakingly along the precipitous shuddering funnel.

* * *

Mouth dry, senses tingling, Kate watched Harry's delicate approach. Smoke drifted across the slender bridge, obscuring the two men from view, but through occasional gaps in the fumes she caught glimpses of their hazardous progress. Harry reached the fallen tree and slithered beneath it, using his arm to keep from tilting over the edge. Malheiro followed, his black face glistening.

Eeeerrrooowwwww. The screech was like a roll of distant thunder rising above the clamor of the wind, and Kate felt her stomach contract. A second tree was falling, this time from the opposite clifftop.

"Harry, look out," she screamed.

The tree came down slowly, its great trunk tilting, toppling, tumbling, trailing smoke and flame through the air as it plummeted straight toward the spot where Harry and Malheiro lay trapped. It caught the aqueduct in its branches, bending the metal trough to the left. Kate heard the trestle tearing and felt nausea gathering in her stomach. The gutter snapped, one end plunging into the inferno beneath, the other rearing crazily to the side. The two trees, jammed together, formed a delicate triangle with the aqueduct's last remaining support post, balancing precariously above the roaring tumult. Malheiro was caught between them, his lifeless body ripped completely in two. His limbs dangled obscenely, and viscera dripped into the roaring tumult below. Directly in front, Harry lay trapped in the narrow channel, his chest cage pierced by a jagged branch. His eyes were closed, and he was groaning incoherently. Flames danced along the trunk top toward his unprotected face.

Kate felt herself abruptly losing control. "Harry," she shrieked, her voice lifting in panic. "Harry."

Elliot listened to Kate's scream and tried to shut off his hearing, as if he could, ostrichlike, blot out the awful reality confronting him. But Kate's voice was desperate and insistent, and he couldn't ignore the evidence of his eyes. Malheiro's decimated body. Harry Fuller, helplessly impaled. Well, he thought, what now? The way that runnel was swaying, one end completely gone, it was ready to plummet at any second. There was nothing holding it except the solitary support post. If he ventured down, he'd be asking to die, for the slightest slip, the slightest misjudgment, would tear the gutter from its socket and plunge him into the barbeque pit below. And what did Fuller mean to him anyhow? Nothing but trouble.

Elliot heard Kate's voice again—"Help him," she cried, "help him, for God's sake"—and something tightened in his stomach, something he couldn't quite put a name to, a sense of hopelessness, of emptiness and desolation, because he knew then, knew beyond any shadow of a doubt that it was Harry she cared about, Harry she wanted, and nothing he could do would alter that simple and inalienable fact.

"Okay," he snapped, glaring back at her. "Okay, but sit tight, damn you, just sit tight."

Carefully, he eased himself into the mouth of the tilting aqueduct, which shivered ominously under his weight. Balanced on its final stanchion, it was slanting into the gully at an alarming angle. Spreading his legs, he dug his heels against the parallel rims and gently, delicately lowered himself downward.

Perspiration was pouring off him, slithering down his skin. No sense hurrying, no sense doing anything at all except inch down this infernal gutter. He was doing all right, fingers strong, feet sure, shutting his mind to the horror below, making his eyes turn inward, seeing only himself. It was not that he didn't care for Fuller, he thought wildly. Fuller was a human being when you dug beneath his prickly exterior, but God knew, he looked dead down there. Maybe he was risking his life for nothing more than a corpse.

Elliot tried to shut his mind from that as delicately, gingerly, he worked his way toward Harry's supine body.

Sobbing deep in her throat, Kate watched Elliot's progress, pressing her fist against her lips. She peered out at Harry through the drifting smoke. He looked grotesque with his burned hair, his shriveled skin. Like a creature from some distant universe. Please, God, don't let him die. She couldn't bear that, the thought of Harry dying. It had been Harry's indomitable spirit which had kept them going, which had dragged them through the fiery inferno. She'd been wrong when she'd thought he didn't care. Harry cared all right. He was no quitter, not Harry Fuller.

Elliot reached the tree boughs and, pausing to balance himself warily, tugged his bowie knife from the sheath at his waist. He hacked at the branch piercing Harry's chest, and Kate shivered, her skin crawling. Elliot was holding on to the chute with one hand, slashing frenziedly with the other. Smoke wreathed his glistening cheeks. On the opposite cliff, the flames cast an incandescent glow over his singed black hair.

Elliot grunted as the branch came apart, its tip still embedded deep in Harry's chest. Hooking one of Harry's arms across his shoulders, he began to work his way painfully upward. Kate watched, trembling with fear. "Will he be all right?" she called.

Elliot ignored her. Feet straddled against the aqueduct rims, he was shuffling up inch by inch, Harry clutched awkwardly against his chest. How could he do it? Kate wondered. How could he keep coming like that? One man. A big man, a strong man, but a man nevertheless. Didn't care that Harry was his enemy. Didn't care that Harry had almost fractured his jaw in a fight. Was poised now, directly over the inferno, dragging Harry up that desperately sagging incline. God bless you, Elliot Chamille.

Elliot scarcely knew what he was doing anymore. He couldn't think straight, couldn't breathe even, every fiber in his body focused into the stupefying effort of clambering desperately up the pitching chute. He could feel Harry's breath against his throat, feel the strong sinewy rib cage beneath his fingers. Not so tough now, Harry Fuller. Not so testy and arrogant. Helpless as a baby with Elliot dragging him up the steep slippery gradient.

Elliot risked a swift glance upward, feeling his spirits leap. Almost there, he realized. Another few feet. Ten. Five. One good push should do it. Gritting his teeth, he gripped Harry's body closer and struggled remorselessly on.

As the two men approached the summit, Kate heard a terrible ripping sound and, with a chill of panic, saw the aqueduct rising slowly from its foundations. It hovered motionless for a moment, its trestlework buckling and twisting, then it slewed to the side, dropping vertically, the two trees plunging into the maelstrom below. Kate felt her insides knot as the water chute slammed the wall of the canyon, almost dislodging Elliot from his perch. Eyes glistening with alarm, he was clinging tightly to the swaying gutter, Harry, barely conscious, hanging on to his neck and shoulders. The chute dangled over the cliff edge. Below, the fire raged remorselessly on.

"Timol," Kate shouted.

Timol ran his fingers down his smoke-grimed cheeks. In the ripples of light, his eyes rolled wildly. Ignoring the fierce wave of heat rising out of the chasm, he lowered himself over the rim, hooking his arms around a narrow spruce trunk. Inching downward, he braced his legs against the rocky wall, his waist level with Elliot's head. Kate watched in silence, scarcely daring to breathe. She realized dully that one mistake, one minuscule error of judgment, would plunge all three men to a certain and instantaneous death. She loved Harry, had never stopped loving him, not for a moment, not even through her long harrowing months in Africa. He was querulous, exasperating, intransigent, but he was purely and utterly himself, and she loved him for that. Now, with a small sense of shock, she realized suddenly she loved Elliot too. How could that be? she wondered. She was not capricious, she wasn't the type. A one-man woman, she always called herself. She couldn't love two, that didn't make sense. But Elliot's was a different kind of love, he excited her senses, galvanized her emotions. It was a mind-stunning revelation. She loved them both, wanted them both. She couldn't bear to lose them now.

Somehow, Elliot managed to transfer Harry's grasp to the belt at Timol's waist, and Harry hung on grimly, his blackened face weak with pain. Kate saw Timol's muscles rippling as he used the spruce trunk to drag himself upward. Whimpering, Kate seized his parka, adding her own strength to his desperate battle for ascendance. Harry's hands came into view, then his sleeves, and Kate reached down, seizing him by the coat collar, heaving and straining as they hauled him over the precipice edge.

The aqueduct dropped suddenly lower, and clutching its tip, Elliot stared desperately up toward them, his body suspended above the raging blaze. There was no fear in his face, that was the surprising thing. He simply hung there, dangling over the chasm, fists clenched, knuckles gleaming white through the skin. Kate started to shout, and then her voice froze in her throat, for she saw with a sense of horror and anguish that Elliot's clothing had already ignited. In a whoosh, the fire took him from below, darting impulsively along the full length of his powerful frame. One minute he was a recognizable human being, the next a billowing ball of flame.

Kate screamed, "Elliot."

Transfixed and petrified, she seemed unable to move as, engulfed in fire, he watched her calmly, his gaze bereft of pain, bereft of fear, bereft of any emotion at all except perhaps a strange and elusive awareness. For a full moment he hung there, a macabre lantern lighting up the smoke-filled sky, then his grip slackened and he rocketed earthward, vanishing mercifully into the heart of the blaze.

Kate closed her eyes, stricken. Dear God, she thought. She could see his image seared into her memory. It was something she knew she would never forget.

She shook herself. She hadn't time for sorrow or despair. She had to move, move quickly, or Elliot would have died for nothing. Sobbing hysterically, she hooked her wrists beneath Harry's shoulders, dragging him forcefully to his feet. He stood swaying as he struggled for balance, and she stepped in close, supporting him against her side.

"Fetch the minister," she snapped at Timol.

Somehow, staggering and stumbling, she manhandled Harry through the underbrush, and Timol followed, assisting McAuley. The minister's cheeks were pallid with pain, but thankfully he had reached some semblance of awareness at last.

Ahead, the trees parted, and beyond them she glimpsed virgin woodlands, luxuriant and untouched. They halted at the rim of a jagged cliff, and Kate spotted, far below, the passive flatness of a mountain lake. It was a staggering sight, its calm surface contrasting incongruously with the fury through which they had passed. Beyond, the land lay green and verdant.

"We'll have to jump," she said.

Timol stared at her in disbelief. "It is nearly a hundred feet down there. What if there are boulders underneath the surface?"

"There'll be no boulders. You heard what Harry said, they used to float logs over this precipice. Now jump, damn you. It's our only way out."

Heart pounding, she watched Timol shuffle to the rocky edge, poising himself on the cliff rim. He stood framed against the azure sky, McAuley's arm still hooked around his shoulder. They looked so vulnerable standing there that Kate felt a sob lodge deep in her throat. Timol glanced back at her, his yellow eyes rolling, and Kate smiled encouragingly, but he gave no answering flicker. For a moment, time hung suspended. Then, still clutching McAuley against him, Timol launched them both breathlessly into space. Kate gave an impulsive cry as she watched the twin bodies hurtling down through the smoke-filled air, drawing apart as the awesome momentum tugged at their flailing limbs. They hit the lake with a momentous splash, and Kate felt a wave of relief as she saw two heads break the rippling surface.

Taut with strain, she took her stance at the cliff edge, supporting Harry against her. She closed her eyes, afraid to look down. The mere thought of stepping off the edge filled her with panic and dread. You've got to do it, she told herself, you've got to.

Hugging Harry against her, she gritted her teeth, trembling helplessly; then, with a deep breath, she leapt over and down.

Kate gasped as the icy slipstream hammered her face and throat. Her ears rang with a curious whistling sound and she was filled with the awful stomach-plunging sensation of falling. There seemed no end to it, she was dropping down, down, down, the world flitting by at a devastating speed. Her mind and body separated, each caught in a reverie of its own choosing. She felt as if she were floating on air, moving through a land of long-lost dreams and memories.

Then her heels drove into the foam-tossed wave crests, and with a muffled groan she felt herself plunging into the inky blackness of the mountain lake. Panic swept her as her feet sank into the muddy bed, and thrusting out with her legs, she battled her way upward. Her head broke the surface, and blinking, she spotted Timol dragging McAuley out at the water's edge. She groped desperately beneath her, felt Harry's head bob against her fingers, seizing him under the arms, dragged him alongside, kicking expertly with her feet. We're alive, she thought thankfully, then the memory of Elliot flashed into her mind like the return of some dark and morbid specter. Oh Elliot, she thought, tears streaming down her cheeks. She recalled the sickening moment when, eyes locked into that terrible awareness, he'd begun his last fateful plunge. He hadn't deserved to die like that—wouldn't have, if he hadn't gone back for Harry. And God knew, she couldn't have blamed him, not truly, if he'd let Harry fall. He'd been such a strange man, so complex and intense. In the singular horror of his dying, she was filled with a sense of loss from which there could be neither solace nor escape.

She began to swim, the roar of the fire echoing in her eardrums. Then she realized it wasn't the fire at all, but a brace of helicopters hovering above them. The helicopters settled, and Kate stared in wonderment as troops spilled from the metal hulls and came sprinting toward them across the wind-tossed moorland.

Harry stirred in her arms, his eyelids fluttering. "Harry?" she gasped. "Harry, are you all right?"

He blinked weakly, water spraying across his stubbled cheeks. "Did we make it?"

Suddenly she began to sob. She was laughing and crying in turns, she just couldn't help herself. At least she still had Harry, she thought, wonderful fiery Harry. Everything she cared about, every single good thing in her life, was here in the ravaged features of the man beside her. "Of course we made it," she cried. "As long as we have each other, we'll always make it. I'm going to take care of you, Harry."

His lips twitched into a parody of a smile. "Big mistake. I'm a terrible patient."

"Terrible patients are my specialty. I think this time, Harry Fuller, you'll find you've met your match."

Harry didn't answer as she propelled him toward the distant shoreline. He had a happy feeling Kate was right.

In the fire control tent, the marine lieutenant gave a crisp salute. Waldo noticed his mustache had been singed by the raging flames. "We've got them, sir," the lieutenant announced with a triumphant grin. "Our choppers just radioed in."

Waldo heard Palmer's intake of breath. "McAuley?"

"Safe. He's injured, but still alive. They're airlifting him to the hospital now."

Waldo felt his muscles relax. The tension flooded out of him in a breathless rush, and he was filled with a tiredness so intense he could scarcely keep his eyelids from fluttering. It was a difficult thing to come to terms with, success, he reasoned, especially after such a catalog of disaster.

"We've done it," he breathed.

Palmer nodded. "So have the fire crews. The Forestry officer says the flames are blazing along the summit of Blackcleugh Sill, but the wind's dropped sharply and they're showing no sign of jumping the lake. If the weather remains smooth, the blaze stands a good chance of burning itself out by morning."

The lieutenant glanced from one to the other, hesitant and uncertain.

"What about charges, sir? Do we leave those to the police?"

Palmer frowned. "I don't think so, lieutenant. The situation's embarrassing enough without dragging it through the courts. Get the casualties to the hospital, and I'll decide what's to be done with them afterward."

Waldo studied Palmer warmly. Palmer was quite a character, he reflected, in his own idiosyncratic way. It had been a turbulent couple of days—a stimulating experience in many respects—but not one he'd care to live through again. Waldo's own position had been embarrassing enough, but for the little British security chief there'd been the awesome burden of responsibility to consider. Not once had Palmer wilted. He'd kept his nerve. Waldo liked the man, had learned to admire him during their hours of acquaintance.

"You'll want to telephone Washington," Palmer said.

"I guess so."

"We'll find somewhere. Preferably with a bar. I don't know about you, but I could do with a good stiff drink."

"That's the best idea I've heard all day."

They strolled to the tent flap and the lieutenant stood watching them, his eyes strangely disappointed. He'd been expecting more—excitement, elation, congratulations for a job well done. Their lack of response had taken the wind out of his sails, and he struggled to think of a fitting finale. "Did you hear the news on the radio, sir?"

Palmer glanced back. "News?"

"Joshua Matshoba. They've turned him loose. They put out a special bulletin. His plane's just landed in Angola."

"Thank you, lieutenant," Palmer said gently.

He smiled at Waldo as they crossed the loading bay toward the waiting helicopter. "With McAuley laid up, it looks as though your PAC talks will have to wait a bit."

"That's true," Waldo agreed.

"On the other hand, Matshoba's release is a step in the right direction. It may not seem much, but it's a start, a gesture, a declaration of intent. And if Option 24 is dropped from the agenda, who knows? We might see peace in South Africa yet."

Waldo's cheeks looked crimson in the firelight. Across the clearing, the crews were working hard to hold back the receding blaze. In the glow of the flames, the smoke seemed like mist wreathing the valley floor.

"Sometimes," he murmured, "I begin to believe there might be some hope for the human race after all."

"Wouldn't it be nice to think so?" Palmer said.

Turn the page for a
heart-pounding preview of
Bob Langley's new superthriller

PRECIPICE

Available from Bantam Books
in March 1991.

Major Zach Garrett steered the submersible deftly, easing it in and out of the twisting tangle of snags and spurs, surprised at the complexity of the seabed, the way it went rolling and dipping this way and that, full of crevices and bulges, much like the country he'd grown up in, the country he'd trained in. He felt at home here—or could have, if it hadn't been for the insufferable gloom.

The route led him along a spine of rock, around a jagged promontory, over a tumbling shale slope, the boulders coated with sediment and slime, and always he was conscious of the breathless void beneath. There were depths even this machine could never hope to penetrate.

Mountain tips reared through the darkness as Garrett nudged the tiny craft skillfully between the spires, operating the control console with a delicacy that had become almost instinctive. Sometimes he felt as if the submersible were part of himself, a second skin responding to the minutest signals of his brain. He experienced no discomfort beyond the inevitable dampness and cold—and the curious metallic odor he was always conscious of at extreme depths. Through the viewing port, he discerned the contours of the seascape, the rocky buttresses and hill slopes, the rolling bulges of forgotten summits, a weird, unreal, unimaginable world.

Their search followed a switchback course, the ANSAAD scanner cutting a swathe nearly half-a-mile wide, and Garrett divided his attention between the screen itself and the control panel in front, picking out the individual signatures, assimilating, appraising, identifying. There was no tension in him now, only the absorption of his job.

"Coffee?" Lieutenant Jeavson asked, filling a plastic cup from a Thermos flask in his lap.

Garrett sipped the scalding liquid, a glow of warmth spreading upward through his stomach. The coffee tasted thick and brackish. "Who made this muck?"

"It's hot and wet, isn't it? What more do you want at 3000 feet?"

Garrett was about to answer when a red bulb flashed on the control console.

Almost simultaneously, a shrill ringing sound echoed through the tiny cabin, and Jeavson stared at him with alarm. "The power module! It's flooding again."

Garrett swore. The damned power module hadn't been right since the hammering they'd received from the Argentine depth charges. If enough seawater seeped through the leaks, he knew the entire system could short-circuit.

"We've only just got here," he growled.

"What are we going to do, Zach?"

"What else can we do? We'll have to go up and get the bloody things seen to."

He stabbed the radio transmitter with his finger. "Submersible to ship-con, are you receiving me, over?"

"Hearing you loud and clear, Major Garrett. What's the problem?"

"We've sprung a leak in the power module again. It's filling up with seawater."

"Bad, is it?"

"Bad enough. I don't want to be wallowing about down here if the control section blacks out. Mark our position and bring us up to the surface."

"Understood. Position identified and recorded. Hang on to your underpants, gents."

The submersible rose slowly through the gloom.

Sergei Malenov straightened from the radio console, his pale face strangely luminous beneath the overhead strip-lamps. "They're in trouble."

The Russian captain said: "So it would seem, Comrade Colonel."

"It could take them hours to fix that power module. This is our chance."

Lieutenant Pertsovka, the submersible commander, blanched visibly. Malenov knew Pertsovka didn't relish the prospect of confronting the British on the ocean bed, but he was filled with an uncontrollable excitement. He could still, with luck and good judgment, outwit Garrett at this moment of defeat.

"You want us to dive, with the British so close?" Lieutenant Pertsovka asked dubiously.

"It's our only chance," Malenov said.

"But Comrade Colonel, you stressed the importance of secrecy. No observers, no intruders."

"The situation has changed. The British already know what we are doing here. Garrett knows. We have to seize our opportunities as they arise."

The captain watched the exchange with a seasoned eye. He said: "If we do find the *Suchko*, how can we raise her in full view of the British warship?"

"We'll worry about that when the moment comes. In the meantime prepare the submersible for diving."

Malenov had no desire to venture into the ocean depths himself. Diving oppressed him, always had, but hopefully such a move wouldn't be necessary—his particle-beams could be directed as effectively from the mother ship.

His voice grew crisp and businesslike. "I will handle the ANSAAD scanner from the control room. Lieutenant Pertsovka, when you reach the search area, you will follow the customary procedure of crisscrossing the seabed in parallel rows."

"If the comrade colonel wishes it."

"I do wish it. I also wish you luck, Lieutenant. If you handle this correctly, we stand a chance, a very strong chance, of snatching the prize from under our enemy's noses."

Clad in his diving gear, Garrett stood on the *Ashbourne*'s deck, watching the submersible being cranked up from the water hole. The sailors waited to receive it, shouting instructions as the crane operator, working his gear box delicately, eased the glistening craft gently over the deckrail and brought it to a rest on the metal ramp.

Standing at Garrett's side, Wesker noticed the frustration in the Englishman's features. "How does it look down there?" he asked.

"Rocks. Mud. Damn all else. Not even fish at that level."

Louis Wesker glanced at the sailors who were pumping seawater out of the submersible's damaged pressure housings. "How long will it take to get the leaks mended?"

"An hour. Two. Maybe all day, if luck goes against us."

Commander Henderson chewed at his pipe stem. "The Russians'll be here then. Like a shot. Bound to."

"Isn't there anything we can do?" Lori Madden asked. She couldn't bear the thought of the Soviets interceding, especially after the President himself had placed his trust in her.

"This is Antarctica," Garrett told her. "Down here, you learn to take things slowly, or you simply don't survive."

He paused as the radar officer appeared, his face taut with concern.

"I'm sorry to intrude, sir, but we've picked up a puzzling signature on the scanner. Something seems to be approaching at seabed level. It's too large for drifting wreckage. It looks . . ." The man hesitated. "It looks like another submersible."

"My God, they're here already," Lori said.

Garrett's face was expressionless. "How close is he, this intruder?"

"He's nearing the search area now. And there's something else, sir. The vessel's giving off strong electromagnetic impulses."

Garrett began to chuckle, and Lori stared at him in bewilderment.

"What's so funny?"

"Malenov. My old rival. He's trying to operate

the ANSAAD from inside the *Orlov*'s control room. He doesn't relish the idea of crawling around on the ocean bed."

"Does it make a difference?" Wesker asked.

"A big difference. It means we can beat him to the punch."

"How?"

"By placing our ANSAAD transmitter directly over the ice hole. Malenov's trying to control his accelerator from the mother ship, but he's weakening the signals, giving us a chance to intercept and slow them down. The ANSAAD's particle-beams are formed by accelerating electrons—or protons—to high energies and velocities. By emitting beams of neutral particles with our own accelerator, we can corrupt the signatures on Malenov's scanner."

"You're sure it'll work?"

"Hell no, not a hundred percent, but I'm going to give it a damned good try."

Garrett slapped Jeavson on the shoulder, trotting toward the dangling submersible. "Come on, Toby, let's get that ANSAAD uncoupled."

Huddled over the instrument console, Malenov stared at the video screen in front of him. The readings were meaningless, senseless hieroglyphics, little else.

Leaning across his shoulder, Captain Gubkin examined the unit, frowning.

"What is wrong, Comrade Colonel?"

Malenov thumped the panel with his fist. "The signatures aren't making sense. Something's corrupting the readings."

"Perhaps you are too far away to operate the machine effectively."

"It has nothing to do with distance. This is some kind of interference, something magnetic getting in the way."

The breath caught in his throat, and his frustration turned to a blind, consuming fury. Suddenly he knew the reason, knew it beyond any shadow of doubt.

"It has to be Garrett. He's using the British ANSAAD to intercept our impulses."

Was there no depravity Garrett wouldn't stoop to? Like a nemesis hovering on the fringes of his psyche, the Englishman's image dominated his senses. There could be no peace, no salve for his troubled conscience, until Garrett was dead—he knew that.

Fear welled up inside him. He'd tried to avoid going down with Pertsovka, dreaded the thought of crawling through those dank dark depths below. Space, he could take any day, he'd never balked at Baikonur, but the ocean bed was something else. He couldn't bear the prospect of entombment, no matter how transitory.

"What do you want us to do, sir?" the captain asked, eyeing Malenov's face.

Malenov came to an unwilling decision. "Recall Pertsovka," he ordered brusquely. "I will have to accompany the submersible myself."

Garrett stood at the ship's rail, watching the squat, cylindrical quadrupole injector, strapped to a metal frame wedged across the ice hole, pulsing its signals through the gently lapping water. From above, it looked like an oversized vacuum cleaner, emitting an eerie blue light from its carefully positioned director-tube. Back in the eighties, Garrett reflected, an accelerator like the ANSAAD would have filled an entire building.

Holding the instrument panel in front of him, he tinkered with the controls, testing, judging, transmitting. It was a delicate operation, requiring years of skill and experience. He had spent countless hours learning his craft, honing his instinct until he could control those impulses better than any man alive, though he couldn't guarantee his strategy was sound. The ANSAAD was mercurial, to say the least, and maybe Malenov had an ace or two up his own sleeve. Nobody in the West knew how far Soviet technology had advanced during the past four years.

At his rear, the others stood watching, afraid to interrupt in case they broke Garrett's concentration.

Feet clanged on the foredeck as the radar operator emerged, running, from the lower companionway. "The Russian submersible is returning to its ship!" he shouted jubilantly.

A ragged cheer broke from the watching seamen, and Garrett felt a flush of triumph as he visualized Malenov's face. Twice during the last twelve hours he had outmaneuvered his enemy, and knowing Malenov, the Soviet colonel would be almost demented by now.

Wesker smiled, his plump cheeks pink with cold. "Congratulations, Major. I didn't believe you could pull it off."

"Piece of cake," Garrett told him modestly.

"What happens now?"

"Well, as soon as Malenov gets his ANSAAD on board, he'll be back like a shot. Only this time he'll find us waiting."

"Without the submersible?"

"Of course not. How else do you expect us to reach the ocean bed?"

"But what about the structural faults?"

"We'll just have to take a chance."

Garrett turned, shouting to the sailors gathered at his rear. "Prepare the vessel for diving."

The chief mechanic looked startled. "She's not ready yet, Major. We've got to plug the power module, otherwise she'll blow again."

"Seal it up with Gaskin tape."

"Too dodgy, sir. It'll disintegrate under pressure."

"Not if you do it carefully. Anyhow, it's my neck on the chopping block, so don't argue."

"Right, sir."

Garrett handed the ANSAAD instrument panel to a watching seaman. He placed his arm about Jeavson's shoulder, drawing him gently aside. "Toby, I want you to sit this one out."

"What are you talking about, skipper?"

"I mean I'm making the dive alone."

Jeavson blinked. "You're nuts."

"That thing's ready to come apart at the seams, and I don't want you getting hurt."

"Developing a conscience, Major?"

"Put it down to my strong moral fiber."

"I know what you're up to," Jeavson accused. "You want to hog all the glory for yourself."

"That's me, squire. A regular prima donna."

"Nothing doing. You can't operate that machine and look after the ANSAAD at the same time. It isn't humanly possible."

"Toby, this is between Malenov and me. Anything happens to you, I'll never forgive myself."

"Zach, stop kidding around. I'm going. It's my job. You need me, and you know it."

"I can order you to back off," Garrett threatened.

Jeavson shook his head. "Make that dive alone and you'll find yourself in front of a court-martial. And believe me, I'll be delighted to testify."

"That's what I like. The devotion of a true friend."

"Besides, somebody's got to keep you in line down there. You're too bloody wild to be let out alone."

Garrett conceded defeat. "Okay, don't say you haven't been warned."

The preparations were carried out in double time. Garrett watched impatiently as the submersible was swung quickly into position. When everything was ready, Jeavson slithered through the narrow entrance hatch and Garrett followed, reaching back to close the cover. The sound of Lori's voice made him pause.

"Zachary?" She was peering up at him from the deck rail. "Why are you doing this?"

"Gallantry," he said. "It runs in the family."

Lori ignored the quip. "Is it because of the Suchko, or because of Colonel Malenov?"

"What difference does it make? They amount to the same thing, don't they?"

"No, Zachary, they don't amount to the same thing at all. You're turning this into a personal vendetta."

Reaching down, he squeezed Lori's arm. "Listen, I'm not planning to settle old scores at three thousand feet, if that's what you think, but somebody's got to stop those Russians. If Malenov reaches that spacecraft first, this whole escapade will have been for nothing."

Without waiting for her reply, he slammed shut the hatch and slithered into the tiny cabin. Time to go. Time to set the record straight. Vengeance was a purifying thing when a man set his heart on it.

Jeavson's cheeks paled as their midget craft was hoisted into position. The A-frame swung out, suspending them over the jagged ice hole, then with a clanking sound lowered them gently into the water. Garrett waited in a fever as the final safety checks were carried out. When everything was ready, the lead diver gave the thumbs-up signal.

Garrett watched the frantic flurry of bubbles as the sea darkened around them. His body seemed on fire with excitement. It was like the culmination of some long-awaited dream. Everything he'd gone through, the anger, the betrayal, was about to find fulfillment. The girl was right. It wasn't the *Suchko* anymore. This was the repaying of old scores, and all the bitterness seemed to flow out of him like pus from some old, but freshly reopened wound.

Outside the viewing ports, the water became black as pitch, and soon even Toby was indiscernible. Their only focal point lay in the luminous dials on the control panel. Like an insidious vapor, the cold again seeped through their insulated hull, and Garrett swallowed an antihistamine tablet to clear his lungs and throat.

They descended more rapidly than prudence demanded, but this was his moment, this was the confrontation he had hoped and prayed for. No tricks now. Just he and Malenov together. And the ocean. The impervious, unbeatable ocean.

They were past the euphotic zone, dropping, dropping, the water losing its texture, losing its substance, darkening against their viewing ports like molten tar.

"How about lights?" Jeavson muttered, his voice wavering.

"Leave them," Garrett snapped. He immediately regretted his harshness. Couldn't blame Toby for feeling edgy. In such awesome gloom, a man lost his sense of perspective, panic became an ever-ready enemy. Besides, Toby was his friend.

"I don't want to use the lights," he explained, "because I want them to take us for the *Suchko.*"

Jeavson didn't answer. Squatting at the viewing port, Garrett could sense his fear.

Garrett did not see the ocean bed emerge, but he glimpsed its proximity on the ANSAAD scanner, and his hands moved deftly across the control panel, bringing their descent to a halt. Their solitary ski-blade dug gently into the silt, and Garrett used the thrusters to settle the craft on an even keel. Dense and impenetrable, the curtain closed around him, blacker than pitch.

"What happens now?" Jeavson whispered.

"We wait," Garrett said grimly.

Malenov's skin felt clammy as he squatted inside the tiny submersible, watching the seabed twisting and buckling. It had been a long, nerve-racking haul from the security of the support ship. Malenov struggled to hide his panic. He'd never liked diving, never, tried to avoid it whenever he could, would have, if it hadn't been for Garrett. Always, it was Garrett.

Beside him in the cabin, Lieutenant Pertsovka hovered over the instrument panel, his eyes trained on the elongated light beam picking out the path ahead. Oh, he was a splendid fellow, Pertsovka, followed instructions to the letter. Cool as a cucumber, when the need was there. But Pertsovka had one big advantage. He lacked imagination. He didn't appreciate the hazards they were facing in crossing nearly half-a-mile of uncharted water 3000 feet beneath the surface. Brains of a rabbit, had Pertsovka, but for the first time in his life, Malenov had to admit that he envied the man.

His stomach jumped as something registered on the ANSAAD scanner. He tapped it with his finger-tips, his reverie forgotten. "We've got a reading," he said.

Pertsovka glanced at him, features tense. "Where?"

"Bearing one-three-seven."

Pertsovka engaged the motors and gently changed direction.

Garrett saw the light beam cleaving the water ahead and heard Jeavson's quick intake of breath. Reaching out, he squeezed the young man's forearm. There was little to see beyond the approaching vessel's headlamp shafts. The hull itself was lost in the blackness of the ocean wall.

Garrett lowered his other hand, his fingers tracing the control-console as the lights locked into position. Slowly and determinedly, the Soviet sub-mersible was inching toward them in a direct line.

"We're going to collide," Jeavson warned.

Garrett's fingers bit deep into his forearm.

"Let them come."

Peering through the viewing port, Malenov saw something hovering directly in their path. It looked at first like a chunk of fallen ice or a buttress from the seabed, but as they drew closer, he discerned a neatly bevelled engine housing. The obstacle was the hull of some man-made machine.

"It's the *Suchko*," he breathed, squinting through the Plexiglas.

Fingers trembling, he watched the vessel take on definition as Pertsovka inched their submersible steadily closer. Something protruded from the vehi-cle's front, an elongated manipulator arm. He recog-nized viewing ports, a hoisting bit, a hydroplane.

"What kind of spacecraft is that?" Pertsovka whispered, his voice hoarse and strained in the clammy atmosphere.

Stupefied, Malenov felt a terrible weakness gathering in his limbs as he stared at the grotesque creature confronting them on the ocean bed.

"That's no spacecraft," he muttered. "It's the British submersible."

"Now!" Garrett bellowed.

Jeavson flicked the light switch. The Soviet vessel was transfixed in the dazzling glare.

Reaching down, Garrett engaged the thrusters and their craft surged forward, the water foaming around them. They soared toward the intruder's vulnerable underbelly, their screws chewing the chill Antarctic current. Garrett saw the vessel's titanium skin, saw the broad bulge of its hatch turret, and the flat, parallel platform that housed its cameras and battery gear.

The Soviet craft seemed to hover, motionless, like an inquisitive insect sensing a prey, then its bulbous hull tilted slightly to one side as the operator—panicked, probably—blew the trimming tanks in a desperate bid to swing to starboard. Filled with a fierce elation, Garrett held their vessel on a collision course, judging timings, movements, positionings.

At three thousand feet, the two submersibles did not move with grace through the inky water; they wallowed for position like a pair of drunken hippos. Garrett reached for the control unit governing the manipulator arms, feeling the chill touch of the handgrip cooling his fingers. The huge six-hundred-pound feelers weaved clumsily through the eddying current, their mechanism filling the cabin with a heavy purring sound.

The pincerlike claws scraped across the Soviet hull, sending vibrations through its titanium shield. A terrible shock wave rippled along their deck, and to Jeavson, watching dry-mouthed, the Russian vessel seemed to rear backward, lurching over on its own axis, its screws thrashing the water in wild, impotent fury.

Garrett threw their craft to starboard, jockeying for position.

"Zach!" Jeavson yelled. "Have you gone crazy, for Christ's sake?"

Garrett scarcely heard. Gripping the instrument

module, he flung out the manipulator arms for a second try. His hands moved like pistons, switching from control panel to manipulator console, testing, aligning, activating. He could feel the shirt clammy against his chest, smell the sharp metallic odor of the submersible's rebreathing system, see, through the viewing port, the enemy vessel pitching and reeling.

This time, the steel claws caught the Soviet port-side headlamp, smashing its reinforced glass. In the arc lights' beam, Garrett glimpsed the severed lamp plummeting into the darkness. He swung the submersible into a lumbering broadside skid, and there was a deafening thud as the two hulls clanged together.

Peering up through the forward viewing port, Jeavson saw the Soviet vessel clip the corner of a craggy outcrop. The rock exploded outward in a starburst of silt and granite fragments, clouding the water around them. For a moment the enemy craft was lost to view, and Jeavson heard Garrett cursing as he struggled with the controls, then the sea swung into focus, and they spotted the vessel retreating desperately among a bristling forest of pinnacles.

Bellowing like a madman, Garrett engaged the thrusters, burrowing through the water in a wild and glorious pursuit. A rock reared up, and he swung the craft deftly to starboard, missing the projection by a breathless fraction.

Jeavson reached out, seizing Garrett's arm. "Forget it, Zach. Let them go, for Christ's sake!"

Garrett glanced at him, some of the fury dying in his eyes. Jeavson saw reason and sanity returning to the craggy features as Garrett's gaze focused, losing its wildness. Abruptly, he slowed the submersible to a crawl. Jeavson felt a surge of relief as the Soviet craft vanished into the darkness.

"Sorry, Toby," Garrett said, his voice suddenly calm and sensible. "Did you do something unpleasant in your trousers?"

Jeavson filled his lungs with air. "That was the craziest thing I ever saw. For Christ's sake, skipper, do you want to start World War Three? You damn near killed the poor bastard."

"His headlamps were hurting my eyes."

Garrett blew the trimming tanks, bringing the submersible around in a gentle arc, and Jeavson gripped his chair, fighting to control the tension inside him. Something caught his eye through the starboard viewing port, a pale, faintly luminous outline amid the curtain of gloom. Jeavson felt his palms turn clammy as he squinted incredulously.

His voice was barely a whisper. "Look, Zach."

Twisting columns of rock traced the rim of a giant precipice, and here, balanced on the craggy edge, something swayed gently in the current. Jeavson discerned a titanium cone, with porthole windows and numbers painted along its upper hull. A deep gash in its side indicated a collision of sorts, and more recent scratches suggested the vessel had rolled from its original position—hit by a rock probably, dropped from the melting ice pack above. Caught in the headlamps' glare, the spacecraft looked like a relic from some forgotten age, its smooth shielding blending into the clifftop silt with no appreciable dividing line.

Garrett stabbed the telephone switch with his finger. "Submersible calling ship-con. Do you read me? Over."

A voice broke through the static, clearing as Garrett adjusted the background volume. "Ashbourne-con to submersible. Everything okay?"

"Everything's fine," Garrett said. "Mark our location and bring us to the surface."

He glanced through the Plexiglas, noting the vessel's delicately balanced position. The battered spacecraft looked as if it might plummet at any second, and Garrett grimaced as he punched the transmission switch.

"Tell Wesker we've found the Suchko."

THRILLERS

Gripping suspense...explosive action...dynamic characters...international settings...these are the elements that make for great thrillers. Books guaranteed to keep you riveted to your seat.

Robert Ludlum:

☐	26256	THE AQUITAINE PROGRESSION	$5.95
☐	26011	THE BOURNE IDENTITY	$5.95
☐	26322	THE BOURNE SUPREMACY	$5.95
☐	26094	THE CHANCELLOR MANUSCRIPT	$5.95
☐	28209	THE GEMINI CONTENDERS	$5.95
☐	26019	THE HOLCROFT COVENANT	$5.95
☐	27800	THE ICARUS AGENDA	$5.95
☐	25899	THE MATERESE CIRCLE	$5.95
☐	27960	THE MATLOCK PAPER	$5.95
☐	26430	THE OSTERMAN WEEKEND	$5.95
☐	25270	THE PARSIFAL MOSAIC	$5.95
☐	28063	THE RHINEMANN EXCHANGE	$5.95
☐	27109	THE ROAD TO GANDOLOFO	$5.95
☐	27146	THE SCARLATTI INHERITANCE	$5.95
☐	28179	TREVAYNE	$5.95

Frederick Forsyth:

☐	28393	THE NEGOTIATOR	$5.95
☐	26630	DAY OF THE JACKAL	$5.95
☐	26490	THE DEVIL'S ALTERNATIE	$5.95
☐	26846	THE DOGS OF WAR	$5.95
☐	25113	THE FOURTH PROTOCOL	$5.95
☐	27673	NO COMEBACKS	$5.95
☐	27198	THE ODESSA FILE	$5.95

Buy them at your local bookstore or use this page to order.

Bantam Books, Dept. TH, 414 East Golf Road, Des Plaines, IL 60016

Please send me the items I have checked above. I am enclosing $_____ (please add $2.00 to cover postage and handling). Send check or money order, no cash or C.O.D.s please.

Mr/Ms _____

Address _____

City/State _____ Zip _____

Please allow four to six weeks for delivery.
Prices and availability subject to change without notice.

TH–11/90

Action on Eighteen Wheels!

Marc Lee and Carl Browne, ex-Delta Force anti-terrorist commandos: They've taken on bloodthirsty Middle Eastern terrorists...deadly drug cartels...vicious bikers...the Mafia...no matter how badly they're outnumbered, Lee and Browne always come up swinging...and blasting!

Don't miss any of the exciting books in Bob Ham's OVERLOAD SERIES!